"UNTO OTHERS"
By
MCKENZIE THOMPSON

SYNOPSIS

The Gabriels are Negroes or Colored people, using the vernacular of the day which is 1935. However, unlike most black people of that generation, they are wealthy and educated, but like all that generation, particularly in the South, they are fettered by the color of their skin. This novel however is not about the struggle for equality, which is well documented and rightly so; instead it is about a family described by one Black leader of the time as part of the "Talented Tenth." The Gabriels are one such family.

The family matriarch is Rosa, born a slave, it is through her courage that the land they call Angel's Trumpet, becomes their home. But Angel's Trumpet is more than just land; it is people and a way of life. Rosa is willing to do whatever it takes to maintain the Gabriel legacy, but she will find that the price may be too dear.

Reese Gabriel loves his wife, but he has never been a slave and Rosa's insecurities have driven a wedge between them, but his idealism will also demand a price and his two sons Jasset and Steban will pay the cost.

Stuart Overfield's privileged world of the southern aristocracy had been destroyed by the Civil War and stripped the Overfield family of everything, except the prestige of the Overfield name. Stuart has returned from the Civil War determined to restore the Overfield plantation to its

1

former glory, but to do so, he must make an unlikely alliance with Reese Gabriel, a Black man. The next generation of Overfields enjoys the wealth Stuart has accumulated; but his son Justin, plots to strip the Gabriels of their land and wealth by any means necessary, even murder.

Rosa Gabriel prepares to face the threat to her family from those who live in the Overfield mansion, unaware, that across an ocean there are those who would destroy her family to obtain a medallion given to her by her dying mother. The medallion holds the key to power in the royal court of Abyssinian, modern day Ethiopia. The elegant Salim Akbar will pose a greater threat to the Gabriels than Rosa could ever imagine.

"UNTO OTHERS", boast no heroes, only flawed characters who are moved by pride, greed, revenge and survival. From the early days of the "reconstruction" South to New York's Harlem of the thirties; from Paris to the country of Ethiopia, a land of antiquity and tradition; each character's personal drama unfolds against a back-drop of historical events. All will learn the scales are always balanced by what you give "UNTO OTHERS."

PROLOGUE

Two royal lovers stood silently in a stone courtyard high above the city of David as the stars faded and the night shadows ebbed before an emerging sun rising over an ancient land of milk and honey. It was a blessed land of promise, given to a chosen people by a benevolent and faithful God. But the new day brought only great sadness for they knew their time was at an end.

Beyond the city gates a caravan of magnificent proportions prepared its journey south, laden with gifts from the King of the Israelites. In the street below a chariot surround by the Queen's Elite Guard, awaited its royal passenger. Their farewells had been said and yet the King would not grant her leave to depart.

"I beseech you my love, do not go; stay by my side and I will make you my queen of queens.

Tears shimmered in eyes the color of desert sands, as she stood before him proudly, her golden-skinned body covered in swaths of fine linen; saying, "My love I am a Queen. I beg you, not to entreat me further, less you break my heart."

The King struggled against conflicting emotions, anger that she would defy his wishes and the impulse to see the ebony mass of waist length hair loosed from its hood of silk one more time. To taste her lips once again and experience the passion she aroused in him like no other. Instead he reached inside his robe to remove a medallion attached to an intricately woven chain, made to a thickness of his small finger. The medallion had been forged of pure gold and fashioned into the shape of a lion's head with eyes of brilliant emeralds. The King wore a matching chain of gold about his own neck that carried the crest of his house.

"For you my love", he said.   Taking her hand to demonstrate the mechanism that released the elaborate hidden clasp.

The regal Queen bowed before her lover, that he might fasten the medallion around her neck, but the King move away from her, turning his back, his eyes glazing stonily toward the caravan in the distance.

His abrupt withdrawal hurt more than she thought she could bear, the anguish of her woman's heart was overwhelming, but the dignity of a Queen saved her. There was more at stake than her shattered core. She straightened and descended to her waiting chariot. "Goodbye my love", she whispered.

The King lingered in the courtyard long after the royal personal guard had led the Queen from the city, until only the dust from their passing remained.

The Queen raised the medallion to her lips as she rode away from the man she loved more than life, but her people needed their Queen. Her hand dropped to her belly knowing his seed already grew there. She felt sad that she could not tell him, but he would have tried to enforce his will upon her to stay. She was a Queen of Sheba and she belonged to her people and her son, his son, would rule after her.

THE BEGINNING

Chapter I

The Overfield Plantation, August 1864

The early morning mists from the river swirled about the moss-draped trees that lined a once immaculate drive, now choked with weeds and the unkempt green expanse of lawn that stretched out from a large white columned house and surrounding gardens. The entrance doors were flung open and a man came out; part running, part stumbling the sound of baying dogs loud in his ears. He ran toward the gardens, tearing though the flowers and thick green foliage that grew in lush profusion. Running until his breathing had become labored and his lungs burned with exertion.

Jamison Overfield was terrified. The mastiffs were on his scent; he had to keep moving before the dogs tore him apart. They were almost on him, then he tripped falling to the ground screaming as they hurled themselves toward his throat, bared fangs dripping with saliva; then disappeared before his eyes, the dogs of Hell evaporating in the mist. He realized he was hallucinating, that the fever had taken hold as he struggled to his feet. He was an Overfield of Overfield Plantation, but his attempt at some semblance of his former dignity was useless.

He continued forward, shivering uncontrollably; his tall gaunt form as unkempt as the land he owned. His wild mane of hair was wet with sweat that trickled down his pale face in salty rivulets stinging his dark ringed eyes until he could barely see; threading through the grime, and the unshaven stubble covering his cheeks. He could not remember when he had last washed and the thought of food made him sick. Sleep came only after his exhausted body fell into a whiskey stupor filled with nightmares. But it seemed the Irish whiskey had lost its mind numbing magic, as the fever gripped him.

The garden was filled with the heady fragrance of gardenia and roses mingled with the scent of rain and fresh turned earth. It had been his beloved wife's pride, now the rich soil housed a different type of fruit, he thought, as the way ahead was hindered by graves. Once the gardens had been a place of solace and peace for the living; now it belonged to the dead.

The strength in his legs gave out and he collapsed to the ground; using his hands and arms to pull himself the remaining distance to Cullum. He leaned his head against the cool headstone that marked all that was left of his beloved son. It was the beginning of Jamison's lonely vigil, there was no one else to mourn his dead son.

The throbbing ache in his head had reached a crescendo, matched only by the dull pain in his heart as scenes from the past lanced through his mind of the day Cullum left home. Cullum had sat his horse proudly dressed in the grey and gold braid of the Confederacy. He seemed to gleam in the sunlight like a blond god of lore, his spirited stallion pawing the ground ready to be off, banners flying, as he took his place as leader of the Regiment.

No amount of whiskey could erase the image of his son, being led back home draped over his horse bloodied and soiled. His precious son, that light stamped out, to be buried under a mound of dirt; while the destruction and bloodshed the South had so arrogantly begun raged on, but he had nothing left to sacrifice.

His fortune consisted of a chest filled with confederate dollars; he occasionally used to wipe the dung from his ass, just to remind himself of how worthless it was and a deserted plantation, with acres of bare fields.

The slaves had begun running off as soon as Lincoln had declared his "proclamation." They had drifted off a few at a time until only the house servants had remained. He had not begrudged them their freedom; he had always known that the system could not continue, but there had been no courage behind his conviction. It had been simply easier to do what his fathers' had done before him; but freedom would exact its' price; it had already cost him dearly.

Jamison was so weary and the stone over Cullum's grave was cool and soothing. He could close his eyes and there was Julianne; she was waiting for him, as beautiful as she had been on their wedding day. But reality cut through the feverish fog clouding his brain, denying his retreat into illusion. Only death could free him and death would not be rushed.

In the past, Jamison had the power to resist the onslaught of grief and guilt; but he could no longer summon the old anger to shield him from the painful memories. If Cullum was the son of his grief, then Stuart was the burden of his guilt.

He had just never understood the boy. Stuart James Overfield, his changeling, his youngest son. Why couldn't he have been more like Cullum? It was hard to believe he could have sired two such different men.

Cullum had been a southern gentleman, but Stuart had nothing but disdain for Cullum's code of chivalry and so-called frivolous pursuits. The boy had persisted in speaking out against secession and war, shaming them among their friends. Instead of joining a regiment like other loyal southerners, he defamed the "cause" as foolhardy.

Jamison had made no effort to check Cullum when he had publicly accused his brother of being a coward. He had shared Cullum's contempt for Stuart's refusal to fight for what belonged to him. He had been so angry he had forced a confrontation with boy; demanding to know where his allegiance lay.

Jamison would never forget the look on Stuart's face as he had stood stoically before him; and later as he packed his bags and left the house. A week later, a messenger arrived with a letter:

> "Father I have followed my conscience the Union must be preserved. I do what
> I must, please forgive me."

But Jamison harden his heart against his son. He had no forgiveness for Stuart's defiance. Cullum was dead. The Union had killed Cullum. Stuart had turned his back on their way of life; and for his betrayal Jamison had tried to erase every trace of his youngest son's existence. Now with his last conscious thought, he wondered if his only child was still alive.

Chapter II

Overfield Plantation, 1864

Of course Master Jamison had been drunk the day the men had found the soldier near the landing. Tilly had suggested he be taken to one of the empty cabins to be tended, but Lillian wasn't having any of that. A white man in a darkie cabin, Lillian was incensed at the notion. She ordered the soldier be carried into the house; when Rosa had tried to reason her with repeating Tilly's concerns, Lillian had struck Rosa in the face, demanding she do as she was told.

Lillian had always been aloof, but since returning home a widow, she had become petty and cruel; abusive not only to Tilly and the remaining slaves, but poor Miss Phoebe. Phoebe spent her days waiting for her husband to return. Tilly had to pull her away as she fluttered about, calling the soldier by her dead husband's name. As Rosa undressed the soldier, her worst fears were realized as he began to retch the black vomit of the fever.

Within a fortnight, she and Master Jamison had buried them all; the soldier, Lillian and Phoebe, Frazier the butler and the remaining house slaves, they were all dead. She and the Master had dug so many graves.

Neither one of them had been handy with a shovel, and since the garden soil was soft ground and easy to dig; they had dragged the bodies to the garden. There had been no coffins, they just wrapped the bodies in sheets and buried them, burning the bedding and anything they had used.

It was late afternoon when she had found Master Jamison atop Cullum's grave. She had begun to dig another hole; being perversely glad he was nearby and she would not have to drag him from the house, until he moaned and she realized he was still alive. But she would be burying him soon enough, Rosa thought wearily, as she watched Jamison toss fitfully upon the bed.

She had been twelve, when the "fever", had last razed the countryside. Miss Julianne, weaken by child-birth had quickly succumbed to the disease along with her baby. Rosa had remembered thinking the Master had lost his mind; he had been so wild with grief.

Rosa had not understood when Tilly had made a small cut on her arm and used clots of blood from the mistress's sick bed to rub into the cut. She had started to scream and Tilly had clamped her hand over Rosa mouth so tight she could not breathe. Tilly had never raised her hand to Rosa, but Tilly had been afraid. She had not been able to help Miss Julianne; to use what she had learned from the old healer from her village on the white folk. If something went wrong, her life would be forfeit. Rose had suffered a mild bout with the disease then she had recovered.

Her beloved Tilly could not even save herself, Rosa thought as she examined the old scar on her arm. Rosa had survived, but now she was alone, except for a sick old man.

She found herself in a unique position; for the first time in her life there was no one to tell her what to do. No go here Rosa or do that Rosa. The first decision she had ever made for herself and it was all wrong. She should have left him there in the garden and ran, but for some reason she could not do it; nor understand that part of her that needed him alive.

He had not been a cruel man, but he had been master and she his slave. Rosa owed him nothing; yet she bathed him in cool water and cleansed his filth; forcing medicines and broths down his throat. In his rational moments, he cursed her to let him die in peace, but those moments were few. Mostly he babbled on to his long dead wife and children.

Rosa had a chance to run with the others after Lincoln had granted the slaves freedom, but she could not leave Tilly. Tilly had felt responsible for holding her back, it had not that it mattered. From the day of Rosa's birth, her adopted mother had loved and protected her.

The older slaves used to tell the story of how Tilly had taken a beating rather than leave her behind as an infant while she worked in the field, and how Miss Julianne had saved her. Tilly had only laughed, telling Rosa that Miss Julianne gave her hope for the white race. Except for fate and a snake bite; they would both would have remained in the fields.

Tilly always told her those early years was for preparation. She had managed to learn English and her skill as a healer became known among the other slaves, and they began to come to her with their aliments. They had come to her while harvesting a crop of rice, standing hem deep in mud, Mr. Asa, the overseer had been bitten by a water moccasin.

The snake had latched on to Asa's leg above his boot-top, as he kneeled down to examined a rice plant. Asa had fallen back into the mud in shock and the moccasin slithered away toward the swamps. Tilly had borne the marks from Mr. Asa's whip on her back until she died, yet she helped him.

She had only been in the next section and reached him quickly. Taking his sheathed knife, she cut him deep, making an X across the snakebite, and let the cut bleed freely while she made a poultice of mud, herbs and moldy bread, a concoction she usually carried in a pouch bound at her waist to draw out the remaining venom. Asa had lived to use his whip again, and brought her once again to the attention of Miss Julianne.

As the mistress of a large working plantation; the health and welfare of the slaves was Miss Julianne's duty. She had been impressed with the way Tilly had handled the snake bite and with her cabin gardens which were always abloom with flowers and vegetables. She decided Tilly would work with her in the plantation stillroom where she prepared various food stuffs and medicines for the family and household. After Miss Julianne died, Tilly became housekeeper.

Rosa fingered the chain of the medallion hidden in her pocket like a rosary. She had never seen anything like it; the weight of it comforted her. Somehow all those years Tilly had kept the medallion hidden, waiting for the right time to give Rosa her birth mother's legacy. After war was declared, and freedom becoming a possibility, she had given Rosa the medallion.
Tilly's dying words continued to echo through Rosa's mind; "You will have to have courage my bebe for what lies ahead; dying may not always be easy, but its living that's hard. If you stay alive, there is nothing lost that cannot be regained."

Tilly could not tell Rosa the exact date of her birth since knowledge of that kind was not encouraged in a slave; but before she had been given the slave name of Tilly, she had been Menesba.

Chapter III

West Coast of Africa, 1835

Captain Jonathan Nils had grown accustomed to Mr. Giles's curses and the whistling, cracking sound of his whip as the "cargo", was herded on board. His first mate was a crude man, with no sense of decorum, but he knew his business. However, the loud melee above was beyond even Mr. Giles' ability to wreak havoc on those miserable creatures. He was a wealthy man now, and vowed it was his last voyage. He was sick of the stench, the noise, and the look of hatred that blazed at him from all too human eyes.

Captain Nils arose from his desk, deciding it might be wise to check on the commotion topside. He put on his jacket, checking his appearance in a mounted mirror. The jacket was blue with gold buttons and braid; the same gold braid trimmed the visor of his cap. He was a vain man and it was a game he played; protocol must be maintained even on a slaver.

As he stepped from his quarters into the companionway, the cabin boy skidded into him; almost knocking him down. "See here boy, what's your hurry", he bellowed.

The boy jumped up tugging his forelock, "Beggin your pardon Captain, sir, Mr. Giles, he sent me", the boy began breathlessly but he got no further.

Nils shoved him aside, "Mr. Giles be damned, what is happening on deck?"

"Well sir, O'Malley and McKinney took aliking to the same wench, McKinney he pulled a knife and they proceeded to have at it," he stuttered to stop once again, as the Captain began to climb the ladder to the deck; but the captain's actions were not his business and he hurried to carry out Mr. Giles orders.

Left unguarded, the "niggers", lay huddled together, chained hand to hand and foot to foot; each muttering loudly while the crew encircled the pair of brawlers calling blood-thirsty taunts and encouragements. Mr. Giles stood apart, arms akimbo watching, a dusky skinned woman sprawled at his feet, the gold glittering about her neck, set ablaze by the sunlight.

Nils had accepted the whole lot as payment from "The Portuguese", in lieu of his debt; which he claimed he had brought off some Arab traders. Damn foreigners, it was his fault for dealing with them. But the woman was something special. Evidently Giles had been holding out on him.

He was surprised to see what appear to be gold around the slave's neck. Items of value were generally stripped as soon as the natives were captured, and Captain Nils wondered why it had not been removed. Although, judging by the scarring that marred her slim throat, someone had tried, he thought disgustedly. He could not abide such stupidity, broken the item would have been worthless and to damage such a magnificent creature, was senseless waste.

His eyes roamed over her still form with lusty regard, the ragged shift she wore revealing more of her supple body than it covered. Slowly she raised her head, her eyes, dark as a stormy sea met his gaze unflinchingly. He flushed as he felt himself harden. By heavens, no wonder the fools fought over her, he thought, turning slightly to adjust his clothing less anyone should notice

his own reaction to the wench.

The cabin boy returned from below gingerly handing Giles a brace of pistols. A shot fired over

the heads of the crew quickly brought them to order and O'Malley and McKinney were clapped

in irons.

Nils cleared his throat, then said, "I trust everything is in order now Mr. Giles?"

"Aye Sir, Giles replied sourly, his own interest in the woman waning at the look in the Captain's

eyes.

"Have the wench properly cleaned and bring her to my cabin later tonight."

"Aye, aye, Sir."

Charleston Harbor, 1840

Menesba looked down at the girl's swollen, sweat drenched body with pity as she wrapped her

arms tightly about her own waist, conscious of the emptiness of her womb. Her child had been

delivered stillborn a few days before, the birth cord wrapped about its tiny body. She had been

raped too many times to know what man's seed had taken root, but the baby would have

belonged to her. Now she was past caring whether she lived or died; content that soon she

would end her life; when the one the men called, Giles had dragged her into the small cargo hold

15

to attend the Captain's woman. Perhaps if Menesba had herbs and medicines she could have helped her, as it was there was little she could do for the girl.

Menesba had never had any claim to beauty and her family had been too poor to give her a dowry. Her father had needed to provide for his sons; she had been traded to the old village healer as a helper; for the price of a cow. The old one had been very wise, and taught her many things, but the baby was in a breeched position, and despite Menesba efforts, the girl was losing blood. Already the plank flooring beneath her was soaked red, as wave after wave of anguished pain torn through her body.

The girl recognized the woman from the village, she was one of them that had brought her food. All the villagers had been afraid of her, but not this one. After the witch-doctor pronounced her "juju", and the medallion cursed they had stayed away from her.

She touched the gold medallion that had once been a part of her dowry, a slight smile curving her dry lips. The scars on her neck bore witness of the attempts to remove it from her. Only their greed had saved her. It had been forged in such a way that it could not be easily broken. The family legend was that it was blessed by the God of the Hebrews. The white one who had used her during the voyage had tried to open it and failed also, although she had discovered his kind had a natural cunning. He would find a way, to open it once they had reached land.

Natives working with white men had attacked the party that she and her lover had been traveling with down the coast, when they had camped for the night. After a long trek through the jungle they had reached the main village. She and her beloved had traveled so far to no avail. He had been cruelly killed as she watched. When the village had been attacked by slavers, she already carried the baby.

She knew was dying, but she was not afraid. Her baby stirred within her and she was determined the child of her beloved live. The medallion was all she had to leave the child. The base of the medallion was shaped like a lion's head, and when pressed at a certain angle released a hidden clasp. The medallion dropped easily into her palm. She repeated the gesture until the village woman had seemed to understand. She gestured to her stomach, and put the medallion in Menesba's hand. "For the child", she whispered although the woman did not speak her language.

Menesba had never perceived such strength in one so young. Looking at the medallion in her hand she flung it away. She was afraid; afraid of the strange quiet that surrounded them, shattered by the girl's resonating scream. Terrified, she looked into the sightless eyes of the dead girl and the infant slippery with her mother's blood resting in her hands.

Menesba fell back against the wall fear oozing from her like sweat. She sat there unable to move, and no idea of what to do. The chain was cursed, the elders said so, but it had been the last wish of the girl that her child have it. Daylight shone through the cracks in the trap door opening. Soon Giles would return. They would take it away.

The child lay upon her dead mother's breast whining softly, as she breathed for the first time outside her mother's womb. Menesba's breast began to fill and ache with the milk that should

17

have fed her own child. Unable to bear it any longer, she bit through the umbilical cord where it had been tied off and lifted the infant from her mother's lifeless body. The baby's small mouth rooted eagerly until it found what it was seeking, latching on to Menesba's breast instinctively.

Menesba smiled, her eyes filled with tears as the baby suckled. For the first time in many months, she felt something other than despair. The fear was still there, buoyed by a fierce, unexpected devotion; as she held the baby close. Oh yes little one, she crooned, stroking the girl child's downy head, you belong to me now.

Above she could hear the crew stirring and the slow measured step of the white man as he approached the trap door of the cargo hold. She picked up the blanket covering the girl and tossed it in the corner where the medallion had landed. She knew she would die before she allowed harm to come to her child and she sat quiet as Giles examined the girl.

Giles looked down at the dead woman and shook his head in disgust at the waste. The woman and baby would have fetched a goodly price. The captain had had his pleasure, and he was left to clean up the mess. The infant had no white blood that he could discern and it appeared one of its legs was crippled. Perhaps it would be kinder just to put the poor little mite out of its misery; but it wasn't right to treat an infant like an unwanted kitten, even if it was only a nigger.

The matter was settled however as Giles watched the midwife huddled protectively in the corner suckling the child. A decent profit might still be made Giles decided. He bellowed orders that the dead body be removed, then turned his mind to his other numerous duties; promptly forgetting both mother and the child.

Menesba continued to sit in the hold long after members of the crew had taken the girl's body away. She no longer craved death; and she knew the change had been ignited by the courage of a girl and a tiny baby's will to live. The pair had rekindled the hope she lost a thousand miles ago on the shore of her home. She would survive, no matter the cost.

She had sat on the blanket covering the medallion while Giles was in the cargo hold. Afterward she had unlatched the chain, torn thin strips from the ragged shift she wore and tied the medallion about her waist. She had waited, expecting to be discovered; but after the ship had entered the harbor, several slaves and two crew members died in a scuffle after the slaves were brought above deck to be aired and cleaned. Later she discovered one of the white men that died had been Giles.

She often wondered why no one had questioned her. She had just been given a clean gown to cover herself and herded off the ship. Maybe with Giles dead, the captain had been too busy after the riot to notice or care about the medallion; it was something she would never know. Menesba had been taught that life held an infinite number of paths. For now, only slavery loomed ahead, but swaddled in the thin blanket that had covered her dead mother was the baby of her heart and a medallion of gold.

Chapter IV

Overfield Plantation, October, 1864

Jamison Overfield was aware of her sewing by the light of the fireplace. She was always there, but until recently he had been too sick to care. He was thirsty, and not long ago it would have been whiskey he desired; now his parched throat craved water.

His mind brought forth ready excuses for his drinking and neglect. His family was destroyed; his son was dead and his beautiful, genteel daughters lost to him as well. He had married them to southern gentlemen who rode off for the "cause" without a backward glance. Rachel had died in child birth unattended, abandoned as her slaves followed the Yankee army. Catherine and Laura's families had been caught in the middle of Sherman's march to the sea and he had not heard from them in months.

Lillian and Phobe had returned home impoverished widows, after their husbands had fallen at Gettysburg; but they were no longer his sweet girls. Lillian's loss had turned her into a shrew; while Phoebe had retreated into her own reality, convinced that her long dead husband would soon be coming home. Jamison had not been able to help them; he had not been able to help himself, only grieve for the past.

The glorious cause had been nothing but a grandiose illusion, and what was left had no appeal to him. He had been prepared to die, ready to die and she had not allowed him a peaceful exit. Instead she had healed his body, frail and weak it might be; with little compassion for his tortured mind.

She left her place by the fire and sat down on the edge of the bed where he lay. He could not

even raise his head and she cradled his shoulders to give him a sip from a dipper of cold water.

She picked up a bowl from a nearby table and began spooning soup into his mouth and soon he

was drifting back to sleep.

Rosa looked down at the old man thoughtfully. Many weeks had passed since she had dragged

him in from Cullum's grave; now it seemed Master Jamison would live.

Rosa sat wearily upon her own pallet near the fire. They had made it through another day; she

had purposed in her heart the task of getting them through one day at a time and trying not to

think beyond that.

They lived in one room. She cooked their meals in the fireplace using the remaining stores in

the cellars and the yield from the small garden. She would not think about what would happen

when it was gone. But she had a decision to make. She was a free woman and she would leave

as soon as he was on his feet.

Overton Plantation, November, 1864

Jamison grew restless as the days passed. He had too much time to think and he was still too

weak to move about. As usual she was sitting near the fire sewing. She never spoke much to

him; just fed him, kept him clean and continued to administer that vile brew she made him drink,

but that was all.

He had once prided himself on knowing all of his people. Little Rosa had grown into a handsome woman. Unlike her mother Tilly, who was small and darker; she was tall and slim yet curved at the bosom and hips with skin the color of coffee.

Payne McClure had once offered him top dollar for her even though she limped, but he had refused. It wasn't that he had never sold a slave; over the years he had sold a few troublesome bucks down south, but he knew how McClure would use the girl and something in him could not allow that regal being to be crushed under McClure's fist; because that is what she was, regal. Her manner always subservient; with a lame leg, an unbowed head and an erect posture that even the nuns at the expensive girl's school could not teach his daughters.

His voice sounded rusty to his own ears as he spoke. "Come here Rosa", he said, gesturing impatiently. "Don't dawdle, come here let me get a good look at you."

"Yes sir, Rosa replied, moving toward the bed warily.

"Don't be foolish girl, you have never been afraid before. I'm an old man and you should know right now I could not lift my finger to hurt a fly, much less you. You are handsome enough, that's for sure, no wonder old Frazier wanted to marry you. I just want you to read to me", he said pointing toward the book lying on her pallet. "Don't pretend; I know you can read. It was you who told the slaves about Lincoln's proclamation of freedom, from that handbill I foolishly tossed aside"

Rosa was shocked. All these years he had known she could read and had never said nothing. As a child, Rosa had been given to Miss Catherine as a body servant and she cared for all the young mistress's needs. She would attend Catherine in the school room to fetch and carry while doing the mending. The lessons had been wasted on Catherine, but not on Rosa. Even as a child, she made sure Catherine or the governess never realized how much she had absorbed.

The lessons had ended after Rosa made the mistake of revealing her knowledge of plants to the governess and little missy had stormed into her father office and declared Rosa was showing off and she no longer wanted a stupid "darky" in her school room. The Master had looked at Rosa speculatively, and a few months later Catherine was sent to a girl's school in Charleston.

The denial was upon her lips, but why should she lie. She was a free woman and in control of her own destiny and if the master of Overfield plantation did not know it, it was time he learned. Rosa said, "Yes sir, I can read and do numbers, when it suits me."

"Of course you can, my little Catherine always had more hair than brains; I am glad the price of the governess was of benefit to someone. My Julianne always said you knew more than you let on. Rosa would you please read to me", he said smiling wearily?

Rosa nodded slowly and pick up a book by Charles Dickens; one of the last books they received before the war began. When he saw it was "A Tale of Two Cities", he shook his head, saying, "No war, please", and she picked up the bible and began to read; he could only speculate at the times ahead for him and Rosa.

Overfield Plantation, May, 1865

Gradually Jamison was able to care for his own needs and Rosa moved to a room off from the kitchen. Eventually they read Dickens, and began making inroads into a library he had never spent much time in. He would correct her mispronunciations and sometimes they would laugh over shared memories of Catherine. Jamison did not ask the question that constantly occupied his thoughts, but finally he had to know. "Why did you stay Rosa; why did you help me?"

Freedom and leaving was never far from Rosa's thoughts and yet she had stayed. She did not have an immediate answer to give him; instead she just looked at him, full into his face and eyes.

Jamison was taken aback; no slave or person of color had ever looked at him that way, directly; face to face. He felt a stirring of anger at her impudence, but as her steady brown eyes continued to meet his gaze without apology, his anger drained away.

He could not put words to what he was feeling. It was like a raw wound hurtful to touch as he stared at her as if he was seeing her for the first time. He saw the years of injustices in those eyes. He saw himself and he was appalled at the wave of guilt he felt. Then she answered him.

"I stayed because you needed me and habits of a life-time do not change overnight."

Their relationship was different after that day, although he nor Rosa could have explained why; but for a time, they were cocooned from the insanity of war. And so they continued together through the long winter and spring.

Chapter V

Jamison knew he could not continue to rationalize his self- imposed isolation. Each day he thought Rosa would leave, yet she did not go and he did not want her to go; but things could not remain as they were.

His closest neighbors were a half a day's ride distance; only the threat of contracting the fever had kept them away and Rosa did not care to venture from the house alone. It was only later he discovered that a band of marauders comprised of deserters; had been raiding, along the river.

To the north, was the McClure Plantation; Payne McClure had been wounded in the early days of the war and it had eventually cost him his leg. The Tatum farm, to the south was closer, but deserted after the women had left to join relatives. Jamison had decided to ride north the following day, when Ben Mantell had rode up to the house.

It was common knowledge Mantell hated the Overfields, yet he was here, walking up to the house, hitching the poor lathered animal to the porch as if he was something other than white trash Rosa knew him to be. Not so long ago, instead of pounding on the door demanding entry, he would have waited on the veranda, hat in hand to see the master.

Rosa waited until she heard Jamison from the top of the landing; softly tell her to let him in. She opened the door only partially, but he pushed his way in. She watched in distaste as he lumbered into the front parlor, his beard sprinkled with tobacco juice, his boots caked with mud and by the smell, horse manure.

Large and thickly muscled, Mantell was the kind who took grim delight in hurting others. Whites who failed to steer clear of him soon learned to their regret, Mantell was not a man to cross; for what Mantell could not solve face to face, a dark alleyway and a knife in the back served him just as well.

It was rumored he had once broken a slave's back, just snapped him like a twig and the slaves were quick to do his bidding.

"You alone here gal", he said, greedily eyeing everything in the room, including her.

"No, Master Overfield is above", she replied. She returned his look with frigid eyes until his heated look became menacing. Rosa's sigh of relief was heartfelt, when she saw Jamison making his way unhurriedly down the stairs.

Mantell watched the old man, his lips stretched in a tight smile. Jamison Overfield and his sons, always the perfect southern gentlemen. Overfield thought he and his was too good for the likes of Ben Mantell.

He had once been foolish enough to take Catherine Overfield's flirtatious nonsense seriously. Catherine had been a pretty piece and Mantell had intended to give her just what she had been asking for. Overfield had ordered him off the place with a buggy whip.

Duels were for gentlemen, he recalled angrily. Even the niggers were uppity; he thought; eyeing Rosa as he relieved himself of a wad of tobacco juice in a nearby vase.

After Payne McClure had discovered Mantell had deserted from the army, he and his women folks had ordered him off the plantation at gunpoint; a mistake McClure would pay for later; but there was no way for Overfield to know that. Overfield's comeuppance was long over-due and now it was time he paid, decided Mantell.

The plantation was a regular treasure trove, untouched by the war and ripe for plucking. He saw no need to inform his band of fellow miscreants that had been raiding in the area of the rich pickings to be had. Overfield was his. His bogus smile faded when he saw the shotgun laid across the crook of Overfield's arm.

"Now hold on, ain't no need for that", said Mantell gesturing toward the gun.

"Speak your piece Mantell, Jamison said evenly. Mantell was of the worst sort; as overseer for Payne McClure, he was known for his cruelty. The McClure slaves could be identified by the scars on their backs, but Payne had done nothing to curb him.

Mantell said, "Just being neighborly that's all; don't s'pose you heard ole Bob Lee surrendered to the blue bellies in east Virginia at a place call Appomattox a couple of weeks back."

Mantell's eyes were narrowed to slits as the older man relaxed his grip on the shotgun giving Mantell the opening he needed.

Elation mixed with sadness as Jamison thought of the destruction and death the war had left in its wake; but it had been a mistake to take his eyes off Mantell. Before he could react, Mantell knocked the weapon from Jamison's hands and drove him to the floor; fighting as Mantell fingers closed about his throat.

Rosa looked down at the shotgun that had landed at her feet. She knew she did not have a choice; Jamison was about to die. She picked up the shotgun and fired.

The shock and amazement reflected in Mantell's eyes as they clouded over in death, was akin to the horror etched on Rosa's face. She had killed a white man and it would not matter why, they would hang her for sure.

Fear griped her as the sound of several horses came from the front of the house, but she could not move. She stood rooted to the spot, unable to do anything but stare at Jamison's still body lying on the stairs and Mantell in a pool of blood next to him.

As the door was flung open, Rosa's knees buckled in terror and she fell to the floor beside Mantell and Jamison.

Part II

Chapter VI

Overton County, Founder's Day, 1882

The confederate soldiers had drifted back slowly, with little more than the clothes on their backs. Some had once owned prosperous plantations, others only small dirt farms where they had barely eked out a living before the war. They were all land poor, without money to cultivate their acreage or to pay the taxes. They had gone to war for different reasons; they had returned tired, defeated men; angry men and even more they were afraid.

The euphoria of freedom that had filled Black men and women with such optimism for the future had faded amidst broken promises, hunger and homelessness. Some were lucky, they made it to the North where there was work or headed out West; but for others they could only returned back to what they knew.......the land.

Slaves and slave owners had come together in a way that only desperate people can; together with the Overfields and the Gabriels as Reese and Rosa had begun to call themselves, they forged the future. They had invested all they had on a dream, promising share for share for each man willing to work.

Rosa would never forget the golden fields of corn and barley; or the huge cotton crops, stark white against the blue sky as far as the eye could see; blue-black and red brown men sweating and laboring under the blazing sun. For a season they experienced utopia. People united in a common effort, fired by Stuart Overfield's drive and determination, but it could not last.

Produce from lush fruit orchards, along with the corn and barley crops had been shipped up river to St. Louis for use in the brewery that had been inherited by Amelia Overfield. A textile mill and manufacturing company had been incorporated by Stuart and soon the old plantations had flourished again with the practice of sharecropping. Prosperity brought the slow emergence of the "middle-class". Shopkeepers, businesses of various enterprises opened their doors as well as the First Bank of Overton County.

A school for Negro students had been built and financed by the Gabriels. Never again would black and white share a school room. It was 1882 and "Jim Crow" laws were in full force. On the eastside from Mulberry Road to the county line the white citizens resided; and to the west the blacks lived in Angel's Trumpet.

Angel's Trumpet, 1882

Rosa did not understand why they continued to have the Founder's Day celebration. They were no longer one community, but two; black and white; that was a fact of life and law. But Stuart Overfield wanted the celebration to continue and like always whatever Stuart wanted, he got; and Reese agreed.

Rosa's smile became forced as she observed Jasset and her baby Steban with Reese. Jasset was like his father in so many ways, and to her way of thinking, not all of it good. Jasset and Reese shared the same dark eyes that concealed their thoughts even from her. She had begged Jasset not to challenge Justin, but he would only laugh and kiss her cheeks; telling her not to worry.

Rosa had known Justin Overfield since the day he was born. There was a word in mother Tilly's language, which described one with a single face and two hearts. That was Justin. She had seen the petty cruelty he hid behind the charming mask; and the hate and jealousy in his cold green eyes when he looked at Jasset.

Jasset would be leaving them again after her birthday and the harvest was done. That was her heartache, but it was not safe for him to stay, not yet. None of them was safe. She wondered if she would ever feel safe again, like in the beginning the day she met Reese.

Overfield Plantation, May, 1865

"Gabriel", Rosa had mumbled. Miss Catherine's governess had taught about the baby Jesus, and how the beautiful angel Gabriel was going to blow his trumpet on Judgment Day, much to Tilly's scorn.

Her mother had spent little time teaching Rosa about religious matters. Tilly had believed in the traditions of the elders, the mystic powers of nature and Allah, which she would just as soon curse or praise. Tilly had said, "The whites have no gods but themselves, how can it be otherwise; and they treat us as they do."

"But mama, I believe what I have read from the bible", Rosa had replied.

"Then believe my bebe, for there'll come a time, when you will have need your of God."

Rosa thought it was strange, her head hurt and she felt so dizzy, but she remembered that conversation with her mother like it had happened yesterday.

She slowly opened her eyes, transfixed on the face above her; fumbling about in her mind for a suitable word to describe the man that stared down at her. He was beautiful enough to be the angel Gabriel. His hair had no African kink but was cut close, emphasizing his hawk-like features, dominated by long lashed black eyes filled with concern as he cradled her in his arms.

Rosa heard her him say, "I think she's coming around, but she keeps mumbling about somebody named Gabriel."

With effort, Rosa shifted her gaze to a tall slender woman dressed in black. Her light brown hair curled softly around her face, and her clear gray eyes were kind. Rosa sighed as she recognized the third occupant in the room. He had never been as tall as his father or brother, she thought as he kneeled down beside her. There was a scar on his face, but the green eyes and smile had belonged to Stuart Overfield.

She discovered her Gabriel was named Reese as he carried her to her room off the kitchen; where she had slept until the next day. Once awake she moved by rote, washing herself and changing into a clean dress. She gathered what was left in the larder to prepare a meal, but first Rosa had known it was time to face Mr. Stuart.

She had not been sure what to expect, white people were dead, with only her word for what had happened. But she was a free woman, nobody's slave and that is how she intended to behave.

Rosa had burst into tears when she saw Jamison seated by the warmth of the fire, but she waited in the doorway; until he smiled and motioned her in, saying, "it's alright child."

Stuart had eyed his father strangely, but kept his thoughts to himself. He had been clearly surprised at Jamison's attitude toward a former slave. Rosa covered Jamison shoulders with a blanket then turned to face Stuart; eyes cast downward, but standing tall and straight before him.

Stuart had said, "Rosa I want to thank you for what you did for my father. He has told me of your bravery and loyalty; that he owes you his life not once, but many times over. Now that the war is over, I know we have no hold over you, but we would like you to stay. We have some land that was never cleared for planting, but has laid fallow for many years. I will be honest with you it is hilly, covered with rocks and bush, but I believe with hard work it can be farmed. My father wants you have it. Over two hundred acres bound by the plantation on one side and the swamp lands on the other to make a home if you choose. The boundaries will offer you some protection, do you understand."

Rosa could only nod, as Stuart continued, "Dangerous times are coming Rosa, the countryside is running wild with carpetbaggers and scalawags a plenty. There are those that cannot or will not accept your freedom or that the war is over, but also a time of prosperity for those willing to work hard and take risks. The land is yours and will be recorded as such. Let me make known to you my wife Amelia and my friend Sergeant Reese.

The land you own is part of Overfield Plantation and you can share in the profits; and you have our oath we will always honor the bond between us." Rosa had wanted to believe those words. After twenty years she remained unconvinced.

She could still remember the fear she felt the day she had killed Mantell; but that same day Reese had come into her life. Her "Gabriel", had held her close in his strong arms like precious cargo and for the first time in her life she had felt protected and safe.

A slave's life was filled with fear, but with Reese in the beginning, she forgot to be afraid. But she had been living in a fool's paradise. She did not want to be lulled into a sense of security that did not exist. Fear kept you sharp and sometime it was the only edge you had; Jamison taught her that. If she had not been scared witless that day, so long ago, they both would have been dead.

Reese had always been his own man; how could Rosa blame him for not understanding something he had never experienced? He had never been a slave so how could he know. One of the first things you learned as a slave is to hide your thoughts and feelings. She had allowed herself to be swept along on a tide of love for Reese and Stuart Overfield's enthusiasm. By the time, she began to come out of her trance, it was too late. Reese did not want to know. Her fears were ungrounded, slave notions based on distrust. When she had tried to explain how she felt he had become angry and she could only swallow her frustrations.

Reese had been the love of her life, and she allowed herself to see him as she wanted him to be instead of who he was. He had never tried to deceive her. Rosa had deceived herself. Now he was determined to raise his sons in his own image, shaping their character not as a reflection of their world, but the world as Reese viewed it. It was not a realistic vision, given the fact they were surrounded by people who saw only their skin color and nothing else. Unless Reese tempered his ways and the boys gained a truer outlook of life, only trouble lay ahead.

She had even believed he had taken the name Gabriel to please her, although he could have legally called himself Amherst. Maybe it had been his intention to please her, but it also pleased Stuart since he did not want the connection between Amelia and Reese to be known.

Amherst Brewery had been owned by Reese's adopted father. He had taught Reese the business and had even made him assistant manager before the war. It had not been easy, but his knowledge of the business had been undisputed. How many times had she told him it was the only reason Stuart had made him a partner?

The life and death experiences of war had created a bond between the two men she could not break. Reese trusted Stuart without reservation. Such absolutes should never be invested in another human. That is what she read in her bible. Jamison had help her learn to read the bible and increase her knowledge of the world. Their relationship had also been based on trust and had remained so until the day he died, but she never forgot who she was.

Rosa remembered thinking Reese was the person she had wanted to share her news after Jamison had given her the land. She had been alone it was true, but she had felt close to him from the start. Yet she could barely meet his gaze, unsure of what she might expose. She could not have borne his pity; but he had listened quietly offering his congratulation, but nothing of himself.

She had tried to talk to him; asking him questions, which he answered with one syllable words; until she had finally turned to leave, when she heard him speak.

"When the Captain got wounded the closest place to take him was my home. Amelia took care of him; and later they were married. The rest I reckon you will find out in time." His full lips had curved in the similitude of a smile, as he replied.

And so, she had found out the rest. Rosa had thought Reese was a sooty, educated man, who thought he was too good for her. Of course, Reese had been none of those things. She had just not been able to verbalize what she had been feeling, but Reese had known.

Sex was common place around a plantation. Having been raised in the slave quarters, she had not been ignorant about such things. Thankfully, the Overfields didn't breed their people like some, nor were they likely to be found in the women quarters at night. Still, bellies were always big and broom jumping had been mostly an afterthought.

She had never been touched or molested in any way; nor had she wanted to be. Besides she limped. She never thought of herself as a cripple, but she knew others thought of her that way. But when Reese had looked at her it had not been like she was a cripple or a joint of meat like the dead man Mantell.

Love for her had not grown gradually; it had been sudden, passionate, and it had taken her a long time to realize that loving and knowing, was not the same as understanding and respect.

Fate had linked their destinies and the rightness of it remained; as tangible and real as anything she had felt then or since. She had never regretted her love for him, only her unwillingness to see what was right in front of her eyes.

She remembered the night she had waited for him in her mother's cabin, never doubting he would come. The cabin had been clean and homey; filled with her mother's loving present. It had been right that she be joined to him there.

He had softly called her name, framed in the moonlight spilling through her door. She had walked toward him wishing she could be perfect for him, but her limp meant nothing to him. "You are beautiful", he had told her.

She had not known desire, but she had ached with the sweet wonder of wanting him. She remembered the gentleness of his hands and the warmth of his mouth as he traced kisses over her body. She had opened herself to him as naturally as breathing.

She felt the heat of his gaze from the end of the table and felt her pulse quicken at the knowing smile, that small curving of his lips she knew expressed so many things. Their eyes met and the noise of the crowd seemed to fade as they experienced a shared remembrance of how it had been.

Reese was honest enough with himself to admit that no matter how much he loved her now, it had not started that way. He had wanted her and the situation had appeared made to order. His future had been tied to the Overfields just as hers. He and Stuart were a team, and still after so many years Rosa could not understand that.

Reese had always admired Rosa's spirit and backbone; but it had been her vulnerability that had attracted him. She touched him in a way he could not define. He remembered how hard she had tried to hide her limp. She hadn't even known how pretty she was. In the beginning, she would have done anything he asked; now she questioned everything he thought or did.

Rosa just refused to let go of the past. But there had been a time when she had looked at him with luminous brown eyes, and he had been filled with the belief that he could do anything. He thought of the first time he had kissed her parted lips; of her beautiful smooth-skinned body and the way she had yielded herself to him so sweetly. How he missed that woman.

Reality brought them both back to the present and Rosa saw the look in his eyes cool as he turned away. She felt sad; but she could not go backward. She knew who she was and where she belonged. She meant to hold Angel Trumpet for her children, and their children; whatever it took.

Chapter VII

Overfield Plantation, 1882

It was a beautiful September morning and a perfect day for a picnic, Amelia decided as she readied herself for the festivities. Amelia Amherst Overton was a gracious woman and after so many years of marriage she had to learned to be a forgiving one.

The day Reese had brought Stuart home wounded and feverish she had been too busy trying to save his life to wonder about his southern accented ramblings. As he recovered it did not matter, she did not care, she was in love. For better or worse she had married him and watched him ride away, back into war; leaving her to wonder if she would ever see him again.

She was already pregnant when he returned for good and she had followed him to his home unsure of the welcome she would receive. She had walked into this house as a bride to find three bodies and blood all over the floor. She had nearly fainted dead away herself, but she was Colonel Charles Amherst's daughter and she was made of sterner stuff than that.

She had worked, washed and cooked right alone side Rosa and the other colored women, while their men worked in the fields all day, right alone side Stuart. To the other white wives, she was just a Yankee, which explained her particularities.

Charles Amherst had found Reese as an infant on one of his treks into the wilderness, lying under the dead bodies of his parents. He and his wife had been childless at the time, but a few years later Amelia had been born. She and Reese had been raised as brother and sister; but she had agreed when Stuart asked her not to reveal that Reese was her adopted brother. People in Overton would not understand he had said and Reese had gone along. It had become a habit, doing whatever Stuart wanted.

She smiled at Rosa and Reese seated at a nearby table. Reese was still her dear brother, but the closeness Amelia tried to encourage between her and Rosa never happened. Rosa would not let it happen. There were too many barriers between them and things Rosa felt she could never share. She would probably be surprised, if she realized how much Amelia did understand her insecurities.

People rarely noticed her when Stuart was around, but she never minded, because it gave her the opportunity to observe and later when the house was quiet she would record her thoughts in her diary. For instance, she knew there was tension between Rosa's boy Jasset and Justin.

Her son was handsome, thoughtless and spoilt. She wanted Justin to be the man his Father was and his Grandfather had been, but she knew in her heart the boy fell short of the mark. However, to Stuart he could do no wrong. He dismissed Justin's actions as "sowing wild oats." She loved her son dearly and it was up to her to keep a watch over him.

Stuart leaned over to kiss Amelia on the cheek; he was proud of his wife and children. Looking out over the crowd of town-folk, he knew some were there because they liked and admired him. Others came because they owed him, but there was none he could trust implicitly, except the black man who sat tactfully at a table on the other side of the grounds.

He had left home with Jamison 's angry words following him out of the door and he had not known what to expect when he returned. Cullum had been killed and he could imagine the depth of his father's despair, but he had to know where he stood. What had greeted him was chaos. He had just been grateful that Jamison still lived. Mantell was lucky, he had got off easy.

Stuart realized that his father had changed. He had watched Jamison as he sat by the warming embers of the large fireplace. He had said very little except about Rosa and the gift of land. The relationship between the two was revealing. She had started to cry when she realized he was alive and he had beckoned her into the room to comfort her as if she was a daughter of the house, patting her hand, and thanking her in a low, whispery voice. Gone was the hearty bluster of the father that Stuart remembered, instead he was a frail old man.

His brother Cullum had been Jamison's pride. Cullum had simply possessed a zest for life, an energetic presence that overshadowed others whether charming ladies in a ballroom or excelling on the hunting field, his dogs snapping at his heels. He was also arrogant and petty. Cullum never backed down from a fight and no slight however trivial had been left unchallenged. He and Jamison were "southern gentlemen" they had understood each other.

Stuart had been one of Cullum's favorite targets; but he had no appreciation of Stuart's humor. His response to Cullum's taunts and threats had infuriated his older brother; and Stuart quickly learned that if he was caught, the price for his disrespect was Cullum's gloved fist or booted foot.

All Stuart had ever wanted, was his father to be proud of him. That was why he had worked become an excellent marksman and horseman. He felt no urge to prove himself or pit his skill against another. He preferred to read a book which only angered Jamison more. Only his mother's support had been unconditional.

Julianne Overfield had been a lovely woman, wise and caring. She handled her husband adroitly as she did most things; after he accused her of making Stuart soft. Remarking quietly that his youngest son was his own man, not bound by others' opinions; and that in time he would find his way.

Jamison could not stop staring at his son trying to find Julianne in the man. Julianne's green eyes had been the color of a grassy meadow on a spring day and her soft auburn curls teased a man to touch it, but when he looked at Stuart's thick bronze hair and hard jade eyes he saw a stranger. A ruddy-ridged scar on his face stood out against his tanned skin in the firelight and the thin body of the scholar had filled out into manhood.

Stuart was not self-conscious about the scar, but he could feel his father assessing gaze, and the truth was he was no longer the young man desperate for his father's approval he had been when he went away. Perhaps he didn't need a father, but he could use a friend. He could not allow the past to dictate the future. Finally, he said, "Papa, I'm home to stay, if you will have me.

Jamison grasp Stuart's hand, tears falling unashamedly down his face. "Thank God you have come home son; everything I have belongs to you."

They both had known all could not be said or set right in one night, but the floodgates had been opened and walls of silence that had been built over so many years started to crumble that night.

Stuart heard his daughter's laughter and smiled. His Sarah had Jamison's coloring with her golden curls and topaz eyes, mixed with her mother's sweetness of spirit. Sarah was a lovely girl and he doted on the child. Julian had Amelia's brown hair and grey eyes with none of her compliancy. Jamison had taken perverse delight in reminding Stuart when he complained about his youngest son's stubbornness; that he had been just as head-strong at that age. However, it was his oldest son that troubled Stuart.

Whenever he looked at Justin, he saw his brother Cullum. Granted their coloring was different, but Justin had the same tall, good-looking swagger; with red-gold hair, green eyes, and a lazy smile that drew women like flies. But despite his faults, Cullum had always maintained the comportment of a gentleman. Justin, it seemed knew no boundaries.

The boy had been adored and spoiled since his birth and Stuart readily admitted to indulging the him, but his cousins in Virginia as well as the school officials had written Stuart some disturbing letters. Only yesterday, Henry Tatum had accused Justin of forcing his attentions on his daughter. Stuart knew he could pay off Tatum, he and his family were barely scratching by sharecropping, but Stuart could no longer allow Justin to go unchecked.

For over a hundred years the Overfields had held the land; Justin was his oldest son, the survival of the family legacy was his duty and it was time he realized that fact.

Stuart had faced many challenges after his return and there had been a point when even Jamison questioned the family ability to overcome the challenges facing them. Already there were whispers concerning the land gift to Rosa. Not that it mattered, the land belonged to the Overfield and they would do with it as they damn-well pleased.

Jamison said, "We have given Rosa the land, but how can we possibly protect her, when our neighbors consider you an outsider." The rest of Jamison's comments had trailed off awkwardly.

He had reassured his father as best he could. "It's alright Papa, I'm aware that they consider me a traitor and an outcast, but I am still an Overfield of Overfield Plantation and anyone who thinks that I will not keep and protect what is mine will soon know better." He had kept the promise.

With Jamison's support, he and Reese had beaten the odds Stuart thought as he looked about him. They had accomplished the impossible; he still marveled at their success. Men like the McClures had resented him, but no matter what the community had thought about him, he had given them hope, and a chance. It was a chance that had paid off.

Overton had started as a small shipping town, boasting a deep harbor inlet, and an ideally situated U-shaped quay, first settled by Augustus Overfield in 1740. The community had grown and prospered during the intervening years, weathering skirmishes with Indians, pirates, and royalists' sympathizers during the struggle for independence from England. But none had ever caused as much trouble as Gregar McClure.

McClure had migrated from Scotland, after most of his family had been slaughtered by the British at Culloden. He had a hatred of the English aristocracy, and the landed gentry, Virginian tide-water antecedents of the Overfield family were all one in the same to him. Many speculated where he had obtained the money for the venture that had him a rich man, but no one asked, considering it was worth your life to know the answer.

The plantation owners had grown wealthy using slave labor to harvest rich yields of rice, indigo and cotton, but a planter had to be able store his crops for market and ship his cotton in a timely manner. None of which could be accomplished except through the Delta Star Shipping Company, using Delta Star warehouses, lest he run afoul of Gregar McClure, the Delta Star's sole proprietor.

Other shipping concerns had suffered remarkably bad luck in Overton; with ships sunk, cargoes lost and crews impossible to keep. There had been no proof McClure was involved, and those who had the effrontery to accused him directly, had found themselves facing McClure across the dueling field.

Augustus Overfield had endured McClure's highhanded ways along with the others until he discovered Gregar was part of a scheme to manipulate the cotton market. It was then he decided to invest in a shipping company out of Maryland; bringing new shipping interests into Overton that Gregar could not break or control, earning the enmity of Gregar McClure tenfold.

Their neighbors had looked on in wary amusement, careful not to offend or take sides with neither family. That had been the nucleus that had formed Overton; personal feuds, births, deaths, duels, marriages; and an ease of gracious southern living from one generation to the next.

Such was the world before Noah and the flood, and for the people of Overton the flood came in the guise of Lincoln and the Yankee army.

The Yankees had decided that although Overton could be of strategic importance, it was too small of an area to waste the deployment of troops. Their solution was to burn the remaining docking ships, the warehouses filled with England bound cotton; and most of the quay to cinders.

It was no secret that the town-folks of Overton had excepted Stuart's help because they had nowhere else to turn. Most considered him a traitor to his own family and the southern cause, but they had nothing and pride offered a poor substitute for their children's empty stomachs. He had offered them hope for the future of Overton.

For two days, the men had loaded the cargo of cotton from the river bank, using boats and rafts to row their crops to a waiting Yankee clipper. Only Reese knew how the ship's Captain had been persuaded to travel down river from Missouri to convey the largest cotton crop Overton had ever produced to Bristol. A third of the profits, shaved from Stuart's share had been the only inducement to persuade the Captain to travel that far south, but they had been able to corner the market for cotton in England, before others could off load their cotton surplus. The money from that shipment had been the beginning of a fresh start for the people of Overton.

Chapter VIII

Angel's Trumpet, 1882

Rosa checked her reflection in the highboy mirror. The diamond ear drops glittered as she turned her head to and fro, then with a sigh she removed them and placed them in their box. Reese had given her the earrings for her birthday the night before. For a while they had set aside their differences causing Rosa to smile at the memory of their lovemaking. Time and age, had added an extra sweetness to their time together that she cherished.

She knew he would be disappointed that she had not worn his birthday gift. She had tried to tell him, she was no pampered white woman nor did she want to be, but Reese just didn't listen. She sighed, Reese was Reese.

The years had been kind to Rosa. Her hair was still thick and only lightly sprinkled with gray. The burgundy gown she wore suited her slender figure and she knew she looked well. She had made the gown herself; her sewing machine was one of the most precious gifts Reese had ever given her; but she doubted he would be satisfied with that knowledge.

Her limp was more pronounced now as she walked into the adjoining dressing room, using a cane of smooth teak wood Jasset had brought her from Paris. She found Reese there; fussing with the stiff collar of his shirt.

"Move", she said slapping his hands away as she smoothed his collar and tie.

"You look beautiful Rose, said Reese, admiring his wife, until he noticed she was not wearing the earrings. "Why won't you wear the earrings or the other things I have bought you", Reese said angrily?

"I am not Amelia, Reese." Besides I am wearing one of your gifts; you know they are my favorites", waiting for him to admire the gold earrings, that dangled whenever she turned her head.

"You are my wife dammit, and if I want to shower you with jewelry, why in hell is it anyone else's business."

"It is not just the jewelry, and you know it. I don't want white men wondering how you afford diamond earrings or their wives' side-way glances. I don't want their envy; it's dangerous."

"Rosa you deserve the best this world has to offer, why can't you believe that? Your body is free, but you still think like a slave. Things are changing for our people."

"For a while I wanted to believe that. That we could began to live our lives like every human being has a right to, but they not gonna let us. When Hayes became president, any hope that things would get better died. I have had to send my sons away to be educated, to keep them safe, because they want to be like their father."

"So, what do you want Rosa, do you want them to grovel; be less than men?"

Please don't be angry, she said softly, tears gathering in her eyes; "I just want them to live, and their children and their children's children to have and hold this land; or it has all been for nothing. Those three babies that we buried on the hill, was all for nothing. They got to be smarter than us Reese, they got to be wiser.

"Listen to yourself; this land was given to you by the Overfields, Stuart would not let anything happen to change that, but if it did, there are other places to go, other land to be had."

"And if they decide you too uppity at that place we could just go on to the next, and the next one after that. No this is my land, I earned every inch of it, and so did you."

"I will not emasculate my sons, not for you or the land or anything else, he replied stonily.

"Then you live with the consequence. Have you seen the way Justin looks at Jasset; he hates him. You and Stuart might love each other like brothers; but Justin, is his son. I want you to remember that."

Tempers had cooled by the time they arrived at her birthday celebration, but Rosa was still upset. She tried to compose herself as they stopped at the Overfield table and she returned Amelia's greeting. Rosa thought Amelia was a fine woman, but how could she explain to her she felt closer to Sally Mack. Or how could she tell Amelia that her son was dangerous, or the threats she sensed aimed at Jasset.

As soon as she and Reese were seated at their table, Jasset headed toward the Delecourt's table. The Delecourt girl was very pretty and Jasset was suffering the pangs of first love. Jasset was too young to be serious about anyone, but apparently, she was the only one who thought so as Reese winked his eye smiling. She watched as Jasset and Mae Delecourt walked down toward the river, wishing she felt as sanguine as Reese evidently did.

Sally Mack leaned over and said, "Look at her Miz Rosa she ain't no better than she should be; flaunting herself around every man here."

Sally had been hired by Reese to help Rosa with the heavier work in the house. Originally, she had grudgingly accepted the help, but over the years Rosa had come to appreciate the Macks and their unfailing loyalty. Rosa had to admit that the Delecourt girl garnered her share of attention, including Sally's husband, Lucias. Even the white men had been gawking, which could be dangerous.

Rosa said, "Sally it's not the girl's fault that nature has been more than kind to her."

"Uh Huh and she knows it too, remember how she carried on at the baptism, that white gown, sticking to her like a second skin. I'm tellin you Miz Rosa, she ain't got no shame."

"It is not like the girl has a mother to teach how to go on and Preacher Delecourt travels a lot. Mae is a pretty girl, there will always be men looking at her. I'm willing to give her the benefit of the doubt."

"You are a good woman Miz Rosa, but if I was you and Jasset was my son, I'd give her more than benefit of the doubt. Look at Lucias he so drunk now he can hardly stand, 'scue me."

Rosa smiled, as Sally dragged away a protesting Lucias amid much laughter. Sally was probably jealous because Lucias was paying so much attention to the girl. She had notice the Overfield boys looking too.

Justin was particularly eyeing the pair as Mae and Jasset walked along. His was smile was friendly, but his green eyes had darkened to the color of pond scum. Rosa suddenly felt uneasy; maybe Sally was right, maybe she should make an effort to know the girl better.

Justin was aware of Rosa's scrutiny; that old woman always did see too much, but he only smiled. She was so worried about her precious Jasset.

Justin frowned as his father congratulated Jasset on his accomplishments at some school that took niggras up north. When they were boys Justin could best every other boy in the county, but Jasset was always a little better.

His mama was always going on about his manners pleasing; and about how gifted he was on the piano, often delighting Stuart and Amelia's guests. They had actually given him a piano and Justin's resentment had increased ten-fold. It had been bad enough to be compared to anyone, but for daddy to keep holding up that nigger, was just too much. Jasset had sat there smiling, as if it was his due, as arrogant a bastard that ever was.

51

Well he had plans for that boy hell, he had plans for them all, Daddy couldn't live forever; but first Jasset. The boy had been uppity since the day he was born and Justin hated him and his whole family. He was careful that his father not discover his contempt for the Gabriels, but one day they would all know.

And he would be willing to bet his new stallion, that whatever Jasset's accomplishments might be, women were not included among them. Justin had his first woman when he was fourteen, one of his mama's friends had been most obliging and he had not slow down since. He knew Daddy insisted that he attend school in Virginia; where his Overfield kin there could act as his watchdog.

He been home for a month, raising hell and having fun; although he had to admit sometimes fun had a way of quickly turning awry. Stuart had found out about Lib, he had seen that cracker Tatum leaving the house which was why he had acquiesced graciously to his mother's request that he escort her to the Baptism at the colored church.

His mother's fascination with the native rituals disgusted him, but he had thought it best to stay out of his father's way for a while and cultivate his mother's good graces. As far as Justin was concerned, church was for women and old men. The way he saw it, the only thing these fools could be assured of was a Saturday night bath and muddy sheets.

He had tossed the reins of the horse and buggy to one of the young boys milling about and left his mother talking to Rosa Gabriel amid the crowd at the water's edge; while he climbed uphill to a shaded spot overlooking the river.

It was damned was hot and his mother had insisted he dress as befitted a gentleman. He took perverse delight in pulling open the starched collar and unbuttoning his white shirt almost to the waist; knowing that his mother would be appalled at his lack of gentlemanly decorum.

His Mama's particularities were as troublesome as his father's friendship with Reese Gabriel and about as pointless; since Rosa did not like her no matter what she did. Still, it would not do to upset her. He needed her to intercede with Stuart. If she observed him sipping whiskey from the flask he kept hidden or smoking one of those "detestable cigarettes", he could forget about her handling daddy for him.

It was not long before his flask was empty and the preacher still had not run out of sinners to dunk under the water. Justin had had enough; Mama could just get a ride home with the Gabriels. He could not disguise the smell of whiskey anyhow, deciding he would prefer to face his father's wrath than spend one more minute watching wet niggahs; when he saw the girl.

Beaded moisture glimmered like jewels on her dark wet skin; molding the thin white gown to her svelte form. The women hastily covered her with a sheet, all the while, the girl's bewitching eyes sought his, filled with laughter, leaving no doubt she was aware Justin had been staring at her.

The bold challenge in the dark beauty eyes was irresistible and he determined to learn who the minx was.

Until today it had only been about getting under her skirts. It had not taken him long to discover she was the local colored preacher's daughter; but today, Justin discovered Jasset Gabriel was head over heels in love with the girl whose name he found out was Mae.

Justin almost laughed out loud. He could not believe his luck when he saw the lovesick expression on Jasset's face. He just stood there, twisting his hat in his hand, stuttering like an idiot trying to talk to her.

Maybe he could not do anything about the rest of them right now, but seducing Mae would give him the opportunity to rub Jasset's face in the mud and he could hardly wait.

His chance came several days later he saw her walking alone. She was even more alluring up close. Thick shiny braids curled atop up thrust breasts pushing against the bodice of a pink calico dress; that hugged her slim waist, flaring over her shapely hips. He stopped his horse in front of her resting his leg on the top of his saddle.

"Gal you look as sweet as a cherry candy in that dress and I'm a man with a sweet tooth. What a bold little hussy you were at the baptism."

"Oh you was that white boy staring at me from on top the hill. Was you lost or something?"

"You know damn well it was me and you knew exactly what you were doing. You were dripping wet, practically bare-assed naked and that look in your eyes was an invitation, I ain't never misunderstood. I thought you were supposed be renouncing sin not inciting it."

"Is that what I do to you Mr. Justin Overfield, incite you to sin", said Mae, returning his perusal with a sly smile?

"Honey you could incite St. Pete to sin."

Mae moistened her lips with her tongue, as she looked speculatively at Justin Overfield. There was no man she could not have, but since the day she spied him swimming naked, there was only one she wanted.

He dismounted, expecting her to run, instead she continued to look at him; daring him to do what came natural to him. He would have taken her then and there, but they heard someone coming and she dash off through the woods, but Justin was a man, who enjoyed the chase; he intended to have her. And he would make sure Jasset Gabriel knew all about it.

Angel Trumpet, May, 1882

The light of the full moon shone brightly through the open window haloing entwined lovers and tangled sheets. Their breathing was labored as they fell back together, the woman's hand roaming caressingly over her lover's body; lacing her fingers in the red gold hair matted across his chest. Justin rose on one elbow and grinned, "Damn Mae, don't you ever get enough."

"No, but then that's lucky for you cher", she said smiling, moving her hand lower.

"Mae, did you do as I told you, I mean about the Gabriel boy", he said, trailing kisses along her sleek throat."

"Oh cher, why do you bother about him he means nothing to me? You are more man than he will ever be. He can barely speak two words to me without stuttering. I flirt with him, he is in love, it was too easy, but why do you want me to do such a thing?

Suddenly Justin sank his teeth into the tender skin of her shoulder and Mae whimpered in pain. "Don't ever question me again, do you understand. All you got to do is just keep acting demure and virginal. He can find out on his wedding night just how well plowed his little wife is."

"Yes cher", she said tearfully. Suddenly Mae realized he was obsessed with Jasset; but that did not stop her from wanting him. He began to trace the hurtful spot with his tongue, parting her slender thighs and covering her with his kisses she continued to craved him beyond reason. But she was also learning to fear him.

It was almost dawn when he eased away from Mae sleeping form and began to dress. She was really exquisite, too good for Jasset, but she would do exactly as she was told. Soon he would know the humiliation Justin had felt for years. He could hardly wait to savor his victory, especially when he knew his revenge was at hand.

Angel's Trumpet, 1982

Reverend Delecourt was concerned about his daughter. He had returned home to find her heavy eyed and listless, although she smiled at him sweetly as she set the table for dinner. Mae had always been a good girl. She kept the house spotless and she was an excellent cook.

It had not been easy for the girl after her mother died and he admitted that he had not been attentive to her as he should have been. It seemed she had grown up over- night and he could not help but notice the attention she received. All summer she had been courted by Jasset Gabriel and his parents appeared to accept Mae.

She had told him the Gabriel boy wanted to marry her, and he knew the boy was of age. He would have no sin at his door and marriage would be an answer to his prayers. There was a widow who would make him a good wife, but first he had to get Mae settled.

He would be traveling back to Venton County later and Mae had asked once again that she be allowed to stay home. Perhaps if he let her stay the Gabriel boy would finally get to the point.

Angel Trumpet, October, 1882

Justin looked incredulously at the weeping girl, standing before him. Everything had been going as planned. Mae had encouraged Jasset's attentions all summer. It had been amusing to watch that puppy-dog expression on his face when Mae was around. Now his plans were ruined because of Mae's stupidity; he grabbed the girl and began to shake her with a force that rocked her to the floor.

Seducing Mae right under everyone's nose had been so much fun. The first time had been at the pond, after that whenever her father's ministry circuit to the neighboring county began and she could find a reason to beg off.

Jasset returned to school after harvest, and his mother's birthday, which was a big celebration. His parents would be there and so would he. Justin would be watching when Mae turned those sultry eyes on Jasset and before the boy knew it, he would be married to Justin's whore.

Mae was afraid, more afraid than she had her been in her life. She could not erase the image of Jasset face from her mind. That sweet, handsome boy begging her to marry him; his coca brown eyes filled with love for her. How could she tell Justin she could not go through with it?

"I'm pregnant Justin, please don't hurt me", she said crying.

"How could that be", Justin shouted angrily. You told me you couldn't have children."

"All this time we been together, I thought I couldn't, I'm so sorry Justin", she said clutching his arm, but he shook her off cruelly and she sank to the floor weeping.

The dark scowl on Justin's face brighten as he said, "He will be leaving for school in a few days, he always leaves after his mama's birthday. It could still work, just tell Jasset the baby is his. He'll believe anything you tell him."

"But Justin I have never been with anybody but you", said Mae shielding her face from him."

"What! Mae I told you what to do. What have you been doing all these weeks; huh, all the walks and picnics?"

If possible, Mae sank further to the floor. She knew Justin was capable of killing her; she had known it for a long time now. She had seen the mad glow in his eyes when he talked about Jasset Gabriel. Today Jasset had been so sweet, touching her like she was treasured and special. She just could not do it. She had got up running, not stopping until she reached home.

Justin said, "I don't care how you do it, but you get him over here. Your daddy will be away for the next three days. You make sure Jasset has no doubt that the child is his. You do it Mae or you gonna be sorry the day you were born." Justin walked out slamming the door behind him.

Justin had been all she could think about from the moment Mae had first seen him. She had thought she could control him, so wild he had been to be with her. He had turn everything around so smoothly she was lost before she realized he only wanted to use her to hurt Jasset.

She was such a fool; she did not know what to do. Her Papa believed she was going to marry Jasset. She had to convince Justin to find another way.

Suddenly she heard the screen door open and shut. Mae jumped up from the floor; Justin, she thought, he had come back. Instead she looked up to meet the blazing eyes of Rosa Gabriel.

Chapter

St. Louis, 1884

"Mae, will you stop that youngin from crying before wakes up my children", said Lizzie Johns, nudging her awake. Mae got up from bed and poured water from a pitcher she kept for washing. She cleaned her breasts before feeding her son.

"Look at him go, I believe that child is hollow to his feet, said Lizzie as she went out of the door. She would help the cook get breakfast started, then come back to watch the children, while Mae helped serve and started the day's cleaning. Miss Maureen did not care as long as the work got done.

Miss Maureen was a Quaker and her establishment was one of the few that catered to Colored clientele. Lizzie and Mae worked as parlor maids and she allowed them to share the attic room with their children. They worked in shifts, one watching the children while the other worked.

Mae had been working for Miss Maureen Chadwick's boarding house; since the night Rosa Gabriel stepped into her life. She would never forget that woman eyes; cold as death.

She had walked into the house that night after overhearing Mae and Justin without preamble, told Mae to pack up her belongings. Mae was afraid to say a word as the woman took her to the docks where she paid a ship's captain heading up river, a twenty-dollar gold piece to take Mae as far as St. Louis. She wrote a letter to Ms. Maureen and handed Mae a purse with a hundred dollars, warning Mae never to come back.

She never knew what Rosa Gabriel had told her father, but somehow, she must have made it all right. He wrote her a few weeks later her how proud he was that Mrs. Gabriel had been able to find her such a good job. What a joke; Mae thought, but at least she had not told her father she was pregnant.

The baby had been born the following spring and as soon as she was on her feet again, she was trudging up and down stairs empting slop jars and ironing linen. One particularly set of linen she enjoyed ironing belonged to Mr. Louis Templeton Turner.

Louis was one of the most elegant Negro men she had ever seen. His shirts were snowy white hand-stitched fine linen with ruffles down the front. His dark lean hands were soft and his nails manicured. Mae knew he was a gambler by trade and she could listen to his stories about the places he had been for hours. Before long she realized she was pregnant again.

Of course, Miss Maureen had booted her out as soon as she found out she was pregnant; said she would not have such carrying-on in her establishment, but surprised Mae by offering to keep her baby boy. Mae had looked at her as if she was crazy. Where she went, her babies went with her.

She had never expected anything from Templeton, but he showed up with a wagon and loaded up her and the baby she had named Redmond. He told her he couldn't promise to marry her, that he had a wife somewhere, but he kept them with him and a few months later she had another son, Mason.

As they grew older Templeton tried to teach them to poker, but neither had an aptitude for cards, but they displayed a marked talent for malice and mayhem. Templeton decided they would be his watchdogs. He and the boys became a familiar sight on the gambling circuit; some people laughingly called them Dust and Dawn because one was light- skinned and the other dark. The smart ones, however never said it to their face.

New York, 1920

Redmond Turner stood watching the poker game from his behind his step-father; his brother Mason held a similar position in the opposite corner. Temp's hands were shakier than usual, he thought. Maybe he should have let him have that last drink, but he had turned into a complete lush. In their business, you needed a clear head and steady hands.

He looked around the table. Elgin Taffin was a Creole from New Orleans; they had crossed paths with before. Taffin was good, maybe as good as Temp use to be, but he was too quick tempered and prone to use the knife he kept sheaved on a leather throng at the back of his neck.

Theo Farrell was one of the two whites at the table. He had fast hands and tricky fingers; and not above dealing seconds, if he thought he could get away with it. They would have to watch him close, he decided, signaling Mace with a slight nod in Farrell's direction.

He really didn't hold with women at the poker table, but Melina Jones had earned the right to be there. Red watched as she deftly shuffled the cards. Her hands were small and delicate with long white rimmed nails.

Fletcher Monroe III, was the other white at the table. He had the sickness, Red had seen his kind before. A perpetual looser, always looking to the next turn of the cards to change his luck, as the money in front of him diminished. Luckily his family had enough money to fund his addiction. Monroe was a snobbish second generation rich kid, whose father had made the family fortune in the meat packaging business. Unfortunately, he lived in a town of snobs, whose lineages went back further than "Hell's Kitchen".

Red had dismissed Willis Webster as another loser, until his woman came into view. He liked his women dark and she was the color of maple syrup. Every man present turned to watch her as she walked across the room. She moved with a rhythm of body parts; the undulating curve of her ass and the full high breasts invited every man in the room to look his fill. Webster appeared more interested in the card table and that suited Red just fine. He leaned back to enjoy the view as she crossed her legs revealing the contour of her thighs above her gartered stockings.

Leah Webster returned Red's scrutiny with chilly appraisal; neither shock nor impressed at the erection pushing against the front of his trousers which Red made no attempt to hide. Her slanted glance dismissed him as she turned her attention to the poker game, but Red was more amused than angry. Somebody's been real careless in the lady's upbringing, he thought; he would enjoy teaching her some manners.

Willis Webster had noticed Temp Turner's watchdog ogling Leah. It which was nothing new; men liked Leah. He could have warned the poor fool, but he doubted it would have done any good. His wife liked her share of male attention; it did not bother him since it provided a distraction that guaranteed him at least one or two easy pots.

Leah's long lashed chocolate eyes seemed to challenge every male in the room, daring them to try their luck; while acknowledging their perusal, with a slight smile. Her crimson colored lips parted to reveal small white teeth that protruded slightly, which instead of detracting from her beauty, triggered a feline allure that drew men like moths to the flame.

The first time he had seen her, he had been playing in a small south-side speakeasy. She had arrived with the club manager who had become annoyed at her lack of devotion. Leah could have had any man in the room, instead her attention had been riveted on him as he played the piano. She had stayed for every set, and when he left the club that night, she had left with him.

He knew people wondered why a such woman would attach herself to him. Leah would only laugh and say "they have not seen you with your pants off."

They were alike, he and Leah. They both had single-minded passions…… themselves. She knew she was free to comport herself as she liked and he knew it was that freedom she found intoxicating. He never questioned her faithfulness, Leah liked the chase, it was the only way she could control the game. Leah was undemanding; she respected and admired his talent, never demanded money(why should she he gave it to her), and eased his sexual tension, allowing him to channel all his energy into his music.

He was without question a musical genius, but genius required discipline. The self-imposed demands and controlled environment he created for this purpose; spent itself out at the poker table and the excitement of the game's unpredictability, which Temp Turner could have told him was false. The element of predictability was what poker was all about, and using it to your advantage. Yet the lure of gambling increasingly enthralled Webster and even Leah's brand of magic could not cure his fever.

*

"Be-itch at twelve o'clock", said Larry, nudging Mace as he eyed the Webster woman. Mace regarded the effeminate waiter with distaste.

"What would you know about it faggot?"

"Oh, how quickly we forget", returned a sniggering Larry.

Mace pinned him with a deadly glance; "I was drunk that night, and if I ever hear otherwise, you will be sorry for the day that bitch you had for a mother, birthed you." Larry made a hasty retreat, but Mace didn't even notice him leave.

He had seen that look on his brother's face before, and with Red it always came up trouble. He eyed his father disgustedly, Pa needed a drink and he needed it bad, he thought; watching his father's hands tremble slightly, as the next round was dealt.

He was sick of them both; Red and his women; and Pa and the booze. There was over fifty thousand dollars on the table, and Pa was getting ready to piss it away.

He missed his mother and he knew she had staked them for the last time. They had pawned everything they owned to come up with the ten thousand needed to get in the game. You would think Red and Pa could at least try to keep their fucking minds on business.

They had been playing poker steadily for hours, and all of the money seemed to be flowing one way……..Willis Webster.

Melina was dealing again and Mace watched as she made the second pass around the table.

Monroe the Third, was holding a pair of jacks, and he raised a thousand, as Melina started the started the next pass.

"Ace high", she said, as she dealt an ace of spade to Elgin Taffin, accompanied by his snort of disgust.

"Possible straight", she continued as a five of clubs landed next to a six of heart in front of Farrell, who promptly bid a thousand and raised another against Monroe's pair of jacks.

After the flop, Elgin as well as Farrell folded. Monroe made a half-hearted bluff; then folded as well.

Pa was sweating; Mace had never seen him that way before. Thirty thousand dollars was in the pot and Pa had ten thousand in front of him. He pushed half the money to the center of the table. Pa had a Ten of diamond, club, and an Ace of club in his hand and the flop showed an ace and the ten of spade. "I raise", he said, his voice barely above a whisper.

Willis was holding a four of hearts and a deuce of spades, the four diamond from the flop, and his hold cards. Willis could be bluffing, but how could they be sure, the bastard had been grinning the entire game. Willis had at least twenty thousand in front of him. He shoved ten thousand dollars in the middle of the table. "I call and raise you five more", Willis said still grinning.

Mace was aware of what was coming. Pa had no choice he had been called. "I'm in, full house; ace high", Mace heard him say.

There was a collective sigh when Willis flipped his hold cards and the four of club and spade fell next to the other two in suit.

Pa looked as if he wanted to cry; instead he got up with as much dignity as he could, and congratulated Willis.

Mace almost felt sorry for Willis as he gathered his money and woman to leave the room. He had seen the murderous gleam in Red's eye and he did not think Willis Webster was long for this world.

Part II

Chapter

Angel's Trumpet, Overton County, 1935

"You know what, I'm gittin sick and tired of that red bitch comin in here actin like she some queen", said Coralee as she plated food for the dinner table.

"Your problem is that you jealous", replied Jewel Mack laughing. She was a large, yellowed-skinned woman with bright eyes and a toothy grin of gold capped teeth. Her fine hair curled about her head with perspiration as she ladled steaming food onto serving platters.

"If Miz Adel was white you wouldn't be carrin on like this. You think she owes you something just cos she "Colored." I been working for the Gabriels for a long time just like my folks did. Now Mr. WC 's ma and pa was some of the finest folks ever drew breath; and you know what, their money is green and it spends just like the white folks."

The back screen-door slammed shut and a male voice picked up the conversation. "Naw mama, what the gal wants is WC back in her bed."

"You can just mind your own damn business Johnny Mack", Coralee replied, cause it won't ever be you. You may be the handyman, but you won't be handling this", she said, running her hand along her ample curves.

John's eyes gleamed appreciatively at her pose, but he said, "Oh good things come to those who wait honey, and I'm a patient man. In the meantime, I would suggest that you move that sweet behind and get that food on the table before his majesty's collard greens get cold."

*

William Cade Gabriel waited patiently as the servants placed dinner on the table, pointedly ignoring the sultry looks Coralee continued to cast his way. Coralee had been a mistake he decided; wondering if Adel had noticed. Not that it mattered. He did as he damned well pleased, and nobody knew that better than his wife.

Adel had been only seventeen when they had married, and totally self- possessed. She had always known exactly what she wanted and she had no illusions concerning him. After twenty-seven years, three children, and his countless infidelities, he had yet to peel away all the layers she used to shield herself from him.

Maybe that was why he continued to want her. She stirred his senses as no other woman ever had. Even now there was a familiar heaviness in his loins when he thought of the satiny copper colored body she gave and withheld at will.

Sometimes, he wished she cared enough to be jealous of Coralee and all the others, but he knew he had always held second place in Adel's affections. It was Gent she had wanted; and he had been the next best thing. He knew it and it had not mattered; not then or now. He had wanted her that much.

His children were the best thing that had come out his marriage. Sometimes he felt a little amazed that they belonged to him he thought smiling at his youngest, ten-year old Will Jr. Will's conception had been the result of one of those rare evenings when he and Adel had been in accord with each other; after a little too much to drink.

Adel had been furious when she discovered she was pregnant, but cried with joy when her baby boy was born. That was Adel. She was like a mama lioness with her children; fiercely protective, but unfortunately manipulative as hell.

He looked at his wife inquiringly, "Where the old man and Edmond?"

"Uncle Steban is resting, after this afternoon what did you expect."

"Okay, where is Edmond, is he too refined to join his ignorant daddy for dinner?"

"He's gone and it's your fault, your attitude is intolerate."

"Damn woman, the word is intolerable, where the hell is he?

Adele chose to ignore his correction, saying, "He only said he would be back in a few days; and no, he did not tell me where he was going."

WC reached for the cold glass of buttermilk on the table as he felt the usual burn in his gut, a general condition when trying to deal with his family, particularly his son or his uncle. Both of them had a habit of stirring up trouble which they definitely did not need right now in Angel's Trumpet.

He considered himself a good father. Hell, didn't he give them whatever they wanted. Perhaps he had to tighten the reins on Edmond occasionally, but his oldest son had a talent for making him angry. He had been home less than three days after a two-year absence, when he informed them that instead of remaining in Angel's Trumpet now that he had finished his residency, he was going to Africa as part a missionary group to serve as doctor. And he had the gall to leave for parts unknown without a word of explanation.

Once again, Edmond had disappointed him, although he was sure that "bible thumper", Matthew Terrell would be singing his praises.

Maybe a few conciliatory words on his part could possibly have closed the breach between him and Edmond, but he refused to bow down to his own son. Edmond lived a life of unique privilege, yet he seemed to despise everything WC had worked so hard to build.

Two years ago, he had stormed off in anger because WC refused vote in the presidential election or use his influence to encourage the Blacks in the community to do so. Edmond just did not understand; to WC it was a small compromise. His grandmother had taught him long ago that life extracted a price for every act committed and a wise man picked his battles.

His grandparents had been admired and respected by both blacks and whites, but their home was in the Deep South. They had suffered enough disillusionment and death, with the sure knowledge that there was no justice for the black man.   But they never forgot and they refused to let their loss be in vain.   They had paid for Angel's Trumpet with toil, tears and blood.   They believed they had a duty to safeguard the land and the people who depended on them, but it was a balancing act that wearied a man's soul.

The sacrifices of those who came before him meant nothing to Edmond, only being right.   Rosa and Reese Gabriel had not had the luxury of being so high-minded.

There were always whites at the polling place looking to start trouble, embolden by Jim Crow laws, using regulations such as the "Grandfather Clause" or literacy requirements to keep Negro men and women from legally voting, when half them crackers could barely read and write. Reese Gabriel had never been a slave, and the state law could not bar WC from voting, but at what cost.   His vote could not change the outcome of an election, but it could ensure peace.

Edmond accused him of living in a false utopia, when in the outside world black men and women were dying for freedom, being lynched for no more reason than a whim.   WC was not callus, as a Negro man he burned with anger and shame; but life was not simple or fair.   And only God was just.

He had lost count of plots and plans he had supported financially to create a better life for Negro people; to gain a few hard steps forward, only to be lost through white folk political backroom intrigues, or Negro leaders with clay feet.   Riots, back to Africa movements and disappointments; WC had grown sick of all the rhetoric.

The two greatest Black thinkers of his lifetime had been on opposite ends of the pole. One encouraged the skill of the hands, while the other the development of the intellect, but they were both right. The only end that justified the means was money. Money equaled power, the one thing a white man would never willingly share.

He could not save the whole world, only his part of it. Angel's Trumpet was his land, his world. The family had a responsibility to the people that lived and work in Angel's Trumpet. There had never been any lynching in Overton or the surrounding areas and the reason why, was no secret. They had just as much to lose as him.

His Uncle Steban considered him a hothead and his son thought him a coward. He knew fear, it was something a black man learn to deal with. It chipped away at you; day by day, year by year; *but it was the price of survival. A man had to protect his home, feed his family, only a fool like Edmond did not know fear. Time ever came he had to die to protect what was his it would not be swinging from a tree.* He would not die in the dust surrounded by hooded cowards and he would take as many with him as he could. But no matter what Steban thought, he would not lightly destroy what had taken a lifetime to build.

WC shook his head and smiled. Such grave thoughts were not for the dinner table. Let Edmond have his shinning ideals. He would be leaving soon and sooner might be better.

Adel said, "WC you sitting there smiling to yourself, you want to let us in on the joke."

"Just thinking of you darlin", he replied grinning.

"Daddy, you never listen to me when I'm talking to you", said Cassandra pouting.

"I'm sorry Cassy honey, what were you saying", said WC. His daughter was a pretty brown girl with thick hair that had been straighten and waved down to her shoulders. That said however, the phase "pretty is as pretty does", meant nothing to Cassy.

She was a spoilt, little snob; with a full measure of his stubbornness and her mother's ambition; a combination that boded ill for anybody who tried to come between that girl and something she wanted. The problem was Cassy rarely knew what she wanted or at least what was best for her.

Unlike Edmond, WC didn't think Cassy had a serious thought in her head. She and Adel filled their time with frivolous pursuits of high society, where the elite colored folks meet and she could show off. What puzzled him was how Adel got such ideas of grandeur. She had no education, hell when he married her she was living with her family in a three-room cabin surrounded by red dirt; sharecropping and picking cotton.

What Cassy needed was an older man. Someone established, strong enough to handle her, but wise enough to appreciate her. Minton Dorsey was in love with the girl, but neither she nor her mother would have him. The girl could charm the birds from the trees when she chose; she had been practicing on him for years.

"Oh daddy, it's just so boring. Can't I go to Atlanta and stay with Aunt Win", Cassandra whined.

Adel Gabriel had been occupied with her own thoughts as she watched Coralee flaunt herself in front of WC. She would not be disrespected in her own house, but she was determined to ignore the slut. Adel knew Coralee was not the first, nor would she be the last, but if the "cow" twisted her ass around her dinner table one more time, Adel vowed, that she would not be responsible for her actions.

Now she turned toward her husband, one eyebrow lifted questioningly, as she heard her daughter trying to cajole her father into allowing her to visit Win Sinclair.

"WC don't you have any sense", said Adel annoyed. Turning to face her daughter, she said, "Girl you must really think I'm a fool. After all our plans, do you think I would let you throw it all away on Thomas Blue?"

Amused, WC asked, "Who is Thomas Blue?"

"Much time you spent at the Majestic and those low-lives at Win's, I'm surprised you don't know. Thomas Blue is the new bandleader at the Majestic and half the women in Atlanta are infatuated, falling all over him, including your silly daughter; which is why she suddenly wants to visit your Aunt Win."

Cassandra knew pouting would not work with her mother; not if she wanted to see Thomas; instead she said, "Mama I simply wanted to do some shopping before the Gold and White Ball."

WC started to laugh, saying, "The word is infatuated and what Cassy is saying seems reasonable enough. What's wrong darlin, Aunt Win not high enough on the Negro social register. Being aware of your less that aristocratic background, I would think that one reprobate to another, you and Win would have a lot in common. But of course, she's not "high class" like my sweet wife, is she darlin."

Adel refused to allow herself be baited by WC. She was not sure what the word reprobate meant but she would have Cassy teach her just like she did when WC corrected her. She learned long ago that ignorant did not mean stupid.

Instead of the frown he expected, she smiled saying, "I picked up the mail from town today WC and sugar I almost clean forgot, a letter came for your Uncle Steban all the way from Africa, I left it on your desk with the others."

"Damn it woman why didn't you tell me that earlier", said WC scrapping back his chair from the dining table cursing.

He scattered the letters on his desk, noting one from Minton Dorsey; and some fancy glided invitation, before picking up Steban's letter. WC did not stop to consider Steban's reaction as he opened the envelope with the silver letter opener that had once belonged to his grandfather. Reading the missive twice he crushed the letter in his hand and stormed outside.

Adell had barely been able to contain herself as she waited outside the office. After WC stumped outside to the front porch, she retrieved the letter from the floor. She did not bother to hide her amusement, laughing out loud, as she scanned its contents.

**

Angel's Trumpet, 1935

The scent of rain hung on the air as the sun disappeared behind a fat cloud that promised a cooling downpour that never came. For a long time, WC gazed toward the skyline and the farm lands beyond. Looking out over the land he experienced a feeling of peace that was strange considering their present situation.

Angel's Trumpet was the only thing that had mattered to him as long as he could remember. He had been fourteen when he had decided to go to work on the farm under Lucas Mack, to learn everything he could. Later at his grandmother's insistence he had attended agricultural college, but Angel's Trumpet had always been his first love.

He knew some people thought it odd that he should have a passion for farming the land, but they simply did not understand. When he scooped up a hand full of the rich soil, he knew he could plant anything and it would grow. It was like he knew how the Almighty felt on the seventh day. Grandmama had understood, it was a feeling for land that Steban nor grandfather had shared.

As a boy, he had loved listening to Grandmama's stories. He never tired of hearing how their home came to be called Angel's Trumpet, watching her giggle like a young girl. She would hug him tightly and tell him how much he was like her. But WC had always known Gent had still been the favorite son.

Grandmama had loved Gent with an old woman's sentiment because he had reminded her of her son. As for Steban, Gent had been a carbon copy of his uncle. Only he could see Gent for what he was. His brother was an idler, a do nothing, only concerned about himself.

What difference did it make if he had known what was going on between Gent and that white gal? Hell, was it his fault Gent had been stupid enough to get involved with Pris McClure?

Pris was Arlo McClure's youngest child, only daughter and real proud of what nature had done for her. The white boys in Overton followed her around like dogs in heat, but a smart Black man busied himself elsewhere when Pris was around.

His grandmother had always had an uncanny knack of finding out things. He never knew how she had discovered what was going on; but it had been fortunate for Gent, or they probably would have found him ball-less swinging from some tree limb.

Sometimes he wondered why he'd never said anything. It had cost him his grandmama's respect; for she believed what endangered one of the family endangered them all. It was a lesson she had tried to teach him and Grandmama could be very unforgiving.

Maybe, unconsciously he had wanted Gent gone. He had stood in the way of too many things WC wanted. Not that he allowed himself to delve too deeply into his own soul; that was for men like his son and the Rev. Terrell.

One thing he knew for sure, Arlo McClure and his sons, were mean as hornets, always had been; and they were not the type to hide behind sheets. According to Grandmama, the McClures had been rich before the Civil War, although they lacked the aristocratic gentility of the Overfields.

There had been bad blood between the McClures and the Overfields for years. After the War they had refused Stuart Overfield's olive-branch, choosing to go it alone instead of throwing in their lot with their neighbors. The McClures tended to be clannish and the next generation had reverted to the red-necked crackers they had sprung from, staying close to home; farming the land that had not been sold off for taxes and raising hogs.

The McClures however, were not their enemies. Justin Overfield had been trying to destroy the Gabriel family since he was a boy. Justin's attempts to cause trouble had been stymied mostly because Miss Amelia had held the purse strings; but after her death, there had been no one to keep Justin in check. The joke was that Amelia Overfield and grandpapa Reese had been raised as brother and sister; a fact Justin tried to keep secret.

Grandpapa had kept him in the dark, until he collapsed after hiding his illness for months. Their creditors had been demanding cash, instead of extending the usual credit to cover their operating costs and WC did not have to be a genius to know Justin Overfield was behind it all. WC had never seen his grandmother so shaken. The reins of the family fortune had been thrust in his hands, and somehow, he had to stop the financial assault instigated by Justin and his cronies.

WC shook his head smiling, he had learned the meaning of the word "providence", control exercised by God, divine intervention. When the 18th Amendment prohibiting the manufacture, sale or transportation of intoxicating liquors was ratified by Congress, Amherst Brewery had been closed and suddenly Justin was facing too many financial problems of his own, to continue his campaign to destroy Angel's Trumpet, but the damage had been done.

His grandfather had died quietly in his sleep never knowing Angel's Trumpet was on the verge of bankruptcy. WC barely had time to grieve as he and the men worked to get the harvest to market, hoping to stay afloat. He could not believe it when Steban had showed up looking disheveled and ill. Grandmama had been closeted in her room since the funeral; suddenly declares that Steban is in charge, without bothering to consult him about anything.

WC had been furious, what gave Steban the right to question his handling of the family affairs? He was the one who stayed home to work the farm. He was the one that took care of his grandparents while Steban and Gent were running around Europe. Angel's Trumpet should be his, not Steban.

It had Steban's idea was to get the loan from the Maitland Bank; after all they had been doing business with the company for years and he considered David Maitland a friend. None of which made any difference to the Board of Directors of Maitland Bank. The title to the sugar mill for collateral, was not enough, they wanted everything. Steban had agreed to mortgage all they owned, to pour money into the mill which yielded little return.

Just days before the Wall Street disaster in '29, the harvest had been sold for cash at a minimum profit, but they had been able to pay their creditors. However, WC had known it was only a matter of time before the Maitland Bank called in the loan. They had been having trouble just paying the interest and Steban wanted him to play by his rules.

WC had been approached by the bootleggers, who needed large quantities sugar to make their illegal brew. They were willing to pay top dollar and Steban wanted to criticize his lack of "character." For once Grandmama had sided with him. WC had formed a syndicate to supply them with as much as they wanted. Minton Dorsey had arranged the transportation and J. John Tate, the distribution.

But did he get any thanks? Hell no, all Steban had done, was complain. Now Gent was on his way to save the day.

According to Steban's letter, Gent would be arriving in the United States in another week. The prodigal son was coming home, he just hoped Gent had all the facts. Maitland had given them thirty days or the bank would call in the loan and since the "good ole boy" system was still alive and well, you could bet your ass, Justin Overfield knew all about it too; in which case the shit was definitely about to hit the fan.

Chapter

Angel's Trumpet, 1935

Reese and Rosa Gabriel had given over a hundred acres of land to the black men and women, who worked with them to produce the historic harvest that had saved the town of Overton, to build homes and work the land. Later there was a general store along with a blacksmith shop, a church and the school. The Gabriels called the place Angel's Trumpet.

After the quay and storage warehouses were rebuilt, east of the township, a seedier part of the city grew. Along the west side were modest houses of various shapes and sizes. The Methodist church became a focal point as well as the reconstructed school. Office buildings along West Main Street housed an array of black owned business and health professionals, leading to Mulberry Street and the white establishments of Overton County. In the center of town was the Trumpet Arms, owned by Mae Delecourt Turner, but to the residents of Overton she was just Miss Mae.

The Trumpet Arms was a large pink and white Victorian style hostelry that boasted clean rooms and excellent food. On warm Sunday afternoons seated on the wide veranda, the residents and guests could see, and be seen sipping tangy lemonade or sweet iced tea along with Miss Mae's famous tea cookies and buttered pound cake. Of course, there was a side for the whites and another side with a back entrance for the colored; one of Miss Mae's concessions to segregation.

There were scanty details concerning her past and she preferred it that way. Few people remembered her father or realized that she had once lived in Angel's Trumpet. The subsequent years had been filled with bad choices and mistakes; but she made no apologies for her life. Miss Mae had ceased to concern herself about what people thought, or what anyone else did behind closed doors. She had enough peccadilloes of her own.

It was near three o'clock in the morning when she heard the back gate swing open and close with a careless clank. The old fool was probably already drunk, she thought as she waited in the back parlor, with only a kerosene lamp for light, but he knew the way well enough.

"Alright old woman, I'm here, what you want, said Justin Overfield.

Mae peered at him with a smirk, "As gracious as ever I see." She pushed him a glass of whiskey from the bottle on the table; then took a sip from her own. It had been smuggled through Canada some years before.

"I got whiskey at home Mae", he said, downing the drink in his hand just the same.

"Here old man, I got present for you", said Mae, handing him an envelope.

Justin threw the envelope filled with pictures on the table in disgust. "You blackmailing whore, I told you to keep Trent out of here."

"Now how am I supposed to do that? That boy will sleep with anything on two feet, and some of my boarders are not above a little petty larceny", she said with coarse laughter.

"Just tell me how much; before I strangle the life out of you, you lying bitch."

"Well you know they were prepared to sell the pictures to the highest bidder. That Coralee gal, who works for the Gabriels is real fond of one of the picture taking gentlemen, and he with her. I bet WC pay handsomely to get his hands on those pictures"; Mae paused with a crooked smile.

"That boy don't have the balls for something like that and you too smart to waste my time", said Justin sliding an envelope with money across the table to Mae, which she proceeded to count.

Mae said, "You know me so well cher", Mae said, laughing.

"Don't talk shit to me; I want the negatives, now", waiting as Mae tossed him a second envelope. "One day gonna see your throat slit; I needed you before, but the whiskey business is over now."

"You cannot scare me Justin, not anymore." She could not believe it when Justin picked up a knife lying nearby and plunged it into the table with a strength Mae did not think he possessed.

"You think not, I see you again, I'm gonna be the last thing you view on this earth."

Mae didn't stop shivering until she heard the gate clang shut.

**

Overfield Plantation, 1897

Justin Overfield glanced at the still form of his wife to ascertain she was asleep. He loved his dear Anna, but she had no idea of what drove him. His wife was a small genteel woman incapable of unkindness or an act of dishonor. More than once Justin wondered how a man like Josiah Duffy could have sired her. She would not understand or approve of what he had done, but there was no need for her to know. She was the mother of his son and he adored her, but after all these years she could not comprehend his animosity toward the Gabriels.

He had met Anna Duffy during his second term at the Virginia Southern Academy for Young Men, a religious hell hole, where his father had sent him (for his own good of course), after Stuart had been made aware of a few of Justin's youthful indiscretions. Anna was a petite, silver blond beauty with clear blue eyes and Justin had fallen in love for the first time.

Anna's father the right Reverend Josiah Duffy maintained that God (of whom he claimed personal knowledge) had created the white man superior to the colored man and that he and good Christian white men of like persuasion had formed an organization to make sure the coloreds didn't forget their "place." He urged Justin to become a member. Justin wanted Anna, and listening to her father was a small price to pay.

When he had shared his new-found wisdom with his father, Stuart had been incensed and had threaten Justin with a beating. He had never felt more alienated from his father. Justin did not blame his father or Rev. Duffy, he blamed the Gabriels.

Justin did not know whom he hated more Reese, or his sons. He did not think he hated all Coloreds. He had grown up around them and they had always been a part of his life. He had watched his father work side by side with them, but he hated the Gabriels.

Anna's father said the bible described them as a cursed people, born for servitude, a lowly people. Well there was nothing lowly or subservient about Reese Gabriel. He carried himself with a quiet authority that compelled respect. His very present irritated Justin. Reese simply patronized him, allowing him to bark orders before the men; then do as he thought best, consulting Stuart afterwards.

Jasset Gabriel did not bother with pretense. The boy had never known his place and they had hated each other from the cradle. Jasset believed he was equal to any man colored or white.

It was like a damned fairy tale, Rosa had taken care of his grandfather until the day he died and Reese and Stuart loved each other like brothers. Together they had brought prosperity back to the county. Well fine for Stuart, but it had been Justin who had to bare the taunts of "nigger lover", from the boys at school.

Many proponents of the new south acclaimed Stuart's methods as a shining example of what could be accomplished through whites and coloreds working together for the betterment of the land. With the blacks being deferential to the whites and separation of the races maintained, it was easy to slip back into the old ways.

The Reconstruction as dictated by the White House, had wreaked havoc with traditional southern values, but the presidential election of 1878 had brought an end to the reconstruction government and the onset of "Jim Crow" Laws, aimed at keeping the Negro in his place.

What most people did not know, but what Justin understood all too well; there was a mutual respect and trust between the Gabriels and Stuart Overfield that had been forged before he was born. As the scion of Overfield, in the eyes of the community Stuart could do no wrong. He sponsored young Jasset and the whole Gabriel family and what was done at Overfield was considered correct for the county.

Rosa and Reese represented what most of the whites thought proper. They were hardworking and respectful. They were in turn accorded respect and courtesy as perceived merited by whites. Nevertheless, their holdings had continued to increase as those of the Overfields.

Justin had left college and convinced his father to hire him at the brewery. For once, it seemed everything had been going his way. He had married Anna, Reese had retired and Justin had been placed in charge.

The situation with Mae had not worked out as he had planned, but Jasset had not become a problem. He had wanted no part of the brewery business, although the Gabriel family owned a quarter interest in the company. Reese had inherited a portion of the company from Colonel Amherst; a fact that was not common knowledge.

Jasset had earned a degree in Engineering from some school up north; had come home, taken a handsome Creole wife, and appeared content to farm the family land. When Jasset had asked Stuart to buy them out of the brewery and to sell him the swamp acreage, Justin had laughed and offered no objections, especially since Jasset had paid top dollar for the property.

It had taken Jasset three years to drain and clear the land for planting sugar cane and build the sugar mill. He had discovered a new refining process developed by a Negro inventor he met in New Orleans. Justin had been contemptuous of the project from the beginning, but Stuart had invested in the sugar mill over his protests.

To Justin's chagrin, the new method of refining had proved it's' worth over and over again. It was less expensive, safer and had a faster process time. In less time than it had taken to build, the mill became extremely profitable.

Desperate for cash, after making some unwise investments, Justin was determined to find a way to get control of the mill and recoup his loses before Stuart found out. He had allowed Justin free rein and if he found out about the money shortage now, it would be hell to pay

After becoming seriously ill, Stuart had decided to send for his lawyer to make changes in his will and he refused to admit Justin. Justin had appealed to his mother, but for once Amelia had been as adamant as his father. He had been outraged to learn that not only had Rose and Reese Gabriel had been present, but had witnessed the signing of the will.

The flame of the lamp flickered, and held, revealing the document before him. Justin read over the copy of the will carefully, without remorse or shame. As far as he was concerned, it was his father fault he had to resort to bribing a law clerk to get a copy of the will. As his oldest son he should have been privy to its writing.

At first there were no surprises; Stuart had left equal shares in the cotton mill and brewery to each of his children. Justin would remain head of the company. His sister Sarah had been place under the guardianship of his mama and himself, until she came of age or married, and she along with Julian were each left a substantial amount of money. Julian had contracted malaria while serving in the Spanish/American War from which he had never fully recovered and on his death, his wife Carolina and son Andrew would receive his portion.

The will was as expected, but as Justin continued to examine the document he became increasingly alarmed. Stuart had upheld his father's original bequeath to Rosa; all title to the land presently owned by the Gabriels and set up safe guards should Justin challenge the will.

To Jasset he left all his shares in the sugar mill, since the mill had reached its present level of success because of Jasset's management and hard work.

Angrily Justin read on, suddenly horrified there was no mention of him. Was it possible that his father had discovered his pilfering, and left him nothing; no money, only a glorified office position?

Justin had been so sure, so careful, there had been no way Stuart could have found out, he thought; then the answer blazed at him….Reese Gabriel. His world was spinning out of control and he teetered between sanity and a craziness that could destroy him.

Ghoulishly pale in the glow of the lamp light, Justin's green eyes glittered wildly; his body taunt and unyielding. He was gasping for breath and his nose began to bleed; spots of blood staining the copy of the will. Slowly, as a deflating balloon; he sagged limply back in his chair, tasting blood and tears; weeping, not even aware he was sobbing out loud, until Anna rose in alarm from the bed and ran to his side. She wiped his face rocking him as one would a child.

Justin picked up the offending document, damp with his blood and tears, ready to burn it to ashes, when his contemptuous gaze saw words that stilled his hand. Stuart had added a codicil to the will.

**

1898, Angel's Trumpet

Jasset had been so proud of the improvements he had made at the mill, he had planned to take the whole family on a tour of the plant, but the children had been tired, that he and Rosa had decided to take them home and view the mill later.

Miss Anna had just been passing by. She had kindly offered to convey Jasset and Deborah to the mill in her buggy, deciding to join them on the tour since Daddy Stuart had been so impressed with Jasset's work. She had been such a fine, gentle lady; people often wondered why she had married Justin.   Reese and Rosa had only traveled only a short distance, when they heard the explosion and turned to go back.

Reese Gabriel stood immobile beside the graves of his son and daughter-in-law. He was filled with a terrible emptiness; he had to keep reminding himself to breath. Amelia and Stuart were standing nearby; seeing Stuart standing there, aloof; still clinging to life, while Jasset was dead was surreal.

He and Rosa had seen Justin running toward the mill like a madman, screaming Anna's name. It had not made sense.   How could Justin have known Anna was there. The answer was so heinous he did not want to believe it.

He had listened to Justin's lies as he accused Jasset of causing Anna's death through negligence. His claim that Jasset had lured Anna into an unsafe experiment was so absurd Reese could not believe Stuart would side with his son. He had not been able to bear the look in Rosa's eyes, as she viewed Stuart's betrayal.

Weeks before, Reese had sat by Stuart's bedside, sadden to witness his friend's deteriorating health. Stuart had insisted he and Rosa witness the signing of his will and Reese had agreed. Reese had not questioned the codicil Stuart had added; it was much the same as Jamison Overfield had originally added to his will.   At that time, the possibility of the Gabriel land returning to the Overfield in the case of his and Rosa's death without issue had been remote. At that time of Jamison's death, Jasset had been five years old and Rosa had been large with another child.

When Stuart had added the same clause to his will, he had thought Stuart was just being careful. The land legally belonged to Rosa and their family, he saw no reason to be concerned, now he was no longer sure.

It had been no secret that the family planned to tour the mill that Sunday. They all would have been killed in that explosion, except Steban who was away at school. He could not prove what he believed and the thought of making an accusation against an Overfield to the sheriff was laughable as well as dangerous.

He was afraid for Rosa. She would not talk to him and she looked though him like he did not exist. Would she ever forgive him for believing in an unlikely a friendship that began thirty-seven years before in a muddy Missouri field?

**

Missouri Territory, 1862

Reese had been reconnoitering the countryside, looking for a rag-tag bunch of confederate soldiers, using hit and run guerrilla tactics. Those boys moved lightening quick, disappearing into the countryside, leaving behind a bunch of false signs that petered out to nothing.

He knew the back country, since he and the Colonel had explored most of the surrounding territory and the Indian lands beyond. After the Colonel had offered his services to the North, at the beginning of the "rebellion", as he termed it, Reese had joined his adopted father's regiment as scout.

The last skirmish had left several dead and injured and he had stayed behind looking to pick up the Rebels' trail, while his detachment headed west to join the main column, carrying the wounded. He had been two days out, when he had finally picked up the trail, only to be waylaid into a trap by the band of cutthroats, and dragged back to their camp as a trophy.

There had been talk of forming a regiment of Colored troops, but as of yet it had not happened. However, the Confederate government had concluded that the articles of war did not pertain to Negro soldiers, and any man of color being caught in uniform would have been executed on sight. He had been wearing buckskins and a blue linsey-woolsey, Union issued shirt, but he guessed that had been enough.

Bound and tossed to the ground, he found himself face down in the mud waiting for the explosion of a bullet in his brain; when instead he heard the culture voice of a southern gentleman saying, "Just a minute there soldier I believe I know this nigra. Stand up boy let me look at you."

Reese rose slowly to his feet, not understanding the reprieve, but ready for anything, as the next words spoken in an urgent whisper, reached his ears, "If you want to live, follow my lead."

"See here Captain, what the tarnation is going on here", the question posed by Colonel Percy Moreau. Percy was a courtly young man, with more pedigree than brains; and Stuart Overfield quickly decided to take the decision out of his hands.

"Nothing to concern yourself 'bout Percy, just caught me a runaway, that's all. Jasper here is prime stock, my daddy paid $1200 for him to use for breeding. If it's all the same to you, I'll just take him with me. Jasper not gonna give me any trouble, are you boy."

Reese sunk slowly back down in the mud on his knees. "Naw sah massa", he said.

"Then get up out of that mud and get my pack horse and mind you lead him gentle. Percy with your permission, I'll take my leave of you. The dispatches I carry are of vital importance."

The Colonel Percy Moreau saluted the Captain on way; a bit nostalgic as the Captain rode away with Jasper lopping along beside his horse.

Stuart and Reese traveled on about two miles until the bend in the road, stopping only long enough to split the supplies between the horses. There had been no time to talk as they tried to put as many miles between them and the confederate troops as they could. They rode on until they had no choice but to rest the lathered horses, making camp in a small clearing.

Stuart was rubbing down his horse, when finely honed instincts caused him to turn slowly and he found himself looking down the large bore of a two-shot derringer.

"Those Rebel soldiers were a mite careless", Stuart said.

"Some could say the same about you, "massa", now I want you to carefully back away from the horse and drop your gun belt." After Stuart had complied, Reese motioned him toward the campfire.

"That's real friendly like, now just who in the hell are you", Reese said.

"If I am not mistaken, the man who saved your life several miles back."

 "So, you did", said Reese leaning against a rock. Why?"

"Listen I'm tired, hungry and sorely tempted to regret my generosity. Maybe I should have left you back there face down in the mud. If you are going to shoot me, do it, otherwise put it away. I got some bacon and cold biscuits courtesy of the Colonel back there, in my pack."

Reese helped himself before tossing the rest to the Captain. He eased the gun hammer but the gun remained only inches away from his hand. "Don't know your name, but the direction you headed, you best take off that rebel grey."

"You can call me Captain, and if the Yankee line is about two days away, that's where I'm headed, but right now the place is still swarming with Rebs it's safer to keep the uniform on. I did not lie when I told the Colonel I had vital dispatches, just to whom they belong.

"Those troops you talking about are most likely three days west, by now, while the Rebs are less than a day away. Soon as the horses are rested we best be on our way."

They traveled the next two days in an uneasy truce. On the third night once again they set up a cold camp eating hardtack and dried fruit, when a small Rebel patrol rode right into the camp.

Probably part of the bunch he had been trailing Reese thought, as he hunkered down by the fire quietly, while Stuart, still wearing the confederate uniform tried to bluff their way out. He almost had the old Sergeant in charge convinced, when another member of the scouting party rode into the firelight. Reese saw the recognition in his eyes.

"Hey Sarg, I seen this here nigger in the Yankee camp, not five days back."

Reese pulled the holstered gun from beneath his blanket firing from the hip to catch the soldier who recognized him in the chest, swinging around in time to club the unarmed soldier who had dismounted to help himself to a cup of coffee.

Stuart, who had retained his side arm, shot the third trooper and the Sergeant, but not before the Sergeant returned fire, hitting Stuart in his shoulder and he fell forward. Reese's next shot topple the Sergeant from his horse.

The trooper, bleeding from Reese's gun butt to the head, had picked up a fallen saber and landed a glancing blow to Stuart face, opening his cheek. He had moved in to finish Stuart off, when

Stuart kicked out booted feet catching him in the groin, which propelled him a hand's reach from the fallen Sergeant's pistol, but as the trooper reached for the gun, Reese caught him in the back with a knife thrown with deadly precision.

Stuart was bleeding badly as Reese bind and packed the wound with a clean handkerchief. "Come on we got to go. That bunch was just the advance scouting party the others will be here soon", said Reese.

"Just help me get on my horse", said Stuart, gritting his teeth against the pain.

After traveling what seemed like hours to Stuart, they suddenly stopped. Reese lifted Stuart from his horse and carried him to a lightly wooded area that would offer some shade and hopefully some concealment.

"Why are we stopping", he asked, struggling to remain alert.

"You", said Reese disgusted. "You are bleeding like a stuck pig, leaving a trail a blind man could follow. You rest here, I going to scout up ahead; by the way, you better tell me your name, just so I know what to put on the tombstone?"

"I am Captain Stuart Overfield, at your service."

"Well don't you worry none Captain Overfield, I'll be back", said Reese. Looking down to discover Stuart, aiming a gun at his middle.

"If I thought otherwise, you would be dead", rasped Stuart.

Reese started to laugh. "You right about one thing Captain."

"And what would that be", Stuart croaked.

"Those Rebs are sure a mite careless."

Reese cleaned up the blood stain trail as best as he could, but Stuart was already feverish by the time he got him to the makeshift camp he had set up in a cave. No cold camp tonight, he had to chance making a fire. He tossed Stuart a bottle of whiskey from his saddle bag. "Here you gonna need this; that bullet has got to come out."

Stuart drank deeply, while Reese laid the blade of his knife in the flames of the fire. Taking the bottle from Stuart, Reese took a drink to steady his hand; sparing a little for the knife. Luckily, Stuart had fainted long before it was over. The bullet was deep, slick with blood and he had nothing to grip it with. Reese finally flipped the bullet out with the tip of the knife and his fingers. He cauterized the wound with the heated flat edge of the blade to stop the bleeding; binding it with whiskey soaked strips of the Stuart's extra shirt.

Reese hoped a few hours' rest would bring the Captain around, they could not stay longer, the danger was to great; they had to keep moving. The Rebel soldiers could stumble upon the cave anytime. They had probably found the bodies of the others by now and fast on their trail. The safest bet had been to head east away from Union lines and Reese had made the decision to detour eastward toward home and Amelia.

After Colonel Amherst's death at Manasseh, Amelia lived alone except for a few servants. The South was making a determined campaign toward the North, but their home and lands remained untouched. He smiled ruefully, remembering the expression on Amelia's face when he had dragged Stuart through the doorway. But Amelia had always been as steady as they come.

Reese watched as she sewed the cut on Stuart's face close. For days, she nursed him though the fever. During the weeks that followed it was plain Amelia had fallen in love with Stuart. Reese had been concerned, the man was a southerner; but Amelia made her own decisions.

Stuart headed an intelligence gathering network that answered directly to General Grant; and he wanted Reese to be a part of his unit. The work was important, and after some misgivings, Reese agreed. Stuart treated him as a comrade in arms, facing death and the adventures of war, trusting no one and watching each other's backs. Reese had believed that Stuart Overfield was a man of honor.

Through the years, they had become as close as brothers, but no more. Rosa had warned him and he would not listen. Now his son was dead and an Overfield had killed him.

Chapter

Overton Cotton Mill, 1935

Trenton Overfield stood before the large window of his office overlooking the cotton mill yard. He was a handsome man with cool green eyes and red gold hair (one lady friend told him he looked like Valentino). He played golf and tennis to stay fit and descended from the old southern aristocracy. The first Overfield had married a tidewater Virginia lady, back in 1700, and thus beginning the Overfield legacy.

His lineage was not completely pure, since his great granddaddy had actually fought for the Yankees, but Old Stuart Overfield had restored the family fortune, along with saving the county from carpetbaggers and after all he was an Overfield. The only thing lacking was money, but that would soon be remedied. Tonight, he would ask Vera Tatum to marry him.

Old southern gentry were still so clannish; and the Tatums had been red dirt crackers before the war. It might be 1935, but down south, events were measured in time, being either before the War or after the War. The fact that Beauregard Tatum had struck oil in Oklahoma and became filthy rich, or returned home and brought the old McClure Plantation mattered little in some quarters. They still checked his manicured fingernails for dirt, after all, it was after the War.

Still and all, Tatum was a practical man, and what his money couldn't buy outright, marriage to a scion of the southern society could; with the proper settlements, of course. It was what his grandfather wanted, what Tatum wanted; and the Tatum money was what Trent wanted.

Hell, it wasn't his fault the family fortune was practically nil, but he wasn't one to cry over spilled milk. His grandfather and Uncle Andrew had dabbled in the stock market, buying on margin, making an initial payment and the rest on credit.

When the stock market crashed in '29 they had lost everything but the house and cotton mill, and that due in part to Old Stuart's will. Andrew had promptly put a bullet in his head as any self-respecting southern gentlemen, facing ruin, but not grandfather.

Only he knew where the old bastard had got the money to keep the mill running. With his help, they had continued to run a profitable bootlegging operation through Canada, until the law had been repealed; and it stuck in his "paw" like a thorn he could not pull out.

Now they needed money to get the brewery started again, and Trent was to be the sacrificial lamb, but he was no fool. Trent knew that if Jamie had not run off with that gal of Steban Gabriel, his grandfather would not even let him through the door.

Trent walked back to his desk; scattering papers over the floor looking for a file he knew should be there. "Sara where are the annual fiscal reports that were on my desk this morning", he said.

Sara Ludlow, his grandfather's personal secretary hurried through the doorway. "Mr. Justin asked me for them earlier Mr. Trent; if you like I'll buzz to see if he is finished."

"Don't bother", he said, walking past her into his grandfather's office.

The old man was not looking well Trent thought; he was drinking more than usual. He was probably already drunk, but being drunk never seemed an impediment to Grandfather. Drunk or cold sober, only a fool would under estimate Justin Overfield.

"Grandfather, do you have my mother's letter requesting funds, it was in the fiscal reports?"

Justin Overfield looked up as his grandson walked in. As always, his grandson's meticulous appearance annoyed him. It should have been Jamie waiting to take over the reins of the company, not this vain, pampered, pretty-boy, damn Steban and his litter to hell. He said, "You might remind Missy that we are in a depression", Justin replied dryly, his green eyes flashing dangerously. And you make sure she is here for the wedding, Tatum expects it. Have you asked the girl?"

"Not yet, but trust me grandfather; Vera is panting at the bit, ready to be wedded, bedded and enjoy the blissful joys of motherhood."

"I trust you can deliver all that?"

"Why my dear grandfather, whatever do you mean", Trenton drawled. "However, not to worry, I'm sure Jamie has begat a couple of brats by now", he said, laughing.

"Here I got a present for you", said Justin, tossing him an envelope; then watched in satisfaction as Trenton turned pale under his tan.

"Well young whelp, what do you have to say for yourself. I warned you what would happen if you got this family involved in scandal. Nothing can jeopardize this marriage to the Tatum girl. WC could have gotten hold of those pictures taken of you and your latest plaything and he would not have been above using them."

Trenton flushed hotly as he faced his grandfather; regaining his composure, he said, "The nigger would not dare, besides, "Vera loves me and what Vera wants, Papa buys."

"Now you see, that's where you are wrong, that boy would dare anything. Besides he would not have admitted doing it, the pictures would have just found a way into Tatum's hands. Lucky for you, I was able to intercept the photographs and the negatives."

"I know, I'm fortunate you still have a few friends in low places", Trenton finished. "Really Grandfather how many times do I have to tell you I have friends that would gladly deal with the nigger for you."

"Who you talking 'bout, them Chicago hoodlums or those hooded hypocrites we attend church with on Sunday. How many times I got to tell you, boy; WC or Steban ain't the same as your average "coon"; hell, if they were, I'd dealt with them long ago. Your friends ride in there and try to take WC, I guarantee you Adel won't be the only widow. We could lose more than we gain. Steban is one of those "nose to the grindstone" coloreds just like his parents. Hell, some white folks like that and Steban has friends in high places, white friends."

"Yeah Yankees and second generation carpetbaggers, they don't mean anything down here. We'll kill 'em all. I got some boys who would not bat an eye."

"As usual, you can't see any further than your nose. You gonna kill Jamie too; cause that is what you would have to do. You can't kill them all, I know and killing them ain't enough."

"What then," Trent wanted to know?

I am going to take everything they got. I want the land and I want the mill, everything they got is mine by right and I want them to know it. I got a plan and we cannot lose. Angel's Trumpet is gonna fall into our hands like a ripe plum with minimum effort on our parts and I don't want some fancy northern lawyer with a lot of legal mumbo jumbo, coming down here trying to blow smoke up our asses."

Trent said, "What plan, it's the first I heard of a plan."

"Stay the hell out of Mae's and maybe I can trust you to know and I also don't want to hear nothing else about your friends; now get out."

Trenton's green eyed gaze narrowed with contempt. The old man would soon learn it was a mistake to underestimate him. He could rave all he liked; soon all the money and power would be in Trent's hands and he would handle not only the Gabriels, but Grandfather as well.

That conceited puppy didn't know anything, Justin thought, as Trent left his office. Reese

Gabriel and Daddy had done all their business with Maitland Bank and he knew for a fact they

still handled the Gabriels financial affairs.

That old Jew Maitland had been too much of a conservative to get involved in heavy speculation

in the stock market; which was why he had listened to Andrew in the first place; about all the

money they stood to make. Justin had decided to transfer the family accounts, which turned out

to be a mistake. And then if things had not been bad enough, that damned fool Andrew with his

precious honor, had to go and put a bullet in his brain.

It was just bad damn luck; like his daddy finding out he had stolen from the company and Anna's

dying. Or the Brewery closing, and the Stock Market crash; all of it had just been bad luck, but

he would spit in the devil's eye, before he would let it break him and find comfort in a bullet.

After Stuart's death, he had left Justin nothing, except a glorified position as head of the brewery

and cotton mill. Justin knew all it would have taken is a little good will. His daddy had held

this town in his hands by little more than a display of good will; but power and knowledge

worked better. The power and the money had been left in Amelia hands, but that was no

problem, he had been getting around his mother since he had been three years old. Only when it

came to the Gabriels did she become contentious; but Justin had learned patience.

He had the Gabriels just where he wanted them all he had to do was keep squeezing and then

Prohibition had been ratified. Justin had never believed the prohibition laws would be enacted.

They were all a bunch of hypocrites, "Sunday saints", drinking before dinner cordials and brandy after dessert.   However, survival took priority over the Gabriels' demise.

He had trucks and he used them to run a little whiskey down from Canada. With the help of a few of Trent's friends and a few of his own associates it simply became a full- time operation. It had been enough to hold off the creditors and keep the cotton mill going.

Now finally his chance had come at last. The Maitland Bank would call in Steban's loan after thirty days, and he would be there to buy the loan, once it became default. Justin knew they could not possibly pay off the loan and still have operating capital for the sugar mill and farms. Either way he had them, he would buy the loan outright or he would wait and buy the mill and farms at auction for pennies on the dollars.

He had spent whole life trying to rid himself of the Gabriels, but as soon as that puppy married Tatum's daughter everything would be different. He would have enough money to destroy them once and for all.

This day had already cost him more than any man should have to pay, he thought, reaching for the flask of brandy he kept in his desk; swallowing long and hard. Damn the Gabriels to hell, nothing had turned out as he had planned, but he would not think about the past, only how sweet his revenge would be.

Chapter

Angel's Trumpet, 1935

Hollis Terrell had the innocent allure of a healthy country girl; moving with a graceful, hips swaying stride; her plain cotton dress a swirl as she quicken her pace toward the nearby grove and the white frame church where her father was minister. Her brown eyes shone with intelligence and gaiety, but her smiling countenance was often triggered by a self-depreciating humor that few understood or approved; except, of course Edmond.

She always enjoyed walking to church. There was a peacefulness about Sunday mornings that banished dark moods, and today was perfect. The birds chirped, bees hummed; and all around was the faint aroma of wild honeysuckle blossoms that thrived despite the heat.

People tended to act better on Sundays, no matter the sins perpetuated Monday through Saturday; redemption could be found in church on Sunday morning, and there were plenty of churches in Overton County.

On West Mulberry Avenue, well-to-do Negro folks like Edmond's family attended the Pomosa Methodist Church. The minister was young and educated with a desire to do the Lord's will as long as it did not run too contrary to his own. His wife was one of the Atlanta Albrights and he envisioned himself another Adam Clayton Powell.

On the eastside, the white folks attended the Overton Presbyterian Church, where status was denoted by a family pew and stained glass window. The church's overseer, Dr. Tucker Shepard, had been raised in Overton; gone off to divinity school and returned to pastor the church just as his daddy before him. Dr. Shepard had perfected the art of inoffensive sermons, which worked

107

well, considering the whole county knew the church board of deacons were some of the biggest lechers and drunks in town.

For everybody else there were evening tent meetings, foot washings at the Primitive Baptist Church, and on the riverfront, Father Mark welcomed all persuasions.

It was only mid-morning but soon the sun would reach its zenith promising another day of scorching heat and no rain. The well-worn path Hollis walked was scored with tire tread, wagon wheels and bare feet imprinted in dry red clay that gave off puffs of dust at the slightest breeze.

Her father and other small farmers labored daily to keep their crops watered; determined to save their harvest. Papa had talked about Mr. Roosevelt's "New Deal", that promised help for the farmer during his last church sermon, but promises did not fill bellies. Most agreed, that unless Mr. Roosevelt could make it rain, a deal, old or new would not help. They could only continue to labor and pray that a merciful God would see them through.

Praying was something her father was good at. However, Papa had no tolerance for her whimsies. Being late for church was unacceptable and punishment for her lapse in etiquette would begin the moment she walked into the church. Papa would have his "pound of flesh"; and later she would have to endure her mother's reoccurring lecture on her responsibility as the minister's daughter.

Hollis heart began to hammer in her chest as a red roadster came into view, leaving a cloud of red dust a mile long in its wake. She knew the driver could only be Joel Tatum. She could hear the singing in the church and she wondered if she was close enough to the church for them to hear her if she screamed.

Tatum made a U-turn and pulled the car in front of her blocking her way. Jet McClure was riding up front and a third boy in the back, she recognized as one of the Whitlocks. Hollis had known these boys most of her life.

She had played marbles in the dirt with them; but they were no longer boys, but predators of the worst kind. It would be a mistake to show fear but if they tried to hurt her, she vowed they would not go unscathed.

"Holly gal you looking mighty pretty this morning, said Jet McClure, leering at her in a way that made Hollis want to throw up. The Whitlock nodded his agreement, grinning like an obscene Cheshire cat. When he reached out to touch her, Hollis slapped his hand away, but the two just kept laughing and catcalling, suggesting lewd punishments for her being so uppity.

Joel Tatum did not say a word, just continued to drive slowly along beside her, looking at her with eyes like blue disks of ice. McClure and Whitlock were uneducated, redneck farm boys; dangerous but stupid. Tatum was far from stupid and Hollis thought he was not just dangerous, but deadly.

He was forever lurking around whenever she was in town watching. Even coming out of the bank where he worked for his father every time she went by on her way to visit Mae. The last time he had been waiting for her when she had left Mae and she had made it plain she was not interested.

Hollis knew Joel Tatum was capable of taking what he wanted; instead it was as if he wanted her to be afraid. She decided to start taking the longer way down by the docks when visiting Mae. The riverfront was a rough section of town, but at least she understood their crude needs.

"OOwee did yall see the sparks shooting from that little gal's eyes. I swear if they had been bullets son, yall be dead now. What about it Holly gal, can we ride you anywhere", finally Tatum purred in his low syrupy voice. Whitlock and McClure thought his play on words funny as the two sit back sniggering.

The church was just up ahead and Hollis expected to be dragged into the car. She was surprised when instead she heard Tatum said, "Come on boys lets go on down to River Road, the pickings are a lot more plentiful and a lot less prickly."

"Now that's a fact Tat", said Whitlock laughing.

"I say we take her along", said Jet McClure, with a heated glance at Hollis.

"It appears to me old Jet got a mighty big itch to scratch, I say we get it scratched on River Road, what you say Whit", drawled Joel Tatum.

"On a Sunday morning, huh, most of them whores sleep, that aint in church", Whit replied laughing.

"Then we'll wake 'em up", replied Tatum

Whit had seen the expression on Tat's face; that boy could turn meaner than spit before you could blink your eye and it was not pretty sight. With a fixed grin, he said, "Fine with me Tat, let's go have at it."

Jet McClure looked as if he wanted to disagree, but Hollis watched as they left in the same cloud of red dust, which they arrived. Only then did she release the tight control she held over her emotions, trembling with fear as they sped away.

She had told only Mae about Tatum. She knew her father could not protect her and mother would have blamed her; lifting her eyes toward heaven, in her guise of martyred saint.

She wished she could tell Edmond, but she could not. Edmond was a born crusader; passionate to tilt at windmills and right every injustice of the world. It was why she never allowed herself to consider marriage to him, not completely sure she was not another one of his "causes."

But Edmond was right about one thing, people around here took too much for granted; something she would never do again.

Hollis had not forgotten what had happened to the Jones girl last year. The poor girl had been beaten and raped. She could not identify her attackers and nothing had been done, but Hollis had had her suspicions.

She changed her dusty walking shoes for the heels she carried in her hand; tidying herself before going into the church. A mischievous smile touched her lips as she met Edmond Gabriel's mock expression of sternness which dissolved into a grin. Hollis grinned back, winking her eye as she complied with her father's request to sing a hymn. How glad she was that Edmond was home.

Angel's House Church, 1936

Matthew Terrell had broken with the main governing body of the church years before, much to his wife's everlasting humiliation, choosing instead to open the doors of Angel's House, Church of Christ and minister to the small farming community.

The people of Angel's Trumpet were his neighbors and his friends. He understood their challenges and he shared their triumphs and failures as they dealt with the fickle elements of nature and the contrariness of man. Rev. Matt was never too busy to lend a helping hand or give to those who had a need.

He had found contentment in Angel's Trumpet, but he had married a vain, ambitious woman for all the wrong reasons and if occasionally he found solace in the bottle of whiskey he kept hidden, he considered it between him and his God.

Matthew Terrell was an impressive man in any setting, but dressed in clerical robes there was a majesty about him that belied the humble man he was. He did not really care for the robe, but Ruby insisted. She could not accept he was just a plain country preacher.

He bowed his head as he listened to his daughter sing. Hollis had a lovely singing voice and the richness of "Amazing Grace" pour forth over him like calming oil, preparing him; as the congregation joined Hollis in the last chorus.

This was the time he loved best. The beat of patted feet and low harmonious hum of the congregation. He could sense their anticipation and devotion. When he stood in the pulpit, there was only joy.

His vibrant voice moved some to tears, or to offer praise to GOD in a dance of thanksgiving, while others simply bowed their heads and prayed. He preached of faults and weaknesses, with words that scoured the heart. But Rev. Matt's message was not one of fire and brimstone; it was instead the benevolence and goodness of a forgiving God; that filled flayed spirits with hope. Hope that better days and better times were within their reach; that lifted burdens and caused the uncertainties of life to appear surer. At least for a time, Hollis thought.

Custom dictated Hollis stand with her parents while they greeted each person as they exited the church and because it was the second Sunday of the month, custom prevailing, Sunday dinner would be shared. Already the church matrons were preparing to dish up collards, corn bread,

113

fried chicken and sweet tea, each family bringing what they could; to be served on the wooden tables and benches in the back of the church.

Papa always had a special word and a warm handshake for everyone. Mama stood beside him, smiling to mask her weariness of the prolonged ritual. Here she was the reigning queen-bee and there was never a crack in her "preacher's wife" exterior. Who would believe the oppressive atmosphere of cold silences that existed between them or the fights that would wake her from sleep?

Edmond waited until most of the people had gone to the picnic grounds. He wanted to speak with Rev. Matt about Hollis traveling to Atlanta with his family to attend Cassandra's sorority dance. Earlier, when he had broached the subject, Matt's answer had been noncommittal, but Edmond was determined not to give up.

He was greeted with a hug. "I am proud of you boy", said Rev Matt.

"Thank you, that means a lot to me. I'm glad to be home."

"Our Hollis sure did miss you, she has been mopping around for months", said Ruby Terrell.

Edmond smiled, "I have missed you all also", ignoring Hollis's embarrassed expression.

Hollis had been eight years old, when her mother had insisted she attend a birthday party for Cassandra Gabriel. Even as a child, she knew somehow her mother had demeaned herself to get the invitation.

Of course, Cassandra and her friends had ignored her. She had been sitting alone, plotting her escape, when Edmond had arrived. Those silly girls were about to pee in their pants, hoping he would speak to them, instead he had brought her cake and ice cream and spent the rest of the party talking to her; the preacher's daughter whose behavior was always causing comment.

He had taken pity on a lonely little girl prone to mischief and had introduced her to the world of books, taught her to play chess and listened to her dreams. Only Edmond knew she wanted to be a writer. He was her best friend.

Papa could not seem to understand. She did not want stay home or learn to be content with her lot. Her Mama only saw what she wanted to see. Ruby Terrell had determined she knew what was best for her daughter. She would have position in the world, all Hollis had to do was marry Edmond.

As she and Edmond strolled along the church grounds, Hollis said, "I feel like I should apologize for mama, but she will say what she thinks no matter how uncomfortable it might make others."

"Your mother doesn't mean anything", he replied.

"I think we both know better, but tell me about you, tell me everything,

"First can I get a hug", he said smiling.

"Silly", she said, walking into his arms. She could feel the sinewy muscles of his arms as he lightly encircled her waist and pulled her close. His soapy lime scent, so uniquely Edmond, filled her senses and she felt a desire to move closer; instead she willed herself to pull away from him, confused by her thoughts.

Other women envied her friendship with Edmond. She had overheard Shelia Jenkins asking her friends, "Now yall what she gon do with all that man?" The other women had laughed, cackling like hens until they saw her. She was not stupid, she just had never thought of him that way. At least he had never made her feel so strange; she caught her breath, at the achy sensation that swept along her insides.

"Hollis I have a surprise for you, Hollis did you hear what I said."

Edmond was looking at her strangely, after having to repeat himself twice and she quickly apologized with a shaky smile. "I am sorry Edmond. I was wool-gathering."

"Wool-gathering, am I that boring; I said, he repeated, annunciating each word, "I have a surprise for you."

"What is it Edmond", her equilibrium restored, only to be shattered by his next words.

"My family and I will be leaving for Atlanta in a few days"

"Oh", she said, her expression so forlorn, he almost stopped to kiss her. "I had hoped you would be home long enough to visit Mae. She has not been well and she refuses to go to the doctor."

"It has been a long time since I've been to Miss Mae's and It would be a pleasure to see her, but you did not let me finish, I am taking you with me. I want you to attend the White and Gold Debutant Ball with me."

She turned to him excitedly, but the sparkle in her eyes faded quickly. "Oh Edmond, it's impossible, I'm no debutant, I don't have anything to wear, plus Papa would never let me go."

"Ssh", Edmond spoke, placing his fingers lightly over her mouth. "Just say yes, Hollis. I have so much I want to tell you and show you."

Two years ago, he had returned home on her birthday to discovered she had grown up. She had laughed at him after he had carved their names on the large oak that shaded the church yard. Now she pulled back slightly as he traced with craving with his hand. "Do you remember this", Edmond loves Hollis, he read, "I still do you know."

"Maybe; but loving and being in love are two different things", she said.

He smiled at her, "I've been waiting for you to grow up and know the difference."

"Edmond, you treat me like a sister and I think of you like a brother. You just find me comfortable like an old pair of shoes. There should be fire between a man and woman, passion."

"And what would you know about passion?"

"I know what I know", she replied, ignoring his soft laughter.

For a moment, he allowed his imagination free rein, as his eyes strayed from the modest neckline that hinted at soft curves to her smooth bare legs. He longed to pull her close, then she would know just how uncomfortable she did make him, but that was part of her charm.

Edmond loved looking at Hollis. He loved her naivety and the way she could laugh at herself. Her sweet face revealed so much more than she realized, shinning forth from her dark almond shaped eyes, alight with emotion, one following another. He knew she was not indifferent to him, but she was not ready to accept him as a man who loved and wanted her.

She was just so determined to have her way. He had never even kissed her; afraid to overwhelm her with what he was feeling. Perhaps that had been a mistake. He would not deny there had been other women; but since she had been seventeen, Hollis had been the only one for him.

Edmond continued to tease her saying, "Really Hollis have you experienced passion?"

"I'll never tell, but you know what they say about country girls."

"What!"

"Edmond don't be so serious", she said with a relaxed smile; at ease once again.

"I swear Hollis Terrell you are incorrigible", he said, a smile tugging at his lips.

"That's a mighty big word for a country girl. Anyway, as I recall your mother is planning for you to wed a Miss Patrice Albright. I'm sure she'll be at the ball."

"Nobody runs my life, not my mother or anyone else; besides Mama always liked you."

"Whatever that means, do you remember when we met?"

"Of course, I do, you were a nine-year old terror, bent on destroying my sister's birthday party."

"At least I did not act on it, but your mama still views me as that little terror. She has no intention of letting you marry down in the world." "No Eddy, Patrice is the one for you, she is such a marvelous girl; she is so refined. She will make some man an excellent wife." Hollis' mimicry of Adel Gabriel was perfect.

"Girl you are crazy", he said laughing; "and you know what, you are a marvelous girl yourself."

"I know dear Eddy, I know."

The Terrell Home, 1935

Ruby Terrell sat before her mirror brushing her hair as she had every night as long as she could remember, before plaiting it and binding the ends. Strands of silver swirled within the dark tresses, but once it had been silky black. Her mother would dampen it with a little water and oil and roll it on paper twists that set into fat soft curls.

She looked like Mommy, although her skin was not quite as light, she had been as pretty as her mother. It was funny how one mistake could color your whole life, Mommy had once told her. She had been a child and had not understood; now she knew. Some mistakes you keep paying for over and over again.

Mommy had been gay and laughing, but the Bishop frowned on frivolity as unrefined and unbecoming in a minister's wife. Even now she had never thought of her father as other than the Bishop. As his daughter, Ruby was a shadow, not to be seen or heard unless on display.

She remembered when Mommy became ill, a slow lingering disease that robbed her of her beauty and sanity. Every day the Bishop would leave his church duties to sit with Mommy one hour reading scriptures and every day her mother cried when he left. Ruby never figured out if the tears were because the Bishop left or because he came at all. Then one day there were no more tears for Mommy. The Bishop remarried six months later.

He tried to explain to her that a man in his position needed a wife, as if Georgia Smith with her fat curvy body; could replace her elegant mother. He had no shame, marrying a woman like that, nearly twenty years his junior. Soon the little princesses were born in quick succession; Esther, Sarah and Elizabeth. Ruby was reduced to even less, in her father's eyes.

She rarely saw him except at church and mandatory attendance at the dinner table each evening where he dispensed chilly approval on her accomplishments at school or her duties at church. It was how she had met Shelton.

He had had a beautiful voice. She could close her eyes and still see his smile; her brain could even conjure the smell of his cologne and the gentle touch of his hands. It was only later she found out about his wife.

They were sitting at the dinner table and Georgia had been talking, going on and on about Cleopatra Lawrence and her new husband, who were recent converts to the church. Cleopatra Lawrence was a woman of means.

Georgia did not know she was ten years older than Shelton or that he only married her because she promised to help him finish school. He told Ruby that he had never loved Cleo, and she believed everything he said, right up until she became pregnant and he refused to leave his wife.

She never knew what Shelton told his wife, but Cleo wasted no time bringing the tale to Georgia and of course the Bishop. When she had refused to name the father, the Bishop had beat her senseless. He had only been concerned for the scandal and Georgia did not want Ruby's disgraceful behavior to influence her precious daughters.

Ruby thought she really hated the Bishop then. He did not care about her, only what people would say. He decided to send her away to her mother relatives in Atlanta, and she miscarried a week later. She had determined one day to make him regret what he had done.

Aunt Bess and her cousins had been kind. They never mentioned the past and after a few weeks her body healed and physically she was herself again. If her heart remained sore, it only served to make her cautious. When she met Matthew Terrell she believed she had found a man who could rival the Bishop in every way.

Matthew was not handsome, but he was tall and well-built, with a charismatic presence he seemed totally unaware he possessed. No one noticed that his suit was shinny with wear or his resoled shoes. His deep and impassioned voice as he spoke about faith and God ignited an excitement that swept throughout the church.

Ruby had been stirred spiritually like everyone else, but was surprised at her physical awareness of the young minister. She no longer wanted or needed sexual passion in her life; but Matthew Terrell had potential, a diamond in the rough; that needed only her guidance. She could tell he was flattered by her attention; it was simply a matter of blowing on hot coals.

Ruby never questioned her motives; she had been raised to be a minister's wife. She purposed to be a good wife, while she chiseled her husband's way upward in the church hierarchy, but Matthew had proved stubborn. She soon discovered her ambitions were not shared, and that whatever passion he might have for her, his passion for God was greater.

Soon Hollis was born and he accepted the post of assistant pastor at one of the largest churches in town, but Matthew resisted every effort to promote himself. He would only say that the Lord would show him what he should do.

He carried his humility around like a cross and she was soon hardily sick of it and him. But what she could not forgive was Matthew allowing the Bishop to die before she could achieve her aim to see her father humbled by her husband.

She had no patience for Georgia and her fat half-sisters' weeping, particularly after she discovered the Bishop's last action was to reach beyond the grave to dash all her dreams and hopes. He had willed her Mommy's property in Angel's Trumpet.

They had no sooner arrived than Matthew decided that the Lord had called him to build a church there and no matter how she had cried or cajoled he refused to change his mind.

The years passed as she watched him turn down one opportunity after another and she was stuck in Angel's Trumpet, bowing down to the likes of Adel Gabriel. But she was determined it would not happen to Hollis.

Matthew Terrell sat in the back of his house taking another sip from the one glass of whiskey he allowed himself. Soon Ruby would be asleep, he would wait until then to seek his bed. Edmond Gabriel had approached him to ask his permission to take Hollis to Atlanta with his family and Ruby would not let the matter drop if he refused, yet he was tempted to say no.

He was aware that Edmond wanted to marry Hollis, but his daughter had never expressed any feeling for him. Edmond was a fine man, but he knew what it was to marry unwisely.

Matthew had been raised by a maiden aunt; a devout woman who brought him up in the church. She never forced him to go. He knew when he was just a boy he had a genuine calling for the ministry. After his aunt's death, his life consisted of work and study, as he managed to put himself through college and theology school.

He had been waiting tables the first time he had seen Ruby she had been standing beside her voluptuous stepmother and father; wearing a flowing white dress. He had thought she was the most beautiful girl he had ever seen.

There had been no time for women in his life until he had met Ruby and for the first time, his thoughts were occupied with something other than study.

Then he began to hear the gossip of her involvement with Shelton Lawrence. The man had been a weasel, preying on the sensibilities of a young girl. When she went away he was devastated and when he saw her again in Atlanta, he knew he wanted her for his wife.

He had been shocked and outraged when the Bishop had taken it upon himself to inform him concerning Ruby's "transgression", the night before the wedding. The man had been one of his heroes. How could he defame his own daughter?

Matthew had wanted to smash his face in. Instead he had the pleasure of seeing the Bishop shamed after he told him he knew of the tragedy to Ruby; one that could have been prevented had he been a more caring, concerned, parent.

On their wedding night, Ruby had lain stiffly beside him ready to perform her wifely duty. But his inexperience, did not blind him to the passionate nature she was trying so hard to suppress. He decided there would be no pretense in his bedroom; she would be honest with herself if not with him. He could still remember her cries of pleasure that night.

Ruby just refused to be happy. Her sole purpose in life had been to remake him and prove to the long dead Bishop she had been good enough. Now she was intent on remaking Hollis. It was really too bad, she could be such a warm giving woman.

Perhaps if he had told her that he knew about the Bishop, it would have changed things; he could never be certain, nor was he sure he wanted her that way.

He sighed heavily; it was late, Ruby should be sleep by now. If Hollis wanted to go to Atlanta, he would not stand in her way. At least it would keep her out of the Trumpet Arms and away from Mae Turner.

Chapter

Angel's Trumpet, 1935

Mae Turner's "live and let live" philosophy might have made her popular with some, but not with the Ruby and Mathew Terrell. To them she was a "graceless sinner." Their antagonism toward her only increased because Hollis continued to visit her, despite their disapproval. Mae had nothing against them; they were both just self-centered people who occasionally seemed to forget they had a daughter.

Terrell reminded her of her father. He had been a good man who tried very hard to be godly, something that can never be achieved under your own steam. Her father had been infected with the two "G", guilt and god, with a little "g." He could not see beyond his own righteousness.

Sadly, it made you blind to things, like your own hurting child. The cure was easy enough, all it took was honesty. God resists the proud; the truly humble never have to deal with guilt; but then what did an old sinner like her know, she had never had a choice but to deal with her frailties head-on. Mae just figured there was going to be a lot of surprised folks on judgement day.

What tickled her to no end was the fact that Terrell had no idea he ministered in her father's old church. Wouldn't he be flabbergasted (she liked that word) if he knew, Mae thought laughing as she worked in her gardens, convinced that the older she got, the less the world made sense.

As he and Hollis approached the rear of the hotel, Edmond thought it was almost impossible to tell her age as Mae waved to them from the garden. Laugh lines crinkled about her eyes alight with pleasure to see them. Her finely made features had coarsened with time, but her smile was radiant. She rose to her feet, lithe and slender, and he thought what a lovely woman she must have been.

Her greeting was interrupted by a coughing spasm, which she brought under control, but not before Edmond saw the drops of blood mixed in the spittle she captured with her handkerchief. He could understand why Hollis was worried about her.

Hollis kissed her paper-thin cheek, alarmed at her frailness. As usual her silvered hair was braided in cornet upon her head and she was dressed for comfort, in an old shirt and trousers. Hollis pulled Edmond forward. She said, "Mae you remember Edmond, don't you?

Mae experienced an unaccustomed moment of regret when she looked at Edmond. She removed her gardening gloves and extended her hand to him. "Yes, I remember him, what you think I'm senile. You have the look of your grandfather."

"I have been told that", said Edmond

Hollis hid her surprise as Mae greeted Edmond; she had never told Hollis she knew the Gabriels. Hollis said, "Mae, dear I was hoping that you would allow Edmond to examine you."

"It is only a little cough girl, I told you before", said Mae unable to finish speaking as another coughing spasm racked her slim frame.

Edmond helped Mae to a chair on the back poach, while Hollis opened the screened door shouting for Mimi one the maids who worked in the kitchen. "Miss Mae is sick; bring a glass of water for her, please."

"No, no water, whiskey", rasped Mae.

Hollis looked at Edmond, who nodded his head. "Alright Mimi bring her the whiskey."

Edmond listen to Mae chest with his stereoscope, then checked her pulse. "Sometimes Hollis speaks before her brain can process what she is saying."

Mae laughed hoarsely, she said, "Oh you know that about that girl too, huh."

Edmond turned to Hollis, mouthing the words "trust me." "Hollis I'm leaving now, I promised my mother I would be home for lunch; my Uncle Steban arrived unexpectedly yesterday. I'll see you later this evening. Miss Mae I hope you will allow me to call on you again."

"It would be a pleasure to see you whenever you come", she said. The two women watched him go, before Mae turned to Hollis.

The first time she had seen Hollis, she could not have been more than eight years old. She had run through her kitchen door to escape a disappointed gang of roughneck losers she had been pitching pennies with. Her knees were scrapped, face and braids covered with dirt, but she had

had a smile like a sunbeam. She had murmured a polite thank you and scampered off. Hollis had turned up at the kitchen door many times afterward and Mae had lost her heart to the child. Mae said, "Alright what was that about, you mighty bossy today."

"Bossy, oh Mae, I am so worried about you, said Hollis, fighting back tears.

"Oh child, don't worry about Mae, let me get you some tea and a piece of cake; I baked it fresh this morning."

"You sit right where you are, if I want anything, I'll ask Mimi for it."

"Alright Miss Bossy, but I think something else is bothering you, besides old Mae."

"He asked me to attend some high society dance with him in Atlanta."

"Slow down, I assume you mean the Gabriel boy?"

"Of course, I'm talking about Edmond. I believe he is going to ask me to marry him, Mae and I don't know what to do. I'm so tempted to say yes. It is what mama wants and I think papa would be pleased."

"First of all, you getting yourself all worked up and he aint even asked you yet. Besides there's another question here, do you love him, Mae said watching the girl closely?"

"I have always loved Edmond, but I don't know if it's the right kind love. It's mixed with too many selfish motives; marrying him could solve a lot of problems. And another thing, his mother has her sights set higher than somebody like me for Edmond."

"You be very careful baby, cause being married to a man you do not love is a long lonely road. Your ma and pa would not be the one sleeping in his bed."

Remembering her response to Edmond earlier, she shook her head and said, "I know that Mae, but that's another thing; besides a few hugs and brotherly kisses on the cheek, he has never touched me. I know Edmond too well; he wants to right all the wrongs of the world, and that's okay, but I want a husband and lover, not a savior."

"Still the boy seems to be his own man; more important he's a good man, like his grandfather. He just got a lot to learn, and so do you."

"What about his mother, Adel does not like me."

Adel Gabriel should be your last worry, although I imagine she tries hard to wrap Edmond up in her apron strings. Why that gal so high tone, I do not know, considering her family just did have a pot to piss in and a window to throw it out. The funny thing is nobody expected her to marry WC, it was common knowledge she was sweet on Gentry."

"He would be Edmond's Uncle Gent, he doesn't talk about him much."

"Yeah that's right. He was not born when Gentry Gabriel left town. Lordy he was just too good-looking, with too much money and too much idle time; he was bound to get in trouble. A lot of women, including Adel, made fools of themselves over him; hell, I might have myself if I had been younger", Mae said laughing. I even remember seeing that McClure gal making eyes at him; which was just plain stupid, considering a colored man's life wouldn't have been worth a bent nickel if someone had found out, but it wasn't my business."

Hollis began to laugh, saying, "You mean the fat one, is that why he had to leave?"

"Yeah, and well she wasn't fat then", Mae said, laughing along with Hollis.

"Now Edmond's pa, he is a different kettle of fish, depending on who you asking. His wife might say one thing, the people in the community might say something else.

"What you think about him Mae, I don't think he likes my Papa very much?"

"Your papa is not an easy man, but that is another subject. If you ask me what I think about WC, I think he is a "novelty". You don't meet a man like WC Gabriel every day, at least not around these parts. He aint the kind of man to let nothing interfere with what he wants. I know I would not want to be on the wrong side of him."

"A novelty, said Hollis giggling, where did you come up with that."

Mae said, "Huh, I'll have you know I got education. Long time ago I used to know a man that could speak elegant, like nobody's business. Sobering suddenly, she said, "He is dead now."

For a while neither spoke, then Hollis said, "You know the Gabriels pretty well, don't you Mae?"

"Anybody that lives in Angel's Trumpet knows the Gabriels."

"No, I do not mean now, I mean before. Earlier you said Edmond looked like his grandfather and then you said he was a good man like him. You knew Jasset Gabriel?"

Mae paused, reaching into her pocket for a tobacco pouch and leaflets. That's the problem with getting old, you talk too much, she thought as she rolled and formed her cigarette. She inhaled deeply, pulling the smoke through her lungs, releasing it with a satisfied sigh, followed by a coughing spasm, that had Hollis on her feet, but she waved the girl away.

The burn of the whiskey was soothing as she finished her glass and poured another. She leaned back in her rocking chair, her mind drifting with the back and forth motion. "Yes child, there was a time when I knew the Gabriels very well."

Chapter

Morocco, April, 1935

"Ashes to ashes, dust to dust, intoned the minister as first one person then another circled the grave, each dropping a lump of black earth upon the two coffins. The words made little sense to a young boy. His face was wet with tears and each time he heard the sickening thud, his stomach churned.

When it was his turn and he stood clutching Jewel's hand, until she helped him cast a small bit of soil onto his parent's coffins. As he looked into the deep hole and the caskets suspended above it, he closed his eyes sick with the need to vomit. Even so, he knew it would be a disgrace to empty his stomach at his parents' grave site like Jimmy Overfield. They had buried Jimmy's mother on the other side of the cemetery, the day before, and he now he stood nearby with his grandparents.

He understood death; Grandmama had explained it to him when his baby sister died. Papa and mama were gone to heaven; but Grandmama was crying and grandpapa just stood there as still as a stone. If WC had cried, he never let anyone see him do it and he had told him to stop sniveling like a baby.

Gent awoke from a troubled sleep. It had been a long time since he had the dream. It had haunted him for years and was always the same, him standing at the gravesite. Gent could barely remember his parents; just cobwebbed recollections that drifted away before he could fully grasp them; like being lifted high in the air laughing or a low cultured voice reading him a story.

He picked up his Uncle Steban's letter, reading parts of it once again. As a young man he had admired and respected his uncle, but too many years had passed. Their most common ground was a shared guilt that neither wanted to probe, reopening barely healed sores.

He knew what Angel's Trumpet had meant to his grandparents and the sacrifices they had made; although he admitted he had never felt about the land like his brother. With WC was it almost an obsession, Angel's Trumpet was one of the few things he was passionate about; most of the time, he was as cold and manipulative bastard that had ever been born. But then Gent knew he had been no prize.

The sporting life was already in his blood, and at seventeen he had been well known in the less reputable parts of Angel's Trumpet and Overton. He had wanted out and New York was the most exciting place he could imagine. It had been easy enough to convince his grandparents he wanted to attend school there; the Maitlands even helped him get into Columbia.

Gent had been a gambler, and he knew he was good, but he had been so cocky, he sometimes wondered had he managed to survive those days, with his skin intact. He soon learned that there were others better and willing to take his money by fair means or foul.

The gambling circuit consisted of a loosely conglomerate of pool halls, night clubs, and private houses in New Orleans, Chicago, St. Louis, Kansas City and of course New York which catered to high rollers of Color. No one was barred, as long as you were color blind and had the thousand- dollar buy-in, however, standards were maintained and wet behind the ear rookies did not qualify. Gent became a gofer, running errands for the gamblers, anything to be a part of the scene, sometimes watching thousands of dollars, exchange hands.

He remembered watching Templeton Turner, one of the best poker players he had ever seen; play through a 36- hour stretch and walk away with twenty-five thousand dollars. His lessons came hard, but he never forgot; it was business, never personal and skill trumped luck, every time. He watched and learned his craft.

The fact that he managed to graduate from Columbia resulted less from being studious and more as a means of keeping his allowance flowing. When his grandparents had come to New York for his graduation, he had already decided he was not coming home. They believed him when he told them he had to stay in New a York a while longer.

He loved New York and he had never intended to return to Angel's Trumpet, until he received news his grandfather was gravely ill. WC had not even bothered to let him know; only Jewel Mack had taken time to write him. His Uncle Steban still had not returned home from Europe and he felt he had no choice but to return.

Once home, Gent had tried to help, but WC had been ruling the roost, which he had mistakenly thought, included him. Gent's rebellion only led to more excesses, which grew worst after his grandfather died. Finally, his grandmother had no choice but to send him away.

He sighed as he got out of bed to answer Steban's letter. He was not sure what he could do; Gabriel Imports was barely making a profit now with Mussolini and the Italians on the prod. He thought about Nathan and Lowe, but he knew that they would be all right in Djibouti. Tomorrow he would contact Omar Bey to arrange for the long trip home.

Morocco, April 1935

Omar Bey hung up the telephone, satisfied with the results of his conversation with his friend at the French Consultant in Morocco. He had arranged comfortable traveling arrangements for Gent Gabriel, at least until he reached New York.

He looked around his elegant apartment and smiled; the gods had been most kind the day he met the three men behind Gabriel Imports. Nathan, Low and Gent Gabriel were his partners and his family. Before Gabriel Imports, life had become extremely tedious after he had been foolish enough to become involved in Salim Akbar's intrigues.

Omar's mother had been a dancer, the daughter of a lowland tavern keeper, who caught the eye of Adi Akbar, while he was traveling through Djibouti to the Ethiopian royal court in Addis Abba. Akbar had no use for another bastard child and he granted her leave of him most benevolently, with enough gold to use as a dowry to wed Hussein Bey, a widowed shopkeeper.

After his stepfather died, he left everything to Omar and for a time the fates had been gracious. He took a wife and was making good living trading in goods and cattle. His mother had told him of his birth, so he was surprised when Salim Akbar made himself known to him.

Omar had relished the acknowledgement of his high born half- brother and soon Salim had persuaded him to act as a courier. Brother Salim had repaid him by implicating Omar in the murder of an Anglo named Dennison with whom Salim had been doing business. Omar had no choice but to leave Djibouti.

The next years were hard ones, as he made his way as best he could, mostly smuggling, until one of his associates, a fellow smuggler named Hamail, was found floating beneath the docks in the Red Sea.

Weeks earlier Hamail had been approached him with a scheme that he swore would net them more money than they had ever seen. Omar had been agreeable until he discovered that Salim Akbar was involved.

In the sewers of the underground, Omar had occasionally heard rumors and he had recognized his brother's involvement in several unsavory enterprises. People were afraid of Salim and with just cause. Omar knew there was little Salim would not do to turn a profit, as long as he kept his hands clean and his name was not one you bandied about publicly, not if you wanted to remain in the land of the living.

He had tried to warn Hamail, to no avail; now he was dead. Omar had cursed his timing. He had come upon a small fortune in medicines and arms to sell to the rebels in Morocco, but suddenly no one wanted to know him. His connections disappeared and he had no pilot. Omar had no doubt Salim was responsible; and no one was willing to cross him.

Mired down in his own problems, he had been only mildly curious when the three Negro

Americans had walked into the bar; this part of world, attracted all types.   However, when he

heard one of three men use the name Salim Akbar; Omar decided he needed to know more.

The trio had traveled down the Mediterranean through the Suez Canal, where they jumped ship

at the Port of Agadir, hoping to find transport continuing down the Red Sea coast. As a young

man, Nathan had heard about the exploits of Menelik II of Abyssinia and his victory against the

Italians invading his country. He had been excited as the others when it had been rumored that

an Ethiopian Air Force was being established.

 Gent had been flying since his early days in Paris before the war. During the years he was in the

Army he had spent his leave honing his skills at a private flight school in Canada, but to become

a licensed pilot, he knew he would have to leave the United States; an Ethiopian Air Force might

give him the opportunity he needed.

They soon discovered however, that Ethiopia was not a country you could enter at will and that

the Air Force rumor was a hoax. They were drowning their disappointment with some passable

whiskey, when they became aware of a thin man dressed in robes, observing them intently from

the bar.

He was a dark complexioned man; although his beard and visible hair was as silkily textured as a

Caucasian. As he drew near to their table, he bowed from the waist, greeting them in halted

French using the flowery salute of peace typical of the Islamic religion. Gent listened in surprised as Nathan responded in kind.

Omar said, "Ah a true believer; that makes my mission much sweeter. I could not help but hear your conversation and the name of Salim Akbar. I should warn you, that name is one you should not use so freely in this place."

Slightly drunk Gent peered at Omar, saying, "Salim Akbar was once a friend to my uncle, what is that to you."

"And your uncle instructed you to seek him out?"

Gent replied slowly, "No, I just remembered my uncle speaking of his friend Salim when they attend school together in France. My uncle said he and his family was Abyssinian nobility. I simply thought perhaps he could be of help to us in joining the newly formed Air Force, which of course was only a myth."

Such rumors are numerous in this part of the world, most come to nothing; and your Uncle, is he still alive?"

At Gent's nod, Omar continued, "Then he is fortunate, most associated with Salim, are usually found in back alleys, quite dead." "Do I understand correctly, that you are a pilot?"

"Wait a minute, you have asked a lot of questions and I have tried to be polite, but just who in the hell are you."

"My pardon, I am Omar Bey; I thought perhaps we could be of aid, to one another."

Lowe said, "Just how is that supposed to work "offendi", seeing as how we don't even know you."

"I think we could have mutual interest, if you would permit me to sit down."

"Why cause we are Americans, Negroes, and supposed to be easy pickings."

"Lowe that's enough", Nathan spoke with an authority that both Gent and Lowe still respected. Turning to Omar Bey, he said, "How can we be of help to you?"

Once Omar had explained his proposition, the three had opted to join him. Omar had introduced Gent to Philippe Dupris a French expatriate and former pilot who lost his legs in the war. Gent had offered Dupris enough money to negate his fear of Salim Akbar, at least temporarily, but they had a plane and pilot. Philippe did not need legs to teach Gent the terrain or enhance his flying skills.

The safe delivery of the contraband to the rebels had established a partnership and the beginning of Gabriel Imports. The group had smuggled and sold whatever the market would bear; weapons, food, sometimes medicine.

When the rage in European Café Society for the rare and exotic became the new craze; inspired in part by the discovery of a pharaoh's tomb containing priceless artifacts in Egypt, the group decided smuggling antiquities would be no different.

Omar had the expertise and Gent Gabriel had the money. Gabriel Imports cultivated a well-earned reputation for discreet acquisitions. For a price, Gabriel Imports could provide it.

Morocco, 1935

Omar had left Gent's itinerary and passport on his desk. There was little else for Gent to do but pack and telegraph Nathan and Lowe. The two men were certainly more brothers to him than WC had ever been. He would probably be buried somewhere in an unmarked grave or washed up on some beach if not for the two men.

Years before Gent had used scandal and fear to loosen his grandmother's purse strings. It had been a dangerous game he had played with Pris McClure and it could have gone very badly. He felt ashamed when he thought of how frighten his grandmother must have been; but he wanted he to live on his own terms and for that, he had needed money.

She bought him a one-way train ticket to New York and had given him enough money to see him to France. It was only later he discovered how wise his grandmother was. Rosa had answered his first cable for money with four short sentences:

"I love you, write me, there will be no more money, grow up you are on your own."

So he had learned to rely on his wits and card play, traveling through parts of France and Europe; where the color of money made the man and not the other way around. He picked up a lot of things along the way; but he was always alone; one-step ahead of trouble. He might be running still if not for Hezekiah Nathan and the war.

He had bummed around Italy and France, spent some time in Morocco, but Europe had become one big powder keg. There were so many treaties and alliances you needed a scorecard just to keep up with the players. He had been trying to find a ship; anything to get home, but German U-boats were having a field day and had he found a ship, it would have been at his own peril.

His money had gotten low, and high stakes poker games were none existent. There was no more elegant card play; only war, and death. The Germans were dug in, fighting on the French border and there were reports that thousands of Frenchmen were being slaughtered with each assault. Russia had cast in her lot with France, until some up-start named Lenin began raising hell in the motherland, now things did not look good for France or her allies. The war to end all wars had become a royal pain in his ass; and he found himself playing cards with a less than desirable element on the docks of Le Havre on the northern coast of France.

Gent had been wining steadily most of the evening and his fellow players' mumbling overtones were becoming louder. As he expected, the sore losers were waiting for him after he left the bar. A scuffle ensued until one of their number lay bleeding on the street; with a knife lodged in his chest. The rest of Gent's attackers scattered and he didn't wait around to ask questions. Somebody had alerted the watch, and he could hear the whistles blowing as French police ran toward the docks, and once again he was running for his life.

He had been standing in a pitch dark alleyway that smelled of rotting fish, breathing hard; and clueless. He knew he would not be hard to find; he was in a small pond and there were very few fish his color; or least until yesterday.

Suddenly the humor of his situation struck him funny and Gent began to laugh, he could not help it. He was in deep trouble and the only thing he could come up with was crazy. His impromptu brainstorm might border on insanity, but he did not have a whole lot of options. By dawn the police would be on to him, daylight offered no dark alleyways. He needed to blend and it just might work. Hell, not only would it save him from his present predicament, but it could be a way to get back home.

Of course he had never bargained on the HN. He would never forget his first view of Hezekiah Nathan. His size alone was imposing, but when added to the spit and polish of a career soldier, complete with razor sharp creases and seams; his belief in his own cleverness began to fade.

After he had stated his business to a couple of incredulous sentries, they had promptly marched him to Sgt. Nathan who had been neither shocked nor fooled. Nathan had studied him over tented fingers as if he was a stupid fly caught unknowingly in a spider's web.

"What's wrong with you boy, don't you have no ditches to dig at home?" Sgt. Nathan spoke with a Texas drawl, his voice low and intense, and it began to dawn on Gent, that perhaps he had made a serious error in judgment.

He said, "No sir, oh that is Yes Sir."

"And, if I am not mistaken educated", Nathan continued leaning back in his chair. "Let me see your hands boy."

He examined the smooth hands with a bark of laughter and glitter of white teeth that resembled a crocodile at feeding time.

"Now tell me, he said still laughing, are you one of them poets over here to indulge in Greek love?"

"No sir, he had replied angrily

"Or are you that rarest of birds, an educated Negro man with means", Nathan had continued without pause.

"Why you arrogant black" …before Gent could finish however, the sentries reentered the tent, following close on the heels of one of the French police that had chased him, accompanied by one of his attackers.

Nathan spoke sharply to the sentries, "What the hell is this."

One of the sentries answered, "I'm sorry Sgt., I tried to stop him, but he says he is a police officer. From what we can make out, this man here is a fugitive, they say he stabbed one man and tried to rob the other, nodding at Gent's attacker, not more than thirty minutes ago."

Nathan had looked at him, saying; "Translate this boy, I am sure you can. Explain to the policeman that he is technically standing on United Stated soil and that you are an American and a member of the armed forces and therefore not under French law, but U.S. military justice. Tell him also that he might examine his witness a little closer, he might notice that the front of his shirt and trousers are covered with blood."

The police officer argued, but the Sgt. proved persuasive and the police officer left dragging his witness with him.

"Come with me", Nathan said to Gent, leading him through the camp to the temporary headquarters.

"Captain of the Guard, the Sgt. requests a word with you, sir."

Captain Nelson and three other officers were playing poker, and the Captain was clearly annoyed. He said, "As you can see Sgt., I am busy."

"Begging your pardon sir, but I have an eager recruit who would like to join up and we are in need of men sir."

"Can never have enough ditch diggers can we Sgt.", said Captain Nelson with a smirk, the other white officers laughing with him. "Very well Sgt. Nathan, I trust you have checked his identification and all is in order; Lt. Hughes will process the necessary papers and he will be sworn in on tomorrow morning; dismissed."

As he and the Sgt. started back across the camp grounds, it occurred to Gent that he might have jump waist deep in trouble.

The HN was smiling like a crocodile, said, "Well boy, by the end of this war, I can guarantee you one thing; you gonna be an A-one ditch digger."

Sgt. Hezekiah Nathan proved a man of his word. Gent's hands had blistered, peeled and finally harden callus thick, no longer resembling the hands of a professional gambler. However, the changes in him were not only physical. Gent had been drifting for so long, he discovered the constancy of the Army life was not as objectionable as he had assumed.

He ate three square meals a day, had plenty of mind numbing work and suckers to fleece at poker every night and he made a few friends, something he had never had before. If there was a drawback, it was the HN. Sgt. Nathan continued to watch him, scrutinizing his every move. Gent kept reminding himself he had had his own reason for becoming Army bound. However, three separate incidents changed everything.

Le Havre, France, 1917

Gent had been carousing with his fast friend Private Lowe, who upon meeting Gent had dubbed him "Little Lord Fauntleroy", a misnomer that had stuck and was echoed by the whole regiment. They were both a little drunk when they spotted Smity, a member of their unit in an argument with an agitated French shopkeeper that was quickly drawing a crowd.

Lowe said, "Well Fauntleroy 'pears to me old Smithy might need our help, what ya think?"

"Since you know about as much French as Smithy, I guess you mean me, not we."

"Wee, Wee Monsurer", Lowe had replied with a drunken grin.

The situation between Smity and the shopkeeper was handled in a matter minutes, but after he and Lowe had returned to the barracks, everyone seemed to know he spoke fluent French. The place had been like a beehive, soldiers rushing about and all leave had been canceled. Ole "Black Jack" had decided to send the Colored troops to the French front.

What happened next was just rotten luck. Lt. John Malcolm was one of a handful of Negro officers assigned to the black troops and the only one who spoke fluent French. Rumor had it that he had gotten into a fight with some white enlisted men and was stabbed. Nobody knew for sure, but there was no Negro officer to act as translator and there was no one to replace him.

Lawrence Oliver Washington's mama once told him that a fancy name was the best start she could give him in life. His mother's intentions fell short of the mark however; since people had been calling him Lowe as long as he could remember and the only other thing he had inherited from his mother was the gift of gab. The hot temper was his alone.

"Black Jack can kiss my black ass."

"I think you better be careful what you say and where you say it."

"I don't give a damn. Everybody knows he ain't been in no hurry to commit American troops, even though the French have been desperate for reinforcements. Now he wants to send us to the front. Hell what we gon do, throw shovels of dirt at the Germans. Naw, just send the niggers, they ex, ex, shit Fauntleroy what's that word again."

"Expendable, Lowe, expendable."

Gent had finished stowing his gear, listening to Lowe's endless commentary, when Sgt. Nathan had walked in, his gaze falling first on Lowe. "What we gonna do first is tell the general about our secret weapon, we gonna let Private Lowe talk the Germans to death." Turning to Gent, he said, "Get your shoes on boy, you coming with me."

Gent had followed the HN through the camp as he had that first night to headquarter. Major Cook was waiting and got straight to the point.

"We find ourselves in a bit of a quandary soldier, but Sgt. Nathan has assured me that you are the man for the job. Private, I understand you have a degree from Columbia University and that you speak French fluently is that correct?"

"Yes sir, that's correct", said Gent. The HN had a look in his eyes that dared him to refuse.

The Major continued, "I would like to offer you a temporary field commission as 2nd Lt. as a replacement for Lt. Malcolm. You will act as our interpreter with the French command, effective immediately. I know you are inexperienced Lieutenant however you have able help in Sgt. Nathan. If there is nothing further, you are dismissed."

Gent was outside and walking back to his tent before he realized he had never even said yes. "Sgt. I am not equipped to handle this."

Nathan's answer was a crocodile grin, "I taught you to dig ditches didn't I?"

To Lowe he simply became Lt. Fauntleroy.

The French soldiers had welcomed them as brothers-in-arms, teaching them what they needed to know to stay alive through some of the worst trench warfare devised. And yet, they had left so many friends buried in French soil, a fate Gent might have shared if not for Nathan.

Gent watched as a nun had gently arranged pillows under Nathan's bandage shoulder after the removal of a bullet that had been meant for him. Nathan had had the good fortune to be hospitalized at a nearby French convent under the tender mercies of the Anglican nuns; since some of the white nurses took issue with treating Negro soldiers.

Nathan had studied him from beneath hooded eyes, speaking in that soft authoritative voice Gent had come to dread, because it demanded the best of him. "You have come a long way, are you gonna keep those bars, Army is a good place for a man who don't know where he's headed."

"I guess that would depend on the Army and the powers that be", replied Gent.

"No that depends on you", Nathan had said as he drifted off to sleep.

Gent knew he had changed. He was no longer that boy with a talent for cards, and a taste for wine, easy women and generally raising hell; despite his grandfather's teachings. Nathan reminded him of Reese. His Grandfather had been a man of honor, integrity and respect, who believed in doing the right thing just because it was right. There were times he wished he was the type of man his grandfather had been; a man like Nathan, but he guessed men like him had their own type of honor.

Chapter

New Jersey, 1923

Amazingly, Gent's commission had stuck and for a while things had been good, up the until the moment he had struck Lt. Randall. Provoked or not, he had "KO'd" a white officer, case closed. The life he had built in the army had quickly been flushed down the toilet by a white bureaucracy, red tape and equally red necks. He had no regrets, Randall got what he deserved.

After being court martialed and thrown in the brig Gent had no doubt of his fate. Military justice moved swiftly and a stint in Leavenworth had been looming large; when help had come from an unexpected source.

Colonel Raymond Timms; was a "by-the-book", career soldier; an Iowa farm boy, son a Pentecostal preacher. The Colonel had personally investigated the matter and obtained affidavits from several people who witnessed the fight; something no one else had bothered to do.

Once the facts had been confirmed, in addition to his sterling service record, his sentence had been reduced to a dishonorable discharge. Randall had been returned to duty without loss of rank or pay. Maybe he should have been grateful, but all Gent felt was anger.

The Colonel had sat behind a desk that seemed too small for him, his steely blue eyes unwavering. The Military Code of Conduct was clear, yet he knew justice was another matter. He said, "I regret what has happened here. You were a good officer and it had been my hope that you would be reinstated. Negro or white, every man under my command is treated fairly."

"May I have your permission to speak freely sir?"

"Granted."

"Colonel, I stopped Randall from raping a friend of mine and while I do appreciate what you did for me, the fact is there are more "Randalls" in this army than men like you. The men in my division have received more recognition from other countries, than from our own."

"I do not understand, if you feel so strongly, why did you continue to serve?"

"To be honest sir, I am not sure you could understand, there are times I question my own rationale. Most Negro men joined because they hoped for an equal shake in this country and a better life for their families. Instead, they returned home to a nation of apathy that bleeds for everyone except its own citizens."

"I lost a lot of friends in France. Good men who gave their life for this country; I guess that is why I stayed; I owed them a debt as does this country. The price has been paid up in the blood and sweat of those that came before us; and the rights we are denied, are worth protecting."

"The country is changing Lt. eventually the "Randalls" will be weeded out. One day the troops will be integrated, despite the challenges ahead. You see I am also a believer in the nation I love and serve and in the potential and promise we have yet to achieve."

He had offered his hand to the white officer, saying, "I hope you are right sir and God grant, I live to see it. I owe you Colonel and I will not forget."

"You are dismissed Lt. and I wish you God's speed."

Gent had returned to his quarters to pack, still angry but resigned to his fate. Fate had lead him to join the Army in the first place; so when a couple of men from his unit had interrupted his packing with their hard-luck story, he figured it was just more of the same. They had tangled with the wrong people and now one of their crew was in the hospital seriously injured and thirty thousand dollars was missing.

It had been a while since he had heard from Lowe or Nathan, but he knew Nathan was in France. He had a little money and Paris might not be such a bad idea, but first he decided he would go to Chicago and ask a few questions. The military police had come up empty. Perhaps he might have more luck; what the hell else did he have to do.

Chicago, 1923

Outwardly, there was nothing special about Tate's. Dozens of "tea rooms" had opened since the start of Prohibition; you could find the same bootlegged gin in any speak-easy in the city. The regular customers could have perhaps told a different story, but nobody did. J. John Tate took a dim view of people sticking their noses in his affairs.

There were rumors that some found the "tearoom" conductive to more nefarious deals, where for a price, privacy could be assured. Nobody cared or asked questions. It was enough, that a man could have a discreet drink with his friends after the drudgery of the work day. You minded your own business, it was not smart to do otherwise.

The evening had begun no differently than a hundred others, as J. John had stood in his usual spot behind the mahogany bar. A large, ponderous man, with a beatific smile, that often disarmed others to their regret; J. John was a hustler who did favors for a price. A percentage of every moneyed deal conducted in one of his private rooms went directly to him and no one ever tried to cheat J. John twice.

Hatching larceny was his specialty; he knew the value of cultivating profitable contacts and how to bring the right people together; cementing his reputation as a man who could get things done. His allegiance was bought with cash money and those foolish enough to trust him, soon discovered his loyalty extended only to covering his ass.

After the Prohibition laws had been ratified by the United States Congress, J. John had been approached by a couple of gentlemen interested in establishing a northern route for their bootleg enterprise out of Florida. J. John brought together the two elements missing in the operation, sugar and transportation, arranging a smuggling connection with his two silent partners; WC Gabriel and his old buddy Dresden. Unfortunately, the business had become "organized" and he had to make some concessions, which though less profitable, had proved to be a lot healthier.

His love of easy money was equaled only by his love of food; and having assured himself of the evening's profits, decided to heed his growling stomach and have his dinner, until he saw Lilly. He hitched his belted pants over his paunch, only to have it slip back in place under his belly as the girl walked by carrying a tray of drinks without even a smile.

He had been trying to bed the young waitress for weeks. The girl had been playing fast and loose with him long enough. She been had taking his gifts and money, it was time she paid the piper. After dinner he decided he would have Lilly a' la mode for dessert, he thought with a grin, his hand dropping down to his sagging crotch.

The glimmer of lust in his eyes suddenly became ominous, as he watched Lilly flash her willing smile on a customer that had just entered the bar. Jealousy twisted J. John normally placid expression as she leaned invitingly close to the man, practically brushing him with her tits. He motioned to Ed, who worked as the bouncer as well as tending bar. "You know who Lil is talking to?"

Ed shook his head, "Naw, never seen him before; he knew the password Boss, so I let him in."

"Yeah, probably after your sorry butt got paid. What he do, grease your palm with a dollar?"

Ed grinned, "It was a fiver", he said, retreating swiftly from J. John's angry glare, signaling Lilly from the bar.

Ed was giving her a rolling eyed stare and Lilly wheeled around to meet J. John's steely gaze. "Damn", she said with a sigh of regret; as she walked to where J. John was standing, with just enough wiggle, so the pretty man would know what he had missed. "Did you want something baby", Lilly cooed?

"You damn right, who was he", said, J. John grabbing her arm in a painful pinch?

"Let go of me. Hell, I wish I knew, I would be with him instead of talking to you."

"Lil girl you got lots of sass and I like that, but I got other uses for that mouth than smart-talking me. Now get your ass to the kitchen and take my dinner upstairs to my office; and you be there, waiting."

"Bitch", J. John muttered, as Lilly flounced to the kitchen with a swing of her hips and her middle finger extended; before riveting his attention back to Lilly's "honey-man", who continued surveying the room, his back against the wall.

J John prided himself on knowing all the players; it was his stock and trade. This was a new face, the college boy type; that attracted women. J. John noticed a couple of the regular girls had tried to gain his attention, all with no success.

"Maybe he doesn't like girls", J John snickered; about to signaled Ed to get rid of him so he could get to his dinner and Lilly, when the college boy pushes himself off the wall and walks toward the bar.

He was maybe six feet and compact; slimmed hipped and long limbed, his movements smooth, almost like a cat, giving J. John the creeping sensation of being stalked.   J. John motioned Ed away, his smile of greeting waivered as a growing disquiet prompted him to forget both Lilly and his dinner. J John did not like mysteries; and another mistake could be fatal.

Gent cursed softly as Ed walked away. The bartender would have been less of a problem, but then nothing was ever simple and he wondered for the umpteenth time what the hell he was doing in this dive, mixing in an Army investigation; instead of on his way to Paris. Old habits die hard.

The men in his unit had bought themselves a shit load of trouble; thirty thousand dollars' worth, to be exact. Johnson was a born hustler, somehow he convinced the men he could double their money if they agreed to pool their resources together to use as the buy-in at an exclusive gambling establishment called the Crystal Club. Johnson was good, but he never had a chance. All, the men knew, was the money was gone and Joe Johnson had been beaten so badly, he might not make it; and whatever the scam, it had started in this bar.

Gent had the answer to at least one question, as he had watched the round bottomed waitress sashay toward a fat man that had been glaring at her from across the room.

The men had called J. John Tate a chocolate snowman; which seemed an apt description; judging by the stone-cold glance he directed at Gent and his large pudgy body. By all accounts, he was unscrupulous, crafty, and a very nasty customer if crossed. To underestimate the man could get you dead in a hurry. Now whether J. John's greed outweighed his caution Gent had yet to determined; he needed that introduction to the Crystal Club and J. John was the key.

J. John's welcoming smile never quite made it to his eyes and Gent thought J. John's pretense as the jolly fat man could use some work.

J. John asked, "What you drinking, tea or coffee?"

"Tea, straight up", Gent said.

Reaching behind a panel beneath the bar for the appropriate bottle J. John scrutinized the man in front of him. His suit was tailored; his watch and cufflinks expensive looking and J. John would have sworn on his mama's grave, (if the bitch was dead) the ring on the man's manicured hand was studded with real emeralds and diamonds. Looks, however, didn't mean squat.

The man's cool, appraising eyes seemed to miss nothing. Disquiet had elevated to apprehension churning in J. John's gut like a bell ringing. Continuing to smile affably, he said, "I never forget a face and I ain't ever seen you around before; you passing through or did you just lose your way."

"Depends", Gent replied, grimacing at the taste of the raw gin. "You own this place?"

"Yeah, and everything in it", said J. John, his smile fading slightly, remembering Lil's flirtation.

"Place looks profitable."

J. John gave a grunt of agreement, then said, "Money is just a commodity; you can never make enough."

Gent finished his drink and J. John moved off to another customer at the end of the bar. The fat man had tallied his net worth down to the change in his pockets, but it was plain he was suspicious. It was time to raise the ante. Motioning for a second drink, he removed a few "presidents" from his wallet, his fingertips resting lightly on the money. "I'm looking for some entertainment."

J. John eyed the money; this was a game he understood. He gestured at young woman sitting at the bar, saying; "What's your pleasure, I got better than that, any color you want."

"That, I never pay for, I was thinking more in the line of a game of chance", said Gent as he stacked several more bills upon the smooth mahogany bar.

Shrugging his shoulders, J. John pocketed the money, then said, "If you're looking for plenty of action try the Crystal Club on Lexington Avenue. Just ask for Red Turner, I'll tell them to expect you."

J. John eyed the man warily as he left. Maybe he was a gambler, maybe not. That tight-assed, upright, way he moved still bothered him. Or that hard gaze that saw too damn much. J. John had an aversion to losing sure money, but the burn in his gut obstructed his pleasure as he fingered the money rolled in his apron.

The damned Army MP's had been all over the place last week like stink on shit and he could not afford to take any more chances. He had survived this long by following his instincts. If the dude was what he appeared to be, no problem; and if not……he reached for the phone, it rang only once. J. John said, "Let me speak to Mace."

The Crystal Club, Chicago, 1922

Leah was bored and hung-over, which usually meant trouble for somebody. She slumped down in a chair; lighting another cigarette with the last. Her life had taken a drastic change for the worst after her husband had been murdered. She had gone back to work singing in the bar where she had met Willis, but she had needed somebody; she could not help it; she could not change who she was. But Red Turner had been a mistake.

She wanted a drink, but she refrained, knowing Red wouldn't like it. He had no tolerance for drunks and she had definitely been drinking too much. She was just so tired of Red's jealous rages fueled by Mace's lies. Mace had little use for women, even less for her and Leah returned his regard ounce for ounce.

She had found a way to be rid of Mace for good, but she had to be careful. The rumors surrounding Red and Mace Turner could cause nightmares. Leah had learned never to ask Red about his money or his business. She did not want to know; and what she believed, she kept to herself. She had enough trouble sleeping already.

It was early, but soon the guests would begin arriving. The Club's plush mirrored lobby was a constant source of entertainment for Leah. Red was about as sensitive as a rock, but he had a surprising insight into human nature. It was one of the reason the club had become such a success; he knew how to cater to people's foibles. The rich, the beautiful, the notorious; none could resist the impulse to preen and admire themselves as they strolled through that mirrored lobby. Socialites, mobsters, sports legends, and women with only their faces and bodies to barter; the Crystal Club was the playground for their fantasies and they paid for the privilege.

Leah did not immediately notice the man when he came in. He was tall and attractive, but many such men came through the Club. What captured her attention was the way he moved; purposefully, without a single glance at his reflection. He was also well- dressed, with nice shoulders and Leah decided she liked what she saw.

A waiter motioned him in the direction of Mace standing in the rear of the dining area. Mace was immaculate as usual in a white tailored dinner jacket that fit his muscular body to perfection;

but the frown on his face boded ill for the newcomer. He turned to walk away and Mace grabbed his arm. He shook off Mace's restraining hand, and the two squared off.

Leah's gaze flickered between the two men. He was as tall as Mace, but slimmer. His demeanor appeared calm compared to Mace's deepening scowl, but Leah knew that look, it could only mean one thing…trouble. She knew what Mace was capable of and the other man's chances of survival was less than zero. Instead, in a flurry of movement, it was Mace who lay on the thick red carpet gingerly testing his jaw, blood dripping from the corner of his mouth.

The scent of her perfume disrupted Gent's battle stance as he waited, his eyes fixed upon Mace, legs apart, feet balanced, ready if Mace decided to continue the fray.

"Mace I will take care of this gentlemen, tell Mr. Turner we'll be in the lounge", said Leah with a satisfied smirk.

That feminine voice had cooled his blood for the fight and fired up his lust for something else as her sweet aroma played havoc with his thinking. Gent turned and she was beside him, her hand resting lightly on his arm. "Shall we go", she said.

Mace stared in hatred as Leah led his adversary toward the lounge. "That's all right bitch, you'll get yours, I'm gonna see to it personally."

Crystal Club, 1923

She was the kind of woman his grandmother would have called "high juiced." Glossy and exotic as a wild orchid, she was well aware of her effect on the male species and used it to her advantage.

But he could not stop himself from admiring her smooth flawless skin, highlighted by a yellow silk dress that clung enticingly to her mocha tinted curves and long legs, he had to remind himself why he was there. Gent was not sure what she wanted from him, but she had his undivided attention.

She spoke to an old man clearing tables before leading Gent to a secluded booth. She said, "I took the liberty of ordering our drinks, the real stuff. You strike me as a bourbon man."

"You can take any liberty with me you like."

Smiling she said, "I was impressed with the way you handled Mace; that is not something you see every day around here."

"Your friend needs to learn some manners", he replied.

"True, but no one has ever succeeded in teaching him any and walking away. Besides, he is not my friend."

"Better, but since he brought you to my rescue I owe him for that", he said with a grin.

She laughed; the sound low and husky, "You did not exactly need rescuing and believe me, whatever Mace thinks you owe him, he will collect."

"And I will make sure he gets exactly what he's asking for; but enough about him, I want to know about you. Are you going to tell me your name", he asked?"

"No, I don't think I will", Leah teased, feeling an unaccustomed shyness as he continued to stare at her with admiring eyes.

"Now I'm intrigued; but alright no names. What do you do here, besides being easy to look at?"

"A lot of things. What about you? You don't look the type to hang around a place like this."

"A delight to the eye and intelligent too; now I am impressed, but you're right, I'm here on purpose and you are making it difficult to concentrate on my business."

"I'm willing to bet that doesn't happen too often, so I will take that as a compliment."

He reached for her hand, lightly stroking her palm with his fingertips; "You are a beautiful woman and that is compliment enough. The line may not be original, but true."

Leah was shocked to feel herself blushing. She was accustomed to worshipful gazes, not this hot appraisal. This man was far too sure of himself. It was her game and she made the rules, she was in control. She was almost relieved when she saw Mace coming toward them.

"Mr. Turner will see you now", Mace muttered, his lip cut and swollen.

"Your business is with Red; I have to go", she said abruptly

"Yes, but wait a minute", Gent said as she hurried away. "This isn't over", he said softly, ignoring Mace's impatience snort.

The modern genre of the décor gave the room an antiseptic aura; Gent felt like he had stepped into a morgue. Red Turner's chilly grey eyes were the same color as the silvery drapes that covered the windows and the pale tinted walls of his office. There was no extra fat on his lean body, no affectations in his dress. His complexion was fair and lightly freckled, his deep auburn hair was straight; combed back from his face.

The man ushered into his office seemed familiar, but his name had meant nothing to Red. In the old days with Templeton, they had sat down with a lot of wantabes and taken their money but only a stupid man would come up in his establishment without being bona fide. Red did not think he was stupid. Which left the question; who was he and what did he want.

Red would have to remind J. John that the love of money was the root to an early grave. The greedy fool should have dealt with him; which was a conversation he and Mr. Tate would have in the near future. None of these thoughts surfaced however, as he cordially waved his guest toward a chair. "I understand you have business with me."

The casual observer might consider Mace Turner the dangerous one; but Mace was all muscle and flash from the tailored dinner jacket to the diamond ring on his little pinky. Red Turner could have been mistaken for an undertaker; but his hard, silver eyed scrutiny could cut glass.

Gent had walked freely into the lion's den; the problem was walking out, especially since Red was already staring at him like he was a dead man. Gent said, "I'm looking for action; high stakes and no limits, I understand you are the man to see."

"Why me", said Turner, his thin lips stretched in a mirthless smile.

"It's your world, Mr. Turner, and a certain large gentlemen suggested I ask for you", he replied smoothly.

"It is true, we do provide certain types of entertainment for our guests and Mr. Tate does provide introductions from time to time, but my brother, waving his hand toward Mace, does not trust you."

"Your brother tried to rough me over, but I'm willing to let bygones be bygones, if he will." Mace looked ready to chopped Gent into tiny pieces with malice and forethought.

Red said, "You have the money of course."

Anticipating such a request, Gent produced a stack of neatly wrapped bills. "Shall I count it?"

"That won't be necessary, welcome to the Crystal Club. Mace will conduct you to the gaming room." Red Turner's thinned lip smile faded, as a furious Mace lead their "guest to the gaming tables.

Red brooded angrily as he thought of Leah's interference. The woman was like slow poison in his blood, reaching for the cold milk he kept in his office to ease his knotted stomach; adding a splash of scotch whiskey.

He knew Mace had always hated her, but it did not matter; she belonged to him. No one trespassed on what was his; but business first. First he would take the money from their arrogant guest and then he would let Mace and the others have him.

A knock at the door interrupted his thoughts. A lean youth stood in the doorway. "Mr. Mace said you had a job for me Mr. Turner."

"Yeah, come on in and close the door."

Chicago, 1923

Once he had made his way in the world with a deck of cards and it had nothing to do with luck.

He had played with some of Europe's best, he knew all the tricks and he never forgot it was

business.

Dawn was still a couple of hours away when Gent cashed in his chips. As far as he could tell,

Tuner ran a straight game, but then the odds were always in the house's favor. Turner would not

be happy when he discovered Gent had walked away with fifty thousand dollars of his money,

but he could get his cut from the thirty thousand Tate and Mace had stolen from Johnson.

All things considered, it was possible Red did not know about Tate and Mace's little scam.

Johnson had never made it inside the club. He had been found a few blocks from Tate's beaten

and stripped. Naturally when the Military Police questioned Tate and his customers, nobody

knew anything. The two had probably arranged to set him up as soon as he left Tate's and had

split the money. There was no way to know for sure since Johnson was still in a coma.

The old man who had served him earlier was waiting for him as he headed for the front entrance.

"Ms. Leah told me to give you this", he said, handing Gent a letter. "Come on, I'll lead you out

the back way; they probably waiting for you out front."

So her name was Leah, he thought, with a smile of satisfaction as he read the note. Gent

followed the old man who told him his name was Jack, through the back alley behind the club until they were a block away.   He handed Jack a handful of money and walked away, leaving the old man to stare after him.

"Arrogant young bastard", Jack muttered to himself as he walked the other way toward home. He had never seen such luck at the card table; nor had he seen Ms. Leah look at man like she had this one.   But one thing was for sure, anybody with the bad judgment to break the bank of one of Red Turner's tables and then infringe upon his woman, was just plain asking for trouble.

Jack did not notice the thin shadow of the young man as he detached himself from the corner of the building and followed Gent.

She answered the door on the first ring of the bell, wearing a pink satin peignoir and matching robe.

"Nice outfit", he said, smiling. "Are you going to invite me in?"

"A gift from an old friend", she said as she waved him through the doorway.

He could hear a flowing piano melody, playing on a phonograph drifting across the room. "Nice music", he said.

"Composed by an old friend", she said, determined to keep her distance as he followed her across the room.

Gent said, "Nice place you have", he said looking around the apartment which was tastefully decorated in warm shades of coral.

"Belongs to an old friend", she said, unable to resist the urge to giggle. He continued to move aggressively toward as her until they both stood in the middle of the room.

Leah said, "You are a most unusual man, I was almost certain I wouldn't see you again, at least not alive."

"And yet you left the note", he said smiling.

"Call it wishful thinking. I know what happened at the Club; you've been extremely resourceful so far, but I wanted to warn you. You are out of your league. Red Turner has far reaching connections and vindictiveness without bounds."

"You know I would have torn this town apart until I found you", Gent said, reaching for her.

Again, Leah eluded his touch; ignoring the thrill his words caused. What she wanted and what had to be, was two difference things. She said, "You are not listening, I thought you understood I am Red's woman. My life is complicated enough without adding more trouble."

"We both knew how it would be, that's why you sent the note."

"I sent you the note to try and save your life. He will kill you."

"That's gonna be harder to do than you might think."

"A lot of people have thought the same thing."

"It doesn't matter I'm here. Come to me Leah."

The nuance of intimacy in his voice as he spoke her name sent little currents of pleasure through her, as he stared deeply into her eyes willing her to trust him. It was an unspoken promise that all her secrets were safe with him. She could no longer resist him, nor did she wish to. It had been so long since she had felt anything. Her desire for him was cleansing.

His heat, his scent, his long slow kisses, one following another, swept past all her self-imposed barriers, until only the present and its pleasures mattered. He was in control of the game and she sobbed out loud her release not once, but twice; their bodies in perfect sync as he possessed her. And then she slept, naturally, instead of in a drunken stupor.

Gent lay back for a long time admiring the sweat sheen beauty of the woman lying next to him. Leah had not been part of his plans. He had known a lot of women in his life and he had even cared deeply for a few, but he never made promises he couldn't keep. Leah had managed to get pass his guard with a surprising adore, generously giving as much as she received. Passion was a fleeting of emotion, something more had happened between them that he had not expected.

The sounds of splintering wood shattered his lethargy. The money and more importantly his gun were in the living room. He jumped from the bed running, but before he reached either, the door fell away from the lock admitting Mace followed by two others into the room.

He felt the icy coldness of a gun barrel pressed against his temple; then blackness as he was struck from behind. The last sounds he heard was Mace's laughter, mixed with Leah's scream.

Chicago, 1923

He did not know how much time had passed before he regained consciousness. The pain in his head unbearable and he stumbled into the bathroom, splashing his face and head with cold water, wondering why he was still alive.

He found Leah lying on her back near the fireplace. The delicate features of her face battered into a bloody caricature. More blood was flowing from the back of her head, covered his hand when he tried to lift her.

She was struggling to speak and he had to lean close to hear. He had to tear open every drawer until he finally found what she wanted. Gent kneeled beside her, seeking some explanation, but it was no use, poor Leah was dead.

He mourned for the lovely, vibrant woman he had held in his arms, now a lifeless corpse. His sense of loss and anger felt thick enough to choke him, until sirens in the distance penetrated his fury forcing him to think.

They had left him alive for only one reason….to take the blame. He had to get out of there. Somebody had called the police and it didn't take a genius to know who made the call. He pulled on his clothes; grabbed the envelope and headed for the fire escape. There was only one person, who perhaps could help him.

He waited for what seemed like hours in the alley near the rear of the club, before he spied the old man coming out of the kitchen exit. "Hey old man, hey Jack", he said, looking around cautiously.

Jack turned at the sound of his name, his expression icy cold as he recognized the man in front of him. "I knew you were trouble the minute I laid eyes on you. I warned Ms. Leah, now she's dead."

"So you know."

"Yeah I know, what the hell do you want?"

"Listen to me, I know you cared about Leah, I cared too. I made a promise to her and I need your help."

"I heard the police was looking for you", said Jack."

"I know you don't have any reason to trust me; but police deal with only what they call facts. Too many things don't fit. To them Leah will be just another dead colored woman, victim of a domestic dispute. They were not going out of their way to find another killer, when I was handy. We both know who did it and I'm going to pin his ass to the wall; you gonna help me or not."

"The first thing we need to do is get the hell out of this alleyway. I got a place a few streets over; we can finish talking there. And youngblood it had better be good."

Jack's place consisted of a kitchen and living area combination with a small bedroom in the back. It was clean, but nothing could hide the shabbiness. "You want some coffee, Jack said."

"I've been freezing my ass off in that alley, coffee sounds good."

"Alright youngblood, why you come to me; what makes you think I won't rat you out to Red."

"Leah trusted you. I need you to take a look at these", Gent said; spreading what appeared to be ledger sheets across the worn table.

Jack glanced down at the papers as he served Gent his coffee. "Huh, did she give you those ledger sheets?"

"Yeah, but she died before she could explain, but it is plain Red is up to neck in something."

"Hell youngblood, everybody knows that, but one thing he ain't is dumb.

"Maybe you can give me a clue old man", Gent said impatiently.

Red Turner runs the club, but he lets Mace manage the gambling. The control is in the hands of a syndicate boss named Rossetti people call him the "Rose"; maybe you heard of him. Anyway the Crystal Club is in his territory and he gets a slice of everything the club grosses. Now I can't tell for sure, but maybe Leah figured someone's skimming off the "Rose" money."

"Now both Red and Mace are mean, clean through, but Mace is mean and not half as smart as he thinks he is. He's just stupid enough to believe he could get away with something like this. He was the cause of a lot of grief between Red and Leah. My guess is she planned to use the papers as weapon against Mace in some way."

"Did she care so much about Red then", Gent said; unwilling to believe it could be true.

"Not in the way you mean, I think it had simply gotten too hard for Leah to break away."

"Old man, how do you know so much?"

"I'm the invisible man, youngblood. I just look, listen and learn." A small boy stood in the bedroom opening, rubbing the sleep from his eyes. Jack got up and led him back to bed. "Excuse me I'll be just a minute."

He returned a few minutes later and poured the younger man a second cup, ignoring Gent's inquisitive look.

"You are full of surprises old man."

"He's my grandson, Jack finally said. His mama died a few years back. Anyway I am all the boy's got and he is all I got. Now you've asked me a lot of questions youngblood, what are you planning to do?"

Jack listened incredulously as Gent began to outline his "plan". "Are you crazy, you can't deal with a man like Vic Rossetti, not if you like living. If that ain't bad enough, you gonna try to blackmail Red too. I'm beginning to think you suicidal boy."

"Well the "invisible man" should know a way for me to get to the Rose and I will take care of Red myself", Gent said.

Jack said, "Now maybe I know a friend, who knows a friend, that could possibly arrange what you want, but it is gonna cost you. You want your money back from Red and to settle the score for Leah, well I want something for my grandson. If I'm gonna stick my neck out, I want exactly half of what you get from Red."

"Seventy - Thirty, old man", Gent said dryly, not surprised by the turn of events.

"Sixty - Forty", replied Jack stubbornly.

"No more haggling old man, Sixty - Forty."

With a satisfied grin, Jack said, "That's the smartest thing you said all night youngblood. I think for the time being you should stay here, cause Red knows the police don't have you which means he is looking for you and I'm a man who believes in protecting my investment."

Gent tried to sleep, but his thoughts were like leaves in a windstorm. His original plan had been simple; a quick score to settle accounts for his men. Add Leah, Jack and his grandson; and he was stuck in the middle.

In the past, he would have just cut his loses, but imagines of Joe as he lay unconscious in a hospital bed and the face of the beautiful Leah after being crushed under brutal fists would not be banished. The money belonged to him and he fully intended to get it back.

Chicago, 1923

"Gawd damn Mace, what the hell did you think you were doing", shouted Red Turner.

"I still say we should find the old man, he knows something", Mace replied.

"Forget the old man, I had Ajax following him, he didn't turn up nothing. You want to worry about something, worry about that son of a bitch who is blackmailing us to the tune of $100,000.

Worry what will happen if that bastard Rossetti gets hold of those ledger pages. Worry about yourself, you got shit for brains Mace and I ought to serve the Rossetti your ass on a platter.

"You think the Rose will give a damn, who did what, he will cut your throat just like he will mine unless we find a way to get those sheets back. Anyway, maybe you would like to explain how the bitch got the ledger sheets in the first place; maybe you might want to explain that Red."

"There would have been nothing for her to find if not for your stupidity. You too stupid to breathe; first you steal from the Rose, and then you leave a paper trail a blind man could follow. You killed my woman, but you leave him behind alive. You should not have hurt her Mace she belonged to me."

Mace regarded his brother thoughtfully; he had never seen Red like this. He could not believe Red was actually grieving for that conniving bitch. Not that he was afraid, but he knew what Red was capable of. Mace said, "I told you it was an accident; I only slapped her around a couple of times because she kept getting in the way, trying to protect him. She fell and she hit her head. I don't know how he got out of there so fast. I thought sure the cops would nail him, but not to worry big brother, we'll set up the meet, and then I will kill him for you real slow.

Chicago, 1923

Vic Rossetti was thoughtful as he hung up the telephone. Rossetti considered himself, a businessman. He hated Coloreds; Red and Mace were a constant pain in his ass, but he allowed them to remain because their operation was very profitable.

Rossetti was also a very cautious man. In the organization hierarchy mistakes were often fatal and he had no intention of letting anyone discover those two niggers had been cheating him. Rossetti motioned to one of his lieutenants; and handed him a slip of paper; "I want you to take care of this meeting. If the information is legitimate, handle the matter in the usual manner. And make sure, there is no loose-ins."

Chicago, 1923

It had to be the coldest night of the year, Gent thought; pulling his collar over his ears as he walked along the train track leading to an old depot. They had agreed to make the exchange at midnight, along a strip of back road that led to an abandoned train depot, dead-ending into a few dilapidated warehouses; a bootlegger's paradise until the Feds had busted it up a year or so back. Jack had insisted on coming along and was none too happy at being left behind in the parked car, about a quarter of a mile from the meet. The old man was stubborn, but hopefully had enough sense to stay out of the way.

Mace and his boys had been surprisingly low key in their search for him, no doubt to keep Rossetti in the dark. Jack had managed to pick up his things, including the military issued revolver which fit snug against the small of his back.

Gent knew the Turners did not intend to let him walk away with their money. In fact, he was counting on them, to follow their natural inclination for murder, in order for his plan to work. Maybe he was taking a chance, but chance encounters and situations had become a part of his life. It was not that he allowed himself to be swayed by a fickle fate, but rather the adventure of the moment. With any luck, he'd be out of there before Mace and Red knew what hit them.

His steps faltered slightly, when he saw the dark sedan parked in the shadows. Damn, he should have figured there was a back entrance into the place. It had been a stupid mistake, and he felt his odds of survival slip a notch.

The car door opened and the driver got out. He was six-four in his socks and broad across the shoulders. In his meaty paw he carried a satchel he like a lady's purse. The light from the full moon illuminated the craggy features of a used up boxer, devoid of emotion and the outlined bulge of a gun beneath his jacket.

Gent realized things were not going the way he planned; killers, you cannot count on 'em, they or either too early or too late he thought with a quick grin. His humor faded as the unmistakable sound of a double-barreled shotgun choked to fire reverberated in the night. The driver must have heard it also, for he reached for his holstered gun but he was too slow and the double barrels cut him in two.

Dropping to the ground Gent pulled his own weapon from his waistband and fired in the direction of the shotgun blast. The shotgun welding shooter staggered from the shadows, falling into the dirt.

A pistol echoed behind him and a second shooter crumbled beside his partner. Gent turned to see a jubilant Jack grinning at him from across the depot yard. Suddenly Mace lunged from the black sedan firing and Jack's smile froze on his face as a red stain began to spread across the front of his shirt.

Volleys of bullets were coming from all directions as Rossetti's men moved in, racing from the deserted warehouses. "About damn time", Gent said to the dead man, before grabbing the satchel and running toward Jack.

The old man grunted in pain as Gent pulled him up dragging him along. A bullet whizzed pass Gent's ear and another grazed his arm but he kept on running. He could still hear gun-fire after he had reached the car, wheezing so hard he could not speak. He pulled open the driver's side door and shoved Jack inside, relieved to hear the old man curse him profoundly.

He put the car in gear and on the highway in full throttle, checking his rear-view mirror as he drove. The Turners' and Rossetti's men were keeping each other busy, but it would not last for long. Soon they would be on his trail, which led right back to Jack.

"Dammit old man, why didn't you stay in the car like I told you?"

"Then you be dead", said Jack with a ghost of a smile. "You keep your promise", his breathing was labored and he struggled to speak.

"You know it old man, now stop trying to talk", Gent replied, but Jack didn't hear him.

He turned on to a quiet street; Jack had shown him earlier and pulled the car to the curb. He patted the old man tenderly as he placed the ledger sheets in his lifeless hands, confident that Rossetti had enough cops on his payroll that the sheets would eventually get to him.

He got out of the car and began to walk until he came to a rundown tenement apartment. He knocked and knocked until a woman opened the door. She tightened her robe about her thick waist and stood back to let him in. Jack's grandson was sitting on the sofa where he had been sleeping. "I'm here for the boy", he said without preamble.

The woman dressed the boy hurriedly and tugged an old suitcase forward which contained his clothes. Gent thrust some money in the woman's hand, hoping it would keep her quiet at least for a time. Turning to the boy, he said, "Will you come with me?"

The boy looked at him with a maturity he should not have possessed; his eyes were shiny with tears. He nodded slowly, saying, "Daddy said I should trust you."

The two made it to the train station without incident and boarded a train headed south. The sleepy child looked up at him. He said, "What's your name?"

"They call me Gent Gabriel", he said, smiling down at the child; but he was already asleep. His name was Fontaine and he was six years old.

Chapter

Marseille, France, 1924

Gent sat brooding into a glass of wine, for the first time in his life uncertain of his way. The problem was he could not drift aimlessly making his living on the turn of a card as he had done in the past. The military life had changed him. Nathan had changed him. Gent had no luck in tracing him; his old friend was on the move.

After the clash with the Turners and Rossetti, it had seemed a good idea to get lost for a while. He had left Fontaine with Aunt Win and Sinclair; he knew the boy would be safe with them, before traveling to Boston. He continued along the Atlantic sea coast, hanging about the ship yards until he found a passenger freighter sailing for Europe. He had to bribe his way aboard, and spent the crossing working as a steward. It had not been easy, but he did his job and kept to himself. No one would have guessed he had fifty thousand dollars sewed in a hidden bottom of his sea bags.

Tossing a coin on the table for the wine, Gent shouldered his gear to leave when a familiar voice, with the worst French accent he had ever heard, asked where he could find Lt. Little Lord Fauntleroy.

Lawrence Oliver Washington had changed little; he was still quick with a razor, and able to talk himself out of trouble, almost as fast as his mouth usually got him into trouble in the first place. Gent soon had the whole story of how he came to be in France. Lowe first informed him that he was an escaped felon.

"Gent my friend, I don't know how it was with you, but you ask me, the only thing I can tell you is that being over here messes with a Negro man's brain. You leave there feeling like a man, like you somebody. You got medals on your chest and all you want is the feeling to last, but it's all just dumb thinking, and dumb thinking can get you killed or in my case 5 to 20 years at hard labor."

"I had heard about the riots and lynching in New York and other places, but I made it all the way home with no problems; maybe because a lot of white boys in uniform wus returning home too, I don't know. Anyways, I just wanted my folks to see me arrive home in that uniform with them medals. They lived about six miles from the train depot, close enough to walk to rest of the way; besides it wasn't like I had a choice"

"Anyhow, I had to pass by the general store on the way home; and I still had all my mustering out pay. My folks didn't have much and while I knew they would like the trinkets I brought back from France, I figured that a sack of flour and a slab of bacon, they'd like that even better. "You see dumb thinking only leads to more, dumb thinking."

"Mr. Early, the white man who owned the general store had been a fair man, but Mr. Early was dead and his pea-head son Rupert had taken over the store. I knew I had made a mistake the minute I walked in that place. All Rupert's cracker barrel, 'bacca spiting friends was sitting in the store, eyeballing me like I had shit on the floor."

"Hell, the Frenchies thought I was a hero, but them redneck crackers don't respect nothing. I even tried polite. I said "Hello Mr. Rupert how you doing. Could I please get a twenty- pound sack of flour and a slab of bacon? Well Rupert just grunts and goes to get my order. Then what do you think I did, yeah, more, dumb thinking I pulled out my wad of money to pay for the food. The next thing I know I'm waking up in a two by four jail cell, smelling like piss and puke; with a knot the size of a baseball on the back of my head charged with armed robbery. You remember that German gun I kept as a souvenir; well it was in my pack. Things wus looking bad; those crackers had my gun, all my money, stripped the medals from my uniform, so I looked and smelled like the town drunk."

"Now my Ma and Pa they didn't know what to do, so they went to Mr. Bud, to try and get me a lawyer. You remember I told you about Mr. Bud Willis, my family sharecrops on his land. Well Mr. Bud advises them that I should through myself on the mercy of the court, which must equal five years of hard labor; cause when the Judge sentenced me, he told me he was being lenient cause he knew my Mama."

"Well there I was, lookin at five hard years on the chain gang so deep in the Georgia woods I never thought to see the light of day again. Men lookin at you like you the last pork chop on the platter, and I didn't even have a rusty nail to protect myself. I'm gonna tell you something, after the war, it takes a lot to scare me, but I was scared. I prepared myself for the worst, but nothing happened; I mean they avoided me like the plague.

Then finally one of the older prisoners explained why; seems this big white guard was a damned fairy with a taste for black meat and he had picked me to be his new girl -friend."

"After all that dumb thinking, I figured I deserved some dumb luck. I got assigned to a work detail that should have gone to one of the prison trustees. We were cutting and hauling wood for heat during the winter, when I was ordered into a dense section of trees. That fat cracker wanted me to handle his business then and there, or he would my make my life hell. I move in on him then bite down until I tasted blood. When he fell back howling I laid him across the head with a log. I still don't know if the fat bastard was dead; but the way I see it, he had it coming. Since he had obliging taken off the leg irons, I just started running."

"I knew I couldn't have more than an hour before they got out the dogs and it would take that much time to make it to the river. By the time I got there I could hear the far away sounds of dogs baying. The current was strong but it was going my way. I had stripped down to my underwear and scattered my clothes before I dived, hoping to throw the dogs off my direction or maybe they think my ass had drowned. I grabbed hold of an old log and it carried me along until I came to a narrowed gap and I made it to the other side."

"About three miles from the river bank I came on a farm. I stood there shivering in my under-drawers, but there was no one around and the barn door was partially open, so I crawled in and up into the loft. The place looked deserted, but the following morning I saw a woman hanging clothes on the line. For two days I lay in that barn, she never came near it. I even saw the sheriff when he came to the house asking questions. Heard the woman tell the sheriff her husband wasn't there and she would be picking him up at the train depot the following day."

"There was a barrel of apples in the barn and an old pair of overalls that smelled so bad I decided to forget about the apples. The next day before light I was in that truck crunched under old burlap sacks and wooden crates used for produce. When she left I sat up in the back like I belonged and when I walked away, nobody paid me no mind. That day I discovered that people see what appears to be. White folks see, what appears to be a docile nigger waiting in the back of the truck for his mistress, hell that's what he is."

"For the rest I would have never made it except for the bible. You laughing Fauntleroy, but it is the truth. The old minister at home told this story that when King David was in trouble and running for his life, he drooled and played crazy. And he got away. You would be surprised, white folk like drooling, simple-minded niggers. I got work and food all the way to Savannah."

"I got me a job working on one of the shrimp boats. I tell you I traveled some before I came to be on a freighter as cook's assistant. I had been forced to use my razor and a couple of the crew members had decided to teach me a lesson. I thought I was a gonner when I heard that Texas drawl. They parted like the Red Sea and there stood the HN."

Gent reached out and grabbed him. "You know where Nathan is?"

"Well yeah, aint that what I was just saying."

Hezekiah Nathan was thinner than he should have been. His skin stretched over the prominent cheekbones of his narrowed face, emphasizing the deep set eyes that missed nothing, but slid away from Gent's gaze at their first meeting. His friend and mentor had always been strong and forthright, now there was a dark grittiness Gent had never seen before. He had too much respect for Nathan to question the changes that were plain to see. It was much later while sharing cramped quarters on a ship bound for North Africa that Nathan told him. He had murdered his wife.

Gent had never met Madeline Nathan; he had only seen the dogged-eared picture that was never far Nathan's side throughout the war. They had met when Nathan was on leave and after a whirlwind courtship he had married her before his last deportment. She had been so beautiful he could hardly believe she belonged to him. Maybe that's why it happened. Afterward it was like watching himself in a bad dream.

He had wanted to surprise her. He had wired her when he was coming home, but he had been able to get an earlier transport which put him there two weeks earlier than expected. She had even mailed him the key to the apartment which he wore around his neck like a crucifix.

They were so busy they did not hear him come in. He had walked up the stairs slowly the sounds of their lovemaking was loud in his ears. The door had been left ajar and he saw her through tear clouded eyes astride her lover. The peach gold body he adored being caressed by another. He didn't remember how he came to have his service revolver but it was in his hand and he shot them both dead. Then he left as quietly as he had come in.

Dazed he was not sure how much time passed as he wandered through the streets, but it seemed the whole city block had gone crazy. Buildings were burning and groups of white men were brandishing clubs, some with guns were marching down the middle of the street.

People were running, some throwing bricks and bottles and that's when he saw a Negro soldier hanging from a lamp post. Something hit him from behind and when he awoke he was laying in an alleyway. Everything was gone, even his dog-tags.

The buildings were still smoldering; black people and some whites were laying everywhere. He noticed some folks trying to help and he just started to help too. When it was over he discovered they were local Red Cross workers and he just stayed with them.

They needed volunteers, strong enough to lift the wounded vets and clean. Soon he was on another ship headed back to France to help evacuate the wounded. When he got to Le Have, he got a job shoveling coal on a freighter to Marseille where met up with Lowe.

Gent could not judge his friends. He knew what kind of men they were; they were good men, loyal friends and circumstances had dealt each a bad hand. Home was not an option for them and once again he was traveling by ship, but this time he was shoveling coal beside the HN and Lowe.

Chapter

Angel's Trumpet, May, 1935

Steban had not planned the trip to Angel's Trumpet. It had been his intention to wait in Atlanta, until he had heard from Gent, but after his dismal failure with the bank in New York, he felt a longing to be home. The confrontation with WC was inevitable.

Steban was more tired than he cared to admit. He could not muster enough energy to be angry after he discovered WC had opened his letter from Gent,. Steban was just glad the Gent was coming home.

At least he had tried to mend matters between him and Jennet. He was not sure he would ever be reconciled to his daughter's marriage, but he had decided to release the money that Rosa had put in trust for her. He had delayed the probate of the separate trust; but Mama had stipulated in her will that it belonged to Jennet.

Steban had just been so angry over Jennet's elopement. There were things in play that his daughter had no idea about; the potential danger her marriage could mean to the family. He could have told her, but what would be the point. She loved James.

He had explained to WC many times they could not touch the trust legally; Steban could see no reason to tell WC about the money until it became necessary. His nephew would only state the obvious. Steban knew they desperately needed that money. WC would just have to get over it.

Their outlook on the family situation was drastically different, but Steban was willing to admit that although he did not agree with the methods he used, it had been WC who had kept their finances afloat. Somehow, he and WC had to find common ground if the family was to survive. The argument had just gotten old. When he got home it was more of the same.

Steban said, "If you would just stop fighting me boy; we both want the same thing, to save Angel's Trumpet. I take full responsible for our situation, but paying off the loan is not going to be helped by your tactics. We have held this land for seventy years; Justin has no legal claim to the land and he is hurting financially worse than we are. We have got to trust in the Law, we have right on our side. Your way would cause us to lose the few friends we have. And we need friends."

WC said, "You think it matters that legally Justin does not have a case? When are you going to wake up? It is 1935 and you are a Negro man in the South; that means white man law and white man justice. Have you forgotten what Overfield's done, what he's still trying to do; can you really be that naive? After Grandmama explained about the codicil attached Stuart Overfield's will, the danger to the family is clear. She had known how it would be after Amelia Overfield died. If something happens to us, what's going to stop James Overfield from inheriting the property through Jennet and God forbid, Trent?"

"I have not forgotten anything; and I am not a fool, but either is Justin. He knows all he has to do, is wait. He will be able to buy the note from Maitland for a pittance. You think with your gut WC, which puts you at a disadvantage when dealing with a cold-blooded reptile like Justin.

I made your grandmother a promise that I would do everything possible to maintain the peace and hold the land, and this I will do. That arsenal you have hidden is going to lead to more trouble."

"You think you knew her, but I was here and I know Grandmama would have done anything to protect Angel's Trumpet. I saw her smiling, standing at the back door to do business with men who thought her less than their hound dogs. You are an educated man, you've traveled abroad, speak foreign languages, and even have a few white influential friends, but you still have to go to the back door, just like Grandmama Rosa.

I have done my best to avoid trouble, even losing my son's respect, but I refuse to be a victim Steban. Justin is not going to stop until he regains the property and unlike you he is not squeamish about how he gets it done."

"We need money to save the farm and the mill, any other argument is moot", said Steban

"You are right, first we got to get the money, and then I'm going to handle it my own way", replied WC.

Angel Trumpet, 1935

Steban sat at his father desk, for a long time after WC stormed from the office. He wondered what his parents would have done. He regretted taking so much for granted and now his parents' legacy was in danger.

Angel Trumpet was 700 hundred acres of good farm land; more than triple the gifted acreage given to Rosa by Jamison Overfield. Jasset had purchased and developed the additional adjacent swamp land for planting sugar cane and built the sugar mill. His brother had been a brilliant man and Steban still missed him.

He could remember warm spring mornings; his mother's white hand stitched curtains blowing in the breeze. Jasset would be at the piano, a gift from Stuart and Amelia Overfield, playing Mozart's Piano Concerto #21; which had been his favorite. Even as a boy, his brother was gifted. Jass could have been a great concert pianist; instead he chose to be a farmer. It had taken many years before Steban had understood why.

On the day Jasset died, his mother had taken an axe and would have chopped the piano into kindling had not Reese stopped her.

The house had always been a work in progress, Steban thought nostalgically. The original cabin had been expanded and enlarged over the years. It was what Mama wanted, although his father had wanted to tear it down.

Inside the house was spacious, with smooth wood floors aged to a rich butternut patina and wide airy rooms with large windows that filled the house with sunlight and everywhere were the plants that Mama had loved and nurtured.

Steban admired the sheen of the mahogany dining table set with a pewter bowl filled with roses from the garden. The dining room furniture had been Mama's joy. Reese had the furniture shipped from New Orleans, created by a Negro artisan. The table would seat twelve and Mama had imagined it surrounded by family. The massive matching cabinet was filled with fine Wedgwood china that had once belonged to Julianne Overfield, a gift from old Jamison before he died.

Many pieces of the furniture had been created by the men on the farms, some of them, gifted craftsmen. WC and his wife still slept on the bed built for the master bedroom. Touches had been added by the wives of her sons and grandson, but the essence of the house was still Rosa. There were times when he felt her presence so strongly it was hard to believe she was gone. So much had been left unsaid between them.

He had not been there when his family needed him; and WC never missed an opportunity to pour salt into an old wound, but his nephew wasted his time, the heaviness of the guilt he bore never left him.

However, WC was wrong about his knowledge of Rosa. Steban understood his mother very well.

After his father's death, she simply lost interest in Angel's Trumpet. Her grief and despair had just been more than she could bear. Rosa's answer had been to lock away her feelings to cloister herself against further hurt. It had been the price of her sanity and what little peace she could garner. Only her great grand-children and Jennet were allowed access to her and she refused to involve herself in the running of Angel's Trumpet.

They had stood in this room the day he had returned from Ethiopia. He had almost lost his life and Franz had been badly wounded. The treasured medallion had been lost and he was consumed with grief and guilt over his father's death. Facing his mother had been the hardest thing he had ever done; he could see the sadness and disappointment in her eyes.

Rosa said, "I had thought when you returned from Panama with Jennet you would stay at Angel's Trumpet, but you did not. You regret the loss of the medallion; but it did not really mean anything to you; you feel bad because you lost a valuable heirloom. Maybe it was valuable, but it meant so much more to your Papa and me."

"All your life I tried to instill a love of the land in you; but it was never in your heart. My birth mother sacrificed her life so I could live and Tilly the mama who raised me risked her life that I might have that medallion. Not because it was valuable, but so I would never forget."

"The people of Angel's Trumpet for better or worse threw in their lot with us. They gave their loyalty and we owe them whatever protection we can. Maybe if you had thought about that, the medallion would not have been lost; but you see wherever a man's treasure is, that's where his heart is. Your heart was never in Angel's Trumpet. You wanted to be free.

Steban had wanted to deny what his mother had said, but he could only stand silent as she continued.

"You think we didn't know what you were feeling; that yearning just to live your life your way; but you learned there was a price to be paid. It ain't free to be free. It cost your brother his life, it cost your father his faith; I don't know which is worse. Now stop feeling sorry for yourself, be the man we raised you to be."

And he had tried, but from the beginning he and his nephew had bumped heads. WC had enjoyed playing lord of the manor, and he resented Steban. As a peace offering he had given WC control of the home farms, and the sugar mill, while he established an office in Atlanta to handle their finances and marketing. But they had been barely breaking even; just living on borrowed time and now time was up.

Regrets were useless; his mother had taught him that lesson. And yet as they faced the prospect of losing everything, he wondered if he had stayed home after returning from Panama instead of traveling to Ethiopia would things be different now. His motives which he had thought so important, seem so trivial now. Much too late he had discovered his mistakes.

Chapter

South America, Panama, 1911

"Senor Gabriel I have your hot water, yes", said Benito, as he entered the one room house; his perplexed expression nothing new, as he pondered the Negro man's obsession with hot water.

Steban had quickly sent the boy happily on his way with the jingle the coins in his pockets. The hot water was a welcomed luxury.

The past three years had not been easy. From the beginning, Franz had put him in an untenable situation, but he had never considered leaving. Some of the most important construction in history was taking place and he had been a part of it.

The Colonel had insisted that Steban list his nationality as French in an effort to head off trouble with his white engineers, but the color of his skin could not be changed. It was useless to be angry with Franz or the Colonel.

The Colonel had arrived in Panama faced with a major crisis. The project was at a stand-still. Mountains of mud and rock, disease, a worker's strike and a U. S. Congress breathing down his neck and the President wanting solutions, not excuses. The task before the Colonel had been daunting and the pride of one man was insignificant.

Every day Steban had watched the men work tirelessly on. They were its body and soul; their life's blood mixed in the soil and cement. They were black men the same as he; constantly exposed to danger and under paid in silver, while the white supposedly skilled workers were paid in gold. It was "Jim Crow", wrapped up in clean linen and Steban found himself in the middle, neither fish nor fowl. The Panamanians had been gracious while his fellow Americans ignored him when they could, and pretended when they could not.

Steban was glad of his small quarters; its purpose of course was to separate him from his white counterparts in the camp, but it afforded him a measure of privacy for which he was grateful.

He looked at the two letters on his desk. The first of the letters was from Franz, outlining a future venture in Africa the engineering company was considering, and the other letter was from his parents.

He knew his parents wanted him to come home, but the world that his parents lived in had become foreign to him. His brother had been murdered, but even if it could be proved; what jury in the south would hang a white man for killing a Negro. He could not reconcile himself to the injustice of the system, despite his misgivings about leaving his parents without his support. He did not want to cause them more grief.

His time in Panama had taught him patience. He had seen too many men die and his personal disappointments had faded in significance against the backdrop of such a huge undertaking. He was thankful for the opportunity he had been given; despite the fact it had all started as one of Franz's jokes.

Twenty-five years earlier, the d'Abbadie engineering firm had been involved in the construction of the Suez project and while the prestige of the Panama enterprise could rival that great work, they were fully aware of the finances needed for such an enormous undertaking and the risks involved. The firm's board of directors had decided to terminate their interests in in Panama and had transferred all rights to the building of the canal to the U.S. government. The transfer had gone smoothly, with all parties satisfied except perhaps the Panamanians.

The Panamanians had not been happy with the turn of events after their fight for freedom, having their country become little more than a protectorate of the United States. They were openly resentful and distrustful of the U. S. military presence, which threaten to create more problems.

The Colonel's appointment had not been well received in some quarters. The President had taken the heat; but politically the skeptics did not need another bone to chew on. So when Panamanian government's request for a civilian engineer to act as liaison between them and the U.S. military, landed on his desk soon after he arrived, the Colonel acquiesced as gracefully as possible.

Using a civilian engineer from the d'Abbadie firm had seemed ideal. The Colonel had believed that the established accord which already existed between the French firm and key Panamanian government leaders, would prove invaluable in smoothing, ruffled Panamanian feathers.

Franz had sent a letter of recommendation from the firm to the Colonel highlighting Steban's qualifications and a formal letter had been sent offering him the position. Franz had simply decided to omit the fact that Steban Gabriel was a Negro.

Steban remembered the Colonel's look of bemusement as he scanned his letter of introduction. It had been plain that Steban was not what the he had expected. Steban had been angry and embarrassed as he stood waiting for the Colonel to acknowledge his presence.

Steban's qualifications had been impeccable and the Colonel had been momentarily at a lost as to what he should do with the tall, distinguished man. Steban Gabriel was an American, fluent in both French and Spanish. His scholastic credentials and experience made him eminently suitable for the position. There would be no trouble with the Panamanians; the same could not be said of his staff.

Most of his men had been Union Officers, but what they would fight for and who they would live and work with were two different things. They were competent men; but few possessed the level of expertise as the man who continued to stand stiffly before his desk.

The Colonel was not a politician; he was a soldier. He had a monumental task to complete and he would do so with all dispatch. Finally, he stood and offered his hand to Steban. "Welcome to Panama, Mr. Gabriel.

That had been three years ago thought Steban as he closed his journal. Three years was long enough; he had done his bit and now he believed his usefulness was at an end. His position had dwindled to that of a "glorified office boy", with emphasis on "Boy", but he had been a part of a monumental undertaking, whether he shared in the accolades or not. Even now, his suggestions that further precautions be taken against landslides were being stonewalled.

He rose wearily from his makeshift desk to put the hot water Benito had brought him to good use. Cleanliness was essential in the tropical climate.

Steban thought of Franz's letter again. He had not seen Franz in the three years he had been in Panama. He had written several letters asking Steban to forgive him for his actions and his damnable humor. His latest letter was more of the same; but he had included details concerning a project in Ethiopia. Franz had known traveling to Ethiopia would be of interest to Steban; and the prospect of seeing his friend Salim Akbar again.

Steban had met Salim Akbar while they were both attending E'cole Poltechnique in Paris and they had become friends. Salim had been intrigued by the medallion Steban wore, claiming it was the family crest of minor nobility in the Abyssinian court. There had no opportunity to investigate Salim's claim, due to Jasset's death. When Steban returned, Salim had left school.

Steban studied the medallion he still wore. His mother had often told him the story of her birth aboard a slave ship and that the medallion had been the legacy of her birth mother. Rosa had presented it to Reese on their wedding day. Reese had given it to Jasset and Jasset had given the medallion to Steban before he left home. The medallion was another reminder of his responsibility to those who loved him; a responsibility he had yet to honor.

His thoughts were interrupted by a knock on the door. He smiled slightly, thinking perhaps the lovely senorita he had met in the square had decided to accept his invitation. Instead he stared into the calm face of an Anglican Nun holding the hand of a young child.

"May I help you Sister", said Steban, feeling foolish.

"You are Steban Gabriel, senor", the nun inquired.

"Yes I am", he said.

"This is for you", she said, handing Steban a letter. "Please allow me to introduce you to your daughter Jennet."

Overton County, 1912

My daughter, Steban thought, as he sat listening to the animated little girl chatting away in French; wondering once again how she came to exist. One look at the tumble of black curls and hazel eyes, he knew she was Maria's child. He found it hard to believe that Marie would keep such a secret from him. He knew his parents would have questions, he just had no answers.

Lucas Mack was waiting was waiting for them at the train depot when they had arrived; for some reason it surprised him that Lucas was old.

"Mr. Steban it's good to have you home", said Lucas Mack.

Grabbing the old man's hand, Steban said, "Since when is it Mister, it was not Mister when you were swatting Jasset and my behinds."

"Lawd-a-mercy, you two wuz a hand full and who is this pretty miss?"

"Lucas let me introduce to my daughter Jennet."

"Then lets git this wagon loaded, I expect there gonna be big doings at the house tonight."

Angel's Trumpet, 1912

Returning home had been more difficult than he had imagined. His father and mother had always been such vital people, and it came as a shock to him that they were old. They had cried when they saw Jennet, and his eyes pooled with tears as he explained she had been named after Jasset. But he had not been able to squelch his feelings of guilt, because he knew he must leave again.

His father had been waiting for him later that evening. There was something solid about Papa as he sat behind the large mahogany desk that Mama had insisted he must have. His tall board-shouldered father had been his hero and all he had ever wanted to do was to make him proud.

Perhaps all children worshiped their fathers, but as Reese enveloped him in a hug, Steban knew it was because Papa's love had always been unconditional.

"Your mama and I are glad to have you home from Panama. Your last letter said you were resigning your post there. Does it have to do with this Major O'Brien you wrote me about?"

"No Papa it was time, although I just don't understand men like O' Brien. He's Irish; there are places they would bar him as quick as me and yet he was the worst of the lot."

"That's because you are too young to remember the race riots in the Five Point area of New York. It's human nature, for some to demean others, when they are being demeaned. Negro men it seems have only each to put down. I am glad you are here. So much has happened; your Mama wrote you about Justin Overfield?"

"Yes and about Amelia, but not many details, you know how Mama is. And she did not tell me about William and Gentry. They had been precocious boys when I left, now they are young men."

"Gent is still precocious, that's the trouble, said Reese smiling, but we hope school will settle him down. WC it appears has developed a taste for farming. He and Lucas Mack have been a great help to me. As for Justin, you know he tried to challenge the original land gift to Rosa before the dirt was shoveled over Stuart. Thank God for Amelia, but with her gone, it will all start again and this time there will be no one to stop him."

"Why does Justin continue this senseless pursuit of land that does not belong to him?"

"It is one of the things I have wanted to talk to you about. I should have told you long ago, but we did not want to burden you. When your brother died and you were so angry; we just wanted you to have your chance. You wanted answers. I failed you then, but I thought that if you knew we might have lost you too. Your mother was already blaming mc for Jasset's death in every way but words. I lost her, but your Mama's sanity was at stake, I could not convince her Jassett's death was in an accident; we both knew better, so I let her use up her anger on me."

"It was a bad time Papa", said Steban, his eyes wet with tears.

"After decided not to come home from France, the years just seemed to pass. Amelia was alive, I thought I had time, but now time has run out. I must tell you about the codicil to Stuart Overfield's will. To put it simply, if the Gabriel family ceases to exist, all the land we own could revert back to the Overfield."

Steban was shocked; he could not believe what his father was saying. "Papa what are you saying; how could you keep something like this from me all these years?"

"Son forgive me, I was not trying to shut you out, but on your visits home there never seemed to be the right time. Jamison Overfield had added the codicil to his will to protect Rosa. You know the original gifted 250 acres he gave to your mother was tripled after Jasset purchased the swamp lands. I had not been overly concerned when Stuart added the codicil to his will. The land belonged to us. But after your brother's death, I began to see the danger. We all could have been killed that day. You see I trusted Stuart Overfield with my life, but I had no right to trust him with your future."

Steban laid a comforting hand on his father's shoulder, "It is Okay Papa I just need to know everything. What about Amelia, was the codicil included in her will also?"

Reese nodded his head sadly, "Yes son, it was prepared the same time as Stuart."

"I don't know what to say, I always thought Amelia a true friend."

"Amelia was family son, no matter how it might appear. We both made our decisions long ago."

For a time, they were silent each occupied with their thoughts. Steban spoke first. "Papa please understand that I cannot stay; I must leave again, just for a while. It is important that I find out what happened to Jennet's mother and why she was kept from me all these years."

"The child is precious to us son, I have not seen your mother so happy in a long time, but if Maria is dead, why must you go?"

"What happened to Maria has haunted me for too long. Once I find some answers, I will be home for good."

Reese knew Steban was conflicted, and if he asked, his son would stay. But he would not ask. It was Steban's decision. Reese said, "Son, tell me about Maria?"

Later when he was alone, Steban thought over his conversation with his father. After Jasset's death he had been so sad and confused. He had been unable to share his feelings with anyone until he had met Maria. He had always thought his parents had understood, but now he realized how hard it had been for them each time they watched him go.

He had one last trip to make; there were too many unanswered questions and the answers could only be found in France.

Chapter

Trigray Province, Ethiopia, 1912

The Ras of Trigray read the dispatches on his desk with a pleased nod. Adi Akbar's displeasure with his son had truly been a stroke of good fortune for him. Nevertheless, even Adi would have agreed Salim had a certain aptitude for intrigue.

Lord Adi Akbar had been ambitious man, who had nourished high hopes for his son. He had sent Salim away to be educated so that he would be conversant with the Europeans that continued to seek a stronghold in his country. Adi had groomed Salim to be the essence of the modern courtier. However, Salim's varied sexual appetites had proved too much an embarrassment to his father. Consequently, Adi decided to send Salim to Trigray and his cousin's princely court, taking advantage of the blood ties between their families.

Salim had proved invaluable. He was cultured and intelligent, but more, he possessed the hypnotic charm of a snake tamer. People trusted him with their confidences and secrets. Over the years, he had developed an espionage network that rivaled the Emperor's nest of spies. Salim's sexual interludes meant nothing to him. Whispered secrets from the wife of a highly placed official or a naïve young priest were all the same to him. It put him closer to obtaining the crown for himself.

The Ras was aware that Emperor's last illness was more serious than anyone outside of the royal family knew. If the Emperor had indeed suffered another stroke and the rumors that the grandson and pretender to the throne had embraced Islam could be proved the Ras felt certain he could gain of the support of the northern chieftains and the church hierarchy could be persuaded to favor his claim, given the right inducement. His musings were interrupted by a servant.

The servant bowed low, saying, "Highness, Salim Akbar requests an audience."

"Yes, sent him in at once."

The servant returned with Salim close on his heels. As was his custom, Salim was garbed for riding. His ripcord jodhpurs molded long muscular legs and thighs and his knee-high boots were made of the finest leather. The red silk shirt he wore clung to his lean yet powerful torso, his tall body as sleek and strong as a panther.

He carried himself proudly with the supreme knowledge that the blood of kings flowed through his veins. The disdainful curve of his full sensual lips betrayed his contempt for his princely cousin, which he masked with charming indifference.

Salim bowed, saying, "My Prince, I hope today finds you well."

The Ras smiled dryly, "Quite well", turning to the waiting servant, he said, Wine."

Salim grimaced and said, "My liege if I might beg your indulgence, a sifter of your fine cognac, if you please."

The Ras nodded to the servant, waving his hand in dismissal. The servant completed his task, bowing low as he exited backward until he reached the door.

Salim laughed and said, "Really cousin, you simply must join the 20th century."

"Leave my servants to me; what news do you bring from the capital."

"It is as I dispatched you my liege, the Emperor has had another stroke."

"And the other", the Ras said with a lowered voice, perversely aware that open ears could be found in his court as well as the Emperor's.

"Everything is going as planned, even as we speak Highness."

Salim arrived at his apartments sometime later, weary and in want of a bath. His royal cousin was becoming a princely bore, he thought, but he had grown accustomed to his comfortable lifestyle, one he would hate to lose. It had been a mistake to tell the Ras of the medallion, knowing his insatiable ambition. His princely cousin had become convinced if he possessed the Medallion of Sheba, the church officials would support his claim to the throne.

Salim had learned many things while in the capital; things his liege lord would recognize if not for his overwhelming sense of importance. The church hierarchy nor the nobles would never support him, no matter how many medallions he possessed. That of course had little to do with its monetary value and who knew better than Salim what the possessor the Medallion of Sheba was due, it was his heritage.

Salim had heard the story of the medallion all his life. He had been stunned when he recognized the medallion being worn around the neck of an American Negro. Steban Gabriel had no idea what he possessed. Salim had not been able to examined the medallion closely, but it had all the correct marking. Before he could formulate a plan to steal it, Steban had been called away from school. Unfortunately, Salim had been asked to leave the school a short time later, after his conduct with his professor's wife had been discovered; but he had never forgotten the medallion.

When he chanced to hear through his network of spies that Steban and the Frenchman, Franz D'Abbadie occasionally involved themselves in espionage for the French government, he decided he would have the medallion for himself.

Salim prided himself on the successful execution of his plans. They were always meticulously constructed and once put into action, flawlessly played out. A word here, a whisper there and it was done; although this time he admitted to having the advantage of knowing all the players.

He beckoned to Bela, his manservant since childhood, "A hot bath Bela and my pipe."

"It is done my lord."

Chapter

Paris, France, 1912

Francoise d'Abbadie was an aristocrat from the top of his head to his expensively shod foot; a

fact his demeanor often concealed. He was at that moment slouched in a chair one leg crossed

negligently over the other, as he waited for his friend to calm down.

A cheroot dangled from one hand and on a nearby table sat a shifter of brandy he which he

sipped between pauses to stroke his meticulously groomed mink colored mustache; that was self-

admittedly his only vanity. He continued to twirl it between his fingertips, as he pondered the

problem at hand.

Most considered him an elegant buffoon, more concerned about the cut of his suit than politics.

In truth he was a highly intelligent man and a gifted engineer, but for a time it suited him to play

the court jester.

Steban Gabriel had been his friend for many years, but even he was not sure what Steban's

reaction would be when he discovered the entire truth. Steban had a right to his anger, but there

were other important matters at stake, and he would need Steban's help as he had in the past.

"How could you do it Franz, how could you keep my daughter from me", Steban shouted.

"Mon ami, it was not my secret to tell. You were already in Panama. The child was young, her mother gravely ill. When she begged me not to tell you, what could I do?"

"But I loved her", he whispered, filled with all the grief and bitterness he thought he had put behind him.

"I am sorry Steban. When the child's mother died, I sent the child to you as her mother requested, did I not?"

"You are a cold sonofabitch Franz, what you were doing was hedging your bets, you were not sure I would come back to France and you knew that the child would bring me be back, if only to confront you."

"Ce le vie, Mon ami, I did what I thought best."

"Ce le vie my ass, you tell it to me straight right now Franz, or get the hell out of here."

"Alright dammit, I did what I did. You would have thrown everything away, trying to find her as you almost did once before. It suited my purposes and it was how Maria wanted it. I only hoped, sending you the child would bring you back to France."

"You call yourself my friend; always playing your little manipulative games, but there is more isn't there? You'll tell me now or I'm going to take a razor to that mop under your nose."

213

"You mean bastard, I believe you would", said Franz, stoking his mustache defensively. "But, whatever you may think, I am your friend. I thought you would be interested in the assignment in Ethiopia. You have always wanted to research the origins of the medallion you wear."

"Bullshit, you always said Salim's stories were just myths."

Franz shrugged his shoulders in typical Gallic fashion, and said "Alright, I needed someone I could trust to watch my back."

"Just as I thought, spying for the French government again. What's the rest of it Franz?"

"Spying is such a harsh word, mon ami. We have been requested through government channels to make inquiries concerning the railroad that is being built from Djibouti to the Ethiopian capital at Addis Ababa. Someone is inciting the workers to strike; miles of track, has been sabotaged and several workers killed."

"And what else?"

"As you know my cousin is an undersecretary in the diplomatic corps, and quite naturally recommended our firm to look into the problem. Djibouti is a major French seaport and trading center in that area and we have a vested interest in the building of the railroad, just as the British.

We are of course concerned with protecting French holdings and commerce, both of which could be seriously affected if armed conflict breaks out."

"The Head of Operations, overseeing the project believes that a rebel fraction from Ethiopia is involved and the British would not hesitate to bring in the militia, for any viable reason which could start a full-scale war. We are being asked to investigate and hopefully defuse the situation."

"Your cousin doesn't want much does he Franz? You could have explained this to me from the beginning; instead you choose to dangle my daughter and Ethiopia in front of me like carrots in front of a horse. Nobody uses me Franz, not even you. I owe you a lot, which is why I am going back home, instead of breaking your face."

"Wait, there is more, but Steban I beg of you please do not do anything rash."

"What is it you're not telling me; spit it out Franz."

"The head of operations is Maxwell Dennison."

Franz remembered his friend's last encounter with Dennison, and the look on Steban's face had been frightening, just as it was now.

Maria had never told Steban that she had known Dennison or that her parents had owned an inn in village outside of the family estate of Dennison's French grandfather. He did not know of their relationship or that she ran away after her parents' death to get away from him. Steban did not know, and Franz had seen no reason to tell him or break his word to Maria.

It had been by chance that Dennison had seen the two of them together and he had followed them back to Maria's rooms, forcing his way in after Steban had gone. When Maria had refused his advances, Dennison had become violent, brutally beating and raping her.

Steban had blamed himself, believing Dennison had acted out of some warped notion of revenge against him. After he had taken Maria to the nearby convent, where the nuns cared for her, Steban had gone looking for Dennison.

Steban would have killed him that night if Franz and two fellow friends had not stopped him. The police were called, but Dennison had claimed diplomatic immunity, and had left under his father's protection. Steban had vowed to kill him if he ever saw him again.

Steban had returned to the convent to find Marie gone. He had been like a wild man, trying to find her, but it had been useless; she had not wanted to be found.

Watching his friend now, Franz had decided he would just have to take his chances that Steban would not kill Dennison before the assignment was complete.

Red Sea, North Africa, 1912

Steban leaned against the ship's railing looking out at the amber colored sky as the sun began to set over the Red Sea. The waters were not particularly beautiful to look out upon, tending to be rather murky, but the sea was tranquil. He opened his watch to check the time, and gazed at Maria's smiling image, wondering, as he had so many times since this trip began why she had run away from him.

Maria's parents had originally been from New Orleans. Her father had been the son of a white plantation owner and her mother his octoroon mistress. They had fled the United States after secretly marrying and Maria had been raised in a quiet hamlet, in the French countryside. After her parents died she had moved to Paris. Steban realized now how very little he had known about the woman he had loved so passionately.

Maria had been gay and vivacious, with twinkling hazel eyes and when she was around he could not be sad. She had loved away the anger and grief bottled in his heart after Jasset's death.

His memories of those last days with her were as vivid as if they had happened yesterday. He had finished his last examinations of the term with honors, and they had decided to go on a picnic to celebrate. He would have married her without delay, but she refused, insisting that he must finish school.

His graduation had only been a year away and he had been determined to persuade Maria to marry him. She had looked so beautiful that day in a white dress, black curls blowing in the warm breeze, her face delicately tinted with color. "Marry me now Maria, before graduation", he had said.

"Oh cheri, I am sure your parents would want someone better for you."

"I love you Maria, who could be better for me, than you."

She had wept, nodding her consent, and they had made love in the grass. Slightly disheveled and thoroughly happy, they had been returning to her lodging, when he became aware that a man was staring at them strangely. Steban had only been mildly surprised when he recognized Maxwell Dennison. Dennison's mother was French after all, and his American born father was a member of the U.S. Diplomatic corps in Paris.

Dennison was no different from a lot of men he had grown up around. As a youth, Steban's French had not been idiomatic, but it was good enough to know he had traveled across the ocean just to be called a nigger.

A braggart and a bully, Dennison enjoyed picking on his weaker classmates, but Steban had refused to be his victim; choosing instead to laugh in his face. Dennison had been dumbfounded. He was too much of a coward to start a fight he was not certain he could win; nor quick witted enough to verbally spar with Steban. He had wisely decided to look for easier prey and Steban made some friends that day; one of whom had been Franz d'Abbadie.

Steban had recalled hearing Dennison had attended the Sorbonne, but they had never encountered each other until the day he had hurt Maria.

For weeks Steban had searched for her. It had been Franz who had finally persuaded him to return to school and upon his graduation he had been offered an apprenticeship in the d'Abbadie Engineering firm. In the ensuing years he had never seen Dennison.

And now he was on his way to Ethiopia. He did not know what this journey would reveal, but before it was over he would finally confront Dennison.

Provisional Governor's Mansion, Djibouti, North Africa, 1912

"The Suez Canal opened Africa to colonization, and the whole continent was quickly carved up by the European powers, except of course Ethiopia. The Italians have been most persistent in their attempts to take Ethiopia, using force and political chicanery, but after being successfully repulsed by Ethiopian forces at Adwa, the Emperor has managed to keep them at bay.

The Italians however, continued their encroaching ways in the lowlands Territories of Assad and Massawa; but as the Americans say, it is more than one way to skin the cat, eh, Monsieur Gabriel. Already the English and the Russians are encamped at the royal court; each offering their countries' technological advances in exchange for a political foothold."

"The Emperor Menelik is a traditionalist, but he is also a shrewd man. He has been perfectly willing to allow the British and French interests to finance the building of the railroad from

Djibouti to his new capital at Addis Ababa, but he commits to neither one. The building of the railroad would be one of the first steps toward modernizing his country; but his dealings with the Italians have made him wary of Europeans; and the Ethiopian nobles and members of the Church hierarchy have long memories.

From the Portuguese attempts to convert the population to Catholicism in the early 1500s causing civil unrest, to the British attempts to assert their will over Ethiopian politics and infringe on Ethiopian independence, which lead to the more recent suicide of Emperor Theodore; European interference has been problematic. That fact alone; lends strong support to Dennison's assertions that the blame for the troubles on the construction site is being instigated by Ethiopian insurgents, is not without foundation."

"Perhaps that is why Emperor Menelik cultivates the Russians, or so it is rumored", inserted Franz.

The Governor puffed out his fat cheeks, hating to be interrupted, he said, "Monsieur d'Abbadie, let me reiterate our position. Djibouti is a profitable French seaport and it is our intention that it remains so. Mr. Dennison is an American; his mother's family's influence garnered him the appointment as Construction Manager; but like many of his countrymen he lacks the necessary subtlety for this part of the world. If he continues to cry foul against the Ethiopians, the British who have a political, as well as monetary interest, in the building of the railroad, will dispatch troops. We do not see that as advantageous. You are here to see that it does not happen."

"Of course your Excellency", said Franz smiling, while he tugged on both sides of his mustache; a sure sign he was annoyed at the pompous Governor, thought Steban as he watched the exchange between the two.

The Governor said, "Now although we are not privy to all the working of the royal court, we do know that the Emperor has been ill. We believe also, there is an internal power struggle going on and quiet rumblings as to his successor. The Emperor is one of the last male links in direct agnatic descent in the Solomonic dynasty, and Menelik's grandson is considered the heir apparent, but who can say. There are rumors that the boy has a strong leaning toward Islam and the Coptic Christian church hierarchy would never sanction his rule. He also dislikes Europeans, and I am sure the British would welcome his being deposed."

The Governor's voice droned on as Steban listened, his mind sorting facts, fiction, and speculation into each respective groove. They had been cordially welcomed by the Governor of the province and he was certainly knowledgeable; but nothing Steban had heard so far was new or reassuring. He and Franz could very well find themselves up to their asses in political intrigue.

One unexpected complication had already arisen. When their ship docked to take on passengers and Missy Cadwell Overfield had come on board.

Justin Overfield had hoped for a brilliant match for his only son and had not been overjoyed with his son's choice. The Caldwells were modest farmers, but Jimmy Overfield and Missy Caldwell

221

had been inseparable since they were children; no one was surprised when the two married. His mother had written to him after Jimmy's death in Cuba; and six months after burying her husband, Missy had left her two boys in their great aunt Sarah's care and headed for Europe; where she had lived for the last two decades.

She and Franz traveled in many of the same circles and after observing her at several diplomatic parties and he had been convinced that she worked as a courier; gathering and selling information to the highest bidder. Franz did not have any proof, and her appearance in Djibouti could be just a coincidence; but he trusted Franz's instincts. Missy Overfield's presence was just an additional element of danger in an already volatile situation.

Steban shrugged off thoughts of Missy, once again focusing on the Governor's recital, when one of the most beautiful women Steban had ever seen walked into the room.

She leaned over the governor to kiss his cheek. "I am sorry to be late Papa, I was delayed at the school", she said.

The Governor said, "Gentlemen allow me to introduce my daughter, Leonie.

Mademoiselle Leonie Poussin was clearly accustomed to being admired. She graciously accepted Franz's gallant gesture as he saluted her hand and accorded Steban the same as he bowed simply from the waist.

She said, "I am delighted to meet you gentlemen; dinner will be served shortly, until then may I offer you another glass of sherry.

Franz was clearly smitten as she refilled his glass, but when the servant appeared in the doorway to announced dinner, Leonie placed her hand on Steban's arm. Franz reacted with a twirl of his mustache and the Governor clearly surprised, said nothing.

The silence was short lived however, as the Governor once more began his discourse on Euro/Ethiopian intrigue during dinner. Apparently the Governor had no secrets from his daughter, nor did they adhere to the after dinner custom of leaving the men to their brandy.

Leonie enjoyed a shifter of her father's fine brandy with her coffee, listening to her pompous sire rant quite candidly, his personal belief that the outlaws responsible for the attacks, were in the pay of the Russians.

After Leonie finally excused herself, Franz said, "We have heard other rumors since we arrived that that the hill tribes might be responsible."

"Preposterous", snorted the Governor. Those attacks required planning and precision, I hardly think the tribes equipped for such."

Typical Anglo arrogance, thought Steban, but he kept his thoughts to himself.

Franz said, "Nevertheless, do you think a meeting could be arranged with the leaders of the hill tribes? Perhaps with the right incentives we could at least gain some information."

The Governor was immediately offended by what he considered Franz's clavier attitude; particularly since he did not believe the hill tribes could possibly be involved. "Sir you are most casual in risking your life. You are an outsider; attempting to engage the hill tribes could be fatal."

"Forgive me sir; it was not my intention to trivialize the situation. As you can see I am woefully ignorant, is there someone who could acquaint me with tribal customs or act as a guide?"

Mollified, the Governor said, "Perhaps there is a young man that could help you. Kefle was raised and educated by the French monks, so his French as well as English is impeccable. He is also well versed in the different native dialects. As Senior Clerk at the Customs House he has been in charge of ordering and delivering supplies to the railroad campsite so he is knowledgeable concerning the recent troubles. Most consider him an engaging young man."

Franz said, "So the young man is well connected?"

The Governor made a moue of distaste, saying, "Too well connected in my opinion; however, society being what it is here, it is no surprise and as I said he is an urbane young man. Perhaps my hesitation is colored by a father's anxiety, but if you insist on trying to make contact with the hill tribes, I believe Kefle could be of help to you; however, I would advise you to be very careful in your dealing with him."

The Governor abruptly changed the subject, as his daughter reentered the dining room, "Your pardon my dear, have we been over long."

"No papa, I wondered however, if Monsieur Gabriel would care to take a turn about the terrace with me?"

Governor's Mansion, 1912

Braziers of incense perfumed the night air with the scent of jasmine; casting the circular terrace in a warm glow amid an evening so still you could hear the quiet stream of water flow into the courtyard fountain. They did not speak as they strolled slowly along the patterned walkway, pausing only to look out into the starlit sky and the lighted lattice housed square.

It was a night for lovers, but Steban sensed the beautiful woman at his side had something else on her mind. He was taken by surprise when soft arms encircled his neck pulling him close for her kiss. The kiss deepened, fully engaged until he forgot everything but the woman in his arms. It was Leonie who broke away first and he released her.

Smiling sweetly, Leonie said, "I can only imagine what you must think, but you are a very attractive man Monsieur Gabriel, and I was curious. I would add that I enjoyed it a great deal; although I am quite sure there is no surfeit of women in your life.

Steban considered the enchanting puzzle presented by Leonie Poussin. He found her quick-silver changes fascinating and he was undeniably stirred by her loveliness; yet Steban wondered what secrets lie behind that beautiful face and golden eyes, fanned by inky black lashes she used to effectively to shut out his questioning gaze.

Steban said, "As you say Mademoiselle, but even the owner of a rose garden would stop to admire a rare orchid."

"How charmingly put sir", she said with a rich throaty laugh; I supposed you think me very bold in my attentions toward you", she said softly.

Steban smiled, "You are a beautiful woman, anytime you feel the urge to explore or expand your curiosity, consider me at your service.

"Ah you think me beautiful; you should have seen my mother. She was breathtakingly lovely and so very proud. You know Monsieur Gabriel pride in a woman is of little value in this part of the world."

"Please call me Steban; a woman who knows her worth is rare, and a trait I find most attractive."

"I am glad Steban, but I desired to be alone with you for more than one reason. I have a message for you from a friend; his name is Kefle Araya.

Chapter

Djibouti, North Africa, 1912

Kefle Araya had been born on the Kebessa Plateau, a land of fertile soil and sloping grasslands. His father had been a great Highland Chieftain whose legacy could be traced back to the days of the ancients. For three hundred years his family had defended and held the traditional hereditary lands against all interlopers, the Egyptians, Sudanese, the Mogul Sultans, even the royal Ethiopian guard; bowing only to the occasional demand for tribute by the rulers of the Trigray province, when prodded by the Imperial authority of Ethiopia. The people of the Plateau considered themselves a free, separate people; bound to the Ethiopians only by ancient bloodlines and the slender thread of the Coptic Christian religion.

The Italians had long tried to establish a stronghold in Ethiopia. Even after their defeat at the hands of the Ethiopians at Adwa; the Italians had retained control of lowland seaports of Massawa and Assab, and began extending northward into the rich farmlands of the highland territories.

Many of the highland leaders had welcomed the Italians, seeing them as allies against the Ethiopians, who could be ruthless in their methods, and intolerant of the growing Islamic religion. However, Kefle's father had been one of the few who refused the Italian overtures of friendship. He believed the Italians had no place in their land and feared their influence was growing out of control. Soon they had begun passing laws giving them the right to confiscate tribal lands to give to migrating Italians colonists.

When Kefle's father had protested, refusing to obey Italian law, he and his family was murdered and the village burned to the ground. Kefle had been left for dead, covered in his parents' blood when the French monks had found him. The monks had nursed him back to health and he had remained with them.

He had affection for the monks that had cared for and educated him. Perhaps had things been different he might have joined the order, but a festering desire for revenge burned within him for his stolen birth-right.

To pursue that vengeance, he determined to learn the ways of his enemy; perfecting their languages and customs; for the time when he would have his retribution measure for measure. Not only against the Italians, but all foreigners, who came and took what did not belong to them. It was what his father would have expected.

Seated behind his desk in the Custom House, he removed his glasses and rubbed at the furrow between his brows, baffled over the note in front of him. His dress was European, as well as his manner. It was a role he created and immersed himself in; no one knew of his connection with the hill people, not even Leonie, yet as he read the note, he realized disturbingly, someone did indeed know.

He crushed the note in his hand. Someone had betrayed him, and when he found the breech, he would personally cut out his tongue.

Later that evening Kefle donned native dress and he made his way cautiously down the Street of Lanterns as the note had instructed. There were others similarly dressed abroad tonight, but no one noticed him; anxious that their own concerns not come to light.

As he entered one of the pleasure houses that lined the street, the crowd's attention was centered on a girl dancing on a raised dais and the movements of her hips. He stepped into one of the numbered alcoves used for assignations and pulled the curtain close, before turning to his host.

"Ah, my dear Kefle, so punctual, please be seated. May I offer you some refreshment", said a voice from the shadows, gesturing with an elegant hand toward a bottle of wine on the table?

Kefle said nothing, instead he helped himself to the proffered offer wine; taking the opportunity to study his host.

He sat back in shadows of the dimly lit room so that his features were not clear, but his spoken French was impeccable as if he was a native Frenchman. Just as Kefle, he had also chosen to dress in concealing robes, but Kefle was certain he was not white.

His host continued speaking in idiomatic French, "I assure you Kefle you do not know me, nor have we ever met."

Kefle sipped his wine saying, "And yet you appear to be acquainted with my affairs."

"Ah, but you see Kefle I make it my business to know many things, and in this instance knowledge of your affairs suit my purposes."

"Exactly what is it you want", said Kefle impatiently, his anger growing?"

"A man who prefers to get down to business; surely a European trait, be careful my dear Kefle that your adopted ways do not betray you in the end, but very well; I have need of you and your hill bandits."

"I have no knowledge of the", Kefle began, stopped by a lifted hand.

"Now you disappoint me. These games do you no justice. I repeat I have need of the services of your people, and in return I will conveniently forget who and what you are."

"And if I chose not to do as you request", replied Kefle through clinched teeth?

"I shall let it be known in certain quarters who you really are; to the Governor perhaps and his lovely daughter as well. For now, this meeting is at an end; you may go. You will receive instructions from me."

Kefle could barely contain his rage as he departed the pleasure house. He had been so sure no one had any idea of his identity; but this new enemy could put his entire operation at risk. Kefle had allegiance to none, except the hill tribesmen who carried out his orders and he would not be used as anyone's pawn.

Many dispossessed tribesmen had gone into the hills to become bandits after their lands had been stolen by the Italians and Kefle had secretly become one of them, eventually becoming their leader.

His work in the Customs House had been the perfect cover. He handled trade agreement and bills of commerce, translating contracts in three languages, giving him access to valuable knowledge.

However, the tribesmen's forays into the lowlands were for supplies and the occasional shipment of gold, never sabotage or murder of their own.

Kefle considered his would be blackmailer, the rogue had revealed more than he realized. He was educated, of this Kefle was certain, his French was completely idiomatic, much too good just to be pick up like most of the sewer rats of the Street of Lanterns. And the way he spoke, not just his words, but his mannerism led Kefle to believe he was not European, and if he was acquainted with the Governor he had to move in the highest circles.

Kefle would find him and then he would pay. He, Kefle Araya swore it by the blood of his fathers.

Chapter

Djibouti, North Africa, 1912

Maxwell Dennison checked his reflection as he stood before his dressing table. He deserved more than a position stuck in a foreign seaport, surrounded by inferiors. How he missed the gaiety of Paris, but his father had insisted. His mother's relatives still had influence in certain governmental quarters and had gotten him assigned as Construction Manager in this stink hole. Why would anyone want to build a railroad in the middle of nowhere? But he had finally stumbled on to some information that could make him a fortune. He heard a knock on the door. "Enter", he said.

"Greeting Effendi", said a thin stooped man, bowing affably to Dennison. The aroma of garlic, cheap wine and hair oil wafted across to Denison as the man removed his hat which he clutched with filthy fingers.

Eyeing the man with distaste, Dennison said, "What do have for me?"

The man scratched his chin; darken by at least a week's growth of beard, gesturing toward the girl huddled in the corner of the room. "What I have to say should be for your ears only, Effendi."

"Get out", Dennison shouted to the girl.

"Allah would have us avoid excess Effendi", he said slyly, noting the girl's bruises.

"I pay you for information, not advice."

He bobbed he head, "Of course Effendi, the item you seek has arrived.

Street of the Lanterns, Djibouti, 1912

Salim Akbar relaxed in the opulently appointed suite of rooms he maintained in Djibouti, absently stroking the smoothed skin body of the woman lying next to him. She thought his kisses were like drugged wine; which they were Salim acknowledged laughing to himself; just a little aphrodisiac herb to heighten the senses and loosen the tongue. Her father was indeed a foolish man. To trust a woman and to discuss business in front of one was absurd.

Leonie's father had no idea how she resented the fact he had not married her mother or that she involved herself in such political intrigues, breeding a band of rebels in the school where she was mistress. Too much education was never beneficial for a woman. Even Kefle, had allowed the girl too much access into his concerns, which would prove costly to him as well.

That fool Dennison had actually believed the attacks on the railroad were led by Ethiopian malcontents who opposed further intervention into their affair by the British; which was ridiculous and something only a European would believe. Ethiopian politics were most often settled by strength of arms and rebellions from within.

Of course Kefle had hoped that the foreigners would blame each other or the Ethiopian nobles, it had not mattered to him. If the British militia had been called in, civil war could have ensued, perhaps involving the French as well as the Italians in a territorial dispute. He had forced Kefle Araya to bring his hill bandits out in the open, covering Salim's hirelings' tracks. Kefle had daring, Salim had admired that, but his rationale had been flawed from the beginning; his plans contained too many unknown variables.

However, Salim's intricate strategies had no flaws; they simply unfolded like the petals of a rose: Who else would the French government have brought in to assist in a case of this nature, occurring in French territory, but a French engineer, well known in diplomatic quarters and certain governmental agencies for his discreet handling of political stratagem, hence Franz A'ddabie.

Who did Franz A'ddabie trust; only one man, Steban Gabriel. Steban of course would accompany Franz. Dennison was just an added bonus. Salim had known that if nothing else worked, Dennison would bring Steban Gabriel into his sphere.

Dennison thought he had discovered a get rich quick scheme. Salim had needed his diplomatic connections to smuggle the medallion through to his buyer, a man obsessed with religious antiquities and with the money to indulge his passion.

The euro-trash actually thought he would share in the profits. Once Dennison's usefulness was at an end there would be no reason for him to live. Salim would make certain his exit to the next life would be swift and all the blame would point to Salim's bastard brother, Omar Bey after certain evidence was discovered.

And as far as his dear noble cousin the Ras was concerned, the only information he would be given is that the medallion had been disposed of by Dennison. His cousin would have to find another way to obtain a crown that did not belong to him.

Appreciative of his own genius, Salim found himself becoming aroused and he took what Leonie gave so willingly once again.

Somewhere in Djibouti, North Africa 1912

Steban set up slowly, examining his rough prison by the light of a single oil lantern. Darkness would have almost been preferable. The airless cell was just a damp cubicle with no windows, and a straw covered dirt floor.

He had no idea of the time or whether it was day or night and his head pounded unmercifully as the narcotic used to drug him wore off. The temptation to indulge in a bout of self- pity passed quickly as he watched Franz tossed about on a thin pallet in a fever induced sleep.

.

The bullet in Franz's arm was lodged close to the bone and still seeping blood. Franz groaned in pain as Steban tightened a handkerchief around the wound. He had to get Franz out of here before it was too late.

The whole sorry situation began with the proposed meeting between Kefle and Steban. He and Franz had agreed it was a trap; but they needed a starting point. Franz's method of investigation was simple; start at the beginning, no matter how trivial and follow the bread crumbs.

They had heard a lot of rumors since arriving in Djibouti. The opinions varied as to who was behind the attacks involving the sabotage and murders, but all agreed the attacks could not possibly have been random. The Raiders seemed to know the precise time when the construction site and workers were most vulnerable. Somehow they were getting inside information and the most obvious person would be Kefle Araya. The strange part was no one believed he was capable of such an act and their attempts to learn more about Kefle had been a joke.

Leonie depicted Kefle as a hero, tragically deprived of his birthright; while the Governor considered him ambitious and dangerous. Others described him as hardworking and intelligent; witty and urbane; Brother Andre, who had been his mentor had actually described him as devout.

As Senior Clerk at the Customs House, Kefle handled every aspect of the railroad construction; he knew shipping dates and other valuable information that could have been used to plan the raids where gold and supplies had been stolen. There was no proof that he was involved, but there was more than enough circumstantial evidence tying him to the attacks.

They had plenty of questions and few answers. If Kefle was not involved, and he had information, why not report the information to the Governor. And why contact him and Franz? Going along with the meeting had seemed the best way to discover exactly who Kefle Araya was and what he knew.

The man was clever, Steban credited Kefle that much. They had arrogantly thought to entangle Kefle in his own web. But after the net had dropped; it had been he and Franz who had been caught like bare assed rookies.

Steban had entered a small café called the Red Camel to riotous tones of appreciation, as a nimble dancer moved about the room. He had thought the woman looked familiar, but he had no time to enjoy the spectacle. Franz had followed behind in native dress, hoping to be inconspicuous. Steban had started for the numbered alcove, but as he passed the first curtained doorway, he felt a sharp prick in his shoulder followed by a distinctive scent of gardenia as he lost consciousness.

Steban did not want to believe Leonie could be mixed up in something so deadly, but whether the governor's daughter had been a dupe or a willing participant, she had set up the meeting. It was Leonie who had told him that Kefle had information concerning the raids. She claimed Kefle had a source, who, could identify who was behind the sabotage of the railroad. She had not wanted her father to know she was involved and he had foolishly agreed. She claimed not to know anything else, just that she was asked to deliver Kefle's message.

Steban had a feeling they all were just marionettes and somewhere was in the background the master puppeteer was pulling the strings.

He heard steps coming along the stone corridor, and he readied himself for whatever would happen next. There was the grating of the turn-key in the ancient lock, and the door creaked open to reveal a robed figure.

"Salim Akbar", he whispered in disbelief.

Chapter

Government House, 1912

Missy Overfield wore a daring gown of blue silk that drew all eyes to her lush figure and trim ankles, as she entered the government house reception on the arm of Victor Cardio. She had accompanied him on this trip for strictly monetary reasons, despite appearances and not for the pleasure of sharing his bed. Certain parties were interested in how the Count Cardio had acquired his wealth and had offered Missy a great deal of money to find proof concerning the source of the slippery Count's finances.

Once they had arrived, she had been surprised that Victor had made little effort to conceal his business interests. It was later she discovered Victor's past companions had met with unfortunate accidents. Apparently the local authorities had not found it unusual that a poisonous snake had found its ways into one lady's boudoir and another, a champion rider had broken her neck after falling from her horse.

Plainly, Victor had no intention of allowing anyone to communicate his secrets to polite society. Missy did not plan to wait around while Victor tended his poppy fields disguised as a coffee plantation, and plotted her demise.

She and Victor had been greeted by the Governor and his daughter, who ushered them graciously into the main salon; where they were immediately sought out by Maxwell Dennison.

Dennison was well known to her and she had always been repelled by his oily charm. Instead of pestering her with his customary advances, he had requested a private moment with the Count. Curious, Missy had followed them to terrace, positioning herself behind one of the numerous statues in garden. She strained to hear their whispered conversation, watching Dennison smug gestures as Victor listened, smiling strangely.

Dennison was a braggart, the type of man who always thought he was irresistible to women. A little simper, a smile, her undivided attention, and he had been ready to say or do anything to impress her and she made sure he was suitably besotted. The more he drank the more Missy learned how a certain medallion was going to make him a very rich man.

Victor had left her to her on devises, annoyed at her flirtation with Dennison, but not before making sure his man remained at the reception, to escort her back to their hotel suite. Once the guard was gone, Missy had slipped from her room in search of the night porter, a helpful miscreant named Sulcan.

Sulcan had worked at the Hotel since he was a small boy and was accustomed to the oddities of the English and French. The American lady's unusual request was just more of the same to him. He assured her he knew of the Red Camel and would be happy to escort her there; the money he had pocketed and the promise of more to come, guaranteeing his silence.

The following evening, she excused herself after dinner, leaving the Count and his cronies to their pursuits; closing the drawing room doors behind her. She waited in the hallway, while

Sulcan had created a small disturbance to distract the guard, giving her time to leave quietly out of the front door.

She had quickly changed into the clothes Sulcan had provided and wearing a hooded cloak, she allowed Sulcan to lead her through the streets of the Red Lantern. Whatever was to take place would happen tonight at some café in the district call the Red Camel. Regretfully she had to leave her wardrobe behind, taking only her jewels and what could be stuffed into a small traveling bag.

What she had not expected was Steban Gabriel to enter the Red Camel; as she moved about the café in the hip hugging garment of a dancer she had donned. She had been expecting Dennison. At a prearranged signal another dancer took her place, but before she could get through the crowd to reach Steban, Sulcan had carried out her instructions.

Missy's feelings for Steban were complicated, just like her life. She could remember a time however when everything had seemed so simple.

It had been the summer she had turned fifteenth and she had seen the look of desire in Jimmy's blue eyes. How she had loved that sweet boy. But at fifteen she knew her power over a man, and it wasn't enough that she captured the attention of every male in two counties, she had longed to try that power of seduction on someone unattainable.

Steban Gabriel had come all the way from Paris for the Founders Harvest Celebration and his mother's birthday. She knew who he was, everyone knew the Gabriels. Her papa called them proper "nigras." He was no "red-necked farm boy, but handsome and sophisticated. Missy had deliberately tried to capture his gaze hoping for a similar display of desire in dark brown orbs, but Steban had turned and walked away.

What a foolish girl she had been. She could have gotten him killed that day. It was several years later when she met him again and the circumstances were less than auspicious.

She remembered it was after the "yellow jack", had took her family. She could feel Justin Overfield watching her, seen the lust in his eyes he hid from others. She had married her sweet boy, but Jimmy had put what he considered honor and duty before her and died, leaving her at mercy of his father. It wasn't long after Jimmy's death that Justin had made his intentions plain. There was no one to help. Miss Amelia was ill and Sarah could never stand up to her brother; so she had run away to Europe leaving her two boys behind. Missy had not known what lay ahead, but she knew what would happen if she stayed.

Justin deliberately kept her constantly short of funds, although Jimmy's trust had left her well provided for, but she had refused to come home, instead she found other ways to implement her income.

One particular evening, she had been losing heavily at the tables of an establishment owned by an American named Gregory Lord. Her friends had tried to warn her, Lord was no gentleman, but she had ignored their advice. The champagne and lobster supper he had promised sounded heavenly after her bad run with the cards. Once they returned to his carriage after dinner, however he suggested they return to his rooms.

Missy lived by her own dictates, but she was selective. When she declined Gregory's offer to share his bed, he determined to take what he wanted. She fought back screaming, but he was like a madman. He struck her a stunning blow and she fell back to the corner of the coach, unable to stop him as he ripped her bodice, groping at her breasts. Her reticule which had fallen open on the carriage floor and she felt around until her hand gripped her two shot derringer and she fired point blank at his chest. He had realized her intention and deflected her aim but not before she shot him in the shoulder. The coachman had stopped at the sound of the shot and somehow she managed to get out of the carriage, running along the cobbled stone street like a madwoman straight into the arms of Steban Gabriel.

Steban had been in London on business and scheduled to sail back to France on the following day. After finishing a delicious meal at a pub on the quay called the Jamaican, he started to walk back to the inn where he was staying; when a coach nearly ran him down. Suddenly there was a gun shot. The carriage door was flung open and a disheveled woman tumbled to the street. Steban had rushed forward to help, startled when he recognized Missy Overfield.

Missy had been shaken by the attack, but she was not a woman given to vapors or fear. It was an emotion she could ill afford given the life she had chosen since Jimmy's death. Fortunately, she suffered no more than a few bruises and the landlord's wife at the inn where Steban was staying had cleaned and repaired her gown.

She never thought to see Steban again. Away from the old constrains that had separated them, the years seemed to melt away. Steban dried her tears when she spoke about Jimmy and laughed with her over antidotes of her time in Europe. The attraction that had always been there blossomed, awakening a desire that flared hot and sweetly fierce. When she awoke the following morning a single rose lay on pillow, along with a bank draft for five hundred pounds wrapped in a short note, "From one loving friend to another", signed S.

That money had helped her recoup her fortunes. She owed him, but instincts honed over years dictated her next action. She barely had time to hide, before an older robed man advanced on Steban, directing a couple of others to drag him away. She could not follow without being seen, and Sulcan had not lingered after collecting his money.

From the shadows, Missy saw Franz fire his gun, trying to stop Steban from being loaded into a waiting wagon. One of the men carrying Steban fell backward, but in the returning gunfire, Franz was hit. Two more men had emerged from the café and dumped Franz in the waiting wagon next to Steban.

The wagon moved slowly enough for Missy to follow at a distance; moving stealthy through the dark streets. The wagon stopped in front of a house she later learned had once belonged to the Governor's former mistress and she waited while Steban and Franz were taken into the house. A short time later, a tall, elegantly dressed man, arrived by carriage and entered the house. Missy waited until finally they all came out of the house except Steban, Franz and two of the guards who remained posted at the door.

It was well after midnight and the rescue would have to be now or never, thought Missy. It would be dawn soon and she would allow nothing to interfere with her plans. She had already booked passage on a ship, leaving with the tide and she intended to be onboard when it sailed.

Djibouti, 1912

Steban continued to stare in disbelief at the elegantly dressed man who had once been his friend. "Salim Akbar", he whispered.

"My dear Steban; how delightful to see you again."

"I don't understand Salim, are you here to help us?"

"Hardly, my dear boy, I brought you here."

Steban's facial expression harden; "What is this about Salim?"

"Very well Steban, I had hoped to avoid unpleasantness, but I want the medallion now, or you will die a most painful death."

"The medallion", repeated Steban stupidly, "All this just so you could steal the medallion."

"No you were just one piece of the many facets of my plan; a key piece of course, but only one in my plan to take the medallion for myself."

"So it was you from the beginning? The sabotage and the murders; you managed it all? I must congratulate you; it took masterly skill to manipulate events to bring me half way around the world just so you could steal a trinket. But I must admit I am at a lost as to why you would go through so much trouble. Did you arrange for Dennison to be here too?"

Salim began to laugh and Steban thought he had never heard anything so cruel and hard. "Dennison was just a stroke of good fortune. Really Steban, you are as charmingly naïve as you were as a school boy. You had no idea what you possessed."

"So why don't you explain it to me Salim; explain to me why you would create an elaborate scenario to bring me across an ocean so that you could steal a medallion."

"I could tell you a lovely fable that happened over a thousand years ago, but it is really unimportant. Can you understand power Steban, what some people will do to obtain it? Of course not, how could you understand what you have never experienced, not reared in America; reared to be powerless."

"So it was all about gaining power?"

"Look around you Steban, I have power. It is about money. In my world one needs money to survive. Enough talk now, give me the medallion. I could never gain the secret of the clasp from you at school, but you will show me. And maybe I will let you and Franz live."

"I don't know what game are you playing, you have the medallion; your men took the medallion off me after they drugged me."

"Drugged you say, my men were ordered to subdue you, however their methods are unimportant." Salim turned to one of the guard and spoke to him in rapid Tigrinya.

"My men did not drug you nor remove anything from your person. They found you presumably drunk and you came along quite easily. Franz proved a bit more difficult and they were forced to deal with him harshly."

"Then I have no idea what happened to the medallion."

"Ridiculous! Think my friend, who would be interested in the medallion or know it's worth. I know all the players in this little drama. No one could have gotten close without my knowledge. I warn you do not trifle with me Steban. Your life and that of Franz depend on it"

"Perhaps Kefle has it; you are partners are you not? Maybe he has decided not to share. The whole thing makes sense now. There was never any real threat to the railroad or French holdings, except that perpetuated by you with Kefle's help. You engineered what could be tantamount to an international incident. My god, it is unbelievable; you must be mad."

"You haven't a clue. As for Kefle, I shall soon know what unscheduled part he played in my little play. I want that medallion. I beg you to be sensible Steban."

Beckoning to one of the men, Salim said, "Steban I would like you to make the acquaintance of Gustfa. Would you believe Gustfa was once a skilled surgeon, part of the royal court; until he developed a fascination for the opium pipe? If you do not answer my questions, tomorrow Gustfa will relieve you of a hand, the next day a foot, if you continue to be uncooperative, I think you get the picture."

"Salim what about Franz, he is not a part of this. If I knew what happened, I would tell you. I do not know where the medallion is. It means nothing to me just a piece of jewelry. Do you think I would trade Franz's life or risk my own for a piece of jewelry?"

Salim's face became darkly ominous as he spoke coldly, "You stupid American, you know nothing. Not who you are or where you come from." Regaining his composure, he spoke in Amharic and Gustfa took a bundle from his shirt and kneeled to attend Franz. "I would not want Franz's early demise to deprive him of watching you play the hero."

"Franz always knew there was something slimy about you Salim. I'm telling you for the last time, I do not know where the medallion is."

247

Salim shook his head sadly, "I wish I could believe you my friend, but no one could release the clasp unless they knew how and they could not know unless you told them. It was a family secret that you would not even share with me. I would suggest you ponder the matter carefully. Tomorrow Steban you will answer my questions, or you will be less one hand."

Somewhere in Djibouti, 1912

Steban paced restlessly across the small space. Hours had passed and he had no plan to escape or idea where the medallion might be.

"Well mon ami do you plan to wear a hole through the floor from which we might escape", Franz said as he watched his friend?

Franz did not look well. He was deathly pale except for the feverish glow across his cheeks. The wound in his arm was puckered and red, after Gustfa had removed the bullet, but Steban was relieved to see his friend alert.

"Something keeps nagging at me I just can't seem to grasp it. They just took us too damned easy Franz and Salim claims his men did not drug me. I have missed something I just can't think what it is."

"I am sorry I got you involved in this", said Franz hoarsely. Especially since it appears the whole thing was a clever ruse to get to you and apparently, the medallion you wear. It is really funny you know; I never believed a word of Salim's tall tales, now it seems the myth was true."

"So, it would seem but don't blame yourself; once I knew Dennison was here, nothing could have kept me away, a debt that now must be forgone once again. Besides by the looks of you, it is plain you didn't come easy, what happen to Salim's man."

Franz replied soberly, "Dead, then I was hit and woke up here."

Steban nodded, "Soon Salim and his butcher will be here, we need a plan."

"Will this help", said Franz frowning in pain as he tossed Steban a thin sliver knife. While Gustfa was doctoring, I rolled over on it."

Steban smiled grimly for the first time since they had been taken. Sooner than expected he saw the faint light from the glow of a lantern beneath the door. "They are coming Franz, are you ready?"

At Franz's nod, Steban positioned himself beside the door. He heard a rattle in the lock and the door was pushed open slowly. Steban pulled his jailer inside pressing the scalpel to his neck, only the neck was female, belonging to Missy Overfield. "Missy how in the hell did you get in here", grated Steban

"Now you want to ask me a lot fool questions or do you want to get the hell out of here."

Once Missy realized she was close to the docks, she had found a place to buy food and wine. From her belongings she pulled a vile filled with a golden liquid she had been saving for the Count. The guards had been hungry and thirsty and never thought twice; about accepting the food and drink she offered. It did not take long for the drug to take effect; only neither guard had a key. Her frustration had been short lived however, as the ancient lock luckily proved easy to pick and the look on Steban face had been absolutely priceless, when he realized who she was.

Once they were outside, they supported Franz between them to walk the short distance to the carriage she had hired. There had been no time for explanation. Missy bid them farewell from the docks as she boarded a clipper ship, traveling to Massawa; the captain being well paid to keep his mouth shut.

Though weak and feverish, Franz was the gallant to the end, kissing Missy's hand in gratitude. Steban added his thanks, but Missy silenced further questions. "Another place, another time my friend", then she was gone.

The governor had been shocked of course and they had decided to spare the poor man more questions about Leonie. The girl had been found in a drug induced coma.

The journey back to France had not been easy for Franz. He had been ill for several days after they made it back to their quarters, but the doctors had been hopeful of saving his arm. Before Steban left for the States, Franz had promised to send along any additional information he learned.

Steban had arrived in New York, to be greeted with the news of his father death. He had stayed drunk for two days, but nothing lessened his overwhelming guilt and grief. The medallion was lost; and too late he had realized its true purpose.

It was some time later Franz had forwarded some correspondence via the French Embassy in New York to the Maitland Bank, which David Maitland dispatched to Angel's Trumpet. Dennison's body had turn up in an alleyway off the Street of Lanterns; a presumed robbery. Kefle it was rumored he had been killed by one of the hill tribesmen.

There was no trace of Salim Akba. He had disappeared.

Part II

Chapter

New York, 1935

Jennet Gabriel Overfield waited impatiently for her step-mother. Willa had said she was going to visit old friends, but she had been gone a long time. Her father had not guessed her situation and Edmond had been noncommittal, but she had seen the shrewd evaluation in Willa's eyes and Jennet knew Willa had correctly surmised what was going on.

It was nothing she had done purposely; Jennet had simply let people think what they wanted to think. James had given up so much already and his tenure at the school was so close. She knew her father would not understand and she was desperate to talk to Willa before she said something to Steban.

Unaware of her step-daughter's anxiety, Willa Smith Gabriel walked slowly from Hoffman's Bakery through the streets of Harlem. She felt like a stranger in a town she had lived in for five years. Harlem was "uptown", teeming with Black folks from all walks of life. It was a long way from Hell's Kitchen and the Colored bowery she had once called home.

She found the sea of Negro faces, going about their business, an extraordinary sight. The women smartly dressed, plucked and powdered, and the men wearing suits instead of work clothes, you could not always tell those who had a servant, from those who worked as servants.

She had never expected to return to New York again. Looking back, there was nothing she missed, except perhaps Greda's strudel and of course, it was where she had met Steban. Her life had started that day. She needed no reminders of the violent memories in between.

You could see the boys from the Ivy League schools practicing their rowing as she found a bench where it was alright for her to sit and rest for a while. In truth, she was not in a hurry to return to her daughter-in-law's home. Willa did not blame Jennet nor judge her for her choices, but she knew Steban would not understand. Her husband had been sheltered most of his life and still processed a naivety and idealism that was surprising considering his worldly experiences. Steban would laugh if she told him that, but he had never known the desperation that could compromise your principals or cause you to do something wrong for someone you loved.

Jennet's first baby was due anytime, she needed her family. As much as Willa knew Steban needed her right now, she had not been able to bear the look of longing in the Jennet's eyes. She recalled the birth of her twins and how glad she had been, Win was there.

She pulled the letter from her pocket that had arrived from Steban that morning. Her husband wrote that Adel and Cassandra had left earlier that day for Atlanta and WC was out on the farms, so for a time he had the house to himself. He had received a letter from their twins and had enjoyed his first laugh, since coming to Angel's Trumpet. Sherry and Stephanie were attending school at Howard and much too busy for her to mother-hen. He ended by telling her how much he missed her, and appreciated her decision to stay in New York, to be with Jennet when she had the baby. You are a born mother-hen my girl, and I love you more than I can say.

It was what he did not say that worried Willa. She knew he was troubled about Angel's Trumpet. She had even offered to borrow money from Win; which he would not accept. He was too prideful by half, she thought sighing. It was one of the things she loved about him; she just hoped it did not cause him to destroy himself.

Willa wondered had Steban known Edmond was in New York. Jennet had been surprised to see him. She had no idea he would be in the city; and the two had always been close. Greta and Otto's bakery was nearby and she walked there almost every day, so she had missed Edmond's visit. He had left Jennet headed to Grand Central to catch the train to Atlanta in order to attend some society dance with his mother and sister. She had never understood Adel's pursuit of high society; but Negro people had their "haves" and "have-nots" just like everybody else.

For a while Willa watched the teams on the river rowing, but it was time she talked with Jennet. Willa was glad Steban had tried to mend his relationship with his daughter, but there were things he did not know. She and Steban did not keep secrets from each other, but Willa did not want to jeopardize his fragile rapport with Jennet. She felt in the middle and she really hated it. If Steban discovered what was going on it would put an end to everything.

She noticed a well- dressed young man coming toward her and as he came abreast of her, she felt a sharp prick and watched a drop of red blood stained her white gloves. "Mam, may I help you", she heard rather than saw, as the young man took her by the arm. It was the last thing she remembered, and the strudel she had gotten from Greta tumbled from her hands onto the street.

Chicago, 1908

Win watched Sister Elizabeth's retreating back with a sigh of relief. Today was laundry day, and they would never finish if the good Sister continued to interfere. The large black pots were set up in the back yard of the parish, one used to boil the clothes, the second to scrub and the third to rinse; then everything would be hung out on the line to dry. It was long tiring work, but Win didn't mind, it was a beautiful day and if she and Willa hurried there would be time for an outing after supper; it was a rare treat to see the street minstrels perform when they came to town.

Winifred and Willa Mae Smith had been raised in the Perpetual Saints Parish orphanage on the outskirts of Chicago. Their father had done odd jobs around the parish and after he and their mother had been killed in a tenement fire, the girls had been taken in. The Catholic nuns were kind and she and Willa had each other, which was more than those had who came to the back door of the parish looking for food and shelter.

They were taught to read and write, but the nuns were of the opinion that blacks should be taught a skill and to work with their hands, so they learned to sew and wash, cook and clean, polish and care for children. Every day there were unending tasks to be performed, from early morning to night. When Win was sixteen, she and Willa were hired out to a family in the city.

The Kilpatricks were one of the newly rich, a generation from the potato fields of Ireland. Brian Kilpatrick had struck silver in one of the early mining camps in Nevada and had returned to Chicago to marry the daughter of a prosper merchant. Mary Kilpatrick had been raised a strict catholic and a pious one. Any servant caught fraternizing in her household was discharged without references.

Jenny the cook had summed it all up with a "sheeit" said under her breath. "If Miz Killer kept as much watch over her own family as she do us, she would be a lot better off."

Win had dismissed Jenny's comments, but she knew what the word "fraternizing" meant. The nuns had never explained the mystery of a man and woman; only the ethics of hard work and industry were taught at the parish. There was no time or place for vanity, but she and Willa had seen enough in the surrounding tenement neighborhood, to know that lifting your skirt for a man could only lead to trouble.

Win's loose gowns could not hide the fact that she was growing into a woman, nor could she control the looks and leers she received from the males in the household, but they had already learned not to touch, discovering it could lead to painful consequences, as she put into practice Sister Mary Pauline's prudent advice concerning uses of the knee.

Time working for the Kilpatricks passed much as it had with the nuns. They were not ungenerous, and granted their servants half a day off every week. Willa saved what she could, but Win rejected Willa's frugality. For a nickel they could sit in the colored section and see a minstrel show. Then Mr. Tommy Kilpatrick came home.

Chicago, 1910

The baby, called Bridget, had been sick with a cold and fretful most of the day. The exhausted nanny had requested Win to sit with the child while she ate and slept for a few hours. Finally, the baby slept and Win laid the child in her crib, hoping she would not wake.

The child's nanny finally appeared, and Win made her way wearily down the back stairs to the room she shared with Willa, when she heard a loud noise outside of the back door. Cautiously she opened the door and Tommy Kilpatrick fell through the entrance. He was disheveled, his gold curls matted to his head with perspiration and reeking of gin and other equally unpleasant odors.

"Well, he said, looking up grinning, "I lost my key, you going help me." Begrudgingly, Win helped him to his feet. "Ah", he said, you're the pretty one."

"And you stink, replied Win, unable to stand his smell a minute longer.

"Ain't you the bold wench." Still reeling on his feet drunkenly, he bent down and stiffed his clothes, "I believe you're right, he said giggling, I shall go to my room posthaste and wash."

Win rolled her eyes upward toward a benevolent God and got him up to his rooms and his long-suffering valet.

The next morning, he sought her out while she was cleaning and pressed a five-dollar gold piece in her hand. "I want to thank you for what you did last night."

Tommy Kilpatrick was shaky and pale, but this morning he was every inch the son of the house, and Win responded accordingly with a bobbed curtsey. "You are welcome sir, thank you, sir."

"Oh, I trust I don't still offend", he said with a charming grin that was contiguous, which she shyly returned.

It was a rare night when Tommy Kilpatrick came home sober and Win had gotten in the habit of listening for him. Sometimes she would fix him a cup of black coffee or just fetch his valet to get him upstairs. He would tell her amusing stories, sharing things with her as if she was his equal.

He had been expelled from several colleges, until his parent sent him on a world tour, hoping he would settle down. But his parents had never understood him; they simply catered to his whims. His life was a series of peaks and valleys, going from thrill to thrill, and in between bouts of drinking and the opium pipe. What was new and shiny one day he considered old and used on the next.

Kilpatrick was entertained nightly by the cream of Chicago society. He and his friends prowled the late night supper clubs, drinking and carousing; but Kilpatrick had developed a taste for the exotic while traveling.

The beautiful Asians and African women came in all shades of color and the sparkling eyes and enchanting smile of the dusky skinned Win excited him. Her innocence naïveté and worshipful gaze was like a tonic to him, so different from the jaded beauties he met night after night. Through Win's eyes he relived his triumphs, everything new and fresh. He needed that, craved it and he only hoped she lasted longer than the others.

Win realized the other servants had begun to noticed how he continued to seek her out and it was only a matter of time before his mother found out. Willa had told her she was being selfish. They had decent employment in a comfortable household and she was jeopardizing everything.

Win told herself she was a woman and he was teaching her the ways of the world; but the collection of erotica he insisted she view, had embarrassed her. The nagging thoughts of the good sisters at the parish and their teachings, she tucked away to be examined some other day.

Willa observed her sister thoughtfully; to her it made no sense, but then Win could always find reasons to justify the things she wanted to do; but to allow Tommy Kilpatrick to accost her this way was not only stupid, it was dangerous.

At fifteen, Willa viewed the world with ancient eyes. Win might reject the talk among the older servants, but Willa did not. From the parish's back fence, she had seen too many things. The tenement where she had been born, was a cesspool of vices and to her Tommy Kilpatrick was just as bad as the crib owners and pimps luring young girls into a life of prostitution or the man who ran the opium den on Ric Tic Street.

"Win what is wrong with you, are you so stupid you cannot see what he is", Willa had exclaimed, when Win told her about the photographs.

"Willa you are just a child, Mr. Tommy has never laid as much as a finger on me, which is more than I can say about some the rest around here. He has been so many places and seen so many things."

Her younger sister shook her head, wondering how a person could be so smart and dumb at the same time. Win was a stubborn dreamer, but life was not a minstrel show or a nickelodeon film where the hero rode off into the sunset and he and the girl lived happily ever after.

Willa sighed, she understood her sister's thirst for bright lights and excitement, but a husband and a home of her own was all she wanted.

Win laughed at her practical little sister's taste for domestication, but Willa never took offense, this sneaking around with Mr. Tommy was bound to end badly and she would be there when her sister fell back to earth.

Chicago, 1911
A fall to earth was exactly what Win was contemplating as she looked down from ledge of a window and the lattice she was holding on to. She had ignored Willa's advice and agreed to meet Mr. Tommy outside of the house. Now it was too late to regret her foolishness.

She had slipped out of the house after the other servants had gone to bed, and he had been waiting for her around the corner from the house in a closed carriage. When he opened the door to help her in, he seemed so excited to see her, she was glad she had come. On the seat next to him was a large oblong box with fancy gilt ribbons, which he handed to her; "For me Mr. Tommy", she whispered.

"Of course it's for you, silly girl, who else would I buy it for?"

"It's the most beautiful thing I ever saw, she said, gently stroking the delicate gilt ribbons.

"My foolish little love, you haven't even open the box", Tommy said laughing.

Win opened the box and removed the tissue to reveal a gown of diaphanous silk which even to her inexperience eyes was more appropriate to the boudoir, than something a poor Colored girl could wear to church on Sunday.

"It is beautiful", she said shyly, suddenly feeling uneasy.

"I would like to see you in it now", Tommy said huskily, imagining the silky ivory fabric against her skin.
"Not here in the carriage" she said giggling nervously as she noticed the glassy, heated look in his eyes.

"Don't worry my pet I know a place." He tapped the top of the carriage, and soon they pull in front of a red brick mansion.

The house was brightly lit and she could hear music playing as Kilpatrick drew her toward the front door.

"I can't go in the front Mr. Tommy, you know that", she pleaded; wishing desperately that she had listened to her little sister.

"You don't have to worry about that poppet, the mistress of this house is a good friend of mine and you will be welcomed royally I assure you", he said laughing.

He had barely touched the knocker when the door open, and Win found herself standing in the middle of an elaborate foyer, with a wide staircase and thick red carpet. She assailed by the overpowering scent of patchouli perfume, as a tall blonde woman came through the arced doorway to greet them. She was corseted so tightly that her breasts looked like they would spill over her décolleté at any moment and the pink gown she wore left very little else to the imagination.

"Tommy honey where you been, we ain't seen you in ages", she said loudly.

"Hello Maggie my dear, I brought a friend with me", he said, pulling Win around in front of him.

Win curtsied, "Mam", she said.

"Ain't you a pretty piece", Maggie said, lifting Win's chin with her finger.

"Maggie, Win has a dress she would like to try on, do you think you could accommodate her."

"Why of course we can sugar, she said with a wink, your old room is always ready." Maggie motioned to a willowy brunette seated nearby. "Celeste honey you take Win upstairs to Mr. Kilpatrick's room, and make sure she has all the amenities."

Win followed Celeste up the stairs, wondering how she had gotten herself in such a predicament; as Maggie led Tommy back through the arched doorway laughing, his hand on her backside.

The room was garnished in shades of red, filled with nude statues in various poses, painted scenes of satyrs with arrows and hearts upon the ceiling and a mounted gilt mirror large enough to reflect the red brocade covered bed centered beneath it.

Celeste must have seen the horrified look on Win's face, for she could hear the girl giggling above the sounds of running water as Celeste prepared a bath, filling the room with the smell of lavender.

"Well here you go dearie, can I help you with your bath", said Celeste speculatively. She was interrupted by a knock at the door; and a servant handed Celeste the dress box from Tommy.

263

"What a lovely gown! Well you are at sly one, sure you don't need help", Celeste said smiling wickedly.

Win could only shake her head mutely, completely forlorn as Celeste left the room, locking the door behind her.

There had to be another way out, Win thought, searching the room. The small alcove where enclosing the bath was windowless and Win paused to look at the tub full of fragrant warm water longingly. Every morning she washed herself from the porcelain bowl in their room and when possible she and Willa would alternately take turns heating water and filling an old fashioned hip bath; but there was never a moment of self-indulgence, just to soak, or soap herself with a soft lavender bar, such as Celeste had laid beside the tub.

She knew what she was thinking was crazy, any time now Tommy would unlock that door, but the temptation to submerge herself in the warm, luxurious bath was too much for her. Win propped a chair under the door knob, shed her clothes; and eased into the satiny water. She was luxuriating in the bath when she noticed the brocade drapery move slightly on the opposite side of the room.

She leaped albeit regretfully from the tub and hurriedly dressed. The brocade drapery concealed other alcove with a window bigger enough for her to climb through but led nowhere, except a one story drop. To the right of the window, however was an ivy-covered lattice. It did not appear strong enough to hold her weight, but she grabbed for the lattice anyway, deciding she would rather take her chances, than submit to that Irish snot.

Billy Sinclair leaned against a tree at the back of the house, savoring the taste of his first cigarette in hours. He was grateful to escape the stifling room and its cloying odors. The evening was mild by Chicago standards, the air cool and crisp, but he longed for the warm sultry nights of New Orleans.

He had been raised by his grandma near the red-light district of the city. She worked at night as a chamber maid in one of the houses, sleeping most of the day, which left him free to roam the streets getting into trouble. Confrontation was unavoidable where he had grown up, but he admitted, he was rowdier than most. He could never walk away from a dare or swallow an insult; so it was no surprised when he landed in the county home for boys.

Thinking back, he guessed that had been the luckiest day of his life. At the Home he had been introduced to an old trumpet, someone had donated; and he and that horn was the start of a love affair. It was also at the Home that he had met Reef Miller, his nemesis and in some strange way the closer thing he had to a friend. Sinclair had figured from the start; it could only go one way. Friends would have been easier, but it did not matter, backing down had not been an option.

Reef had been a heavy, dirt brown boy with bad skin, a constant snarl on his face and gapping front teeth. Reef was accustomed to taking what he wanted and for some reason he had decided he wanted Sinclair's trumpet.

A harden bully, Reef had not been expecting a fight, but he discovered that even at only half his weight, Sinclair was quicker, and a brawler by nature. Exhausted and bloodied Reef had decided that it might be better to let Sinclair have the trumpet; especially since Sinclair had always been willing to share. The rivalry had come later, after Reef discovered Sinclair had a gift he would never possess.

After leaving the Home, Sinclair had taken a job in the ship yards to support him and his grandma, but his trumpet was never far from his side. Sinclair was a natural and the city New Orleans stopped to listen. Jazz had been born there in the "red light district", and the music community welcomed him like a hero. You could hear twenty trumpeters that played like Reef; but the few, with a true genius for the music were beloved and Sinclair was one of the best.

Reef was a showman. He and his band had become the darling of well- to-do Creole society (some say he bought a charm from the voodoo lady). Everything was the height of sophistication; from his straighten, waved hair to his taste for silk shirts and tailored suits. Yet despite his financial success and appearance, he craved the adulation Sinclair received as his due and his envy of Sinclair continued to grow. Jazz was coming of age in Chicago and soon Reef decided to try his luck there.

Sinclair was satisfied doing what he loved best. He had a large following in New Orleans, people who paid just to hear him play the trumpet. He had money in his pocket, the best room in the Empire Hotel, women when he wanted them and none when he didn't, but his temper was still his worst enemy, and why he was standing in the back yard of a whorehouse in Chicago.

Lael Elliot had been a cinnamon colored lovely, with a nice ass, who convinced him she could not live without him. What she did, was raise hell from morning to night, and when she wasn't bitchin, she was usually drunk. After a month, the thrill was gone and Sinclair wanted her out.

Sinclair had been unaware that she a husband in jail, or that he was released the day after he booted her out, but they had been waiting for him when he stepped out of the hotel. The two were beyond listening to reason; the husband waving a razor, and Lael sporting a black eye, in the background urging him on.

Sinclair had feigned to the left, and then brought his ridged hand down on the pimp's wrist so hard the bone snapped and the razor dropped from his nerveless fingers. Sinclair knew he would have killed him, had not Lael's screams finally penetrated his blood lust and Sinclair had dropped the fool into the dirt gasping for air. Somebody had called the police and with his record he could be facing another jail stretch. Staying in New Orleans was no longer an option, so he accepted Reef's invitation to come to Chicago.

Reef wanting him to come to Chicago, had amused Sinclair. Their relationship was tenuous at best. Outwardly, perhaps Reef had changed, but inside, Sinclair knew he was still the same snarling bully that took what he wanted. He was not deceived by Reef, no matter how much the man deceived himself. Whatever Reef's ulterior motive might be, now Sinclair, had no choice. He threw a few clothes in a suitcase, grabbed his bankroll and horn and he was soon on a train heading for the Windy City.

It did not take long to find out why Reef had wanted him. He needed original music; otherwise his band was just like a dozen others in Chicago. Sinclair knew it would not work. They just did not hear music the same way. Sinclair was a virtuoso, and he knew Reef had no intention of headlining Sinclair in his band.

Sinclair had no hard feelings, but he was sure Reef had put the word out on him. Gigs were getting harder to come by, which was why he was at Maggie's whorehouse tonight; not that it mattered, he was done with Chicago. He had flipped a coin, to decide his direction and as soon as he finished tonight's gig, he would be on the next train to New York.

He had noticed the girl from the bandstand when she came in Maggie's, looking like a bewildered fly caught in a spider's web, but it wasn't his business, he was just trying to get paid. He knew she was in trouble, but the little fool was about to kill herself. He watched her climb out of the narrow window, perched precariously on the ledge, hanging onto a flowered lattice that look as if it was going to break any minute. Sinclair did not have time to debate the question. He moved underneath the window thinking maybe he could catch her, but she was already falling. She landed on top of him heavily and they both hit the grass sprawling.

Win lay there, trying a draw a deep breath. She hurt all over, but nothing was broken and she was alive thanks to her would be rescuer. He had not removed and his eyes were closed. She had started to cry, afraid he might be dead, until one eye opened to peer at her.
"People generally use the front door when they want to leave honey, or in our case at least out the back", Sinclair whispered.

Win stared at him, unable to think of anything to say, strangely reassured by his soft and gravelly voice, and crooked smile. They both sat up as they heard sounds coming from around the house.

"Come on", he said lifting himself from the grass and pulling her along with him into the shadowed garden.

Win bite her lip to contain her whimpers of fear as two burly men circle the house and checked the broken lattice and began to search the grounds.   Sinclair looked down into her eyes, effervescent with teardrops, her soft mouth inviting his kiss.

Win thought she should stop him, but she decided she did not want to. His kiss was so unexpected and tender she did not want it to end. She forgot about the two men searching the streets for her, about Tommy and every lesson the nuns had taught her, as he held her close.

Chicago, Kilpatrick House, 1911

Willa had finished packing her and Win's few belongings, waiting for her sister to return. She figured Jenny the cook would waste no time carrying tales to Miz. Killer. She was mad in love with Thomas the butler, who lately had been paying Win too much attention.

Damn Tommy Kilpatrick to hell. Willa knew Mrs. Kilpatrick would not understand; even if Win could manage a reasonable explanation.   They would be fired, with no references or wages. Worrying about what had happened to Win, she sat down expecting the worst. What she did not expect was a glowing Win, waltzing in to tell her that they were on their way to New York.

Chapter

New York City, New York, 1921

Perhaps Riverside Drive did not have the prestige of a Park or Fifth Avenue address; and it was certain that not all the residents were on Mrs. Astor's list of 400; but they were rich. The avenues were wide and paved and there were servants whose sole duty was to keep horse droppings off the walk. Behind ornate gates were smooth carpets of green turf gracing mansions of grand proportions that sometime bespoke more money than taste.

The Maitland's stately abode of buff-colored stone boasted twenty-three rooms, all of which Willa knew inside and out. She entered the servant's entrance of the house clutching a letter from Win excitedly.

She was the only one of the servants that did not live in, which after her experience with the Kilpatricks, suited her just fine. She did not mind the long walk from the trolley stop; there would still be time to enjoy a cup of coffee and some of Greda's delicious cinnamon strudel and she would share her letter from Win.

She passed Otto, Greda's husband, picking up the dairy products which were delivered twice weekly. Otto was a taciturn man of German descent; he responded to her good morning with a small smile and a nod of his head. Greda and Otto Hoffman like the Maitlands were Jewish and had come to America with dreams to fulfill, but the Maitlands had arrived sixty years earlier, ample time to make their dreams come true.

Willa could smell the pastry as she came through the door and was greeted by a beaming Greda. She was short and dimpled, besides being very pregnant. After ten years of marriage, she and Otto were expecting their first child. "Good morning Greda, I have a letter from Win, said Willa happily.

"Da is good, lipchon, by first I must take a tray up the stairs."

"But why, with the family in Paris, Mr. David never rises till noon."

"Da is right, but Mr. David leave early this morning and his guest on the third floor, he ring for his coffee."

"In your condition, damn folks don't care about no one, but themselves. You fix the tray, and I'll take it up."

"But it is my work"

"Don't argue, the quicker you fix the tray, the quicker we can have a cozy and read Win's letter", Willa said smiling. Willa loved her sister, and she looked forward to her letters, so she kept her opinions about Billy Sinclair and Win's relationship to herself. All she knew was Win had left to meet one man and had come back with another and that had been five years ago.

After they had arrived in New York with no references and no place to stay; Willa had grave doubts about her sister's sanity. People did not fall in love overnight, and Sinclair was not the kind to inspire confidence; or least not her confidence. It was Willa's money that provided their lodging and bought Sinclair a coat.

However, Sinclair had proved her wrong. He was a gifted musician, and although no one knew him in New York, it was not long before he was "discovered." Five years had passed since then, which was about how long she had worked for the Maitlands.

Willa made it to the third floor landing and proceeded down the hall, wondering why Mr. David had installed his guest on the third floor. His parents and sisters were gone to Paris with half the servants traveling with them, and the rest were on a month's sabbatical along with Mrs. Perkins the housekeeper. Otto and Greda had been left as caretakers with Willa to help with the cleaning.

She knocked on the door, and then pushed it open without waiting for an answer. Willa could only stare; at least she understood now why Mr. David had put him on the third floor.

His lean, butterscotch, body was bared to the waist and her eyes followed the thin hairline that lightly fanned his chest to below the pants that fit loosely about his hips, his suspenders dangling on either side of his legs. She became fascinated with his bare feet which were long and firmly planted as he shaved himself before the mirror.

He paused in his shaving, appraising with nonchalant eyes and ordered her to put the coffee on a nearby table.

Willa had never felt so lacking in her life. She dropped the serving tray on the table and fled. Had she looked back she would have seen deep brown eyes alight with appreciation as her petite, rounded form hurried through the doorway.

Steban shook his head and smiled to himself. He had been too long without female company; little housemaids were definitely not in his line. Certainly since returning home from Europe, there had been little time to indulge in carnal pleasures; but that had not brought him to New York. They needed money and Reese had trusted Jacob Maitland, but it would not come cheaply.

Since he had returned home, he had done everything he could to keep the farm and mill going; while Justin had used his influence to destroy them financially. Of course, the first World War had curtailed some of his efforts and more recently the prohibition laws had left Justin scrabbling for cash rendering him less of a financial thorn in the side of the Gabriels. But their credit had dried up overnight. Cash was being demanded for everything and there was less and less to pour back into the farms and mill.

The Gabriel holdings were of long standing and had been profitable in the past, but Maitland Board of Directors had voted to deny the loan unless the farm as well as the mill be used as collateral. Steban had been disappointed; David Maitland was a friend and he had hoped for better terms. David claimed his hands were tied, and that the terms of the loan were specified by his father. Of course, Steban knew better, friendship or no, to David, business was business and he was holding all the cards.

In the past, whenever Steban had been in town he and David would spend an evening together. They shared a love of good food and congenial company, as well as similar taste in women; from ivory skinned to mahogany, tall sophisticated beauties, who knew the rules of the game. Which is why he had invited Steban to stay at his home while in New York. Of course, he doubted David would mention it to his father. Steban was not sure Jacob Maitland's liberalities extended that far.

Steban was due at the banking offices soon and David had instructed his manservant to bring him into town.

The founder of Maitlands, Gideon Maitland, had been born in the Jewish ghettoes of Russia. His father had struggled to provide for his family and educate his son, finally moving the family to Austria, hoping to escape the increasing oppression of the Jewish community in Russia. Gideon graduated from school and was able to gain employment as a clerk in the Rothschild banking center, later migrating to America in 1850.

By the end of the Civil War, Gideon had amassed an impressive fortune. Many had scoffed at his banking practices. The color of a man's skin or occupation never matter to Gideon; only the green of his money. It was a policy that continued to hold them in good stead, from the beginning to the present. Gideon had died comfortably at a ripe old age leaving his son and grandson to reap the benefits of his wisdom.

Steban had exited the impressive gray stone building that housed the Maitland Bank, feeling more lighthearted than he had in many months. Any misgivings concerning the terms of the loan, he shoved aside.

It was a beautiful day so he had decided to walk, and have lunch at a small cafe David had introduced him to on his last visit.

The café was just as he remembered it and the lunch delicious. He left the café continuing his walk, his mind filled with plans for Angel's Trumpet. His outlook was clearer and he felt hopeful they could turn things around.

After spending so many years in Europe, he had become accustomed to going his way; for a Black man however, in the United States, even in the North there were barriers lines in certain parts of the city, places where it be could dangerous if you forgot the rules.

He had been walking for a while, when he became aware of curious looks in his direction and more than a few hostile ones. He quickly concluded that it would be prudent to change directions and if possible maybe hire a carriage to take him back to the Maitland estate, when he was bumped into by a young white woman.

He knew immediately she had lifted his wallet and grabbed the girl's arm to retrieve his belongings when she started to scream bloody murder.

He was soon surrounded by several white men intent on pounding him into the side walk, when he heard the Irish brogue of a street cop, followed by Otto's German accents. The girl was given a swat on the rump and admonished to mine her manners and his wallet returned, empty of money of course. He was lifted on the wagon Otto was driving and the last thing he remembered before passing out was the concern that lighted a pair soft brown eyes.

The doctor had pronounced him lucky, if bruised ribs, a concussion and numerous cuts and abrasions could be called such. The attack had been so unexpected, sobering thoughts of his own mortality, had triggered a heighten sense of appreciation for life that had lain dormant since his father's death. Or maybe, he thought, amused at his own reasoning, it had more to do with his heighten appreciation of Miss Willa Mae Smith.

He had ceased to blame his celibacy on his attraction to Willa. The previous night the chance to appease his sexual appetite had felt curiously flat. Instead his thoughts were consumed with images of the curvaceous, petite girl, for surely she could not be more than that. She reminded him of a statue of craved ebony, he had once seen while traveling through northern Africa, representing some fertility goddess; a shapely silhouette with generous bosom and rounded hips.

For three weeks she had tortured him with her presence. She had the face of a Madonna, with soft sable eyes. He like the way her nostrils flared when she was angry and the pleasing fullness of her mouth. Her sweet scent was more provocative than Parisian perfume. He would be leaving tomorrow and he could not even get her to talk to him, something he had not encountered before. He rang for his coffee and he waited for her to appear.

Below stairs Greda was enjoying a laugh at Willa expense as she prepared the tray to be taken to Mr. Gabriel, while Willa seethed over her untouched pastry and cooling coffee.

"I don't know what to do Greda; I think he's rattled something loose in his head. A month ago he looked at me like I was the last woman in the world he would find attractive, he gets hit on head and now every time I come near him, he's breathing me in like air and smiling at me like a tomcat and I'm a bowl of cream. I am no man's convenience and Mr. Steban Gabriel will soon know better if he thinks otherwise."

Greda started to speak, but she raised her apron to her face to hide her giggles.

"Oh give me the tray Greda", still hearing the echo of her friend laughter as she made her way to the third floor.

So what if he was unbelievably handsome and she had to fight the urge to respond to his charming ways? She admitted she was tempted more and more each day, but she knew it would not do.

She remembered as a small child being given a tin of candy. The tin was so pretty, with brightly colored with ribbons and the bonbons had tasted so wonderful. She had eaten the whole tin despite the Sister's warning that she should eat only a piece or two. That tin of candy had given her a terrible stomach ache and when she looked at Steban, and listened to his sweet talk, it was just a belly ache waiting to happen.

Briefly, she wondered what Win would have done, before deciding that perhaps it was just as well she did not know. She was not a child, she was twenty-one years old and it was time she put an end to the madness.

He was sitting up in bed wearing a black silk robe and a wicked grin. "So you're finally here, I have been waiting for my coffee; you remember how I like it don't you, black with just a touch of cream."

Every word was like a caress and Willa turned with a sigh. "Yes Mr. Gabriel, I know how you like your coffee and few other particulars. The way you look, I guess women are always falling all over you, ready to cater to your every need."

"Is that what you believe", he said? The intensity of his dark gaze sent a warm frisson through her body she refused to acknowledge.

"Yes that is exactly what I believe and I will not lie and say I am not attracted to you; I think you know that, but listen to me, it is not going to happen. The things I want you cannot give me.

We are too different, our backgrounds and our morals. I want to be a wife, not a mistress. I want to give my husband's babies, not have a parcel of bastards. You see I want the promise and the only thing I have of true value to gift the man I am looking for, is me. It will not be squander on a weekend romp with a man who will not remember me a month from now."

Steban was fascinated by the play of gold earrings, against her smooth cheek, and unable to stop smiling, despite Willa's stormy expression. "Well I guess you made that plain enough. I am leaving tomorrow Miss Willa Smith, won't you grant my last request, and let me kiss you goodbye."

Lest she start screaming in lunacy, Willa whirled and fled the room, hearing more laughter echoing behind her.

The Sabbath was Saturday for the Hoffmans and while the family was away, Willa was off on Sundays, so at the end of the day on Fridays, Greda would pack a load of food for her to take home. Otto would give her a ride into town, where she would ride the trolley the short distance home.

The Elliot Boarding house had been her home since coming to New York, but now she lived alone, while Win and Sinclair went off on tour. It had been Mrs. Elliot who had kindly recommended Willa to her sister Mrs. Perkins, who was the Maitland's housekeeper.

The street was crowded with people; mostly men milling about the tenement stoops. She was

not afraid, but you could feel the tension in the air. People were jumpy; everywhere you looked

you could see the anger and despair on their faces; it would not take much to ignite an emotional

powder keg just waiting to blow.

Too many Negro men had returned home from war to find nothing had changed. There were no

jobs, no prospects and now their very lives threaten by equally poor whites trying to hold on to

what they considered their due. Last week a Negro solider had been murdered. She had thought

about moving, but in the city, housing was limited for Negro people.

Willa was glad when she finally reached her boarding house. All she wanted was a bath, and

with any luck she might be able to get a head start on the two families who also shared the

bathroom. She gathered her towels and soap, an old dress from the closet and the wooden bat

Sinclair had left for her protection.

She cleaned the claw footed tub with lye soap, and soon she felt the warmth creep through her

tired body as she lay back in the hot tub of water. She had been feeling blue all day; and

although she refused to acknowledge the source, she could not stop thoughts of Steban Gabriel

from evading her mind.

She had cleaned his room today and changed the bed linen; remembering the faint smell of

sandalwood. She knew she had done the right thing, but she longed for the comfort of the one man that would be hers. She wanted to experience what she knew Win had with Sinclair and the faceless man of her dreams had become Steban Gabriel.

She took time to wash her hair, braiding it in a single plait, then pulled on her old dress and started back to her room. She clutched her bat tightly as she walked down the shadowed hallway thinking she saw someone lurking in the darkness. She breathed a sigh of relief, as Simon, Mrs. Elliot's son came into view.

Simon handed Willa a note, saying, "He gave me a dollar and I was supposed to give you this note, but I guess he can tell you what it says himself."

"Thank you Simon; that was well done."

That voice had haunted Willa's dreams, she could hardly believe he was here, as Steban Gabriel stepped from the shadows.

"What are you doing here", Willa said, furious that her heart had started to beat faster.

"Are you going to ask me in, are do we stand out in the hallway for your neighbors to see."

"I want to know how you found me."

"Before I left, your friend pressed a sheet of paper in my hand with your direction. She seems to think you need rescuing." His pearly white smile assured her he was more than willing to take on the task.

She would deal with her meddlesome friend Greta later, but looking at him, her resolve waivered. Willa grudgingly opened her door and let him in.

"Do you know what, you are really a piece of work; that beating you took should have taught you how dangerous parts of the city can be", she said angrily, in part because she could not control the gladness she felt at seeing him again.

"Anybody ever tell you, you are one serious young lady. What's outside does not concern me, only what's here and now between you and me; I came for my goodbye kiss."

She just stared at him; the last of her resolve drifting away leaving her defenseless against the longing in his voice she knew matched her own. She had no label for what she was feeling, but whether it was love or lust, but she could not resist him as he pulled her close, his mouth covering hers; exploring and seeking, as he gently cradled her face.

"Look at me Willa", he said huskily. Willa raised her eyes slowly, afraid of what she might see, but she had worried needlessly. Everything she had ever wanted was there in his eyes. She touched his face wondrously, and whispered, "I love you too."

He backed into a chair; still holding her in his arms, her skirt drifting over his thighs. She moaned his name as he gently caressed the taunt peaks of her breasts outlined against her damp dress, followed by the warmth of his mouth through the thin material.

She trailed kisses along his strong jaw, and neck, ripping his shirt in her impatience to touch him, spreading her hands across his sun-kissed muscled torso, reveling in his quick intake of breath; feeling empowered that she could excite him as he excited her.

He buried his face in the soft contours of her neck and she could feel his hardness pressing against the bare skin of her leg, as he pulled her forward until they were face to face, his hand stroking along the curve her hip, seeking her warmth. Suddenly there was the crash of glass and the whoosh of a blaze as a lighted kerosene bottle burst into flames in the middle of the room.

Willa heard Steban speaking, but he his voice sounded far away. He shook her roughly and she screamed, terrified. "It's alright Willa, it's alright, I got you, but we have to move", she heard him say.

Steban gripped Willa's hand and they began to crawl through the glass and smoke toward the hallway. Where there had been a window was now a wall of flames. Steban fingers brush the bat on the floor and he used it to sweep aside some of the debris as they moved through the doorway into the hall.

Willa could hear shouts and screams, combined with the sounds of running feet, and thought they would be trampled, but they kept moving to the rear of the boarding house.

There was a window in the back of the boarding house, but the house's foundation was built on stone, and window was up high, but they had no choice as the smoke and flame threaten to overcome them. Using the bat to clear out the windowpane, they jumped, falling eight feet tumbling into a ditch. For a time, they just lay there, cut up and bruised, afraid to move. Steban remembered his horror as they saw a black man hanging from a lamp post on the corner.

In the street an angry mob of white men brandishing guns and sticks were met by an enraged black community; and then there was chaos. A sea of people surging forward as Steban pushed through swing the bat indiscriminately, dragging Willa along in his wake. Steban lost track of the blocks they travel until at last the crowd thinned and they reached Germantown and there was Otto Hoffman waiting.

Steban felt tears running down his face. He felt grateful to be alive, but also ashamed; this fight was every Negro man's fight, his excuses for staying away now did not mean much. This however was just the beginning. The racial tension between blacks and whites had finally exploded that night. The militia had to be brought in to calm the unrest, but it would happen again and again until this country did right by its people.

He and Willa had been married two days later and she had left the past behind her, but he could not. No matter how hurtful memories of the past might be, the pain of the present had to be dealt with now, and it was time to do what had to be done.

Steban smoothed his hand over his father desk lovingly. The desk had been a gift from his Rosa. It had been one of his mother's few excesses. She had taken such pleasure seeing Reese at that desk. It was large and solid like his father. Now Steban set in the burgundy leather chair feeling as helpless as he ever had in his life.

He had all the right intentions, but he had failed just the same and now time had run out. There were arrangements to be made documents he would need. He could not bear the thought of strangers touching his parents' things.

The desk was filled with papers that mapped the pain and joy of living: accomplishments, deeds, birth certificates, old tin-type photographs of him and Jasset, one of WC and Gent as children and Jasset and his wife on their wedding day.

He finished looking though the upper desk drawer, but when he tried to close it the drawer would not completely shut and he remember the hidden compartment attached to the drawer. Steban smiled for the first since he entered the room. How his father had laughed about the secret compartment being useless, with Sally Mack around. "The woman could ferret out secrets at the White House", Reese had joked. Miss Sally and Lucas were gone now, just like Mama and Papa, what would they think about what he was doing today, Steban thought soberly.

Steban thought perhaps some papers were lodged in back of the drawer, and he reached his hand underneath to pry them loose; instead, he triggered a hidden mechanism and a small compartment spring into view.   It was locked.

He had kept the original keys to everything in the house since his mother had given them into his possession, only duplicating the ones necessary for WC's use. Now he looked at the loop of keys lying on the desk more closely, his eyes lighting on a small brass key, and suddenly he just knew.

Steban tried to stem his rising excitement, as the key slipped smoothly into the groove and the top of the compartment drawer flipped up to reveal a folded letter and another large head key. He sat staring at the letter he recognized was written in his mother's hand; hefting the large key in his palm. His hand trembled slightly as he unfolded the letter; reading slowly:

My Dear Son,

Maybe I should have explained, but I figured that you would get around to cleaning out your father desk and if you are, I know something has befallen Angel's Trumpet. You must know your papa and me loved you more than anything on this earth.   You were the joy of our lives.

In my own selfish grief, I did not offer you the assurances you needed. I know you blamed yourself about Reese and I ask that you forgive me son, the blame was always mine.

Now Steban inside this letter are some instructions that go with the key. The black velvet pouch has something pretty for your wife.

Steban please try to get on with your nephew, WC is a good man, just wrong-headed sometimes, like his grandma, which is why the key is left to you. How your papa would have laughed at me. Be happy my darling son.

Your mother, Rosa Gabriel

He wiped unbidden tears from his face and got up; there was no time to enact maudlin tragedies. He went through the house to the kitchen. It seemed like he could still smell peach preserves cooking and could hear Miss Sally joking with his mother. In those days, they would fix the noon meal for all the workers and everyone would eat together. It was a better time, those days.

Steban stepped outside to the root cellar. The cellars were mostly used now days as storage bin for WC's arsenal. He bypassed the weapons and continued into the second compartment, startled by the chilliness.

His mother had missed her calling; Franz could have used her in the old days, Steban thought. He found the loosen brick she described and removed a second key both of which it took to open the safe in the floor of the cellar. Inside was a draw-string pouch, an envelope yellowed with age and a metal box.

He was speechless as he opened the black velvet draw-string pouch his mother described; and a strand of matched pearls spilled into his hand. Next he realized the envelope addressed to him. He could hardly believe his eyes; for inside was a medallion in the shape of a lion's head made of solid gold, with jeweled eyes of emeralds and enclosed was a short note, "From one loving friend, to another", signed MCO.

He had not seen Missy Overfield since she had saved him and Franz in Ethiopia. Steban guessed he had always known it was Missy who took the medallion, she was the only one he had ever shown how it opened. He was not sure which shocked him more; that Missy had returned the medallion or his mother having had the medallion all those years and never saying a word. He thought he had understood what his mother had been feeling; but he had never comprehended the depth of her anger and despair. Steban was shaken to his core.

Steban did not know how long he sat there in silence, consumed by sadness, the last item, a metal container lying on the floor. He reread his mother letter, seeking solace for his troubled spirit. He longed for Willa's comforting presence, knowing she would understand.

He opened the metal box with trembling hands; almost afraid of what he would find. When he saw the contents he wept bitter tears until he was spent. Steban got up slowly and left the chilly confines of the cellar, pausing to splash water on his face from the kitchen sink. He had to pull himself together, there was too much to be done. He could not go the WC, which left only Edmond.

Chapter

New York, 1935

Edmond Gabriel sat back against the worn cushion trying to adjust his long legs to the limited space between the seats in the "Colored" section of the southbound train. He was eager to get under way as he watched people hurrying along the boarding area. He had been away too long and he was anxious to get back to Hollis. Uncle Steban had promised to make sure that she got to Atlanta, and arrive safely at Aunt Win.

He had planned the night of the Gold and White Ball to ask Hollis to marry him. She could accompany him to the mission and they would honeymoon in Africa. Perhaps he should have told her he had accepted an assignment to be part of the missionary team, but he wanted their time together to be perfect not crammed with a lot of life changing decisions. Hollis deserved some fun, to be wooed in the proper setting away from the prying eyes of her interfering mother. When the time was right would tell her everything and she would be just as excited as him. If he had any lingering doubts, he decided to ignore them.

Of course his parents had been disappointed to hear he was planning to go to Africa, at least his mother had been disappointed; WC had just been angry. It was an honor, the dream of a lifetime; although he doubted his father would recognize it as such. Edmond believed in time WC would become reconciled to his going to Africa, but after he discovered Edmond had left Angel's Trumpet with no explanations; to involve himself in some plan of Uncle Steban, all bets were off.

They had not been expecting Uncle Steban at Angel's Trumpet, they were all to meet in Atlanta. The older man had looked tired and WC had immediately demanded to know what had happened at the bank in New York. Soon the two were involved in a heated argument. It was nothing new, the family had all heard it before. Steban was an unrealistic old fool, whose outdated ideals were responsible for their money woes. WC was devious and unpredictable with schemes that could endanger the entire family.

The next day he was surprised to find Steban waiting for him in his room. It had been three years since Edmond had seen Steban and he did not look well. Now his eyes were bright with excitement, his hands shaky as he handed Edmond a package. The urgency in Steban's voice was unsettling as the older man proceeded to ask Edmond a strange favor.

Edmond agreed to travel to New York and deliver the package to David Maitland at the Maitland Bank. Edmond was not to know what was in the package or what it concerned, nor tell WC his reason for leaving; or where he was going. He was to get a receipt of delivery and afterwards meet the family in Atlanta for the Ball just as planned. Steban had never asked anything of Edmond and he found he could not say no; but Steban had put him in an untenable position.

Keeping secrets from WC would only add fuel to the growing conflict between Edmond and his father. WC's disapproval of his choices was nothing new; and the present situation was just one more in a long list of criticisms of how Edmond lived his life. Trying to please his father had been a fruitless, full time job and Edmond had finally quit trying.

The main problem was that Edmond just did not share WC's passion for the land nor would he take sides against his Uncle Steban. His father believed he had more right to Angel Trumpet than Steban and he still resented the fact that great-grandmother Rosa had left everything to Steban. Uncle Steban had never made a point of it, he considered Angel's Trumpet the family home, and he had given but his father control of the farms but it was not enough.

It had been late when he arrived in New York and the following day he met with David Maitland. Maitland had been waiting for him when he arrived at the bank. His behavior had been just as puzzling as Steban's. He had checked the package, given Edmond a receipt and bid him good-day.

Edmond had decided to visit Jennet before leaving New York. She would have questions and he did not have the answers. However, Jennet had news of her own; she and Steban had reconciled.

Steban had vehemently opposed Jennet relationship with James Overfield. After the two had eloped Steban refused Jennet overtures. For ten years Steban would not see Jennet or even speak to her on the telephone. Edmond remembered the day well. Justin Overfield had come to the house raving that Jennet had seduced his grandson. He actually threatened them to keep quiet about the elopement, not wanting it to become public knowledge that James had run off with a Negro girl. What he did not realize that Steban hated it even more than he did.

Pregnancy had enhanced Jennet's beauty and she was positively radiant as she told him Steban had promised to release the trust left to her by Grandmama Rosa. Jennet had always adored her father and Edmond was glad Steban had finally let go of his anger, but he found it hard to believe that Steban had decided to release the trust.

WC had been urging Steban to find a way to break the trust so they could use the money. It was impossible, of course; but once his father found out he had released the money; it was guaranteed not to go well.

Jennet and James had faced overwhelming odds when they had run off to Canada. The couple had not been able to return home without being jailed or worse; but they had been willing to risk arrest, even death to be together.

Those first few years had been hard ones. James had worked as a laborer and Jennet had washed laundry. James had finally gotten a job teaching in Canada and evidently his credentials had landed him a position with a prestigious prep school in New York. Edmond never asked how; he did not want to know.

Once they had returned to the United States, Edmond had spent a portion of his summer vacation with them. During those brief weeks, Edmond felt free, unshackled from his parents' expectations.

The couple's Harlem apartment was mecca for their friends; people of all persuasions and intellects. Edmond's view of world had been challenged by their ideas. They encouraged

Edmond to make his life stand for something; to make a difference, but from the beginning his way had already been mapped out for him.

His mother pushed and petted. His father was willing to give him anything he wanted. All they had expected in return was his life. Edmond was to dedicate his life to Angel's Trumpet. He was to be the prince in his father's pseudo kingdom and the trophy his mother could paraded about the society of the Negro elite. The fact that he had taken what was given was a hard truth and one his WC never failed to mention.

After Edmond had received his degree in medicine he had moved to Chicago to complete his internship and residency. Whatever WC might believe, he had always planned to return home, Hollis was there; until he had been invited by a group of alumni from Oberlin to be part of a medical team of missionaries traveling to Africa.

He had been honored and excited. Edmond needed challenges, to be his own man. The missionary venture was an opportunity to strive for something other than self-gratification; a chance to give back some of what had been given to him.

Edmond had tried to explain how he felt to his father, but WC had greeted with the news with his usual derision, looking at him with that perpetual patronizing smirk that was so characteristic, before saying, "Ain't the day to day struggle of being a Colored man, enough for you, boy?"

His father was such a hypocrite. His parental attitude toward the people who worked the farms and mill was worse than the smiling white plantation master thinking he knows what is best for the "darkies."

WC had accused him of running away from his responsibilities just like Steban and Gent, but his father did not understand. Edmond had seen the poverty and squalor in which Negro people lived in northern tenements. He had not forgotten the riots or the Negro men and women who had been murdered and lynched. He had no patience for his father's complacent attitude, because by the grace of God he had been born a Gabriel.

Edmond suddenly did not feel well; his vision had become blurry and his mouth dry. Earlier, a helpful porter had handed him a cup of coffee, he thought it had tasted strange and too late he realized he had been drugged.

He shook his head trying to clear away the fuzziness but it was no use. He tried to call for help but he could not get the words out, finally he slumped, unconscious onto the seat.

The porter watched as two men took Edmond off the train before it left the station. Any misgivings he might have had were quieted by the wad of money in pocket.

Chapter

New York, 1922

The nuns had taught Win long ago, that whatever seeds you sowed in this life, you would

eventually reap the rewards of indiscretion; of course the nuns were always right. The bond

between her and Sinclair had cost her Willa's respect, and more than a little of her self-respect,

but they were her own seeds, and she had gone willingly enough.

She remembered how close she had come to disaster, shuddering when she thought of Tommy

Kilpatrick. She would never forget how Sinclair had kept her hidden in the shadowy darkness of

the garden, willing to fight if need be to protect her. Sinclair had saved her and life had never

been the same. He was her hero and her lover. Sinclair had taught her how sweet, loving the

right man could be.

That night had been the beginning of an intimacy far deeper than just a physical act. She

remembered they talked about everything that night, giggling like kids. Sinclair had been honest

from the start, she heard the passion in his voice when he talked about his music. The first time

she heard him play, he had made love to her with his music, playing his trumpet just for her.

That night she had realized she would always be second to the music. She had understood and

accepted it; he had said she was his woman and that was all she had wanted to be.

Perhaps if she had not miscarried their child things would have been different. Sinclair had

wept, blaming himself. For days afterwards he buried himself in his music, not talking; hardly eating. He would lose his temper; there would be fights and brawls, his only concern the occasional split lip; that would keep him from being able to play.

He made her countless promises, and then broke his word on a whim. They had dreams of opening their own club one day, but dreams cost money and Sinclair was content buying expensive clothes and trinkets. He had never learned to handle money; he spent it when he had it and when it was gone made more. His recorded collaborations with Willis Webster had made more money than either man had ever seen. By all predictions they had been headed for the big-time.

The nuns would have said it was simply happenstance, the day Sinclair's booking agent had recommended Willis Webster as a replacement for Sinclair's piano player, after Reef Miller had deliberately lured the man away by offering him more money than Sinclair could pay. Win knew Reef and Sinclair had history, but she never understood why Sinclair tolerated the man.

Webster had been a child prodigy; a truly gifted pianist. He added his musical genius to Sinclair's raw talent, teaching Sinclair how to read to music and score his own compositions; creating an opportunity for Sinclair's music to be recorded. Unfortunately, Webster had baggage, in the form of a gambling habit and his wife Leah.

Leah wasn't happy unless she had the attention of every male in her radius. From the beginning she caused friction between the band members. She had never tried her vamp act on Sinclair, after Win had threatened to break her face, if she ever came near him, but it had remained a sore point. Leah always wanted what she could not have. Webster seemed undisturbed by her behavior. Win had only seen the glow of excitement in Webster's eyes when a musical session went just right or seated at a poker table.

When he turned up robbed and murdered after an all- night card game, no one was really surprised, but Sinclair had been desolated by his friend's death. It wasn't long before they heard that Leah had taken up with a hustler by the name of Redding Turner.

Perhaps she should have told Sinclair she had met Red Turner before. At the time she was just trying to avoid trouble. Sinclair and his band had been booked at a club known as a gambler's paradise and Win had bumped into Red coming from one of the private rooms. He had pestered her with his attention several times after that, until Sinclair had moved on to the next club date.

 Redding Turner and his brother Mason were opportunists like a lot of others they encountered once they began to tour. Win had learned quickly, that the entertainment circuit was a feeding ground for predators. Gamblers and hustlers, dope dealers and pimps, all following the money; and Red and his brother were no different.

One night after two years of silence, Leah had walked into a New York nightclub where Sinclair was playing and introduced him to the two brothers. The Turners had offered their "services", in exchange for a percentage of Sinclair's earnings. When Sinclair refused to play their game and pay for "protection", they threaten to get ugly. Sinclair had been expecting trouble, but the two didn't come back around, and Sinclair thought his refusal to pay had ended it.

Several months passed and things had been going well.   The band's recordings were selling and Sinclair had finally settled down. The band was finishing up a month long engagement to a packed house nightly and she and Sinclair had decided after the show ended that night they would take off for a few weeks and spend some time with Willa.

The band was well into the first set, when Leah, Red and Mace Turner arrived along with Reef Miller.   Reef Miller was like a bad penny, always turning up. Somewhere along the way he had picked up a heroin habit and she had interrupted him one evening trying to persuade Sinclair to take a "taste." Sinclair had no need for that type of temptation in his life   Nor did he need, Red and Mace Turner, who were Reef's new managers, hanging around.

According to rumors, Red had opened a club in Chicago, and by the looks of them, money did not seem to be a problem. The Turners wanted Sinclair to sign an exclusive contract to perform at Red's new club, the earlier threats replaced by a thin veneer of business acumen that did not fool anyone.

Leah was still nothing but trouble, and it was her fault Red Turner was determined to own Sinclair.   As usual she was flirting with Reef Miller, who apparently had a death wish, judging by the look on Red Turner's face.

Win often wondered what she could have done differently, but with Sinclair's temper, the end was inevitable.

As the evening progressed both Sinclair and Reef had been drinking heavily. The old rivalry had never ended and when the two took center stage, the crowd had erupted with excitement. While Reef continued to play, Win had tried to hustle Sinclair out back through the stage door, but before she could get him into the car they were attacked.

She screamed but no one heard. One held her while they beat him. Sinclair was drunk but not helpless. He returned as good as he got, but there were three of them. She watched, as two penned him down, while the other slammed his fist into Sinclair jaw line with brass knuckles.

Later it was more than just his jawbone that needed to mend. Sinclair was depressed and drinking. She was afraid he would become dependent on the morphine the doctor had given him for pain while in the hospital.

Win had been desperate to save her love. When Red and Leah had the gall to show up at the hospital, she knew they had to get away. Sinclair couldn't go back to New Orleans, but they had to leave for somewhere soon. She had no idea what they would do, when she received a telegram from Willa inviting her to Atlanta.

Atlanta had been the beginning for them. Sinclair recovered more than just his health, he rediscovered his first love…music. After Gent, had brought them Fontaine, Win believed at last happiness and peace was finally within her grasp.

chapter

Marseille, France, April 30, 1935

A smoky café in Marseille was not exactly the big-time, but it felt good to be on stage playing

his horn again, thought Fontaine Gabriel Sinclair. His affinity with his instrument and the music

brought forth a spattering of applause following his impromptu improvisation, during a sweet

rift. Picking up the tempo, he fell back in sync with the lead clarinet and alto sax. These guys

were good he thought, and they made him better. He would never be as good as his dad, but

Billy Sinclair had been one of the best.

He never knew the man that fathered him and his mother died when he was a baby. His earliest

memories were of his grandfather, but even those images were faded. It was as if he had been

reborn in Atlanta. Win's love had washed away the grief of his granddad's death and replaced it

with all the caring one little boy could ever need. Gent had always been supportive, but it was

Billy Sinclair who raised him and loved him like a son.

Fontaine remembered the day he had walked into his Dad's music room. He had been

immediately drawn to the shiny horn that rested in a velvet-lined case. He had lifted it from the

case his small fingers pressing the keys, while he tried to blow into it. He heard a sound which

startled him and the trumpet fell from his hands.   He had been ready to cry when he saw it was

Sinclair, but instead of the punishing him, Sinclair just smiled, hugging him tight had given

Fontaine his first lesson.

Sinclair could be loving to his family; charming friends and fans when it suited him. People had

flocked to hear him play a single set; he had that something that separates good from genus.

He loved fine clothes and flashy jewelry, but that was the entertainer, few people really knew the

man.

His dad had imparted to him the love of music; and the discipline it took to master the

instrument. That same discipline had flowed over into other areas of Fontaine's life, but for

Sinclair music was an all- consuming passion.

If his parents ever argued about anything it was Sinclair's single-mindedness concerning

Fontaine's career as a musician. Win insisted he must have time to choose, attend college and do

other things until he decided what he wanted. And Fontaine had discovered he had an aptitude

for history, antiquities and languages.

Fontaine had never questioned his father's love, but he often wondered if his father would have

been as accessible to him, had he lacked aptitude for the trumpet. He had seen the hurt

expression on his mother's face and he was not sure he wanted anything to hold sway over his

life like that.

His Uncle Gent had sent for him the first time when he was only twelve and every summer

afterwards, despite Sinclair's objections. They had traveled to Paris where his Gent owed an

export/import shop fronted by a quirky little Frenchman named Henri Millan; to North Africa,

French Morocco where Gent maintained a home and office, and the main trading center in Djibouti, managed by Nathan and Lowe.

The two men were his second family. Nathan had frightened him a little at first, but there was no one kinder. Nathan had embraced the Islamic religion and had taken a wife. At last count they had five little ones running all over the place. Lowe kept two mistresses who vied for his attention, or at least he said they did.

Fontaine's music had continued to be an important part of his life, but he had an appreciation for the antiquity of the ancient cities where they lived and traveled; and the historical artifacts, sometimes handled by Gent which eventually led him to pursue a degree in Archeology.

Although he had spent considerable time in Djibouti, Fontaine had never had the opportunity to travel to Addis Ababa, Ethiopia's capital city. He had wanted a chance to study the old monasteries and churches the country was famed for; and he had been very excited when Lowe had finally been able to arrange for his travel permit, but it had all paled in comparison to meeting the Lady Nemri Tesseme.

Lady Nemri was a widow, who made her home in Addis Ababa, under the guardianship of her brother-in-law. Fontaine thought that she was the most exquisite woman he had ever seen; small and delicate with velvety brown eyes and golden skin. They had spent a delightful month together, exploring the ancient sites during the day and nights exploring each other, until her brother-in-law found out. His visitation permit was immediately revoked and he was forced to return to Djibouti.

Fontaine had fumed all the way back to Djibouti. He was well aware that slavery was still prevalent in parts of the country, but he was shocked when Nemri explained that she belonged to the house of Tesseme.

After Gent had returned from a business trip for Gabriel Imports; Fontaine had been so sure Gent would support him; his adopted uncle was one of the most moral men he knew. He could not believe it when Gent refused to help him remove Nemri from her brother-in-law's charge.

"Fontaine I don't have time for this, I'm leaving for the States after I return to Morocco, why don't you come with me. Nathan and Lowe have enough to do without your stirring up trouble. Stop thinking below your belt. The story is filled with contradictions. Is Nemri lady or slave?"

"You don't know her."

"I know this, if the lady is who you think she is, Tesseme would be honor bound to kill you; in his world you would be as insignificant as a gnat."

Gent had tried to convince him to travel to the States with him. Fontaine had not seen his mother since Sinclair had died in a car crash. Gent had warned him not to entangle himself in a situation that could affect them all. Angry, Fontaine had refused to listen and had stormed out.

Fontaine knew there had been some truth in what Gent said, but he was still angry; they treated him like a child. Gent just wanted to get him away from Nemri and he refused to be separated from her for what could be months. Gent finally agreed to do what he could when he returned if Fontaine stayed out of trouble. Fontaine decided it might be a good thing to get away for a few weeks to clear his head. He and Gent traveled together as far as Marseille.

In Marseille he had friends and his music; with a regular gig at one of the local night spots whenever he wanted since the manager was a long-time buddy. Everything had been going fine, until he received a telegram from Nemri begging him to help her.

It was no longer possible to wait until Gent returned. He was determined too free her. He traveled by train to the coast as far as the Suez Canal, then connected with a ship headed down the Red Sea coast.

As he stood out on deck looking out on the moonlit sea, he had never felt so unsure of himself. Gent would not like what was he was planning. Fontaine knew he had acted impulsively. He had no plan and very little money to execute a rescue. Somehow he had to convince Nathan and Lowe to help him. He had cabled them he was coming, and he felt cheered by the thought that Nathan and Lowe had always supported him.

As he turned to go inside a fellow passenger bumped into him and Fontaine felt a sharp prick in his arm. Suddenly he was stumbling drunkenly, before collapsing onto the deck floor.

Chapter

Italy, 1935

Konstatino "Carlo" Leopardi felt a kinship with the man that sat across from him. They both were sons of nobility; with ancient lineages traceable to the days of Alexander the Great, when great African kings still ruled the continent. And like his friend he knew that the days of the privileged nobility and the monarchy itself were fast coming to an end.

Italy had long been a hotbed of political dissention. His great-grandfather had fought with Garibaldi for a united Italy despite opposition against nationalism and the displacement of the Church. There were others who felt the republic had no need of a king and opposed a continued monarchy. Having witnessed the ineffectiveness of an inept king, Carlo was not sure they were not correct.

There had been violent clashes over political ideologies; since he was a child. The communists, the socialists; then socialists turned fascists, each seeking a stronghold in the Italian government. The black shirted fascists of Benito Mussolini however, had emerged victorious, solidifying Mussolini's power.

Without the solid backing of the military, the King lost control of the government. He finally had no choice but to invite Mussolini in; and the country had fallen under Mussolini's dictatorship.

Mussolini thought it politically wise to accord the King and royal family all the superficial trivialities due their position; and to that affect, Carlo had been one of the young men of noble birth appointed royal attaches to the King and his family; after he had been judged loyal to Mussolini and his faction.

Opposition was dealt with ruthlessly by the "Black Shirts." Even now, Carlo's father cowered on their family estates in fear of the Black shirted Fascisti and the next edict of Il Duce as Mussolini was called.

Carlo played his role well, but despite Il Duce's Black Shirted enforcers, there were still many young men and women of the nobility, who felt as Carlo did, and were willing to die to oust Mussolini. But a fruitless death would accomplish nothing.

Mussolini had stirred the cause of nationalism in the Italian people, puffing himself off as a modern day Caesar. He was hungry for power and colonization of Ethiopia would be the first step in achieving his goal. Carlo believed that if Mussolini could be made to fail in this effort, it could seriously damage his credibility with the Italian people and would be a blow Il Duce's war machine.

Carlo and his fellow conspirators had waited for their chance, and their diligence was rewarded when vital military information concerning the Il Duce's plans for the invasion of Ethiopia had fallen into their hands. Carlo had a contact in the Ethiopian government; Salim Akbar was an old friend and through him the information would be delivered into the right quarter.

Of course Salim required compensation and Carlo was happy to comply. It had just been a matter of calling in a favor from his cousin in the United States. It never occurred to Carlo to question the method of payment or even why payment was required.

Salim Akbar sipped his wine slowly as he listened to his companion. Carlo considered himself a patriot, but Mussolini would not be pulled down with rhetoric; however, it suited Salim's purpose to encourage Carlo in his defiance. He had always found that timing was everything.

Salim was certain the information Carlo provided would be extremely valuable to the Regent; but knowledge of Mussolini's invasion plans would do little more than slow down the inevitable. The present Ethiopian army bore no comparison to the army of Menelik II who had thrashed the Italians at the battle of Elba; and the current Regent was certainly no Menelik. However, Salim had better and more profitable uses for the information.

After the old Emperor's death Salim's father had supported the young pretender despite rumors of his Islamic leanings. In the ensuing route, the Queen and Regent forces quickly put down the rebellion. The young pretender as well as his followers was imprisoned; their lands confiscated. Adi Akbar had chosen death by his own hand, leaving Salim landless and adrift.

His princely cousin had died of some mysterious illness while at the royal court; where for a price murder was easily contrived. Or perhaps he choked on his own overweening arrogance, Salim thought sourly; and his successor had no need of Salim's services.

Under the cloak of anonymity, Salim turned his talents to larceny, using his network of informants and spies to accomplish everything from blackmail to white slavery. In the stews of the city, his name was spoken in whispers and the few who had seen his face lived just long enough to realize their mistake. Salim Akbar had become a man deadly to know.

His half- brother Omar had proved to be more resourceful than Salim anticipated, but framing him for murdering Dennison had been a necessary means to an end. Salim did not begrudge his survival, or the success of Gabriel Imports. Evidently Omar had chosen his partners in Gabriel Imports with more care than the last unfortunate, who thought he could blackmail Salim and he had been wise enough never to become entangled in Salim's interests.

The name Gabriel had haunted him for a long time. The business with Steban Gabriel had been a grave disappointment and failure did not sit well on his palate; but Salim was a patient man. It had not taken long to discovered the connection between Steban and Gent Gabriel. Over time he had acquired quite a dossier on Mr. Gent Gabriel. Bit by bit Salim had become acquainted with the nucleus of the Gabriel clan. When renewed interest in the Medallion of Sheba resurrected, Salim had sufficient information to bring Steban once again under his control.

High church officials in the Ethiopia government believed that the Medallion could rally the people in the conflict that was surely coming with Italy and enhance the Regent's position. The Italians realized that the religious icon might spell the difference between victory and defeat and a great deal of money was being offered for the medallion's recovery.

Salim knew that altruistic value aside, the possessor of the medallion could wield enormous power and a means to reclaim his family estates. The solution of how best to employ his resources to trap Steban Gabriel presented itself in the form of Carlo Leopardi.

Carlo had been part of King of Italy entourage during his visit to the Red Sea coast and the Italian settlements outside of Djibouti. They had met at an exclusive salon that catered to varied sexual pursuits, which unknown to Carlo was owned by Salim.

It was during one of their drunken forays that Salim learned of Carlo's Sicilian antecedents and his involvement with a group of partisans determined to bring down Mussolini. It had meant nothing to Salim at the time, but later he recalled Carlo mentioning that one of his cousins had migrated to the United States, because of efforts by Mussolini to eradicate the Black Hand from Italy.

According to Carlo the groups were mostly territorial, only lending support to protect the family lands. But they were connected by blood ties which were considered honor bound and sacred.

After Carlo had contacted him with information regarding Mussolini's military plans, Salim believed he had found a way to attack Steban even in the United States. Salim set his little play in motion to once again lure Steban into his orbit.

One particular interesting fact concerning Steban and a woman named Maria had been provided by the late, unlamented Dennison.

He knew Maria and Steban had a daughter, named Jennet who presently resided in New York. That Gent and his brother William were Steban's nephews. Subsequent financial inquiries had led him to the Maitland Bank and the family's financial woes. Knowledge had not been a problem; never the less from the beginning, Salim's plans had not gone smoothly.

Instead of kidnapping Steban's daughter in New York, the fools Carlo's cousin provided had taken Steban's wife, which in Salim's world did not always mean much. His own agents failed to get to Gent Gabriel in time, so they were forced to take his adopted son. Carlo's people had also managed to snag another nephew, Edmond, having discovered his identity from a clerk employed at Maitland Bank.

His agents could have told Salim that his information while correct was missing some vital facts, but it was not worth their lives to do so. It was better to pretend ineptness and bad luck, than suggest Salim was at fault.

Salim had been extremely displeased. The people provided by Carlos had been incompetent; their throats would have been slit had they been employed by him. Luck good, or bad had no part in his little dramas, they were always planned carefully and faultless carried out or you suffered the consequences.

However, there was still a chance; perhaps Steban valued his wife more than Salim valued his own.

Chapter

Atlanta, Georgia, May 31, 1935

Hollis Terrell stared in wonder at the scene before her. Turning to her escort, she spoke in low, almost reverent tones, "Everything is so beautiful I have never seen so many finely dressed people."

Minton Dorsey smiled down at the slim, brown-skinned girl wearing a gown of champagne gold satin. Dorsey freely admitted his jaded view of the ensemble, but watching the display afresh through Hollis's eyes; he could appreciate her delight.

The sparkling crystal chandelier reflected a kaleidoscope of color as couples swirled beneath the glowing sphere. Newly inducted debutants dressed in shimmering white gowns melded with shades of palest yellow and the deepest amber of their older sisters, as the partners of their choice, groomed in black and white jackets glided them about the marbled ballroom floor. The hues of their skin ranged from the creamiest vanilla to the earthiest brown and their hair marcelled into chic coiffures. They were people of color, the upper crust of Negro café society and the excitement was contagious. The Gold and White Ball was one of the social events of the season.

Most of the guests were educated, well moneyed and snobbery was as rife among the chosen few as the lords and ladies at Buckingham palace. Dorsey laughed softly as he recalled last year's scandal involving the elopement one of his waiters and a white dressed debutant.

When Win Sinclair, had called to enlist his aid as escort for Hollis, Dorsey had been happy to help. The older woman was a good friend and he had been willing to join any cause that irritated Adel and tweaked little Cassandra's nose.

Hollis saw him smile, and said, "I probably sound as country as you can get."

"On the contrary, you are the belle of this ball. I think Win must really trust me to turn you lose in my company wearing that gown, Cinderella. As for being country, don't let them fool you, everybody in here is one or two jumps up from the cotton fields. Now come along, it's time to mix and mingle."

Hollis smiled brightly at his compliment. After Adel had made it clear she was not welcome in their party Hollis had been grateful for Win Sinclair's sponsorship and for Mr. Dorsey's escort. For a moment she felt lost amidst this glittering crowd. She missed Edmond; she could not understand what had happened to him, but she was determined to enjoy this new experience.

Dorsey had left Hollis in the capable hands of one of the younger hostesses of his acquaintance, who arranged a dance card for the girl. With a reassuring wink; he took himself off to the iron-worked terrace, for a smoke.

Perhaps some might question the legitimacy of such an occasion, there was a time when he had himself, but he was no philosopher, it was a warm starlit evening and for a while the world of prejudices was held at bay.

They were educators, lawyers, doctors and professional entrepreneurs, in a world whose only drawback was the color of their skin; but in their universe, they reigned supreme. Dorsey's understanding was insufficient to explain how black men and women could continue to create and communicate in the face of such overwhelming odds.

Racism was like trying to digest a daily diet of cabbage and cold pork, you vomited it up, you shit it out, but you got through it. But only the strong survived. Everybody else changed countries, religions, political persuasions or let it break their hearts.

Every black man's success was a cause for celebration for all black men. Who had more right to dance under the stars than these? The hypocrisy rested in their attitudes toward one another.

The origins the Ball could be traced to the "Placee" balls of New Orleans where wealthy white men chose virginal women of color as mistresses. Later an annual ball was held by the "Creoles" as a celebration of their heritage and status that set them apart from other black folks. The custom had migrated and was redefined; but admittance was still based on intangibles money, status, and of course skin color.

Dorsey could not plead ignorance or deny the obvious; no matter how educated or wealthy, they were no better than the sharecropper's daughter. But the unenlightened, black or white would always use their own measuring stick to judge such things. But mostly it was about money, which was lucky for folks like Adel Gabriel, since she had nothing else but WC's money.

To them he was uncouth and uncultured, an uneducated gangster turned entrepreneur. He donated money to their causes and charities; invested in their business ventures, but they never invited him to their homes or introduced him to their yellowed skinned daughters. But he had learned to be grateful and much of what he had he owed surprisingly to his parents.

He could remember being angry at his parents. Not because they were servants, but because they seemed too willing to be subjugated. He would listen to his father whistling while he polished the white folks' car and his mother humming a tune as she cooked their meal, when they had so little. But he had come to understand and appreciate who they were.

They were thankful for what they had, they took pride in the fact that although they worked hard for a living, they owed no man and they found happiness and contentment being with each other and having him. He still mourned the fact they had died much too soon.

Alone and on his own, he soon discovered everything had a price. Even a lowly shoeshine boy, had to pay for the privilege, but if you were smart there was money to be made, and he had been a smart kid. Soon he was peddling everything from jazz recordings to smuggled whiskey, until hustling became second nature.

His main hangout had been the Sin & Win, Club Majestic; which was owned by the Sinclairs. Part of what was called the "chitterling circuit", they featured headliners, big name Negro entertainers and like others, he followed the money.

He had seen WC Gabriel around before, but that night, it was his companion that attracted Dorsey's attention.

Syd Jones was a busty, redbone who made a living, relieving gullible gentlemen, of their money. She and her partner, a slick called Quick Wilson ran a scam as old as the hills, but they were good at it. As a rule, Dorsey would have minded his own business, but Syd and Quick had interfered in his affairs, relieving a client of his bankroll, before Dorsey got paid and it seemed a good time for a little payback.

He was familiar with the duo's haunts and waited until Syd and WC left the club supposedly for Syd's apartment when Quick had stepped from the shadows with a pistol.

Fortunately, Quick was a born coward, unless the odds were stacked in his favor and with a gun stuck in his ribs, the odds could not have been worst. It didn't take much to persuade them to look for easier pickings elsewhere.

WC had been grateful. Both men discovered they shared a common streak of larceny that made them fast friends, and before long they went into the bootlegging business.

Since the beginning of prohibition, everybody was making a little home brew, but you could produce the stuff cheaper and on a larger scale, if you access to large qualities of sugar something Mr. Gabriel could readily supply. Together they had formed a consortium, he set up the still operation and J. John Tate had the connections to push the hooch. He would probably still be hustling or doing time, if not for WC.

The cops had picked him up one night, roughed him up a little; and began making a loud noise about arresting him. He had always believed J. John had set him up, but he had no proof. There was no one else, so he phoned WC for help.

WC had stopped by his apartment to pick up the necessary cash to bail him out and had discovered some stock certificates that had belonged to his parents. They had meant nothing to Dorsey, he had never even bother to exam them, but his parent had used their small savings to invest in a cola company, probably through their employers, which despite the Depression had become very profitable.

WC could have taken the certificates for himself. Instead, he had gotten his own lawyer to look into the matter and collect the dividends that had built up over twenty years. Suddenly Dorsey had more money than he knew what to do with, but the contentment of his parents eluded him.

He remembered a bible scripture his parents had tried to teach him; the Apostle Paul had ministered about abasing and abounding; having and not having. It had taken him a long time to understand. He had learned that money was only a tool that could buy many things, but it could not guarantee him what he wanted; and what he wanted more than anything was Cassandra Gabriel.

He told himself that he was thirty-two years old, almost twelve years her senior, that she was a selfish little snob, but he fantasized about a looked of desire thawing the coldness in her brown eyes. He could not hide the way he felt and he knew she was capable of using that fact.

Tonight, she was a vision in lemon yellow chiffon dancing by in the arms of some pimply face college boy, while she continued to remain aloof from him. One day she would come to him, it was the only way it would work, she had to come to him.

As owner of the Regal Hotel he had hosted these events for the past few years, but rarely mingled with his guests, tonight he would make an exception because of Hollis. He had given Win his word, and Hollis looked as if she needed him, as a bevy of gold colored gowns led by the Albright girl, converged on her.

Cassandra Gabriel moved stealthy toward the terrace trying to avoid her mother's sharp eyes. Thomas had asked that she meet him outside. He had been flirting with other girls from the band stand all evening and she meant to make him pay for his defection. She was her father's daughter and she would take that from no man.

She almost bumped into Minton Dorsey as he reentered the ballroom. The man was really annoying, Cassandra thought, but he did have style. Cassandra could not help but notice how well his he wore his clothes; self-assured and elegant. Feminine glances followed him, as he crossed the ballroom.

Tonight, instead of the traditional white dinner jacket, he wore a light tan jacket with dark tan tuxedo trousers, which was not surprising since she had once heard him tell her father, the ball was all a bunch of pretentious bullshit. She knew he didn't give damn about what anybody thought, least of all the people here.

Cassandra smiled complacently. Dorsey had a passion for her and his ill-concealed adoration amused her, yet he only stood and watched, as other men claimed her attention. Not that she cared; all she had to do was crook her little finger and Minton Dorsey would come running.

She assumed it was her Aunt Win's idea that he escort Hollis Terrell to the ball. Cassandra watched him sweep the girl away before her friends could have some fun. She had promised Edmond she would not be mean to the girl, but she had wasted no time in letting Patty Albright know who she was.

Dorsey was actually smiling at that country heifer, like she was something special; leading her onto the dance floor as the band played a popular swing tune. Who would have thought he could dance like that; but she would deal with Hollis Terrell and Dorsey later, Thomas was waiting. She was about to ease through the terrace doors when she felt a tug on her arm holding her back.

Dorsey was aware of the little drama brewing and the thought of Cassy with Thomas Blue made him sick. Blue, with his oozy charm, was as slick as a greased pig and Cassy was in way over her head. Dorsey decided that his little love needed a lesson.

He waited until Hollis danced off with her next partner, then maneuvered himself just in time to block Cassandra's way as she was about to step out to the terrace. Taking her hand, Dorsey pulled her back into the ballroom, and onto the dance floor as the band slowed its tempo. Cassandra sputtered angrily, but people were looking; the cats already had enough gossip to chew on.

It was their first dance and he should not have been so sure of himself. She struggled in his light embrace, as his fingers brushed against the bare skin of her back. She tried to ignore way she fit into the curve of his body and the shimmering warmth that spread through her as his lips brushed the top of her ear.

"You look beautiful tonight kitten", he whispered into her ear.

"Don't call me that, my name is Cassandra and don't hold me so tight, I don't want to dance with you", she whispered back angrily, annoyed at the teasing timbre of his voice.

"Why are you so mean kitten, you know you have my eternal devotion."

"Really, well you can take a number and stand in line with the rest."

"Ouch, is that any way to talk to your intended."

"Listen, I don't know what kind of inside tract you think you have just because you and WC are thick as thieves, but you are wasting your time."

"Relax puss, pull in your claws, it is just a dance", he replied grinning. Before she could protest, he had manipulated her to the edge of the dance floor and through the terrace doors.

"What do you think you are doing you idiot", she said, after he released her.

"I beg your pardon my sweet, I thought you were trying to get to the terrace", he said laughing.

She was tempted to scream, she simply could not bear the humiliation that would follow, but if he thought he could frighten her he was mistaken. A spark of deviltry her father would have recognized, glowed in her eyes, as she determined to bring him to his knees.

Dorsey knew what she was about, he wasn't fooled by her little impish smile, but he could not help himself, it was his fantasy. So he stood there waiting, his expression unguarded, his adoration opened to her scorn.

Cassandra moved invitingly closer until her chiffon skirts drifted over the tops of his shoes; and her hands rested lightly on his chest. But his kitten was seriously in error if she thought she could manipulate him as she did the rest of her male entourage.

She looked up at him teasingly, "Don't you want to kiss me Dorsey", she said, her smile wavering slightly, when he made no move to embrace her. She was close enough to smell his spicy male scent and feel hard contours of his body against her fingertips through the silk shirt he wore. She stepped back from him, unable to see his face in the shadows; no longer certain of the wisdom of her game.

Cassandra was totally unprepared for the heated rush that moved through her like a swift current at the feel of his lips; powdery soft and textured, as he leaned down to tenderly kiss her mouth.

She closed her eyes, yearning for more, but he made no move to touch her. Instead he continued to caress her lips lightly with the touch of his own, until her hands moved about his neck and her lips parted for him. She heard herself sigh as Dorsey's arms finally encircled her; pulling her against him, kissing her with an expertise that would not be denied.

She felt bereft when without warning she was snatched from his arms. She did not have time to scream as a hand covered her mouth and the prick of a knife at her throat held her motionless as three men encircled them. The leader held her back against him, while the other two challenged Dorsey. "All we want is the girl", one said gruffly to Dorsey.

"Now that's a problem, because the girl belongs to me", said Dorsey. Levity had no place just now, but he was amused just the same, as Cassandra squirmed and murmured against her captor's hand, her eyes flashing, cursing him with every profane word she could think of.

The terrace ran the length of the ballroom with stairs on neither end leading to the landscaped grounds. The man who held Cassandra was dressed as a guest, while the others in black had obviously been waiting for their cohort to contrive to bring Cassy to the terrace Dorsey had some questions for Thomas Blue, provided he was alive to do so. He figured they had to keep him quiet; he just hoped their solution to the problem would not be a permanent one.

"Move", the leader said, motioning Dorsey backward with a gun.

Ever vigilant, Adel Gabriel chose that moment to step through the terrace doors, demanding to know what was going on; creating the diversion Dorsey needed. He reached out, knocking the gun from the leader's hand, countering with a jab to his chin that sent him over the terrace.

Meanwhile, a howl sounded from Cassandra's captor as she stabbed her high heeled shoe into his foot, while biting down hard on his hand causing him to fling Cassandra down on the tiled terrace. She lifted herself painfully raining curses on the man's head as he ran limping down the terrace stairs on the heels of his accomplices, as the noise brought several waiters outside.

The crowd poured onto the terrace as Adel and Cassandra screamed at Dorsey, blaming him for what happened. WC quickly took charge, assuring everyone it was a robbery attempt gone wrong and they drifted back to the dance floor. WC took his ladies and Hollis to his Aunt Win's.

Dorsey had stayed behind to have a word with Thomas Blue; but the man had wasted no time getting out of the ballroom before Dorsey could catch him.

Chapter

Overton County, May, 1935

The wedding of Miss Vera Louise Tatum to Mr. Trenton Stuart Overfield was one of the major social events of the year. Invitations had been sent and accepted from Savannah, New Orleans, Virginia and Alabama.

"The bride is the daughter of Mr. J.T. Tatum, a self-made man of vast wealth and the late Susan White Thomasville Tatum of the prominent Thomasville family of Mobile. The groom's grandfather is Mr. Justin Overfield of Overton County. The couple was married from the lawn of the bride's plantation home followed by a magnificent reception. And the bride was radiant in white organdy", Missy Overfield quoted tipsily, pausing in her high-jinks to consume another glass of champagne.

She smiled crookedly, a lady never appeared drunk in public and she had already had way too much champagne. It was the only way she could abide her father-in-law and stomach the lavish excess she was sure had been Justin's idea. Her presence here was a command performance, in any case.

She had plenty to keep her amused as she watched an incumbent Senator and his family toadying to the brides' father and an ambitious former Lt. Governor, whose tactics were so obvious, his lips might become permanently attached to Tatum's ass.

She noticed Justin coming toward her, and from the rosy glow on his face, she was not the only one worst for drink.

Justin still considered himself man enough to appreciate a pretty woman. Missy was surely in her mid-forties, but still mighty pleasing to the eye. Her low-cut pink gown fit like a second skin; outlining her considerable charms and long legs.

Missy had always been a lot of woman, too much for his son to have handled. Justin had always thought she needed taming and he would have been just the man to do it. She had arrived at the wedding with as much aplomb as he could have hoped for, with what he believed to be her third husband, a minor baronet in tow.

Missy said, "Well Justin I see you got what you wanted, I trust you are satisfied."

Gesturing toward the display, he said, "Why shouldn't I be?"

"Perhaps someone should tell Daddy Tatum, there is a depression on", she returned sarcastically.

"I would have thought you ignorant of the fact yourself, my dear, the way you cable me for funds. But since you have another husband, Baroness, I guess I'll be hearing from you less than usual. By the way where is Lord whatchamacallit?"

"His name is Lord Remington and don't start with me old man. As James' widow and mother of his sons, I was entitled to the money he left in trust for me; money that you used for your own purposes."

"As far as I am concerned you are entitled to nothing. It was a blessing James died when he did before he discovered what kind of woman he had married. And as for your sons, hell you've given me one pretty-boy that bed hops like a rabbit and another one with such disrespect for his birthright that he runs off with a nigger."

"Be very careful what you say Justin, Missy warned. Trenton is more man than you think and as for Jamie, I seem to recall you had a taste for dark meat yourself."

"How would you know that, or anything else, besides lying on your backside to get what you want?"

"I know where the bodies are buried Mr. Justin Overfield and you had better remember that", Missy spat angrily.

"Are you threatening me, you lying little bitch."

Before Missy could reply, Trent interrupted them. His Grandfather's face was mottle and red, while his mother's eyes glittered dangerously.

"What in the hell is wrong with you two, Trent said though gritted teeth and a determined smile. Everyone is looking at you. Come along mother, Tatum is asking for you. By the by grandfather, Will Pomeroy is waiting to talk with you."

"Tell Benjamin to show him to the study, I'll be there directly."

"Really grandfather, it is my wedding day, must you conduct business here and now?"

Justin looked at him as if he was a crazy man. "Boy, Will Pomeroy is the last nail in Steban Gabriel's coffin. Don't be stupid, do what I say."

William Pomeroy stood nervously in the middle of the room, mopping his broad face with his handkerchief. It was a man's room paneled in rich dark mahogany with deeply cushioned red leather chairs; redolent with the aroma of fine cigars and brandy.

A week ago he had sat in this room, toasting the future, now he stood in two day old clothes, smelling his own sweat. Justin Overfield was not a man to cross but he knew his information was correct. A week ago the Gabriels were facing bankruptcy; now Pomeroy knew he was facing his own ruin.

"Pomp boy; why you standing there like that? Come on let me pour you a whiskey", said Justin.

Pomeroy accepted the glass gratefully and drain the whiskey in a single gulp. "Justin, I don't know why or how, he said stuttering to a halt"

"What the hell is wrong with you man, you twitching like a cat on a grill. Just spit it out Pomp."

"Justin, they paid the loan."

"They paid the loan, what the hell you talking about boy, who paid the loan", Justin said, grabbing his arm.

"The Gabriels, a week ago they paid the loan in full. I couldn't get no more information, the only thing I know was loan was paid in cash."

"Cash, that means they used all their working capital, we still got 'em. When they can't pay their bills the property will be forfeit and we will get for pennies on the dollar."

"No, all their obligations have been met, paid by the Maitland Bank in cash", said Pomperoy.

Suddenly Justin could not breathe. The first hammer blow moved down his arm numbing his side and he dropped his glass of whiskey. The second blow brought him to knees and he could not see Pomeroy kneeling in front of him. By the third blow his consciousness was swirling in darkness and the last sounds he heard, as his brain functions ceased, was the sound of Jesset Gabriel's laughter.

Overton County, June, 1935

"Leave it to you, old man to die on my wedding day. How dare you spoil my triumph; after you failed so miserably to deal with the Gabriels", said Trent Overfield.

Trent had always thought his aunt a retiring soul, filled with maidenly inhibitions, but to his surprise, Aunt Sarah had taken control of everything. The news of Justin's death had been hushed up until the following day and Aunt Sarah had insisted Trent and Vera leave on their honeymoon. She had instructed that a private ceremony be conducted, including the cremation of grandfather's body. Now grandfather resided in a brass urn on the mantel above the fireplace in the library; to which Trent addressed his remarks.

"Well old man, you thought you were so smart, now I control everything." Of course, Pomperoy had told him about the Gabriel, filled with remorse that he had caused his grandfather's heart attack and Trent had detected more than just a little relief. Somehow Pomp had screw up and Trent knew Grandfather would've cut off old Pomp's balls and used them for batting practice. Trent decided he still might.

Trent knew he had to be careful; Tatum was no fool. As long as Vera was happy there would be no problems. His new wife had proved to be a charming hand-full, eager to please her husband. Vera was as good as pregnant or about to be and then he would be home free. Tatum would deny the father of his grandson nothing. As for the Gabriels, he had friends who knew how to handle arrogant niggers like WC and dear old granddaddy's soul could finally rest in peace, if such a thing was possible in Hell, since Trent had no doubt; that was now his place of residence.

Chapter

June 1, 1935, Atlanta

Gent Gabriel was weary as he exited the taxi in front of his aunt's house. The trip had been fine until he reached New York and had gotten progressively worse as he crossed the Mason/Dixon line. The Whites Only signs decorating the scenery pulled his reality coat tail; you are a Negro and you are home, land of the free and home of the brave.

He had telegrammed ahead, but the hour being late he had not expected to find the house brightly lit in anticipation his arrival. It was large pink colored brick house with a front porch complete with swing, and a wide yard nestled by pink dogwood trees and azaleas all rosy from glow of the house.

He rang the doorbell and could hear Sweetie's soft tread, her reedy voice proclaiming her intention of answering the door.

Sweetie had been with Sinclair and Win since their New York days. The two older women lived in the house alone since Sinclair's car accident two years ago. Fontaine had not been home since the funeral and Gent regretted Fontaine would not to return to the States with him.

Sweetie opened the door gripping his hand in welcome. "Come on in, it's good to see you Gent, but something is going on with Miz Win; they waiting for you in the front room. They don't tell me nothing, she muttered, leading the way."

His puzzlement at Sweetie's words grew as he observed the room full of people in evening dress. WC was pacing the floor and Adel lay prostrate on the sofa with a young woman hovering over her with a cloth; while some others looked on.

Win came forward with a tremulous smile and gripped his hand, her face lined with worry. Before she could speak, Gent pulled her close and guided her to a chair, saying "Win honey you are making me nervous, I'm almost afraid to ask; what is going on?"

WC interrupted, saying, "Sorry to rain on your arrival Brother, but somebody just tried to kidnap my daughter a few hours ago."

"Kidnapped you say", Gent repeated. "Where is Uncle Steban?"

"That a good damn question, considering we have not seen him or my son for that matter in over a week", roared WC.

"Daddy there is no need to shout, you know it has only been a few days since we have seen Uncle Steban and he is expected to arrive tomorrow. Uncle Gent we haven't met but I'm Cassandra."

He smiled down at the girl, and then leaned to kiss both her cheeks. "You are as beautiful as your mother."

"You can save that continental bullshit for later Gent. Something is going on here, and I smell an Overfield in the woodpile."

"What would Overfield have to gain by taking Cassandra; all he wants are the farms and mill; for that he just has to wait until the estate loan is default."

WC said, "I do not have an answer to that question, if I did I would not be sitting here. I seem to be in the dark about a lot of things. Edmond left home with no explanation and now this episode with Cassy. Tell me, who else would want our hurt."

Suddenly alert, Adel sit up and smiled at Gent; "Well, well Gentleman Gabriel it seems just like old times; you appear and everything is stirred up. What do you know about my boy?"

Hollis, who had been sitting quietly, repeated Adel's question; "Has something happen to Edmond?"

"I find out that sonofabitch Overfield had anything to do with what happen tonight, I am gonna kill him and Trent, then I'm gonna make Jennet a widow", said WC.

Bemused, Gent looked around, wondering if crazy was catching. Win had begun to cry; Adel was like an electrical wire with a live current, snapping at Sweetie and another young female hovering between her and Win. His brother continued to pace, shouting and cursing at the top of his lungs, while his newly met niece was busy asking him probing questions about what he had been doing all her life.   Finally, sanity took shape as he noticed the last person in the room,

sipping a whiskey highball. "I could use one of those", said Gent

Minton Dorsey minus his coat, and a rip in his shirt, got up with a shrugged of his shoulders, "I

don't think no one here will mind. "Bourbon", he questioned, extending his hand in greeting.

"By the way, I'm Dorsey."

Gent took the bourbon gratefully, nodding his thanks. "Control appears to be in short supply

around here; I don't suppose you can tell me what the hell is going on?"

Dorsey said, "That is, not all together easy; your family is really unusual, but then I guess you

know that.   To begin with, someone did try to kidnap Cassandra tonight at the ball."

"Whoever they were, they stuck a gun in my ribs and if Adel had not come looking for

Cassandra, we might be having a "wake." Fortunately, she started to scream and with a few

lucky punches and Cassy's high heel, our would-be kidnappers were suddenly out-numbered.

They sprinted out of there so fast, nobody was gonna catch them. Your brother managed to pass

it off as an attempted robbery, so no one called the cops."

"As far as I can tell, your aunt had received a telegram concerning her son before we arrived. I

believe it is on the table in the foyer if you're interested, Sweetie would know."

Gent turned sharply to look at his Aunt. Kneeling in front of her chair, he said softly, "Win has something happen to Fontaine?"

"I just got a telegram from Nathan and Lowe, they say Fontaine is missing. They say he was not on the ship"

Gent shook his head as he read through the telegram, that Nathan had wired to Aunt Win. Fontaine was supposed to meet him in France, what the hell was he doing on a ship bound for Djibouti. And how could it possibly be connected to Edmond and Cassandra? The whole thing was strange; he needed another drink.

Dorsey handed Gent second bourbon. He said, "All I know is Edmond left home a few days ago. No one has seen or heard from him since he left to catch his train. He was to meet the family here, to attend the Gold and White Ball. The young lady over there was his date; when he didn't not show up, I was asked to escort her. WC is convinced that Justin Overfield is behind it all."

"That doesn't make sense"

"How would you know, that cracker is capable of anything; who knows which of us it will be next", said WC."

"Justin is no longer a danger to anyone, he's been dead two days", said Steban Gabriel from the entrance of the room.

Chapter

Atlanta, June, 1935

Despite his fatigue, Gent was restless. He had a bad feeling Fontaine had done something stupid like trying to help the Ethiopian lady, but surely Nathan would have put a stop to that. He could not see a connection between Fontaine and Edmond. He had wanted answers as much as WC, but Steban had clearly been in no shape to begin lengthy explanations.

The older man was exhausted and was it Win who decided to call a halt to the questions and asked them all to leave. Win's composure had been shaky, but she refused to be intimidated by WC's bluster or Adel's foolishness.

He had planned to stay with Win but with Uncle Steban there and Hollis Terrell she had a full house. Gent was grateful when Dorsey had suggested he arrange a guest room for him at the Regal. After all that had happened, he needed some time alone to think.

Was it possible that the situation here had triggered some scheme that involved Edmond as well as Fontaine? He was not prepared to deal with the fact that Fontaine could be in serious danger; at least not now. He had wired Omar to find out if there was any news and until he received an answer to his cable, there was nothing to do but wait.

He had stretched out on the bed, and begun making slow inroads into the bottle of bourbon he had purloined from his aunt's house. He had drunk just enough to make him careless, since he had omitted to lock the door to his room. There was a knock, then the door opened.

Gent was not sure who or what he expected; but surely his visitor rated his undivided attention and he leaned back to give his uninvited guest his full appraisal.

He remembered that perfume. He had bought her first bottle from Hatchets Department store on her sixteenth birthday and then had shown her exactly how to wear it, behind her ear and along her neck, between her breasts, the back of her knee and thigh and she had let him put each drop there personally. Damn, I must be drunk, to remember that, thought Gent.

The black dress she wore was expensive, just like the perfume. Money looked good on Adel. Her red-gold skin glowed against the shimmering black dress and the shapely legs were still the same as she walked into the middle of the room. She was no longer the girl he had known, but most definitely, all woman.

For a moment he closed his eyes, his brother's wife in his hotel room, could shit get any worst this night. Gent said, "I had forgotten was a pretty woman you are Del, now to what do I owe the pleasure of your company?"

"You know you're the only one whoever called me Del. I just I wanted to talk to you Gent."

"OK, I'll play along, you want a drink."

"Why yes some wine would be nice."

"No wine", he said with a snort of amusement, handing her glass of bourbon. "It's a little warm, but that never bothered you too much. Where 's WC?"

Adel made herself comfortable on the bed, sipping the bourbon slowly, saying, "WC has his own interests tonight and I have mine."

Now that don't sound like brother Will. WC usually keeps close tabs on those things that belong to him. How is the old homestead, I suppose nothing has changed?"

"WC change Angel's Trumpet, you must be joking; that would be a sacrilege, don't you know", Adel said as she eyed Gent thoughtfully.

In her daydreams Adel had always pictured Gent as the same carefree boy she had loved, instead she faced a stranger. Perhaps because he needed a shave his features appear so hard. He had become taller, harder and broader; and without doubt remained an exceptionally handsome man.

She waited for that familiar surge of excitement and desire to flow through her, but all she felt was an appreciation for an attractive man and a vague disappointment she could not explain.

There was a time Adel had known Gent Gabriel as well as anyone. She had loved him, with a woman's love, although she had only been seventeen; but she had refused to be a fool. Adel had known she could not depend on him to be there. She had saved herself and married WC. She had no regrets.

It had probably been a mistake to come. It was plain Gent was drunk and he was never a nice drunk. A tingle of apprehension moved along her spine, despite the silly drunken grin on his face.

"Well from what I can see Del, you have only gotten better, but it's been a lot of years my dear, people change; sometime the changes are not the kind you can see. Where are the others?"

"Like I said, WC has his interests, but my guess is he is probably at the Majestic. Cassandra is in her room and of course Edmond's friend remained at Win's."

"Yeah I wondered who she was; Win introduced her as Hollis Terrell. She's a pretty girl, Edmond has taste."

"Oh poo she aint nobody, just the local preacher's daughter. I don't under why Eddie wanted her to come, she was an embarrassment among our friends. Win and Dorsey encouraged the whole thing. Anyway you used to say I was beautiful, there was a time you could not keep your hands off me."

"This is true, but it was not enough, was it, my greedy little Del? You never thought twice; you reached out and took what you wanted with both hands. You said you wanted to talk, OK, we were different people then, we wanted different things. Life is a bitch, so give the dog a bone. You came here uninvited, what do you want Del?"

She leaned down and kissed him without restraint, until he pushed her away.

"Damn woman, is that really why you are here, a sentimental roll in the hay. Do you think I would actually make love to my brother's wife? The family is in a crisis; your son is missing, your daughter almost kidnapped and earlier today your only concern was about your son. Now you here like this. I don't think I'm, drunk enough."

Adel smiled then said, "It was just an experiment; you better come down off your high horse, you are much too drunk; I would hate to see you fall. Tell me, why are you here Gent"?

He looked at her curiously, saying, "You really don't know do you? But to answer your question Steban sent for me and the why is between WC and me. If you want to know, why don't you ask your husband. Now if you will excuse me, I have some more drinking to do."

She should not have come, she admitted to herself. Not that his rejection really upset her; but Gent had a way arousing conflicting emotions in her; that much had not changed.
"Alright I am leaving. I guess I just wondered if it would be the same between us. I have spent too many nights wondering what if. We were not just lovers Gent we were friends; I guess I never stopped missing you."

"It was your choice."

"Choice, did you expect me to leave home and follow you around like a gypsy?

"Well you got the ring, the house and the money; and the status of being Mrs. WC Gabriel, what you want from me? The way I remember it, WC knew his way around a bed pretty good."

She laughed dryly, "You won't admit it but you and Will are two of a kind. You are both hard and you don't give a damn about nothing but yourselves, but you had finesse. Will was crude, still is, but he wanted to marry me, not just keep me around until the good times went stale."

Gent had to resist the urge to shake her; instead he said, "Del do you realize that the family may be on the brink of disaster, and you're playing out your little drama in the "eye of the storm?"

At her stupefied look, he continued; "That quiet calm when everything seems alright, even when you know the winds are coming. It makes people edgy. I'm chasing my demons with bourbon; WC's doing whatever he does and you trying to dissect the past. I never made you any promises then, and I tell you no lies now."

"No, you were a percentage player; taking the good with the bad, what you could, when you could. I believe you have changed, that you truly care for someone other than yourself. But you are right, we were always honest with each other; and the way I see it, the odds are still in my favor."

"Don't fool yourself Del, for you it was always all or nothing."

"In that case, I guess I won."

Royal Hotel, May, 1935

A few minutes later Adel stepped into the darken room of her and WC's suite. She reached for the lamp, when the room flooded with lights and WC sat grinning at her.

"Startled, she said, "Will what in the hell is wrong with you?"

"How was your evening darlin, that dress and perfume is enough to raise the dead", WC Gabriel said, as his eyes roamed over his wife appreciatively. "I thought you would be prostrate with worry over our son, after that pretentious display you put on for Gent."

Adel was not surprised to find him waiting for her; his presence was the only appropriate ending for this impossibly crappy evening.

One thing about WC he did not need whiskey to be nasty, he just had a natural affinity for being unpleasant. He rarely drank and never to excess; he hated the thought of not being in control too much.

"Yeah, I could see you were all broke up too, when you left me to go to the Sin & Gin", she said matching his tone. "What do you want Will? It's late, I'm tired and I am not in the mood for your shit."

She stepped out of her dress and sat at the vanity table to remove her jewelry and make-up; determined to ignore WC. Not an easy task since he was reclining on her bed wearing a cream satin boxer's robe and she suspected little else. WC was all hard planes and contours with skin as buttery soft as expensive fine grained leather, the color of strong brewed coffee.

"What's wrong darlin; you upset he turned you down, don't worry papa is still here. After all he is my brother, what did you expect? Damn woman, you couldn't even wait 24 hours, WC asked with a laugh?"

"Shut up Will, you don't nothing, you never did."

"But you see that's the point, I do know. I know everything and I know you too, better than Gent ever did. You got your own set of rules and realities from the rest of the world. You were upset earlier, crying over your children, maybe a little worried about me.

"Do you have a point WC it has been a long twenty-four hours?"

"The point is, with everything that is happening you still could not resist the urge to see him and show him what he missed."

"Oh what if I did. It meant nothing. It was you that I chose; it was you that I married."

"So you did darlin, so you did and I am extremely grateful, but then you were always smart and oh so sweet", said WC, leaning down to press kisses along her supple neck."

There was time when Adel hated her own traitorous body. She knew WC wanted an emotional scene, but he would not have it. He could think what he liked.

She would guard her bruised ego and feelings, they belong to her to touch and brood over, even wallow in if she liked, and she would not share them or allow him to intrude for his amusement. But she would not fight the pleasure of his touch, or the heat of unbidden desire sweeping through her body, as he gently kneaded her shoulders and back.

Gent's return had rekindled memories of romance, which her husband had never been particularly good at. WC enjoyed sex; like he enjoyed a good meal, or appreciated a fine cigar, and he wasted little time on what he called sentiment.

Making love was a sport with no holds barred. WC knew her body as well as his own, there were no secrets and little sacred. Between them was a raw sexual energy that would not be denied. The frenzy of youth had been replaced by slow, deliberate sensation and continued to be highly satisfying.

She had ceased trying to rationalize their relationship a long time ago. She knew he would never hurt her, and even now if she said no, he would leave her to her thoughts; but not tonight, she decided, as she reached up to be drawn into his arms.

Chapter

Atlanta, May 27, 1935

Win's home was covered with frills and knickknacks, but Sinclair had refused to allow one piece of bric-a-brac in his domain and the room had a decidedly air of masculinity. His instruments still lay in the velvet lined cases and a Steinway piano dominated one wall and a well-stocked bar the other. Overstuffed sofas and chairs fill the room, elegant but comfortable. On the center table was a gilt-edged silver box containing cigarettes, a matching humidor of fine Cuban cigars, and a sliver-plated lighter.

WC admired few people, but the late lamented Sinclair had been a man of style with an appreciation for the finer things and it irritated him to find Steban waiting for them; enthroned in the comfortable living space like a king waiting for his subjects.

Steban greeted Gent cordially. "It is good to see you boy, thank you for coming", he said with a handshake followed by a hug. He acknowledged WC, with a nod, looking inquiringly as a third man entered.

WC said, "This is Dorsey, I decided to even out the numbers, besides he knows all the particulars, and I trust him."

Dorsey stepped forward and offered his hand. "It's an honor to meet you Mr. Gabriel."
Taking the man's measure, Steban decided he liked what he saw.

Steban said, "If you would all sit down, there are some things I need to say. As I told you last night, Justin Overfield is dead", lifting his hand as WC was about to protest. I know that doesn't mean anything, but Trent could not be involved either; by all accounts he is on his honeymoon."

WC snickered, saying, "Oh yeah, him and Tatum's daughter; pudding-faced, but a nice body."

Steban said, "So you see he could not have anything to do with what happen last night or with Edmond. David Maitland informed me two weeks ago that someone had been making inquiries regarding our finances, one of which he traced back to Justin. What concerned me is he could not discover where the others originated."

"Ok, so maybe all that is true, but as soon as the loan is due, what's to keep Trent from following through on Justin's threats", said WC?

"The loan is paid."

"What", exclaimed WC? Gent said, "Steban I don't understand, how?"

"Your grandmother", Steban said with a small smile."

"Damn old man will you stop talking in riddles", said WC

"Perhaps this will begin to explain", said Steban, handing him Rosa's letter.

"I don't believe it", said WC, handing the letter to Gent.

Gent looked up at his uncle, "I take it that there's more?"

"Those keys your grandmother left opened a safe containing some thirty thousand dollars in cash, and in access of 50,000 worth of jewelry, gifts from papa during their forty years of marriage and apparently including some pieces your father gifted to your mother before their death."

"But why didn't she say something, she had to have known we needed the money?"

"I understand why, that is all that is necessary", replied Steban.

"That old woman had more sides than a rectangle barn, but she loved Angel's Trumpet. I can't believe she did not say something. Maybe, I didn't know her as well as I thought", said WC.

"I had not seen her for some time of course, but perhaps old age had affected her mind", said Gent, ignoring WC's hoot of laughter.

"Not, hardly. She once told me everywhere she went she had to wait while they serviced the white folks, said she'd be damn if she would wait in line to give them her money. I guess I never thought she meant that literally", said Steban.

Shared laughter over the woman they had rarely understood, but loved despite everything brought a moment of closeness between the three men, but they sobered quickly.

"But why send Edmond to Maitland, why the secrecy", questioned WC.

"To be honest I did not want another argument with you WC or listen to recriminations against your grandmother. I received a wire from Maitland so I know everything went alright. Edmond should have returned at least four days ago", said Steban.

"Old man, me and you are like oil and water, probably always will be, but we are still family; if, however I discover something has happened to my son, all bets are off", growled WC.

Gent said, "Fontaine was in France, Edmond in New York and Cassandra here, yet somehow I now believe it is all connected. I am convinced just as Uncle Steban that the Overfields could not be involved, which means we are dealing with unknowns."

Steban said, "I did not know about Fontaine until Win called me. She was upset so I decided to take an earlier train. How all this relates to the attempt to kidnap Cassandra or Edmond's whereabouts, I don't know."

WC said, "Steban did you say that Maitland informed you there had been other inquiries into our finances, maybe this about nothing but money."

"Edmond's been gone almost a week, if it was about money, why haven't we heard something. Fontaine has been missing just as long; the telegram Win received did not say much, only that Fontaine was missing, nothing about a ransom, but I have placed a transatlantic call to my partner and as soon as he responds, I'll have some answers", said Gent.

"But if as you say, the family was facing bankruptcy and someone checked the family financial affairs, they had to know they were beating a dead horse, since no knew about the hidden money and jewelry", Minton Dorsey injected softly.

"But the fact that we were facing bankruptcy was not generally known in Atlanta, and even if Maitland Bank had been contacted, it would have taken time to receive the information. The whole thing was haphazard, the timing too chancy", said Steban

I believe locals were involved with a hastily hatched plan, for some quick money; which thankfully fell apart", interrupted WC.

"I don't know; that doesn't fit the little I found out after tracking Thomas Blue down. He admitted after a bit of persuasion, that he had left a note for Cassandra asking her to meet him on the terrace. Blue says he didn't know anything about the kidnapping; he was just accommodating an associate who promised to make his gambling debts disappear. The associate proved to be a dead end." But isn't there somebody else who would benefit", questioned Dorsey?

347

"No, I won't believe it", Steban said, realizing what Dorsey was implying. "I was against Jennet's marriage, but I would never believe Jamie capable of hurting the family."

WC said, "He's an Overfield, I wouldn't put nothing pass him."

The telephone rang in the foyer, and they were all at attention, hearing Sweetie's treading step, "Mr. Steban, you got a long distance call from New York."

"Thank you Sweetie", he said taking the telephone from her. "Hello."

"Steban, is that you."

"Yes Willa honey, I'm sorry but I……

"Steban they are holding me, I have a message, the man from Ethiopia says to tell you, you know what he wants", Willa said, before the phone was disconnected.

"Oh my god", whispered Steban before collapsing on the floor.

Part

Chapter

New York, June, 1935

J. John Tate pushed back from the table, the remains of a large meal scattered about. His lifestyle had slipped a notch or two since he had been forced to leave Chicago, he thought, looking around the three- room apartment, but he had a roof and the pool hall below turned a fair profit. Sooner or later Rossetti would have linked him with the Turners and he would have been caught up in the fallout. They had found Red Turner with his throat cut from ear to ear and his hands chopped off.

J John had always been a master at landing on his feet. He found as in times past, it paid to know the right people. The place had been a dump when he had taken it on, but safe and he had turned it into a paying proposition, taking policy slips for the numbers bank on the side.

He had left Lilly was downstairs watching things, but he knew it was time to return to the bar, else he would find Lilly with her hand in the money till or down the front of some dude's pants. He still couldn't figure out why the hell he married that bitch.

He had been stepping out of the toilet when a shadow loomed across the room. J John was so startled; he fell back against the door; bristling with anger when heard the laughter.

J John said, "What the hell is wrong with you man, why you got to always come sneaking around like some damn spook. You almost scarred the shit out of me. I suppose you here to pick up the betting slips, they downstairs."

Mace Turner viewed J. John's anger with humorous contempt. "Why you so jumpy, somebody would think you had something to hide and how many times I got to tell you not to leave that hustling bitch you married downstairs alone."

Mace had turned up on his door-step a few years back, a little less pretty with one ear shot off. He had money which J John had needed so be had become a silent partner. The only problem was the "silent" partner was never silent.

Everybody believed Mace had died in that shoot-out, yet here he was, hiding in plain sight and being a pain in his ass. Sometimes J. John thought how easy it would be just to make a phone call.

Mace's gaze narrowed, correctly interpreting the murderous gleam in the fat man's eyes, saying, "Now J. John, we both know that would be a wrong move. First of all, there is no profit in it. This dump and your little side lines are making you a tidy pile of cash. And secondly, but more importantly you know I would slit your fat throat and drop you in a hole like the sack of turds you are. Now get downstairs; we got some interesting visitors."

Gent stood outside the pool hall smoking a cigarette contemplating the odds of finding Edmond. Earlier there had been a few people lounging about the pool hall entrance, but they had scattered quickly enough when WC and Dorsey had stepped from the car and went inside. In this neighborhood folks had an instinct for trouble, it was how they survived.

WC had looked at him strangely when he decided to wait outside, but he and Dorsey had asked no questions. Gent was glad for once WC had not pushed, he was not in the mood for explanations. Who would have guessed that Dorsey would suggest J. John might be of help?

Gent had thought it best to nothing about the fact that he and the fat man had history. It could only jeopardize any information he might have concerning Edmond; and Gent was worried. Too much time had already passed and no one had heard from him.

Gent mentally compiled what they did know. After leaving Maitland Bank, Edmond had taken a taxi to Jennet apartment, and had taken another taxi to the train station. Since New York seemed to be the place he was last seen, they decided traveling to New York was the first step; especially after Omar informed them that Salim Akbar had a contact in the city.

Omar has investigated as much as he could on his end and discovered the name of an Italian family in New York with ties to Salim Akbar, that could be involved. If one of the New York families had taken part in Edmond's kidnapping, somebody had the answers. Dorsey claimed J. John's main hustle was still that same; he called him an "information broker."

WC was a little surprised that Dorsey knew where to find J. John, but he shouldn't have been. A man like John never cut the cord to anybody he thought might be able to help him. Dorsey knew J. John, who would sell out his own mama if there was profit in it; and while he was not big on the cliché of "keeping your enemies closer", he had thought it wise to keep tabs on the man.

After Steban had received the call from Willa, the older man had collapsed. Win had immediately called her doctor, and he had admitted Steban into the hospital. The doctor had made it clear that they were risking his life if he did not have complete rest for at least the next 24 hours and had put him under sedation.

The following day Steban was alert but what he had to say was not encouraging. He made it plain, that Edmond and Fontaine were in grave danger. If Salim Akbar did not get what he wanted, they and Willa was good as dead.

WC went crazy. Gent and Dorsey had to grab him as he lunged for Steban; while Win tried to calm the startled nurse as she threatened to call the police.

WC shook off Gent and Dorsey's restraining hold. His voice was barely above a whisper as he reined in his anger; saying, "Now Steban, are you telling me over twenty-five gawddamned years ago, this Salim Akbar tried to kill you because he wanted the medallion; what kind of damned fairy tale you spinning?"

"You involve Edmond without my knowledge; and now you tell me the crazy sonofabitch gonna kill my son until you give him a piece of jewelry, which you do not even have? Old man I'm gonna kill you", said WC".

Gent reached for him again, but Steban said, "Let him go, he has a right to his anger."

WC had spent a restless night, more afraid for his son than he had ever been in his life and he was so angry. He was angry at Steban, and angry at Edmond for not trusting him. He had been in no mood listen to ancient history and Steban's excuses, but until he heard it all, it was no way they could find Edmond.

Steban took an envelope from the pocket of his dressing gown and handed it WC after he returned to the room. WC refused to acknowledge Steban's apologies, as he opened the yellowed envelope and the medallion fell into his palm.

WC stood blinking at the gems gleaming in their ancient settings, his anger stymied, the confused look on his face brought a sigh of relief from Steban.

"Who is MCO", asked WC?

With a nod at Steban, Gent said, "That's not important, but it seems grandmother had it all the long. Evidently it was among the things Uncle Steban retrieved from the cellar safe."

"But why would she do that. She even had rings made for you and me, to replace the medallion she said Steban had lost", said WC?

Steban whispered, "Your grandmother had her own private demons, just as I had my own. What is important is that we have the medallion. It's all Salim wants, we give it to him and he'll release Willa and the others."

"Uncle Steban, Gent began gently, I don't know. My partner has an intimate knowledge of Salim Akbar; and he tells me Akbar is not the type to leave loose-ins. You told us how methodically he drew you in before and I have a bad feeling he has been watching me for a long time. He knows too much about our family and probably our finances also."

Steban dash tears from his eyes, "You are right of course, he has planned well and he knows us. What we need is an element of surprise. Salim likes to stay in the shadows and manipulate people and events. If we could find his contact here in the States, maybe we could get a jump ahead of him. After he learns I have the medallion, he will be ready to negotiate the trade, that should buy us another few days. Maybe long enough to trace Edmond."

"Even if he aint dead or on a slow boat to Africa, how the hell we gonna find Edmond in New York", said WC, after they had left the hospital?

Gent said, "I received a transatlantic call from my partner this morning, and I believe Steban is right, about locating Edmond, and that New York is the place to start. Salim has had business dealings of late with an Italian named Leopardi, whose family just happens to have business interests in the New York, but unfortunately he could not get a full name."

"Who is this partner of yours and how does he know so much", demanded WC.

"Omar was born among these people, and Salim Akbar is Omar's half-brother."

"Then how do we know he aint involved. Italians my ass, do you know how many damn Italians live in New York City, that name is probably as common as "Smith or Jones.""

"I know Omar", replied Gent coldly. "We have to start on the assumption that if they are involved with Salim, they got to be dirty."

"Oh, is that supposed to make me feel better, us against the New York mob?"

"WC you are out of your depth; you need your brother. Gent says he knows this man you got to trust his judgment. Besides, you and I know somebody who might be of help", said Dorsey.

"And me, the girl named Hollis had said from the doorway. If Edmond is hurt, he will need me."

Gent wondered how much they would trust his judgment if they knew the truth. He froze suddenly, as he heard footsteps behind him, and the unmistakable sound of a bullet being released into the firing chamber of an automatic pistol. He did not have to turn around to know that same gun was being pointed at his head.

"If I have said it once, I've said it a hundred times; there is nothing like a little initiative. When the word on the street tom-tom came down, that a contract all the way from Italy for a family of rich niggers named Gabriel, I knew my luck had changed. Evidently the Gabriels must be a giant pain in somebody's ass, to draw that kind of heat; just stands to reason you would be one of them."

"J. John used to tell us stories about his partners Dorsey and WC Gabriel and one day I'm reading one of our Negro publications, doncha know; and low and behold there's a picture of Mrs. W. C. Gabriel and daughter among the hostesses of some big society dance in Atlanta. The snatch of the daughter was a bust of course, but I never thought Dorsey and WC would show up here. Next to seeing you again however, all that is nothing."

"All while I was hiding, so I could heal up, after our little trouble with Rossetti, I wondered what you were doing, with all my money. They left me for dead, but then I don't die that easy. You and that bitch Leah ruined everything for me. Now turn around, real slow."

A shadow merged into the light of a street lamp on the corner and he was standing there; Mace Turner. Just as big, just as mean and missing an ear. "You remember me sweetheart?"

"Hell yes", said Gent, before he shot him dead.

Inside the pool-hall, J. John was all smiles as he greeted his guests, "Hey Dorsey and damn is that Mr. W.C. Gabriel, long time, no see; how the hell is tricks?"

Dorsey just smiled; when J. John was his most affable, that's when you got to watch him the closest. He nodded at WC, who moved to cover the entryway of the small office.

Still smiling, J. John said, "Dorsey what the fuck is all this hostility about?"

"Aw shit, J. John, you know WC aint never been sociable; but me and you, we go way back, which is why I am sure you aint gonna fuck around; cause if you don't answer my next question just right, I might just have to redecorate the room with pieces of your brain."

"Now Dorsey everything is negotiable, no need to threaten, just tell me what you need."

"Alright I want to know about Italians, those that would have an interest in Harlem?"

"Man, I don't nothing about no Italians."

"Wrong answer", said Dorsey

"Wait", said J. John, starting to sweat. I need to make a phone call."

Dorsey let his glance drift from the top of J John's bald head and sweating face to the worn felt bedroom slippers on his feet. "Let me tell you something J. J, just in case you thinking of doing something stupid, no matter whatever else happens, you gonna be the first one to die. Now I want you to keep that in mind, and remember you are a businessman, that there's profit to be made, all you got to do is give me a name."

"Just give me a minute", J. John said. He had dialed Mace's number twice, but there was no answer. He was supposed to be just around the corner at the news stand. Then J. John recalled Mace asking him about WC's family; what the shit had he got him into and where the hell was he? He should be here to handle this mess. And Lil, he was gonna kick her ass. She let them in without a word and was probably somewhere hiding.

He was not sure about WC, but Dorsey was not a man to play games with. Mace might be the devil to come, right now he had to deal with the devil that was; and saving his own ass had always been his number one priority.

Dorsey could almost see the little wheels turning in John's brain as he waited for him to weigh all the odds, but then J. John was always smart. He turned to Dorsey and said, "The name you want is Joe Tosellini; Harlem is considered his territory."

"And where might one find Mr. Tosellini?"

"Yeah, I hear he's a big jazz fan, you should find him at Club Gibson on 52nd Street. He owns the place."

"Now you see how helpful you can be", said Dorsey, tossing J. John five one hundred dollar bills. You keep your mouth shut and there will be five more to match those in your hand."

"One more thing Dorsey, consider it some free advice, unless you got an army with you, Joe Tosellini ain't nobody you want know; you will be a dead man walking if you get on the wrong side of that white boy."

Outside, Gent looked ruefully at the blacken hole in his coat pocket. There had been no time to debate his action. It had to go badly. Mace might have known something, but it had to die with him, Gent thought as he pulled Mace's body into a dimly lit alleyway.

It was too late to worry about what anybody might have seen or heard, but he did not think Mace was the type to generate a lot of mourners.

He saw no need to inform his brother or Dorsey about the body lying a hundred yards from the car; at least not yet. Things were getting more complicated by the minute, but Dorsey had a name.

Chapter

Joe Tosellini was seated in a private alcove above the club's main floor, surrounded by plastic palm trees. He liked the fan-fair created when he arrived, greeting friends and enemies alike. Once he was seated no one walk up those three stair steps into his private domain without his permission. When he left he used a private exit that led to the parking lot.

He was an attractive man who loved fine clothes and women of all persuasion. He had risen through the ranks by mayhem and death; making his "bones" with his first "hit" when he was only fifteen. He was ambitious and some of his associates thought he lacked the proper respect, but Tosellini ran his territory with undiscriminating violence; he knew how to handle the Jews and the Coloreds and all they cared about was profit.

One of the bouncers came in and whispered to one of Tosellini's body guards seated at the tables on either side of the stairs and handed him a card. The guard waited until he could pry Tosellini's attention from his female companion.

Tosellini looked up saying, "Go powder something baby." The guard waited until she was gone.

"Mr. Tosellini"

"What is it already?"

"You have a visitor sir", the guard said handing him the card.

Tosellini read the card laughing, he said, "Is this on the level." A prince of Ethiopia to see me; oh yeah, send, ah Lord Tesseme on in.

Hollis had sat in her room unable to sleep, her mind on Edmond. She had read books where people wrote about broken hearts. A lot of foolishness, she had always thought. But she felt that if something happened to Edmond, her heart would break. She loved him, and she regretted that it had taken her so long to realize it.

Her insecurities had not permitted her to believe that he truly wanted her. He had never acted like a lover; he was always her friend, treating her with a careless brotherly affection. She realized now that she needed to know once and for all that he wanted her as a woman and not a pet project. If she lost him now, how would she ever know? She been waiting for him all her life; waiting to give herself to the right man. She could not imagine being with anyone except Edmond.

At the moment she was trying to keep her knees from shaking with fear. Earlier, however she had almost regretted her decision to come along. She had wanted to be there for Edmond and she had begged the three men to allow her to accompanied them, pointing out that she as well as Dorsey was unknown.

Edmond's life depended on his father and uncle and the two had bickered continuously since they had left Atlanta. After the trio had returned to the rooming house where they were staying, it was more of the same.

"Why did we come back here, we got the name, let go find Edmond", grumbled WC.

"Use your head WC, two Negro men cannot walk into that club demanding to see Tosellini. Money and threats got you what you needed from J. John; but you try that with this crowd, the only thing you gonna do is make Adel a widow", said Gent.

"And I suppose you got something that's gonna make you magically white in that suitcase you keep rifling through."

"Not white, I had something a little more exotic in mind", Gent had said laughing.

After Gent had explained the plan to Hollis it seemed easy enough. She was to be the distraction, but as she stood arrayed in lavender silk that display every curve of her body, she was shaking so bad she couldn't think.

Gent squeezed her hand, and whispered, "All you have to do is look beautiful and remember you are a royal lady. You already got the first down pat. Just stay close by my side and keep your head up, your eyes downcast, I'll handle the rest, Gent said as they followed the guard into Joe Tosellini presence.

Hollis watched Gent take on another character as he clicked his heels and bowed formally from the waist, wearing a tuxedo complete with tails, speaking with a thick foreign accent. She in turn curtsied low, leaning on Gent for support, not daring to raise her eyes if she could. She could feel Tosellini's eyes on her, stripping away the silk cloth wrapped around her body.

"Alright Prince, what can I do for you?"

Gent bowed again. "Gracious sir, if I may present myself, I am Lord Jeffa Tesseme, emissary of the ambassador to his royal imperial highness the Emperor of Ethiopia and this is my consort, Lady Bebe. I have been sent to offer my government's profound thanks, in addition to the monetary reward for aiding us against that usurper, Mussolini and those that serve him. The information the two traitors would have sold could have been detrimental, to our country's defenses. On behalf of his imperial highness, let me once again…."

"Wait a minute; hold it, what information, what monetary reward?"

"Why gracious sir, we were informed that the two had been apprehended by a member of your society here in America, that one of your, how do you say troops in a place called…ah yes, Harlem."

"Ah excuse me prince, he said motioning to a one of his men, "Johnny where is Vincente?"

"I aint sure Mr. Tosellini, he said you give him the night off."

Vincente Leopardis was his mother's youngest sister's son by one of the bastard Leopardis. The boy was family and he had promised his mother he would help him after the Leopardis smuggled him out of Italy; once Mussolini began eradication of the Black Hand society. Tosellini was a third generation American and Italy's woes with Mussolini, while tragic were not his concern, but his family and territory was.

"Listen I want you to take Pauly and find Vincente. Check out the riverfront warehouse first; and Johnny, if Vincente should have any guests, bring them too.

Tosellini turned around, "What happen to the Prince and the broad."

"They went out the back Boss; I thought you were finished with them."

"Yeah, well they won't be hard to find; you just find out what's going on."

Hollis looked at Gent curiously as they hurried toward the car, "Where did all that come from?"

Gent smiled, "I just made it all up, he said, not bothering to explain Omar's speculations. "Alright, so far so good; all we got to do is follow Hansel and Greta and the bread crumbs."

"Who the hell is Hansel and Greta", said WC?

"Just follow the car", replied Gent.

Chapter

New York, New York, June, 1935

They followed Tosellini's men east, toward the Bronx, trying to keep them in sight, without revealing they were being tailed. They crossed the Third Avenue Bridge, and everybody was getting jittery, knowing they were out of their element, when the car made a sharp right toward a small outcropping of buildings.

"Pull over Dorsey, I think we are going have to walk in the rest of the way", said Gent. They watched as the car went straight ahead at least another quarter of a mile and the headlights of the car dimmed.

WC watched as Dorsey pulled a canvas bag from the back seat. "What's in the bag?"

"You can bet it aint nothing exotic, just good ole American made", Dorsey replied, handing WC a .38 caliber revolver, smiling appreciatively at the .45 Colt semiautomatic in Gent's waistband.

"Are you ready", Gent said to his brother; having recognized a kindred spirit in Dorsey.

"I don't guess nobody gonna questioned your expertise, you and me should have a long talk later", said WC.

Gent grinned in the darkness, "Yeah we got to do that", then more soberly, "you ready?"

"Damn right, let's go get my son."

They moved swiftly, through tall grasses, until they got to the graveled driveway, couching silently outside the front of the building. Dorsey moved to the right; Gent to the left, signaling WC to stay in the shadows out front.

Removing their shoes, the two men moved as quickly as possible. Once in position, Dorsey peered through a small sooty pane, his visibility was nil so he maneuvered around until he could see through a corner on the opposite side of the window. He spotted the two they had followed speaking to a third guy in rapid Italian; then saw Edmond tied in a chair. Blood ran down the side of his face and he was unconscious. Dorsey crawled on his belly to the end of the building looking for Gent; rolling backward as four men step out, two dragging Edmond toward the car.

Damn, thought Gent, as he viewed the scene from the shadows; nothing was ever easy. Tosellini would not be amused at being made to look like a fool, but after all, Tosellini was only interested in his territory and money; maybe he would just let the matter drop. But after the body he left in the alley, Gent was past being fastidious. His family's lives were at stake.

Gent eased along the side of the building, pausing at the corner; he spoke to the men in halting Italian. "Don't move, we just want the boy, it is not worth dying over."

The two carrying Edmond dropped him to the ground, all four men pulling their guns, peering into the darkness. Two of the men circled to the right, stepping directly into the line of Dorsey's aimed revolver. Dorsey's gun acted as his interpreter as he edged the duo back the way they came.

Suddenly they all heard the gun fire. The two held at bay by Dorsey suddenly surged forward, only to be brought up short as Dorsey emptied a couple barrels, one in each man's foot. "Alright move your asses, and next time, it'll be a knee", Dorsey said gesturing with his gun.

"Hey partner, you OK", he shouted to Gent.

"Yeah as long as you keep shooting them in the foot", said Gent as he motioned the other two men toward the front door.

Watching from the darkness, WC waited until Gent and Dorsey took control of the four thugs, before rushing to his son. Edmond was still as he lay on the ground, but his pulse was steady. WC paused long enough to remove the distributor cap from the car, and slit all four tires; before lifting Edmond from the ground, and carrying him back to Hollis.

Dorsey said, "Hey, you speak their lingo, ha I didn't expect that. I was wondering how we would handle that piece of business. But you know these two are not really important", pointing to the two Tosellini thugs he had shot.

"Now our new friends look like they might have a lot to say, and I would be willing to bet they could say it English, but just in case, why don't you explain in Italian they should face the wall, hands up and wide."

Gent spoke the words and they moved slowly to comply.

Dorsey, continuing to gesture with his gun said, "Move! I aint as polite as my friend, I would just as soon put an American bullet in your fucking Italian brain. You wanna keep breathing, you better keep them lips as close to that wood, as you do Tosellini's ass."

"Grinning widely, Gent said, "You remind me of a friend of mine."

"Man can never have enough friends, Dorsey said", reaching into the canvas bag he had taken from the car and tossing Gent two pairs of handcuffs. "Why don't you show the boys all about togetherness?"

Dorsey covered the group with his gun, while Gent handcuffed two men on each side of the metal poles supporting the awning over the front entrance. The two Dorsey shot limping badly.

Dorsey said, "The one on the end was doing all the talking, when I saw them through the window."

Walking passed the driver and his partner, Gent came instead to the last man, shoving his gun underneath the soft flesh of his chin. Again he spoke in Italian. "Where is the woman"?

"Fuck you nigger", he said plainly in accented English. Gent brought the gun butt down hard across his face smashing the man's nose into a bloody mess.

Dorsey said, "Partner that aint how you translate, you pointing at the wrong end; his brain is located further down."

Dorsey rammed the barrel of his pistol up between the man's buttocks; saying, "Now then, I got your attention, Man asked you a question; if you want to keep having two balls to scratch I suggest you tell him what he wants to know."

"Where the hell you two been this ain't no cops and robbers", WC said, as Gent and Dorsey finally emerged from the darkness; fifteen minutes later?

Gent said, "WC your friend Dorsey is a very resourceful man to have around."

"Yeah well he has his moments, right now we need to get the hell out of here."

"How is Edmond?"

"I think he's OK; but still unconscious."

Turning to Dorsey, Gent said, "I just got one question; where in the hell did you get those handcuffs?"

"I'm a boy scout, don't you know, always be prepared."

WC looked at the two of them, as if they were crazy. Gent said, "Come on, I'll explain it to you on the way to the docks."

"The docks?"

"Yeah, we're going to Chelsea Piers, dock 94; The USS Columbia."

"Gent thank you for saving him", she said, cradling Edmond's head in her lap", said Hollis timidly.

"It could not have been done without you my dear, you were superb tonight."

"There is something I need to tell you. While you were out earlier I was reading the newspaper and I got to looking at the sailing times and arrivals. I don't know why, except I knew it might be a possibility that your aunt and Edmond were no longer in the country. What I am trying to say, the Columbia was scheduled to sail for France at midnight and it is already 12:45."

"Damn, we're too late."

Chapter

Willa woke in a daze. Her head was pounding, her mouth so dry she could not shallow. She was lying in some type of box, but when she sat up the top opened easy. She tried to stand, but lurched dizzily, the floor beneath her feet seemed to be moving and she realized she was below deck of some type of boat; Willa grimaced at the thought, she disliked the water.

She sat down on a shipping crate trying to get her drugged mind to work. She remembered walking from the Hoffman's bakery and suddenly feeling faint. The other memories came back slowly. She had spoken to Steban on the telephone. She was in trouble and Steban was too far away to help her.

When she was young and got into trouble, she would often pose the question, "what would Win do", but it never helped, she lacked her sister's imagination. Now, like always she would have to figure it out for herself.

.

She guessed the boat was docked; she could not hear anyone moving above, only the lap of water against the side of the boat. The first thing she needed to do was to get topside. She looked around for something to use as a weapon until she stumbled over a wooden pole near her feet. Clutching the pole in her hand, Willa started to creep slowly up the few steps topside.

It was a moonless night with a few lights scattered along the Marina. It took a moment for Willa's eyes to adjust to the darkness, as she took inventory of her surroundings. In the distant she could see lights from what she thought might be the facilities on Ellis Island.

The boat was not exactly a boat, but a yacht gleaming whitely in the darkness, the deck and trim of polished wood. The Marina moorings housed other yachts of various sizes, but the area seemed to be deserted; there was only the quiet splash of water. So far, so good she thought, as she eased off the yacht down the docking bay to the pier, until she saw the glow of a flashlight.

Could it be someone coming back for her? Panic clouded her thinking; whoever was out there was still far enough off, but she hesitated, not knowing whether to hide or run. She chose the latter, which prove to be the wrong decision, for she had not gotten very far when she heard a shout as a uniformed guard closed in fast on her heels, calling after her to stop.

Willa's adrenaline was pumping, but she was no shape for a sprint. She was fighting for breath as a sickening ripple of nausea engulfed her. She continued to grope forward, but her feet became entangle, and she toppled headlong into the dock.

The night watchman finally reached her side. He kneeled down for a closer view, pushing back the visor of his cap in surprised to discover she was Colored. She was unconscious, but her pulse in her throat was beating crazily against his fingers. He looked around, but could see no one else and guessed it would be alright to leave her while he called the cops. What was a woman her age was doing prowling around Mr. Tosellini's yacht; he wondered, as he moved off toward the nearest call box.

New York Harbor

WC had insisted that they drive to the docks, but aside from the usual bustle of activity, it seemed the Columbia had sailed on schedule. They were at a lost as to what to do next. They hadn't a clue to Willa's location and Edmond needed a doctor.

Dorsey said, "We got to move. Tosellini men are gonna be looking for us and since they gave us the information they will know exactly where we are.

WC said, "We are missing something."

"That's evident", returned Gent dryly.

"No think about it, if the ship's departure was at midnight, why was Edmond still being held at that warehouse. He was still tied up when Tosellini's goons got there."

"Lying bastards, OK, maybe that means that they were putting them on a later ship. Hollis do you recall any other sailing."

"Why yes, the USS Libertine, at 7:00 p.m. this evening.

"They had Edmond on the riverfront; it stands to reason that Willa must be nearby also."

"Yeah but where", said WC.

"Wait a minute said Dorsey, Tosellini didn't know about Edmond or Willa. They must have stashed them close to the pier so he wouldn't find out about them before they could get them on that ship. Come on, we need to find a telephone."

Five minutes later Dorsey returned to the car. Our mutual friend, J. John, was a little more forthcoming since I promised him another five "large." "It appears Mr. Tosellini keeps a yacht."

Gent said, "The Marina."

"It's worth a try."

After arriving at the Marina the group recognized they were faced with a few problems. First was the Marina lacked the bustle of the docks, which meant two Negro men, wandering about at this hour would immediately be stopped and questioned. They had remained parked in the lot overlooking Marina long enough to observe the watchman complete his rounds and had spent since at least another hour trying to come up with a plan. Soon the night watchman would be coming around again.

Gent moved to get out of the car. "Let's go", he said

WC said, "In that fancy getup, what are you going to do; I don't think that prince bit is going to work twice."

Gent was about to argue when Dorsey interrupted, "WC is right, this calls for something else." Dorsey quickly removed his jacket, his white shirt and shoes. Then he put his jacket on again, buttoning it close at the neck; urging WC to do the same.

"Camouflage", said Dorsey grinning

Choking back laughter, Gent said, "OK, what is the plan?"

Dorsey said, "Don't have one, we just gonna play it by ear, WC you let me do the talking."

Finding Tosellini's yacht would not be easy. The Marina was not brightly lit, but a flashlight would alert the guard to their presence. That didn't mean they could not take advantage of the watchman's flash light.

The watchman followed his regular routine, and never noticed the two men moving stealthy behind him; checking each docked yacht as they passed.

They had moved along about a hundred yards, when the watchman stopped and shouted. The two men froze; sure the watchman had realized he was being following.

Dorsey was about to try to talk their way out when WC grabbed his arms and pointed. Someone was running ahead of them. They heard the clatter of heels and a woman scream, then nothing.

Dorsey and WC dropped to the ground rolling into the shadow of a nearby yacht; just out of range of the watchman flashlight as he circled the area with the beam of light.

They waited, pressed into the hard planking as the watchman kneeled down to examine whoever had fallen. Finally, the watchman stood and starting walking hurriedly along the walkway.

Pushing himself up, WC said, "We gotta get closer fast, he is looking for a call box and we are going to be up to our asses in cops."

WC began calling out loud, "Mama, mama." Dorsey looked surprised but started echoing WC, as they moved closer to the body laying so still.

WC could have almost shouted with relief when he got close enough to see it was Willa. However, the night watchman had turned back after hearing WC and Dorsey.

"Who the hell are you two, what are you doing here", he demanded, his hand resting atop his holstered gun, his light shining in WC and Dorsey's faces.

Looking confused, WC began babbling, "Unh, I'm sorry sur, but we been looking for our mama. She old you know and a little tetched in the head."

"I said who are you, I won't ask again?"

WC said, "Well see that what I wuz saying. You see my nephew Roy he got a job as a cook on one of them big boats and we wuz just seeing him off and somehow my mama just wondered away. We been looking all along the piers when some man told us they saw an old Negro woman wandering toward the Marina.

Dorsey said, "We been looking for her since late this evening and I tell you I am bone tired."

"Your mother you say, OK don't move, I got to call it in."

Wait a minute sur if you do dat the police will come and she just an old lady and we might be held cause we let her get away", said Dorsey, silently praying the flashlight not shine on their stocking feet.

"Shut up Luther its yo fault she got away. This here my brother Luther, officer, but what I trying to say if you would just let us take our mama home we would be willing to pay; meaning no disrespect of course", said WC.

"You trying to bribe me boy?"

"Noo sur, it just that together we got 40 dollars with tips and our weekly pay and you can have it all if you just let us go."

The night watchman looked at the two skeptically, saying, "Well I don't know, let me see the money."

Yes, sur, we got it right here, give me your half Luther and I don't want to hear your mouth." Dorsey reached in his pocket and pull out a crumbled five-dollar bill and some ones and WC did the same.

"Here you go sur, that forty-five dollars", said WC, dropping the money into the night watchman outstretched cap"

"Ok you two get your mama and get out here and don't let me see you apes around here again."

They stooped a still unconscious Willa up and hurried along the Marina, back to the car as fast as they could.

Dorsey said, "I wonder what he gonna do when Tosellini's men show up."

WC said, "I don't know, but I hope he can swim."

Chapter

Fortress of Naqura, Ethiopia, June, 1935

Salim Akbar viewed the young man chained before him. He considered himself a man of

infinite patience, but boy's behavior was beginning to weary him. He had only been bait after

all, to draw in Gent Gabriel; when Gabriel had unknowingly side-stepped Salim's trap and his

hirelings delivered the boy instead.

The boy was as stubborn as Steban, as a result his men had not been gentle and he was quite

battered. Yet he continued to be difficult, refusing to speak or answer questions. Perhaps a

different method of persuasion might be more effective. The boy was still alive because Nemri

had urged Salim not to be hasty in killing him; however, if he continued to prove valueless to

Salim, it would be swiftly arranged.

Lady Nemri Tesseme sighed regrettably as she glazed at her young lover. She would mourn his

passing, because whether Salim got what he wanted or did not, Fontaine would surely die. He

had been so sweet and what he had lacked in experience he had made up in vigor. She had been

rewarded as his instructor in lovemaking with much pleasure, but life was filled with difficulties

and disappointments. One had to look for the advantage in every situation to survive

comfortably.

As a young girl, her family had married her off to a man old enough to be her grandfather, but

she had quickly learned to please the old man and he had showered her with luxuries, catering to

her every whim.

She had discreetly taken a lover and was extremely content; until the fool decided he could not bear to share her affections and had dispatched her elderly husband to the next world.

Disavowed by her husband's family and her own, Nemri escaped death with the help of her nursemaid who had cared for her since she was a child.

Women of her class were sheltered and most would not have survived alone in the world; Nemri however, was intelligent as well as resourceful. She had absconded with all of her jewelry and managed to set herself up advantageously. Soon her delicate beauty attracted a protector in the guise of Salim Akbar.

The fact that he was a kinsman mattered little. Their relationship which was tenuous at best. Nemri's mother had been the daughter of one of Adi Akbar numerous female children; fathered, on one of his several mistresses, while Lady Lydia, Salim's mother, turned a blind eye.

Nemri loved Salim as much as she was capable of loving anyone other than herself. She ordered his household, caring little about the wife he had at Court. As a lover, Salim had taught her the sensuality of her young body, lavishing her with pleasure in a dozen ways.

Salim enabled Nemri to live in the comfort which she felt entitled. If occasionally he asked that she do him small favors, such as seducing Fontaine Gabriel, it was little enough to her.

She dipped a cloth in the bowl of cool, herbal scented water and carefully sponged Fontaine's bruised face. His eyes fluttered then open, staring at her wondrously.

"Nemri you are safe."

"Yes my poor darling, I am well."

"I was on my way to you; then I can't remember. Those men, who are they, what do they want from me and how are you here?"

"Shh, you must rest now my sweet, do not try to talk. I am safe and you are here with me, nothing else matters."

Fontaine struggled to remain alert, but soon he had drifted into a drugged sleep once again, lulled by the softness of Nemri's voice and comforting entreaties.

Salim was waiting for her outside the chamber door. "Well", he questioned?

"He must sleep off the effects of the drug, but do not worry my love; whatever he knows, soon you shall also."

Chapter

Djibouti, June, 1935

Nathan banged his hand on the table. Anger was an emotion he had not allowed to rule his

actions for many years; with much effort, he reined in his temper.

"Omar we need answers, Gent left Fontaine in our care, we must find him."

"I have done what I can, we must wait. People are afraid to speak, even to me."

Nathan observed how quiet Lowe had become. He knew the man blamed himself, but no one

could have anticipated what had happened. Self-recriminations were useless at this point.

He said, "Lowe let it go man; we need to know everything Fontaine has been involved in for the

last few months. You spent a lot of the time with him; maybe we have overlooked something."

"Ah Nathan, you know the kid had been grieving over his daddy, I was just trying to help. He

had wanted to travel to Ababa Addis for some time, but I had been unable to obtain the travel

permits. Then out of the blue I received confirmation from the English consulate through an

assistant secretary by the name of Grantham. Later when I checked, no one had heard of an

assistant secretary by that name."

Fontaine supposedly had been granted permission to travel with a group of archeologists from

England after one of the group had become ill and someone was quickly needed to replace him.

The research had been sanctioned by the government and Fontaine was to assist in the labeling and cataloging of religious artifacts. Fontaine had been so excited. I realize now that the whole thing must have been a set-up from the start."

Omar said, "Fontaine was asked to leave because of his conduct with an Ethiopian lady of rank. Gent and I discussed this before he left and we agreed that it made no sense. Fontaine was convinced that the lady was being held against her will. It had taken quite a lot of talking on Gent's part to persuade Fontaine not to pursue the matter until he returned from the States."

The letter Gent had received from Steban Gabriel was most urgent, and the trip to the States could not be postponed. I made the arrangements myself; Fontaine would travel with him as far as Marseille and wait. I don't understand why Fontaine would leave France."

We must cable Gent as soon as possible and let him know of Fontaine's disappearance. I will travel back to Morocco to discover what I can find out on that end."

A week later Omar returned and neither of the three men was pleased with the news. Gent had wired him to let them know he had received the information concerning Fontaine and that his nephew Edmond and Aunt Willa were also missing.

Omar said, "I heard from Gent this morning and what he had to say connects with everything I have been able to discover. According to Gent his Uncle received a threatening call from my half-brother Salim Akbar. It seems the kidnappings were all part of a blackmail scheme concocted by Salim. Only his Uncle Steban knows what he wants and he has suffered a stroke. But I know Salim, it is always about power."

"What I know is that Fontaine boarded a ship traveling back to Djibouti. Henri made the trip from Paris to Marseille to ascertain the truth. I myself discovered that he had gotten as far as the canal where he transferred to another ship continuing down the coast. His present was verified, at least until he got to Assab where he became ill and was taken off the ship.

My search was at an end, when I received word from an informant. The news I obtained was costly, but one of the men who carried Fontaine off the ship was recognized as a henchman of my brother, Salim Akbar, which supports what Gent has discovered", said Omar.

Nonplused, Nathan, fingertips arched before him in a pose Gent would have recognized, as he sought to come to grips with Omar's recital. "Salim Akbar, why would he kidnap Fontaine?" "And how would he get to Gent's nephew and his aunt; were they not in the United States"

"I have no answer right now, but we know Salim is involved. I have telephoned Gent with all I have been able to find out concerning Salim's recent dealings. I can only add that whatever Salim's reasons I am sure Fontaine is just a pawn in some larger game. Killing him would mean nothing to Salim. We must find him at all cost."

"Damn Omar we don't even know where to start", shouted Lowe.

"No my friend, you are wrong. Fontaine quarreled with Gent concerning an Ethiopian lady of rank of whom he was enamored; Lady Nemri Tesseme. We will start there."

When news of Omar's inquiries reached Salim Akbar he was incensed. Questions were being asked about Nemri, but he would use Omar's inquiries to his advantage. He just needed to plant the correct answers in the right source. His brother would soon regret his decision to interfere in his affairs. He would send him the boy's body back in pieces.

Nemri had informed him that the boy knew nothing about the medallion and Salim had ordered his throat cut, when he had received a garbled message from Carlos, that his cousin had met with an accident and that both his packages in United States had been lost.

Salim was not accustomed to having his plans thwarted and his rage had been explosive. The servants hid in fear and Nemri had locked herself in her room.

Nevertheless, reason reasserted itself, for Salim prided himself on his cool resolve. He was too much of a pragmatist to be truly passionate about anything, but he wanted that medallion. He would not lose to Steban Gabriel again. He swallowed the anger that threatened to resurface; channeling his analytical thought process toward another solution. It had been a mistake to permit control to be place in other hands on so many levels and allow Carlos's cousin to complicate matters. But there was another way. Soon Omar and his friends would be like flies in a spider's web. Gent Gabriel would deliver that medallion or he would take great pleasure in killing them all, one by one. He still needed bait, and luckily, he had not killed the boy.

Chapter

Atlanta, Georgia, July, 1935

Edmond and Willa had been hospitalized. The doctor diagnosed Edmond as having a concussion, and both were suffering the effects of being drugged, but they would recover.

They owed Dorsey a debt of gratitude they could never repay. Without the information, he had squeezed from J. John they could not have located the two in time, but Gent hoped it had not been at the cost of his friends' lives.

It had been too long since Gent had heard from Omar. He had received his last transatlantic call before they had travel to New York to find Edmond and there had been no communication from either Nathan or Lowe.

He had promised Steban he would come to Angel's Trumpet for a short visit, but that was no longer possible. Now he knew he had to return without delay after receiving a cable from Henri Milan, earlier that morning. He had managed to convince Win that Fontaine was safe, but the cable had confirmed his worst fear.

His friends were missing and no doubt in the hands of Salim Akbar. Steban was waiting for him when he came downstairs.

"I am very sorry Gentry."

"Uncle Steban they are my family. If I am to have any chance of freeing them, I must have the medallion."

"I already knew you would need it, it belongs to you now. He placed the medallion about Gent's neck. "I think you have already discovered its meaning. Come back son."

WC and Dorsey were seated in the taxi when he came out of the door. WC said, "Don't look so surprise, brother; I have never seen France, it is high time I found out what all the hullabaloo, is about."

Nonplus, Gent stared at his brother. "I don't know what to say WC."

"Don't say nothing, I owe you and I believe you are gonna need our help."

Once they arrived again in New York, Gent booked passage on a chartered plane to Paris; from there they would travel by train to Marseille.

Dorsey said laughingly, "I have never been on a plane; can we do that now?"

Gent said, "If you know the right people and have sufficient money, yeah some things can be done, but remember nobody asked the white man in front of me anything except for his passport and designation."

Angel Trumpet, August, 1935

Soon it would be harvest time. Angel's Trumpet was free of debt, but they needed this harvest to cover their operating expenses for the coming year. Nothing could happen to hinder that crop from being delivered to market.

Steban stood looking out from the window of his office. It was his office he thought; for the first time and not his father. He glanced lovingly around the room, running his hand over the smooth leather of his chair, reveling in this sense of reprieve from past mistakes, and forgiveness since discovering his mother's safe.

Mama, he thought, I understand many things now. She had taken the medallion away because she wanted to punish him, for he had not valued it until he thought it was gone. He had taken, but he had not given anything back. He wondered if she had ever forgiven Reese, after Jasset had been killed. He knew that she had loved him. Maybe she could not forgive him or herself. There surely had been enough guilt to go around.

A weight had been lifted from his heart but he was troubled as he watched his nephew's restless pacing. Edmond had not been the same since he had returned home.

And they had not heard from Gent or WC.

Angel Trumpet, 1935

Life had become unexpectedly complicated, thought Edmond. As a doctor he knew that he was

experiencing some post traumatic anxieties, like a solider after battle, but as a man it was an

unfamiliar feeling of helplessness he found hard to bear. He felt like a fool being taken like that,

knowing he could have died, that those men could have killed him at any time and there would

have been nothing he could have done to stop it.   Now everything had change. Everything he

had thought important had become shaded and warped.

He regretted not making the trip to Africa as he had planned; but the trip had only been a mean

of postponing questions about his life. He could at least he be honest with himself about that.

There had been plenty of grandiose ideas for the future, and no plan to implement them. He

always thought he had time.

He remembered his talks with Rev. Matt. Science verses spirituality; life and death, but he had

just never viewed it in terms of here and now. Death was something for the old. Death was

appointed to every man and when he was an old man, he would be appointed to die.

Maybe he was a coward, just as his father had once said. WC had accused him of running away

where life for a black man was easier, but his father was wrong, he did not believe such a place

existed. Even self-imposed exile offered no escape from your thoughts.

He knew what had happen had not been about racism; the one who had perpetuated this against

his family was not white, but his ordeal had stripped away the blinders he had worn too long. He thought about WC a lot these days. It was like being reintroduced to life as a Black man. His feelings for his father had just been wrapped up in so much anger and disappointment. Edmond was suddenly living with the terrible awareness that no matter his accomplishments he was considered less, because he was not white; that bigotry was a certainty and there was no escape.

It was the tightrope WC walked every day. To lose control could mean your life or the lives of your family. Yet, his father still got up every morning in pursuit of his dreams, pushing and pressing forward.

He did not know if he could live like that. Somehow he had separated himself from common black folks. He had sympathized with their sufferings, but he had never really seen their problems as his problems; and he had accused his father of being arrogant; he thought ruefully, his self-disgust complete.

He got up, pacing through the garden his great grandmother had created. She had constructed a patio floored with smooth stones of slate, and on either side vast amounts of roses, and flowering shrubs that she loved. Along the graveled path were pink and white dogwoods and cherry trees that had been imported by great-grandfather as a gift. Beyond was a clear vista of blue skies where the peach orchards grew, and the planted fields that lay ready for harvest.

He remembered as a child on warm evenings the family would gather here after dinner, his great-grandmother rocking contentedly in her chair looking out on the land. He would crawl into her arms and fall asleep every night. His great-grandfather had died in this garden, looking out on the land. He stopped for a moment and looked out as she and grandpa must have done so many times. What had given them the courage to go on, despite the obstacles they faced? He wished he understood what they had seen when they gazed out over the land.

He was still standing there, when a running figure snagged his attention back to the present and he recognized Hollis rushing frantically through the trees, toward the patio.

He still loved Hollis, but loving her would not be enough. She deserved more than he could give her right now. That day in the church yard seemed far away. She came every day to see him, but there was a strain between them that had never been there before. How could he make her promises and guarantees when his own world felt so uncertain?   His concerns dissolved, as Hollis ran into his arms.

"Oh Edmond, I hoped you would be back here, I didn't want to come into the house…I….

"Shh Hollis slow down, tell me what's wrong honey"

"It's Mae, Edmond I need you to come right now."

Mulberry Arms, Angel's Trumpet, 1935
Edmond finished his examination, putting away his stethoscope. He closed the door to the old woman's bedroom, watching Hollis jump to her feet anxiously.

"She has TB, Hollis; a very advanced case. I knew that when I examined her the first time. We don't have any facilities here; she needs to be in a sanitarium."

"Why, didn't you tell me?"

Edmond sighed tiredly, "Because Mae asked me not to and it was her right."

"Can't you do anything to help her", said Hollis crying.

"I can try to stabilized her condition and make her comfortable, but too much of her lung tissue is destroyed. It is only a matter of time."

Hollis broke down weeping, Edmond said, "Hollis Mae needs quiet and rest. To see you like this would only upset her, do you understand?" Hollis nodded and he continued, "Now I'm going to give her something to help her sleep, I thought you would like to see her first."

"I'm sorry Edmond, she said wiping her face. I am better now."

When they came in Mae looked so tiny lying amidst the pillows covering the bed. Her silvery hair had been loosed from braids, waved about her face. She was trying to speak, but it seemed to take great effort. "You two fighting bout me. Don't, I got to tell you; They coming tonight", she paused struggling to breath.

Edmond said, "Everything will be all right Mae, Hollis is here."

Mae clutch at Edmond's sleeved, "No, you don't understand, warning, coming for your family, overheard that boy; she said gasping for breath, Trent Overfield, nightriders."

Overton Plantation, August, 1935

It was late when Trent Overfield returned home, not so late, however, that the ever diligent John Henry was not there to take his hat and jacket.

"Will there be anything else, Mr. Trent."

"Yeah John Henry fix me a nice tall whiskey and soda, hell fix one for yourself, I feel like celebrating.

"And just what would you be celebrating, Trent."

Grinning broadly Trent came forward hand outstretched. "Papa Tatum, I had no idea you would be coming by this evening."

"Cut the line boy, I want to know what you doing agitating those rowdies at Kate's, this evening?" "Got 'em all liquored up; sprouting off about the supremacy of the white man; what you doing, planning to run for election", he continued sarcastically?"

"A man has a right to his opinion; I believe we gotta stand up for the white folks in this country."

"Don't give me that bullshit boy; you don't give a damn about them poor gape-seeds. You just using them to do what you and your granddaddy couldn't do for yourselves, take the Gabriel land."

"The affairs of Overfield have nothing to do with you Mr. Tatum. I am looking after the future of my offspring." I'm sure Vera has told you the happy news."

"Yeah she told me, but don't you be misled; my little gal is a lot of things, but don't make the mistake of thinking she's a fool."

Trent continued stiffly, "Your daughter is my wife and an Overfield; and I will conduct my marriage and my business affairs as I see best."

"Don't get on your high horse with me boy, not when you using Tatum money to finance your little enterprise", said Tatum, interrupting. You think I didn't notice them boys you brought in to stir up trouble."

Trent cross the room and seated himself behind his desk. No matter what he did, Tatum still looked like a dirt farmer, Trent thought. His faded blond hair stuck out in grey and blond turfs, and his hands were large with prominent knuckles sprinkled liberally with hair and freckles.

He had body proportions of the proverbial china shop bull and was just as awkward; but looks were deceiving. He was no country yokel, nor was he stupid. He had wanted Vera to be accepted in society, to breathe the rarified air of the Overfields and he had been willing to pay to accomplish that feat.

Trent did not want to alienate his father-in-law. He had been so sure once Vera had announced she was pregnant, that there would be no question of Tatum lending his support in eradicating the Gabriels from Overfield land; with the help of a few friends of course. It seemed however, he had misjudged his father-in-law as he looked into the man's brooding gaze.

Grandfather's death, had relieved Trent of the pretense of being a dutiful grandson, and he had no intentions demeaning himself before a man, that except for the fates, would have been sharecropping his land.

As if he had read his son-in-law's mind, Tatum said, "You tread lightly around me boy, you hear me, you tread lightly", abruptly he stopped speaking, his eyes focused on the window and the huge orange glow lighting the sky.

Angel's Trumpet, 1935

They were on horses, their white robes and hoods gleamed eerily in the glow of their torches as they slowly approached. Twelve riders, Steban thought humorlessly, come to pay their respects on the Gabriels.

Edmond stood silently beside his uncle. He thought of his father and the harsh words he had spoken to him in defense of his convictions. Now his father's words came back to haunt him.

"The Overfields or some other white man could come in and try to take everything we have worked hard for. You always talking about freedom and rights, those may be the words men live by, but my question to you is, are you willing to die for your ideals. "Count the cost boy, talk is cheap. A man oughta know what he is willing to face death for."

Looking out on the danger approaching his family and home, he realized he still did not have an answer to that question; living had become very important to him. He was jarred by the sight of his mother and John Mack walking into the room carrying rifles and ammunition.

"Mama what are you doing, you don't know how to fire a gun, Edmond whispered; the thought of his elegant mother loading and firing a rifle unnerving.

"My dear son I would have you know that your grandfather Ruben Tiggler could shoot the eye out of a possum at 100 yards and he taught me well, that's how we kept food on the table; just don't tell the girls in the Essex Club." More soberly she added, "Your father is not here, but I know what he would expect. Do you agree Uncle Steban?"

His uncle nodded, but he did not take the rifle she handed him, instead he walked out the room to the front door as the shouting from outside became louder.

"Steban Gabriel, come on out nigger, we want to talk to you. You come on out now, or we gonna burn the house down around your ears."

Steban paused, turning to those in the room, saying, "I don't know any more what is right or wrong, but whatever happens, just, stay alive. No matter what is lost here tonight if you stay alive, it can be rebuilt."

Outside the wind stirred, and the horses pawed the ground nervously, perhaps knowing instinctively the murderous urges abroad this night.

Steban heard someone said, "Let's burn the fields." To a man they stilled, looking out on the ripening crops. They were farmers and each knew the work and sweat it took to bring such a harvest to fruition, but the reflection only lasted the span of a few seconds.

Grif Miller thought of his own acres of land; him and his wife and family all working in the fields, barely getting by. Something turned in his stomach at destroying the fruit of the ground, but they were niggers. What right did they have to own so much when he and his family had so little. "Give me that torch", he shouted.

"Don't be a fool Grif."

"What's wrong Bobby Joe, you scared Arlo gonna tan your hide."

Bobby Joe McClure spat a stream of tobacco juice on the ground in the direction of the speaker.
He was nothin but an outsider brought in to do Trent's dirty work. He was not afraid of his
father but he knew Arlo would not be please that he was a part of this group. McClures tended
to their own. He just couldn't back down. They were mostly only local boys, except for Trent's
thugs and Grif was his friend.

Trent Overfield had been stirring them up with talk and liquor about how a white man got to look
out for his own. He was no nigger lover and neither was his pa, but his family didn't have no to
do with the Overfields or their affairs and the whole county knew they wanted the Gabriels'
property. But Bobby Joe's words of warning went unheeded as his friend rode toward the fields,
swinging the torch.

After the summer drought, the fields went up like kindling; the crackling flames blazing a swath
through the corn fields, as the wind picked up moving rapidly eastward toward the several farms
that lay in its path; one of them belonged to Grif Miller.

Their lust for blood and envy had blinded them to everything else. They were gonna kill them a
nigger tonight and they moved forward across the yard toward the house. Steban stood on the
front porch his face was streaked with tears, as he watched the farm's acreage, burning out of
control.

He shouted, "My god, do you realize what you have done."

"Well boy you should have thought of that 'fore you start smart-mouthing white men. You Gabriels ain't never known your place, but you will after tonight."

Steban smelled the heavy, choking scent of coal oil and he realized they meant to burn the house as well. Burn his mother and father's home; he would have to be dead before he let that happen. Steban lunged toward horse and rider carrying the coal oil; grabbing the horse's bridle. The rider leveled his revolver at Steban's head.

When the shot rang out, Steban wondered why he was still alive, until he saw the rider clutching his shoulder. His arm hung uselessly and his pistol had dropped from his hand, discharging as it hit the ground causing his horse to shy.

Suddenly, the horse and rider were engulfed in flames; as the oilcan attached to his saddle splattered, as simultaneously someone hurled his torch at the front porch. He fell from his horse rolling on the ground screaming. Steban began to run, stripping off his jacket using it to smother the flames consuming the rider while his horse mad with pain galloped toward the burning fields.

After the first gunshot, things began happening so quickly, Steban had been caught in the middle of a cross-fire as the riders surged as one to take the house, peppering the front with buckshot.

The skilled gusto of gunfire coming from the house had surprised them and they scattered to find cover. Steban had made it as far as the barn when he felt a searing pain as bullets passed through his flesh. The sounds of the gun battle faded away as he lost consciousness.

In stunned silence Edmond watched, unable to comprehend the scene that had erupted in just a matter of minutes. He saw one of the riders aim and fire at Steban and was catapulted into action.

"Uncle Steban", Edmond cried, dashing through the fire lancing along the floor boards of the front porch, his mother's screams echoing in his ears as he raced toward his uncle.

Adel and John Mack continued to fire into the group with deadly accuracy, keeping the riders off- balance, as Edmond dragged his uncle into the barn. Buckshot laced through the back of his thigh as they made it through the door. He saw his mother aim and fire and another rider topple forward, as he crept along the side of the barn with a bucket of coal oil.

"Did you kill him Miz Adel", whispered John Mack.

"No, I only wringed him, but that devil was trying to kill my son. If I wanted him dead, he would be; don't want no dead white trash around here, WC would not appreciate the mess."

Had everybody lost their mind, or was it just him.   There was no time to figure it out.   Edmond's leg was hurting like hell as he tried to staunch the blood coming from several gunshot wounds covering Steban's body.

Steban hands were surprisingly strong as he grabbed Edmond by his shirt. His eyes were filled with tears and blood dripped from the side of his mouth. "Just stay alive", he said with a deep breath and then he was gone." Edmond looked down at his uncle, a sob caught in his throat.

In the house, Jewel kept her son's rifle loaded, while Coralee huddled on the floor nearby. Moving closer to Adel, she said, "Ms. Adel, I aint no good at shooting, but I know how to load it well enough, if you want me too."

Adel looked down on the frighten girl and nodded. She didn't know how much longer they could last. They had to get Steban and Edmond out of that barn. There was a momentary lull in gunfire as the bunch outside rallied; soon they would attempt to rush the house. Suddenly the yard was flooded with the headlights and sounds from a blaring car horn.

"Damn, the shit just hit the fan, that's Tatum out there", said John Mack

But Tatum's motives became secondary, as they all look toward the horizon and the bright red-orange glow as Overton County burned.

Chapter

Djibouti, July, 1935

WC Gabriel was ready to kiss the ground, just thankful he was not in the air or on the water, even if the ground was Africa. The trip had taken ten days instead of three weeks and he was still trying to adjust to the foreign sounds and smells

He and Dorsey were seated in a small courtyard attached to the outer quarters of Nathan's house. Both men had removed their jackets, sweating heavily; were seemingly the only two affected by the heat. Everyone else walked around looking serenely cool.

"WC is there shade anywhere in this blasted country?"

"It must be a well-kept secret."

"WC has it occurred to you that we are a long way from home, and this is some deep shit."

WC just looked at Dorsey before replying sarcastically, "It has occurred to me." "You scared?"

"Hell yeah, but I like your brother's cut. A little too damn polite mind you; but a good man in a fight just the same."

"Yeah my little brother inspires confidence, don't he, thing is, it ain't us he's got to impress."

But it doesn't really matter; he helped save Edmond; if not for you and his friends we would not have had a clue. I'm here to help him get them back." I just hope he knows what he is doing."

"One thing I know, we sure as hell don't", Dorsey sagely concluded.

Inside, Gent questioned Nathan's wife. Shartar was a tall woman of generous proportions, smoothly muscled with light brown skin. She was surrounded by her children in what would be the women quarter. In most Muslim house-holds only male relatives were allow in the women quarters, but Gent was her husband's brother in all ways that mattered and she knew he was her only hope of seeing Nathan alive once again.

She spoke slowly in English, "I have told you all I know. They left two weeks ago, he would not say where but he packed for a trek across the desert and they had the services of a guide."

As Gent took his leave of her, she said, "Gent Gabriel, you will return my husband to me?"

It was because of his family that Nathan was lost to his loved ones Gent thought, as he looked into the woman's worried eyes and bowed before her. He knew WC and Dorsey would not understand, but things were done differently in this part of the world. "On my life", he said.

As he exited to join WC and Dorsey, Malik, Nathan's oldest son bowed formally before him; "My father knew you would come", he said, as he handed Gent a sealed message

Djibouti, North Africa, July, 1935

Philippe Dupris was indulging his favorite habit when they arrived. His hair and beard was dirty grey and his unwashed body reeked in the small interior of the room. He was seated upon the sofa, his opium pipe close at hand, his legless thighs supported on pillows.

"My god Philippe, what are doing to your-self, said Gent appalled at the state of his former teacher?"

"Ah Gent Gabriel my friend, come on in, Yasmine will get you some wine."

"Forget the wine Philippe, we need your help, Omar, Nathan and Lowe have disappeared."

"Ridiculous, it was only last", he paused, his mind fumbling about for the time. Taking a puff from his pipe to clarify his thoughts, only becoming further lost in a hundred other dreams.

Yasmine came back into the room and bowed before Gent, saying, "Perhaps I can be of help." "Omar and the others left seeking your son. He rewarded my husband for the information which he provided. But as you can see his mind wanders. They travel to the mountain fortress of Narque, my brother leads them there as guide."

There was little else Yasmine could tell them. Gent gave her a hand full of money, leaving Philippe's house more frustrated, than before.

If Salim Akbar was holding his friends at Narque he did not have many options. He recalled Omar's stories of the impregnable fortress of Narque. According to Omar, a Calvary could charge the fortress and be cut down before they reached the doors. Hundreds of years ago it was used as a prison to house the royal brothers and sister of the emperor; and no one ever escaped.

Gent was tired when they had returned to the living quarters he kept in Djibouti, but the hour grew late and Gent could not sleep as he wrestled with the dilemma of how to rescue his friends. He poured himself a glass of wine as he sat alone in the dark. Dorsey and WC slept soundly; nothing had prepared them for what might lay ahead. Gent was just thankful they were here.

The more Gent learned of the Salim Akbar, the more he realized the man left very little to chance. One thing was in their favor, Salim wanted that medallion; all they had to do was wait.

He felt sure was Salim's men had been watching them since they disembarked from the ship. Akbar knew exactly where to find him; and the game would be played by his rules. Even if he got the medallion the odds of Salim Akbar releasing the others was unlikely.

There was a knock at the door; armed, Gent positioned himself before responding, "Yes, what do you want?"

"I am a friend; I have a message for you. What I have to say is of great importance to you."

"Oh yeah, convince me."

"I have a message from Salim Akbar"

The Fortress of Narque, 1935

Omar glared at his brother from his cell, but he did not bother to berate Salim. He had allowed himself to fall into Salim's trap. There had been no other way to get into the fortress, except they let themselves to be captured. He had thought they could bribe the guards, but whether out of loyalty or fear the guards seemed impervious to his offers of money.

There had been no sign of Fontaine; and he had been forced to watch as Lowe was beaten senseless by Salim's guards. Afterward he and Nathan had been transferred to another cell. He only hoped Gent would get there soon.

"Really Omar, we are family after all; you have noble blood in your veins, yet you choose to align yourself with this American cafee trash. Like our esteemed father, you choose lost causes."

Omar said, "Unlike you, I am told our mutual sire was an honorable man and he died as such. I feel no shame to be called his son."

Annoyed, Salim said, "Enough, for I assure you, no quick death will be yours. You are ungrateful; did I begrudge your success or interfere with your business? Yet you presume to come between me and my destiny, and for that betrayal I promise you a slow agonizing death. Not however before you watch the others die first.

As we speak Gent Gabriel travels to a place of my choosing to exchange the medallion and where he will shortly thereafter be very dead.

Fontaine Gabriel Sinclair presently resided in a lady's boudoir, but no less a prison cell. Akbar had decreed he be chained once he had regained his senses and unlike Omar, he had plenty to berate himself with.

His former paramour and her lover had seen no reason not to enlighten him concerning the events that would swiftly culminate with the death of his friends.

Salim had said, "My young friend let me assure you, there will be no rescue for you. We are in the mountain fortress of Naqura; no one can save you or your friends. You would be dead before anyone could breach the entrance."

Nemri visited him daily; at first with words of affections and constant questions about the Gabriel medallion, and later sensing his growing hostility, actually commiserating with his predicament.

It was strange thought Fontaine, her beauty no longer moved him; all he felt was an urge to encircle her slim throat with his hands and squeeze, but that emotion had been short lived. His pride was rubbed raw, and he was angry, yet had his hands been free, he was not sure he could really hurt her.

He had loved Nemri and maybe some part of him loved her still. In truth, she was as much of a pawn as he, despite being a willing subject. He wished he could appeal to her better instincts, but since he had discovered she had none, he decided money might answer.

"Nemri I don't believe I have ever told you my family is rich and I am sure they would gladly reward anyone who aided me in returning to them."

"Really, from the things my Lord Salim has said concerning your country, I did not think such a thing was possible."

"Certainly I would not say that it is commonplace, but it is not unusual. "Think Nemri with money you could leave this place."

"And why would I, a mere female want to leave the comforts of my home?"

"To be free of course", impassioned Fontaine.

Nemri looked thoughtful, giving the impression she considered what he said. Fontaine, like most of the men in her life, failed to recognize the intelligence masked behind her doll-like exterior. Salim had explained why Fontaine and his fellow-countrymen were so passionate about rights and freedom; but in her world, it could be fraught with liabilities.

The murderous glare in Fontaine's eyes when she had told him of his friends, had been replaced by something akin to pity as he looked at her. Pity was an emotion that had rarely been extended to her during the course of her short life and she found herself reluctantly moved.

Her sense of self-preservation however, was too well engrained to allow sentiment to lead her into crossing Salim; that would be folly indeed. But with enough money perhaps losing Salim would not be insurmountable.

She would return to her suite and give the matter additional consideration. She turned to Fontaine touching his face caressingly, "Your words have much beauty my love, and I will consider them carefully. Now I must go, until tomorrow my sweet", she said as she glided from the room with blown kisses, fluttering silk and perfume, leaving Fontaine feeling more desperate than before.

Chapter

Somewhere outside of Djibouti, July, 1935

Gent felt a gloomy sense of déjà vu as they rode out of the city. They were traveling on horseback as Salim's man guided them to the appointed meeting place.

Grandpapa had taught him and WC to ride as soon as they were old enough to sit a saddle and Gent glanced back with sympathy as Dorsey sat his horse in pained silence. They had attached a guiding rein to his horse's bridle; that was led by WC.

They had traveled for a day, and continued traveling in darkness, alleviated by lanterns and a half-hearted waning moon settled amongst the mountain peaks. It occurred to Gent they could be seen from miles ahead, confirmed when their guide executed a signal with his lantern and received an answering signal in return.

The rode for another hour before they came to a clearing surrounded by mountainous hills and no opening except the one through which they had come. The area was illuminated with lanterns encircled about the clearing.

Gent was disappointed, but not surprised that Fontaine or the others were not present. The guide ordered them all to dismount; and he got his first look at Salim Akbar.

It seemed impossible that the man was an old as his Uncle Steban. His face appeared unlined in the dim light and only the merest touches of grey highlighted the temples of his hairline.

His bearing was regal and athletically fit. He was dressed in riding clothes, with a holstered gun belted about his waist.

His onyx black eyes, glittered dangerously at him from across the firelight, but the suppressed violence that radiated from the man could not be detected in the soft-spoken tone of his cultured voice. He was welcoming them to their death, as if he was welcoming them into his home.

Salim said, "Well, we meet at last. How curious you don't really look like Steban, but blood will tell, you have that same arrogant stance", he said to WC.

WC started forward, but Gent pulled him back, saying, "I really don't give a damn about what you have heard or what you think. Where are Omar and the others?"

"But you should", Salim said ignoring his question. "Do you know that the blood that flows through your vein stems from the line of Mandeb; a noble house from the days of Sheba. Your sire many times removed, was a great nomad chieftain whose devotion to the great Queen, replaced his wandering ways and he became a man of great wealth and prestige.

You and I are distant kinsmen, but alas the line ended with the death of the last of the male line in the wars for succession many years ago. But enough of old history, do you have the medallion?"

"I have what you want, in a safe place."

"I hope you will not waste my time with empty threats."

"Do think I am stupid enough ride in here without some assurance that we would be allowed to ride out, including my son and friends?"

"One thing you may be assured of my friend, if you do not produce the medallion this instant, this one will die right now", said Salim, his guards restrained Dorsey, a knife placed at his throat.

"Wait, I have what you want, said Gent, pulling the medallion from inside one of his packs.

"Finally, said Salim taking the medallion from Gent's hand; stroking it reverently, the emeralds, gleaming from the dull gold casing in the lantern light.   "Kill them" he instructed his guards.

It was his faithful Bela's frantic plea that finally penetrated the aura created by possession of the medallion; and Salim noticed the commotion among his guards. His eyes widen as he saw that they were trapped and outnumbered as bandits surrounded the hilltops.

Salim propelled himself toward his horse, but Gent leaped at him knocking the medallion from his hand, but he fell to the ground, unable to stop Salim as he rode out of the canyon, leaving his men to be slaughtered.

Couched behind rocks, Gent, WC and Dorsey watched in horrific awe at the ensuing blood bath. There was nowhere to hide, or run as they found themselves cornered like rabbits.

Dorsey closed his eyes, as they shivered in the shadows, filled with regrets concerning Cassandra. The eerie silence brought him back to the present; he and the Gabriel brothers were surrounded by dead bodies.

II

As Salim raced through the portals of his stronghold, he noted with relief, that his sentries were still posted. The medallion had been in the palm with his hands and he had lost it, but that was a problem he would contemplate later. Now he must marshal the remaining guards, should the hill bandits be foolish enough to attack the fortress; but first he would finish his brother Omar, and the others.

His booted feet echoed loudly as he walked across the stone floor shouting orders, as he proceeded up the staircase leading to the bedchamber where Fontaine Gabriel was chained.

"Akbar."

Salim whirled in the hallway, but he was too late. "You", he whispered, blood bubbling on his lips as he clutched at the dagger buried deep in his chest.

His killer looked down impassionedly at the corpse at his feet, pausing only to retrieve his dagger and wipe it clean on the dead man's robe. He pushed open the door of Nemri opulent bedchamber, taken aback by the beauty of the woman before him.

"Welcome My Lord Kefle."

Chapter

Overton County, September, 1935

Edmond Gabriel drove slowly along fire ravaged countryside, disgusted at the useless waste. He thought of his Uncle Steban, unable to believe he was dead. They had buried him on the hill next to his parents and siblings.

He was filled with anger that had no outlet. No arrests had been made because no one knew who had tried to destroy his home and killed his uncle; only Grif Miller's charred remains had been identified.

The fools had destroyed themselves as well as Angel's Trumpet, that night. With one single swoop they had turned back the clock seventy years, and there was no Stuart Overfield or Reese Gabriel to save them.

Edmond had cabled his father, but had received no reply and his mother had deemed he should handle matters as he saw fit. His father had entrusted his beloved Angel's Trumpet to him, unfortunately there was little that he could do.

The front of the house would have to be repaired, and by some miracle the orchards and the garden had been spared. He had been able to negotiate a price for the fruit; but it was too little too late.

When he had received the letter from Tatum, inviting him to meet with him at the bank, Edmond experienced the tortures of the damned. The harvest was gone and they had no way to meet normal expenses, much less to recover what was lost, but how would he be able to face WC if he gave up without a fight.

Without operating capital they would still lose everything and Trent Overfield would buy his grandparent's life blood for pennies on the dollar. Or perhaps Tatum was going to make Angel's Trumpet a gift to his daughter husband. Either way, Justin Overfield would have reached out from the grave and won.

Edmond did not know what to do; but he remembered Steban's words, the night of the fire. As long as they stayed alive, so did the Gabriel legacy. But how did a man put a price on his heritage?

Edmond ignored the startled looks of the people in the bank. They were probably as surprised as him, at Tatum's affability as he stepped out of his office to greet him, but then he and the Overfields had won, he could afford to be generous.

"Have a seat young man, have a seat. I understand you are a doctor. Your grandmother would be very proud of that you know.

"Yes sir, thank you, I believe she would."

"You know them boys are plum ashamed of themselves for what they done. It won't bring the Miller boy back or you uncle, but you can't throw the baby out with the bathwater can you now." Anyway if you just sign here, he said, pushing a paper at Edmond and our business will be concluded."

Edmond looked incredulous at the document before him. "I don't understand."

"It looks simple enough to me. I have included an estimate for the damages sustained by the burning of your crops and the cost of running expenses and enough to get you started."

"You are offering us a loan?" Edmond could hardly speak.

"That's right, with interest of course."

"But why would you do that?"

Tatum leaned across his desk and the expression in his eyes was one very few men, white or black had seen. He said, "I would like to tell you a story."

"A lot of years ago, my family had a small farm. It was not much, but me and my Ma and sisters we worked that patch of land from sunup to sundown. My daddy was a traveling man, coming back just long enough to get Ma with a baby and take was little we did have. Beat my Ma black and blue when she tried to stop him. Then one day he didn't come back no more. I reckon somebody put a bullet in him, Ma always said it was bound to happen."

"The year I turned fourteen, my Ma and sisters they come down with the fever; and none of them fine women who would sweep back their skirts when we passed by, could be bothered to help a Tatum. But your grandmother she came. She nursed my Ma and sisters though the worst of it. My sisters they got better, but I guess Ma was just too weak.

"On the day I buried my Ma, Miss Rosa, she comes and she put some money in my hand. Says to me, to take my sisters to my Ma's kin in Mobile, go out, and make a life for myself. Says to me the world is a big place, and you a good boy; learn to trust God and keep your own council and you gonna do well one day. She put a fifty-dollar gold piece in my hand that day. I took care of my sisters and headed for the oil fields. That was the beginning for me.

The people who have shown me a kindness are few in this world. I never saw Miss Rosa again after that but I ain't never forgot her kindness."

Epilog

Atlanta, Georgia, April, 1936

The bride wore ivory lace and satin, her face aglow, and her eyes shining with love for the man who would shortly become her husband. They were surrounded by well-wishers, the cream of Atlanta Negro society as Miss Cassandra Renee Gabriel pledged her troth to Mr. Minton Dorsey.

Hollis Terrell viewed the wedding with her own personal heartache. She was happy for the couple and wished them well, but her own life was filled with more upheavals than she knew how to handle.

Her father's farm had burned with the others, but with the help of the Gabriels it seemed the people of Angel's Trumpet would come about. Her dearest Mae had died the day after the night riders had attacked the Gabriels and she had been heartbroken. The biggest heartbreak of all had been losing Edmond.

So much had happen and with his uncle gone, all the responsibilities fell on Edmond. She wanted to be there for him, but he was less lover-like than ever. She had waited for him to tell her he loved her that he wanted her, but he said nothing.

It seemed that she had been right after all, to Edmond she had just been another of his "causes." Weeks had passed and everyday was like a hundred years. She had been home feeling sorry for herself when she received a visit from a man claiming to be Mae's lawyer and just yesterday she discovered that Mae had not only left her the Trumpet Arms, but an unspecified amount of cash.

She had made arrangements through Mae's lawyer about the hotel and she thought of Edmond and how she loved him, but Edmond had to figure out what he wanted.

Well if he was the man she thought he was, he would work things out and find her. Mae had made it possible for her to choose a different life for herself and the means to live it, at least for a while. Her mind was made up and her bags packed. She was on her way to New York.

The End